Hyunjin, thank you for waking me from my own curse.
*Stray Kids, I'm so glad to be **star lost** with you.*

FAIREST IN THE FOREST

LORE GRANT

ASIN: B0BSLT22L9
Ebook ISBN: 979-8-9876020-7-2
ISBN: 979-8-9876020-2-7
Library of Congress Control Number: 2023901991

❀ Created with Vellum

BEFORE YOU READ

Below are the tropes/kinks/trigger warning materials. Please read at your own discretion.

Blood, mild gore, blood play, blood consumption, knife play, voyeurism, exhibitionism, under discussed kink/boundaries (in one specific situation), orgasmic vampire bites, murder, human heart consumption (cannibalism), dubious consent (in one specific situation), threesome (imaginative), swordscrossing (imaginative), raw sex, creampies, self inflicted injuries, on-screen character death, cliffhanger ending

PRONUNCIATION GUIDE

People:
  Miro (Meer-oh)
  Seok (Say-ock)
  Hyunjin(H-yeon-jin)
  Taesung (Tae- sung)
  Filix Hallows (Phil-liks or Fee-liks)
  Seiji (Say-G)
  Iyena (Ee-yen-ah)
  Novenol Pace (No-ven-nol)
  Aleiah (Ah-lay-uh)
  Terephine (Tear-ah-feen)
  Madam Mezarae (Madam Meh-za-rae)
  Iseul (E-seul)/Jotkai (Jot-kai)

Places:
  Neverhelm (Never-helm)
  Nithsdale (Nith-ss-dale)
  Everacre (Ever-acre)

PRONUNCIATION GUIDE

Kiruna (Kih-roo-nah)
Yenta Ga (Yen-ta Gah)

THE GLASS COFFIN

He had been rotting beneath the earth for centuries, according to legend.

But most legends have been twisted and misinterpreted over the course of many generations. Because the prince inside the coffin before me was not buried beneath the earth and he had only been here for about four hundred years.

At the center of a budding lavender field, nestled at the edge of a deep forest sat a frosted glass coffin. The land had long since begun to reclaim the final resting place of the Feywild's prince. Vines grew and stretched across the thick panes of glass, twisting and turning in intricate filigree patterns, obscuring anyone's sight inside.

Wiping the sweat from my forehead with the back of my hand did little to help cool me off as I came to a stop, casting a worried glance up at the dark sky off to the south. I yanked off my gardening gloves and stuffed them both into the back pocket of my jeans.

From the opposite side of the coffin I heard a grunt, a tiny curse and then pure silence which sent a smile stretching across my face.

"What do you think he's dreaming of?" I asked as I stared down at the prince's coffin.

Filix popped up from behind it, leaves scattered in his silver hair and dirt was splattered across his face, adding to his freckles.

"Gosh Mare, you scared me. Warn a guy next time," Filix yelped, pink tinting his cheeks and the top of his ears. A pair of gardening shears were idly held in his hands as he leant against the coffin, his elbow perched on the thick frosted lid.

"Do you think he's run out of things to dream about? I mean he's been asleep for like hundreds of years," I continued on, staring at Filix.

The coffin had been overrun with vines and underbrush again, despite Filix and I coming every year to this clearing to clean up the prince's resting spot.

This tiny, tucked away alcove wasn't far from my house, fifteen minutes at best and another thirty to make it to the heart of town; yet the prince's coffin was hardly ever disturbed. Humans whispered that the coffin was cursed - that should the prince be woken, terrible things would befall whoever had the misfortune of waking the Feywild's prince. The few fey that lived here often avoided speaking of the prince; it brought back memories of the Feywild, of home and how it couldn't be reached anymore - because of the prince and his curse.

"He's not bored," Filix said as he used the gardening shears to cut through several barbed vines that had begun to encapsulate the coffin. He forcefully yanked the vines away, clearing the glass.

My gaze cut over to him, an incredulous look morphed across my features. "Oh yeah?"

A nervous laugh bubbled from Filix as he rose from his knees and shifted his weight around. With his hands completely plastered against the glass, he looked down on the prince and thoughtfully studied him, his gaze growing distant as he focused on something, almost like remembering a memory.

"He's... he's dreaming about my a– about– about a lake of milky water. How the roses in it make him feel sad," Filix said, his eyes never leaving the coffin lid. Using his sleeve, Filix tried to brush away some moisture that had gathered on the glass, but found himself unable to fully see inside. I watched as his dark brows furrowed in frustration.

I stepped closer and put my own hands on the lid of the coffin, copying Filix's stance.

"Oh, I'm sure he is. I bet he can even hear us talking and is able to incorporate us into his dreams now," I said, being sarcastic.

Filix's head popped up and jerked to look at me, a worried look passing behind his eyes. A smile broke out across my face the longer Filix looked at me. It took Filix a second to catch onto my teasing tone, but when it finally clicked his expression morphed into a devious smirk. He set the shears down near the foot of the glass box and faster than I could process, was darting over to my side. His hands wrapped around me and hauled me upward, depositing my body onto the top of the coffin.

Shrieks of laughter bounced around the clearing as Filix began to tickle my sides. No amount of wiggling or squirming could stop Filix's relentless assault. I tried dodging but Filix anticipated my move and went to trap my hands in his.

I miscalculated how much space I had between me and the coffin, because my hand slapped against the glass and the distinct crackling sound of glass beginning to break echoed around us.

The glass beneath my hand splintered, a dozen tiny shards shattered and pierced my skin. I yelped and jerked away from the cracked lid, trickles of my blood dripped down my fingers and splashed against the lid of the coffin.

Filix surged forward, his hand reaching for mine when he realized I had been hurt. I pulled away rapidly, trying to keep from bleeding everywhere, and Filix's hand ended up smashing into the broken glass. A jagged edge cut into the side of his palm, making blood well in the cut and running down his wrist.

Our blood marred the frosted surface, ruining the beautiful glass.

Filix and I slowly looked up at one another, a tense silence passing over the clearing. Birds no longer chirped and insects no longer buzzed. Even the thunder clouds in the distance were quiet.

"You're hurt," Filix pointed out in a whisper as his eyes drifted downward to my injured palm.

"So are you," I retorted, nodding at his own injury.

Filix didn't seem to register that he was hurt as well until he looked down and saw blood smeared across the edge of his palm. A panicked flurry of emotions passed across his pretty features, as he looked from his hand to the splintered glass and back to my face.

"Hey, it's okay. We can clean off the coffin in a minute," I said, placing my hand on his shoulder to ground him, to calm his overactive imagination.

"Mr. Park is going to kill us," Filix mumbled.

"Mr. Park doesn't even know we're the ones who come every spring to clean this place up," I pointed out. "Now let me see your hand."

Filix reluctantly gave me his hand as his gaze dropped back to the prince's coffin. I gently turned his palm over, closely inspecting the wound for any stray shards of glass that might have sunk into his skin when we miscalculated our movements to help each other earlier.

His cut was deeper than mine, still slick with fresh lines of blood running down to his wrist. Twisting his hand back and forth in the light I tried to see if there were any shards of glass in his skin, but I wasn't able to see anything. With a gentle, ghost-like touch, I gently ran the pad of my finger over Filix's wound, searching for any minute, miniscule pieces of glass that my eyes couldn't see. Filix flinched as I touched his cut, a hiss of pain escaped his heart shaped lips.

"Sorry," I apologized and let go of his hand when I was satisfied there wasn't any debris in his cut. "I think you'll live."

"If I die by papercut I'm going to be so mad," Filix grumbled as he rolled his eyes and grabbed my own hand to inspect it.

"You don't have a papercut Lixie," I teased him.

Filix absentmindedly hummed, ignoring my sarcastic comments and focusing on the task in his hand. I glanced away from him to inspect the damage that had been done to the coffin.

A compact break spread out in a flowery pattern, our combined blood gave the shattered glass flower its coloring. It was eerie looking at the coffin with a drop of color on it. The hazy, frosted coffin had always been milky white at best. Blood red wasn't a color I was used to seeing near it.

I hissed as warmth engulfed two of my fingers, something wet had reopened the cut on my hand. My head snapped back to Filix, gasping when I realized he'd stuck my fingers in his mouth.

His tongue moved against my skin, his plush lips closed over my fingers keeping his teeth from biting down. His eyes fluttered shut as he sucked on my fingers, a deep but quiet moan left him, making me press my thighs together. My chest felt hot as I watched him enjoy himself as he licked sweat and blood and dirt from my fingers.

"Filix," I breathed out, my eyes unable to look away from his pretty mouth and my fingers.

Filix sucked harder on my fingers, the action making me bite back a moan as I breathed heavily through my nose, arousal beginning to burn in my veins. His teeth grazed the edge of my knuckles as he tried to pull my fingers deeper into his mouth.

"If you wanted to get me hot and sweaty we could have done something else besides physical labor," I said, breaking whatever trance had been cast over Filix.

His muddy brown eyes popped open, a glazed over hazy look clouded his vision as he looked up at me. He slowly let my fingers go, giving the one with the cut a kitten lick in a last attempt to taste me, or my blood.

When the glazed over, drunk look vanished from his eyes, a deep tint of pink dusted his cheeks and ears. Filix's head dropped as he attempted to hide his embarrassment. He coughed and cleared his throat, taking a step backward to give me space. Filix raised a hand to scratch at the back of his neck.

"Sorry, I'm not sure what came over me," he admitted, stealing a quick glance in my direction.

I slid off the coffin and stepped over the discarded vines to stop before Filix. Reaching out for him, I noticed the way he stiffened immediately when my hand grazed his arm. Slowing my movements, I made sure to catch his attention and held onto it.

"I'm not mad Lixie," I reassured him, "Don't apologize for something you're into. Besides, I'm into it too, I just didn't realize a tiny drop of blood would bring out your blood kink."

A deeper blush covered Filix's face as he rolled his eyes at me again. I laughed a little under my breath as I slid my hand up his arm across his shoulder, stopping at the base of his neck. His breath hitched, making his chest puff up instinctively. I let my fingers glide feather light down his neck, watching with rapt fascination as goosebumps spread across his skin.

"Shut up," Filix grumbled, his voice dropping.

Trying to keep the smirk off my face was nearly an impossible task.

"I won't tease you anymore," I promised him, taking my hand from his neck. "But seriously don't apologize. I liked it."

Giving him a small smile, I stepped around him and walked to the edge of the clearing where we'd dropped our things for the day when we first arrived. I rifled through my bag, searching for the mini first aid kit I kept for emergencies exactly like this one.

Unzipping the bag I pulled out two bandaids. Keeping them cradled in my palm I zipped up the bag and tossed it back into my pack while simultaneously grabbing one of the few water bottles we'd brought along with us.

Spinning back around, I watched as Filix stood before the prince's coffin, his shoulders drooped and his head hung low in a somber stance. Filix's shoulders jerked as if he were laughing or crying at something he'd said before he shook his head and tossed his hair out of his eyes.

A heavy melancholy feeling ebbed across the meadow as thunder rumbled across the sky. Tears filled my eyes rapidly for no reason, the sudden shift in the air making my chest feel heavy.

Filix's head whipped around at the sound of the thunder, his eyes shot to the sky before intensely scanning the clearing for anything threatening. His gaze softened just slightly when he settled on me. I quickly willed the tears from my eyes and took a deep breath to steady myself.

Reaching behind him, Filix grabbed the gardening shears and jogged over to me. Whatever shift had changed in the air had really set him on edge.

"What's wrong?" I asked when he got closer.

"It's gonna rain," he replied, going straight to our bags, hastily packing all our gardening supplies away.

"Filix, we're not done. Ten more minutes and then this whole place will be back to normal," I argued with him.

I wasn't sure why I was arguing with him, the rain was coming in faster than either of us had initially anticipated. Ten minutes from now and we'd be completely soaked to the bone no matter where we were unless we left now.

"Please," Filix begged me. Something in his muddy eyes looked panicked. Like a nervous deer encountering a person for the first time. He wanted to bolt but was too stunned to move just yet. "Please, I don't want to..." he trailed off, glancing back at the prince's coffin.

Everything within me protested at the thought of leaving our clean up job unfinished; but the expression on Filix's face had me worried. He was never this spooked before.

"Okay, we can go," I relented.

Momentarily forgetting our injuries, I stuffed the bandaids back into one of our bags and slung the straps over my shoulder. Filix picked up the duffel bag of yard work tools we had, and turned to look back at the prince's coffin.

His full lips turned down into a sad frown, his brows creased again. He looked puzzled, torn even. Something was bugging him and I couldn't figure out what was wrong with my best friend.

Filix forced himself to turn his back to the coffin. With a shuddering breath he offered me his free hand and gestured toward the pathway home with the duffel bag.

"Let's go home, baby," he said, his voice quiet.

I nodded at him as I gripped his hand tightly and tugged him away from the clearing.

THUNDER RUMBLED AGAIN, this time the boom felt much closer than it had been minutes ago. We hurried our pace, knowing full well that we were going to get wet any minute now. My childhood home wasn't any closer than it had been five minutes ago.

A tight knot had begun to form in my stomach, the anxiety of knowing Filix and I could get in trouble later for getting blood all over the prince's coffin lingered at the back of my mind. No one knew how to wake the prince, but it had been prophesied that the blood of his kin would wake him when the time came.

I hoped the rain would wash away evidence. It made me wonder if Mayor Kim would make us pay to replace the coffin's lid after it nearly shattered beneath our palms.

Could the coffin even be opened?

Rain poured down on us without warning, startling me from my thoughts.

My laughter filled the air as the rain continued to pour down. Filix's annoyed frown twitched, the corners of his lips lifting the longer we walked in the middle of the road.

Tipping my head backwards, I threw my arms wide and spun in a circle beneath the downpour.

"I don't think I've ever seen you so carefree before," Filix mused above the rain.

"You bring out the best parts of me."

"Mother, you are cheesy."

"You love me!" I teased him in a sing-song voice.

I turned to face him, my hair plastered against my face. A look of adoration had spread across my face when I saw Filix staring at me in a similar fashion.

"I'm beginning to wonder if I chose the wrong person," he teased back.

"You would be lost without me."

We looked ridiculous as we walked through the pouring rain, our clothes soaked and clinging to different parts of our bodies. I was incredibly thankful Filix had worn a white shirt today, the rain had given me free access to see his abs beneath the wet fabric.

I reached for his hand, wiggling my fingers to try and entice him more. With a raised brow, Filix took my hand in his and continued to walk with me back to my house.

"Gah! Why do I have to live so far from everything?" I complained through my laughter. We were nearly at my house. Another 2 minutes and we'd be inside drying off.

"You're the one who lives on Lonely Street."

I shoved Filix, the rain water beneath our feet making him slip and slide. Our laughter rivaled the volume of the rain.

"I didn't name the streets when Neverhelm was formed! Don't blame me for living on Lonely Street. You live on–"

"Yeah, yeah, yeah! I get it!" Filix shushed me, his hand coming to cover my mouth completely as he pulled me into a headlock.

I squirmed and dodged half of his attack. My feet slipped on the wet pavement much like he'd done seconds ago when I had shoved him.

"Careful baby," Filix said as his hands rested against my waist holding me steady. He looked down at me, his deep voice sent shivers down my spine. "I couldn't live in this world without you," He declared with a smile.

I felt my cheeks and ears get hot at his words. I had to distract him or myself to get one of us to calm down.

"How about in the Feywild?" I asked, trying to get my heart to stop doing flips inside my chest.

Filix was quiet for several seconds. Rain water clung to his hair, plastering it to his forehead. The droplets ran over his lips, dripping off his chin.

His eyes filled with tears as he studied my face, taking in every detail he possibly could. His full lips pressed together.

I felt my stomach drop when it dawned on me just how quickly the mood had changed. How serious Filix had gotten.

"It hurts to be alone. I never want to be without you."

"I'm never leaving, Lix. I promise."

I watched as Filix suppressed a flinch or a shudder. He rolled his shoulders and quickly looked away from me, toward the gate that led into the garden, into the house.

"Let's dry off, yeah?" I asked, moving past the intense conversation we'd just had. I couldn't linger on it, or else I'd begin to overthink and then I wouldn't be able to stop thinking, analyzing every word of every conversation we'd ever had.

Filix silently nodded as he slipped his hand in mine and tugged me forward.

ONCE WE HAD SHOWERED, thrown our wet clothes into the wash and dressed in cozy clothes, we curled up on the couch to unwind after a day of physical labor.

A prince cursed to rot beneath the earth until the blood of his kin awoke him.

My thoughts had been plagued by the prince and his now bloodied coffin since we returned home.

There was no way the prince was actually asleep inside the coffin. He was a myth. A legend.

Filix's laughter echoed from my living room snapping me back to reality. Something funny must have happened in his book.

I smiled down at the block of cheese I was cutting up, my heart felt warm and happy to know my best friend was enjoying himself. I dropped the chunk of cheese we weren't going to eat back into its bag, and then placed it back inside my fridge. With a twirl, I picked up our plate of chips and cheese before joining Filix again.

"What's so funny?" I asked as I plopped down onto the couch with him.

He immediately draped the blanket back over my legs and let me curl into his side. When I had settled and balanced our snack plate between us, Filix passed me back my own book before snatching up a slice of cheddar cheese.

"I forgot just how unapproachable Miro can be at first glance," Filix chuckled to himself, his voice dropping the longer he laughed. He ran a hand through his silver-blonde hair, making the messy locks even fluffier. He looked incredibly pretty, even though he was just in sweats on my living room couch.

"I doubt he was really like that. I bet the legends get it wrong," I told him as I glanced at the cover of his book.

The Lone King.

"Oh trust me, he's exactly like that," Filix huffed with a roll of his eyes.

With my head on his shoulder it was a bit hard to look up at his face, but I ignored the slight pain that throbbed in my neck as I looked up at him.

Nine hundred and fifteen freckles were smattered across his cheeks and nose, which seemed like a ridiculous number to know but Filix had been my best friend since we were teens. We did everything together growing up. Wherever one went, the other was right beside them. We're inseparable, unless you factored in me going away to college.

"Oh and you know Miro so well?" I teased him, staring into his muddy brown eyes.

Filix's dark eyebrows twitched just slightly, the movement so miniscule I barely even caught it, but I knew he was hiding something. He swallowed and blinked, trying to move on. I arched an eyebrow at him, but didn't press him on whatever he was hiding.

"I know him better than most," he answered me as he shook the book back and forth in my face in a teasing manner.

I laughed, snuggling further into his side.

"Oh, I'm sure you do, Lixie."

I turned back to the page I'd left off on and continued reading. The occasional sound of a page flipping was the only sound to break the silence that the heavy rain outside couldn't chase away.

A chapter or two farther into my own book, I found myself growing bored with the story. I had been excited to continue reading about an alpha werewolf and his human mate falling in love with a fairy, but my mind kept drifting back to the prince inside his glass coffin.

A prince cursed to rot beneath the earth until the blood of his kin awoke him. Sounded like the cruelest fate one could ever suffer.

Snapping my book closed, I looked up at Filix and gave him the poutiest puppy-dog eyes I could muster up. Filix sighed deeply, but ignored my pleading look.

I stayed silent, keeping my eyes on his face. When another minute passed and Filix hadn't acknowledged me I decided to see how much I could do to annoy him before he snapped and acknowledged me.

I raised a hand and at an incredibly slow, annoying pace inched my finger closer and closer to his cheek. Filix side-eyed me as my finger pushed into the little fat he had on his face and hit his cheekbone. His brows furrowed, confused about my actions but his attention went back to his book rather quickly.

"Filix!" I whined, failing to stifle my laughter as I pulled away from him.

"Yes baby?" Filix asked, dropping his voice to an incredible low rumble.

I rolled my eyes and struggled to keep the smile off my face as I felt my ears and chest growing hot. His deep voice always made me feel flustered. I smacked his shoulder before snuggling into his side more.

"I'm bored," I whined, my words were muffled by his shirt.

"I'm not making you brownies right now," he denied me.

I gasped dramatically, clutching my heart like he'd shot me.

"But flicking flour at you would cure my boredom. You're killing me by denying me this."

"And that's my problem?" he asked, teasing me. His heart shaped lips pulled back into a beaming smile as he looked over at me. He was so pretty, it was nearly hypnotizing.

"Can I lick whipped cream off your abs?" I asked innocently.

Filix's eyes crinkled at my question as he held back a laugh. "You don't have any in the fridge."

I groaned.

A deep boom of thunder shook the house, causing the both of us to jump just slightly. We burst out laughing at our ridiculous reactions.

"When do your parents come home?" Filix asked.

"Next week. Over the weekend I think," I said, trying to recall what my mum had told me before she and dad had left for their vacation. Truthfully I had not been paying attention, I was excited to have Filix all to myself in an empty house.

"Hm," Filix hummed.

"Would you read to me?" I asked sweetly.

"You hate this one," Filix pointed out.

"I don't hate it!" I protested a bit too loudly. "I just hate that it has no real ending. It's stupid. It deserves an ending."

"Not all stories get happy endings, baby. Half the books on your shelf are angsty heartbreaking love stories," Filix pointed out.

"That's not– would you just read to me? For once I want you to bring this story to life," I begged him, giving him another round of puppy dog eyes.

Filix stared down at me, his lips slightly pursed in thought.

"You know I haven't read to you in like, years?" Filix pointed out, sounding a bit sad. "I thought you grew out of this."

"I could never get tired of this Filix. I love spending time with you."

"Why the sudden interest in 'The Lone King?'" he asked.

Cleaning up the prince's coffin had reignited my mild curiosity in 'The Lone King.' Everyone in Neverhelm had heard the King's story, and the prince's story; parents used their stories to lull their children to sleep almost every night. It was only natural for me to want to re-hear one of them.

Filix was quiet for several seconds, his face contorted into a myriad of different emotions, as if he couldn't quite wrap his head around being asked to read to me again.

"Fine, but you can't interrupt me every five seconds," he relented.

"I love you," I sighed as I leaned my head on his shoulder again and waited for him to begin reading to me.

"I love you too," Filix said before he kissed the top of my head and opened the book to the beginning again.

"Eternities are hard to bear. They are harder to bear alone. Their weight can break you down, strip you of yourself until there is nothing left," Filix read aloud.

My eyes felt heavy the longer Filix continued to read. I gently closed my eyes, hoping to rest them for just a moment but ended up falling asleep instead.

"Baby," his deep voice called out to me.

I groaned, and threw my arm over my eyes hoping to go back to sleep.

"Baby," his voice called out again, dragging out the word.

His arm slid across my stomach, his fingers dipped below my shirt and caressed my skin gently before they stopped just below my chest. Filix's fingers traced feather light patterns against my ribs, his thumb rested just below the plushness of my breast.

"Filix," I breathed out, dragging my arm away from my face. He must have carried me to bed last night after I fell asleep on the couch.

His warm breath fanned out against my collarbone, drawing me farther from the depths of sleep. The gentle plushness of his lips met the side of my neck, and pressed down.

Blunt nails dug into my flesh at my side the harder Filix pressed his lips against my neck before he eased his grip. A soft noise came from the back of my throat as I pushed my head farther back into the pillows, trying to give Filix more access. His lips met the junction of my neck and shoulder, his teeth scraped over the sensitive skin there, earning him a shudder at the action.

I felt him smirk against me before he shifted his entire body to hover over mine. His chest pressed against mine, our ankles and legs tangled together. With a roll of my hips I felt Filix's hard length against my thigh.

A delightful, broken gasp left Filix's swollen lips as he rolled his hips, grinding against me. I pushed back against him, wanting more of what he was so keen on waking me up for.

Mid-morning sunlight illuminated him from behind, granting him the illusion of being ethereal. His hair stuck up in random cow licks, his eyes were heavy lidded with lust and the barest remnants of sleep. He was the prettiest human alive. I reached out and pressed a hand gently to his cheek, before I closed the distance and kissed him.

A deep groan left Filix as he kissed me back, his hands tightly gripping my hips. His fingers pressed harder into my flesh the more I squirmed beneath him. His fingers gripped the hem of my shirt, and pulled up, removing the article from my heated body.

"Fuck," he chuckled as he pulled away to look down at me, "How did I get so damn lucky?"

I laughed as I stared up at him, "I need you."

A fire lit behind his muddy eyes, as a challenge was issued before him. Cocking his head to the side Filix stared down at me with a dark, hungry gaze. The hand that wasn't supporting half of his weight slid up my body and settled against my neck. Filix licked his lips slowly as he watched my chest rise and fall faster, the excitement of choking setting us both off.

"You need me? My baby needs me to take care of her?" Filix questioned, purposefully dropping his voice into a lower tone.

"Mhm," I whined, not trusting my voice.

Filix dipped beneath the sheets and kissed his way down my body, leaving a trail of love bites along the way.

His covered form hovered above my thighs for a moment, his stillness made me worried I'd done something wrong. I tossed the sheets off our bodies and glanced down at him.

"Everything okay, Filix?"

My question was left unanswered as Filix licked a stripe up my still-covered pussy. The panties I wore were thin enough already, and they were soaked through with my arousal, and now his saliva. They might as well have not been there at all.

Filix licked into me again before closing his lips around my covered clit and sucking lightly. My hips bucked only for an arm to settle over them, Filix's strength kept me pinned to the bed.

He continued to tease me over the material of my panties until I was mewling, begging for him to please take them off. Filix took pity on me, hooking his thumbs in the elastic of my underwear and dragging them down my legs at an agonizingly slow pace, teasing me further.

He cast them aside and was back between my knees in a flash.

I squirmed slightly, hyper aware of the fact that Filix could now see all of me, despite how many times we've been together. I tried to close my legs, but between his broad shoulders and his strong hands on my thighs, it was impossible.

Filix mouthed at my inner thigh, leaving a few more little bites and hickeys. Then he was using his thumbs to spread open the lips of my cunt, blowing softly against me. I could feel my arousal dripping out of me already and he'd barely done anything.

"That's my messy girl," He praised me.

And then he dove back in, tongue dragging up my cunt before stopping to lap at my clit before I could feel embarrassed by his words. My hands fisted in the sheets as I tried to writhe against the iron grip that kept me exactly where Filix wanted me. I wanted to reach down, to tangle my hands in his hair, but some part of my mind registered the fact that he had not given me permission to do so.

So all I could do was clutch at the sheets while Filix brought me more pleasure than I had ever felt in my entire life.

The juxtaposition of sensations was what had me reeling the most. There was his tongue, of course: soft and dexterous, it alternated between playing with my clit or dipping slightly into my tight hole. His fingers were hard inside me, two slipped in whenever his mouth was busy with my clit.

All that combined had my edge approaching quicker than I had expected. I clamped down on Filix's fingers, as I struggled to hold off on cumming.

He pulled back slightly when he felt me tighten around his fingers, although he kept his fingers buried in my cunt and stroking softly. It was a nice gesture but nowhere near enough stimulation to get me to cum. I whimpered and pouted, but that only made Filix laugh.

"Aww, what's the matter, baby? Do you want to cum?"

I whined, squirming, but Filix just shook his head.

"If you want something, baby, you have to ask for it."

"Filix, please," I begged. "Please can I cum? I want to cum for you. I want to be your good girl."

"Well, how can I say no to that? Don't worry, I'm not going to edge you anymore," Filix smirked sadistically. "We can save that for another time."

He continued to tease me, lapping at my slick like a man starved, his mouth continuously working over every part of my pussy. He pulled back ever so slightly, admiring how wet my cunt was, slicked with my arousal and his spit. His tongue pressed deep inside me, my cunt clenching down tightly against the wriggling appendage.

"Fuck," I gasped out as I squeezed my eyes tightly shut. My temple became damp with sweat against the pillows, my toes began to curl. All the while, Filix never let up. His tongue was stuffing me, nearly overwhelming me, but I never wanted it to leave me.

"Cum for me, baby," Filix ordered.

And I did. Stars flashed before my eyes as my orgasm crashed over me in a powerful wave. I thrashed against Filix's arms, but he just held me down and continued to lick me even through my high.

"Too much, baby?" he asked in a husky voice when he moved up the length of my body.

"No – never enough," I panted, pulling him down for a kiss. "I can never get enough of you."

Filix hummed into my kiss, before his tongue licked against my lips. I let him in and grunted at the way I could taste myself against his tongue. Knowing Filix tasted of my arousal had my clit pulsing with need again.

"As much as I want to lay in bed all day, we have things to do that we neglected to do yesterday," Filix said as he pulled away from me, leaving me wanting.

"You're such a cock block!" I groaned as I flipped back against my pillow.

"I can fuck you all night long baby," Filix reminded me.

"Fuck me now," I bargained with him, batting my eyes at him for good measure.

Filix fixed me with a dark, lustrous gaze that had me squirming beneath him.

"Be a good girl for me and maybe I'll reward you tonight."

"Promise?"

Filix barely managed to suppress a shiver that ran through his body, yet he played it off as if nothing had happened. He leaned down and pressed a quick kiss to my forehead, silently promising me, and then he was leaping off the bed and walking into my bathroom.

"Come join me!" he called out as he turned on the shower.

"Come back here and fuck me!" I called back with a laugh as I pushed my body off the bed.

I silently wished for the day to pass quickly as I stepped into the steamy bathroom, going to join Filix.

HE'S REAL HOLY SHIT

There was a ton of buzz inside Clé's bar, which wasn't unusual but on a weekday night it was rare to see so many people here. The lights were dimmed low which paired nicely with the gentle rock that played softly in the background from the speakers above the bar.

Clé Jekeil waved at us as we stepped through the front door, their thin lips spread into a wide smile that revealed their sharp teeth. Clé was one of the last living fey in Neverhelm. They'd originally lived in the Feywild but had been trapped on this side when the doors were ultimately sealed when the prince was cursed.

Filix raised a hand in greeting as he placed his other hand on my lower back and urged me forward, deeper into the small crowd that gathered in the bar. As I weaved toward the bartop I tried to get a look at who was here.

Neverhelm's doctor, Novenol Pace, another fey trapped on this side, was seated at the bar with his girlfriend, Annalisa Dupree and a dozen of their close friends. Lydia, our librarian, sat at one of the booths near the pool tables, where some of the town's teenagers were goofing off.

20

Mr. Park, Neverhelm's previous mayor, and Mrs. Kim, our official mayor, were at one of the booths near the back; Sheriff Radley at their side with his husband, Oliver. The four of them barely registered the commotion around them, their attention focused on whatever topic they were discussing. Even from across the room it was clear that whatever they were talking about was serious.

Filix's hand sliding around my side to rest around my abdomen had me tearing my eyes off of the town's leaders to look back at him. I barely managed to move out of Novenol's way before he was barreling past us with his girlfriend giggling hysterically behind him, the two hand in hand and clearly drunk off their asses.

"Be careful Noven!" Callie shouted over the crowd.

My eyes connected with hers across the room. A teasing eye roll graced her round features before she glanced at the front door where Novenol and his girlfriend had disappeared through.

"*You'd think our doctor would be more careful,*" she mouthed at me.

"*You'd think!*" I mouthed back, tapping my head in a 'no duh' gesture.

Callie's laughter filtered through the rest of the noise in the air as Filix guided me toward the bartop once the pathway was less crowded. Ever the perfect gentleman, Filix pulled out a free barstool for me and waited for me to sit down before he closed the gap of space between us.

"What's with the crowd, Clé?" Filix asked, leaning against the back of my chair.

"Haven't ya heard?" they asked, wiping down the counter space in front of us.

"Heard what?" I asked, a chill ran down my spine.

Clé stopped what they were doing and looked at Filix and I. Their slitted eyes jumped back and forth between the two of us, trying to gauge if we were messing with them or not.

"Did someone die?" I questioned them, making my voice lower so as to not be overheard. Clé's floppy calf-like ears twitched before they straightened their posture and continued to wipe the bar down.

21

"The prince's coffin is open. Someone broke the curse," they said, grabbing various glasses and bottles of liquor.

Filix and I threw worried glances at each other before we plastered shocked expressions on our faces, acting as innocent as we could.

"Whoa, really?" I asked, shifting in my seat.

"Mhm, their blood was all over the lid of the coffin. Smashed it up pretty good too, like they wanted to break the poor fella out of there."

Clé passed Filix and I our drinks, a jack and coke for Filix and a vodka soda for myself, the two of us subconsciously reaching for them with our injured hands, our bandages in full view.

"Ouch. You two playing too rough or something?" Callie asked as she slipped behind Clé and grabbed a cocktail shaker and a bottle of tequila.

"Uh…" Filix tried to come up with an excuse but failed. Even in the dimmed lighting of the bar, I could see Filix's ears getting pink.

"I dropped one of my mum's vases. Glass went everywhere and my prince over here wanted to be the perfect gentleman and clean it up himself but you know me, " I said throwing in a fake laugh that got Callie and Clé chuckling under their breath. "I was too stubborn for my own good and we both got cut by some stupid shards of glass."

I kept my gaze on Callie, but I saw Clé's slitted eyes flicker down to our bandaged hands for a brief second. I dropped my injured hand into my lap and grabbed my drink with the other, hoping to avoid any more lingering stares.

"Do they know who opened the coffin?" Filix asked as he tried to take a nonchalant sip of his coke and rum.

"Radley ain't too sure yet. He's got some ideas though," Clé stated, frowning at the end of their sentence.

I hastily brought my drink to my lips and looked down at the countertop.

Fey couldn't lie, that was a well-known fact around here; and as a community, the people of Neverhelm - and the surrounding areas - had made an unofficial rule about demanding the fey to speak truths. It felt unfair and somewhat violating to do such a thing. Thankfully most of the remaining fey that lived around here were pretty understanding when someone slipped up by accident.

"I don't get what the fuss is over," Emily spoke up from a couple barstools away. She had been in that group with Novenol and his girlfriend before they split. She and her twin sister, Violet, were primary school teachers but I could never remember which grade they taught.

"Oh?" Callie asked, a pink brow raised at her.

"We aren't even sure if the prince was inside. Like no one's ever even tried to see if the lid could come off that obnoxious looking glass box."

I felt Filix stiffen beside me, his grip on the back of my chair making the wood creak. Quickly setting my drink down, I shifted in my seat and slid my arm around Filix's side, pulling him into a side hug. His stiff posture relaxed the instant I pressed myself against him. The arm draped across the back of my chair wrapped around my shoulders, keeping me close.

"You've had enough to drink tonight Emily. Let's stick to water, yeah?" Callie asked, leaving no room for Emily to argue with her.

"He was in there. Myself and a select few watched the whole thing," Clé said, their eyes blowing wide as they walked through their memories. "The prince didn't deserve that."

"Did you know him?" I heard myself asking. I immediately regretted opening my mouth. "Sorry! Don't - Don't answer that. Ugh I mean - forget I apologized!"

"S'okay Mare," Clé reassured me. "I was closer with his kin than I was with him."

"Filix," Sheriff Radley's deep voice boomed from behind us.

The two of us froze momentarily before we spun around to face the Sheriff, friendly smiles plastered on our faces. Filix's hand on my shoulder squeezed tightly, in a reassuring manner, reminding me that everything was going to be fine.

"Mare, how are you two doing?" Radley asked, crossing his buff arms across his chest. In that stance he looked powerful and imposing. Intimidating.

"We're doing good. A little surprised at the news we just heard," I answered, hugging Filix tighter. I was nervous, but then again I always was around Radley. He intimidated most of the folks here in Neverhelm.

"You heard then?" Radley asked, his thick brows rose on his forehead creating a dozen wrinkles before they disappeared again.

"Is he really out?" Filix asked.

I glanced up, worried about him. There was something off in his tone, and his body language was still stiff from earlier. It was like he was on edge, waiting for something bad to happen.

"Looks like it. It's been hard to tell how many people tried to break 'im out 'cause of the heavy rain we had last night. It'll be even harder with the rain we're gonna get tonight."

"You and Tindol will figure it out. The two of you have never not solved a case," Callie said as she loaded up her serving tray with another round of drinks.

"Tindol's away on vacation in Nithsdale. You know this," Radley sighed, running a meaty hand over his buzz cut.

"He gets back in like a day or two," She drawled with an eye roll.

She walked off into the crowd before Radley could respond. Clé shook their head as they continued to polish some glasses that had been recently washed.

"How are your folks Mare? Still enjoying their vacation?" Sheriff Radley questioned.

"They're having a blast," I said, with a fake smile.

"How've you kids been?" Radley asked, shifting to a safer topic.

I took another sip of my drink, and let Filix speak.

"We've been good. Had a busy day," Filix said, raising his drink to his lips.

"Oh yeah? What were you kids up to?" Radley asked, his question completely innocent.

Filix choked on his drink and began to cough violently as he clearly thought back to this morning. He spun to put his drink down so as to not spill it as I pat his back, trying to keep my laughter at bay. I gathered myself for a couple seconds to answer him but Radley cut me off with a hurried wave of his hand.

"Ah ah ah, I don't want to know," Radley back tracked, catching on to what we'd done this morning. "Just be careful out there. The prince is bound to be very confused now that he's awake."

"Sure thing Chief!" I smiled, laughing more openly as he walked away.

My gaze was drawn to Mayor Kim across the room. Her beady black eyes refused to look away from Filix. Her undefined, thin lips, and slightly snubbed nose were tugged up into a scowl - one she did not try to hide.

Filix, thankfully, paid no mind to Mayor Kim. He was too enthralled with a conversation he was having with his aunt and uncle, who had arrived at the bar not too long ago. I paid no mind to their conversation, my attention focused solely on our mayor and her displeased expression.

Shifting in my seat, I slowly moved my body in front of Filix's, blocking Mayor Kim's line of sight to Filix. She blinked rapidly when our eyes connected, very obviously surprised that she had been caught throwing daggers across the bar. With a gentle shake of her head, Mayor Kim turned to focus on the conversation Sheriff Radley and his husband were engaged in.

Filix's arm around my shoulder tightened, drawing me into the conversation he was having with his family. He looked down at me for a brief second, silently checking that I hadn't reached my limit on socializing for the evening. I gave him a cheesy smile, one that had my eyes closing fully and my cheeks squishing cutely.

I felt a quick peck on my nose seconds before I opened my eyes, completely forgetting about Mayor Kim's weird stares. I stared up at Filix, with a warm happy smile on my face.

Conversations flowed as freely as the drinks, especially when Callie returned behind the bar. Music played softly in the background as we talked about literally anything and everything. Filix's aunt and uncle eventually moved off, going to hang with their friends, leaving us to our own devices.

We mingled for quite a while, moving from the bar to a table near the entrance, hanging with friends from high school that had also returned to Neverhelm during the semester break before classes began again. It felt great to catch up with them, it had felt like an eternity had passed since we'd all seen each other.

At some point I began to feel hot, my hairline damp with sweat. The alcohol in my system amplified the heat inside the bar, turning the cozy, warm atmosphere into a stifling, near suffocating environment. My mouth felt dry and my nose was agitated with every breath I took.

I looked over at Filix, shifting in his loose side hug to reach his ear. I leaned in close and whispered to him that I was going to go outside and get some air. He nodded, sobering up slightly.

He gently excused us from our friends, his hand rested on the small of my back as he maneuvered us toward the front door. As we stepped past the threshold, Filix's hand dropped from my spine, leaving the space cold.

I turned to look at him as I stepped farther outside, confused about why he wasn't touching me any longer.

"Give me two seconds. I need to let Kyomi and Minjae know I'm staying with you tonight."

"Why don't you just move in? You're with me more than you are with your aunt and uncle," I laughed, just a bit tipsy.

"When we move in together," Filix began, "and yes - when. Not if, but when we move in together, every room within that house will need to be fucked in."

"Filix Hallowes!" I screeched as my ears got hot and laughter escaped the two of us. I moved to try and hit Filix for being so brash and outright dirty but he darted out of the way and dashed back inside the bar, laughing the entire way.

The cool, crisp night air felt good against my flushed and heated skin; the momentary solitude was an added bonus. I dismissed Filix's comment about fucking in every room with a small smile. My brain instead focused on what his words meant - what they implied.

Filix wanted a life with me. A future together.

Butterflies flipped inside my stomach as a giddy, euphoric feeling washed over me. Being with Filix wasn't something that was up for debate, or something to question.

Being with him, together until time stopped was a given. A fact that would never change. My feelings for Filix were not complicated. I loved him, and I couldn't wait to graduate and start a life with him - far, far away from Neverhelm.

Clangs and the shattering of glass made me jump out of my skin. My hand flew to my chest, like a Victorian woman clutching at her pearls. A reflex that wasn't helpful in defending myself at all.

Muffled screams came from down the alleyway, making my heart race faster. Sweat broke out across my brow as I clamped a hand over my mouth to dampen the sound of my heavy breathing. The muffled screaming turned into rough grunts before a heavy thud finished the fight.

I hastily moved forward, wanting to inspect what was happening in the alleyway. Something tugged in my chest, drawing me toward the darkened alleyway and whatever lurked in the shadows.

The cobblestone beneath my shoes was slippery from the rain, and Clé had not replaced the lightbulbs that had burnt out last month, which plunged the back area into complete darkness.

A wet squelch and the crunch of bones had me reeling backward, freezing instantly as to not draw attention to myself.

Something dangerous lurked in the darkness.

A sudden bang from the roof had me stumbling backwards and searching the skyline. Lightning illuminated the building in front of me, revealing a figure perched on top of the room of Miriam's Inn right next to the bar.

He sat perched up on the roof, his back illuminated by the faint light that reached him from the lanterns below him. Bright, blood red hair stood out, even in the dimly lit darkness. I watched as his posture stiffened, his pointed, pierced ears twitched as he listened to something. With a quick jerk of his head, his eyes bore into mine. His eyes glowed a vibrant crimson color, making my heart sink into my stomach.

A bleeding heart held in his hands, so close to his mouth, had me silently gasping as I froze up. His illuminated eyes raked over my rigid form, taking in the frightened expression I had plastered on my face.

I felt cold and nauseous as I stared up at him – at the prince. The very mythical prince that Filix and I had accidentally awoken.

"Mare?" Filix's voice called out.

I refused to look away from the prince, afraid he'd disappear completely or come and attack me. His eyes snapped in the direction Filix's voice came from, a look of hungry desire passed over his face.

Fear gripped my heart. Filix couldn't get hurt.

"No!" I breathed out, panicking, my words quiet.

I stepped forward, drawing his attention back to me fully. He completely forgot about Filix's approaching figure and stared down at me. He studied me intensely; his eyes flashed neon again. His head tipped sideways, like a wild animal's would when they were interested in something foreign to them.

"There you are," Filix said, his voice right beside me.

I jumped in the air and yelped loudly. My hand flew to my chest as I spun to look at him. Tears clouded my vision immediately.

"Whoa, easy. It's just me," Filix said, his face full of concern.

My eyes darted back up to the rooftop, searching for the prince with the bleeding heart in his hands. His silhouette and luminescent eyes were gone.

"I - I know, you just startled me," I said, swallowing.

"What are you even doing down here? Home's the other direction, baby," Filix pointed out.

The cold of the night sent a shiver down my spine that I wasn't able to suppress. Filix saw the shiver wrack my body and was immediately sliding out of his sweater and passing it over to me.

His eyes looked over my entire being, still worried about my well-being. With a serious expression he looked down the alleyway, his eyes sliding up to the rooftops. Filix looked back at me with a forcefully neutral look, which made the hairs on the back of my neck stand on end.

"Let's head home, yeah?" he asked, looping his arm over my shoulders. He drew me away from the alleyway and began to steer me back in the direction of my house.

Every couple of minutes Filix would try and casually look behind us, as if he were checking to make sure no one was following us. Knowing Filix was also on high alert made my anxiety spike.

"Filix?" I whispered, afraid to speak out loud.

"Hm?" he hummed, tearing his eyes from glancing behind us to look at my face.

Do you think we really woke the prince up? I wanted to ask, but asking meant acknowledging that we had royally fucked everything up. I wanted to play ignorant for just a little while longer.

"You know I love you, right?" I asked instead, needing to calm my overactive nerves.

He immediately pulled me closer to him, as if I weren't already molded to his body to begin with.

"Of course I know. What's on your mind, baby?"

I hesitated, forcing my mind to shift gears to focus on something else besides what I had just witnessed for the remainder of the night. I adjusted my arms around him and continued walking home.

"I'm just wondering when you're going to propose."

"Whoa, who says I'm going to propose? What if I wanted to be proposed to?" He teased, his cheeks growing pink at my sudden conversation shift.

"You'd deny me the only good part of getting engaged?" I grumbled, pulling one arm away to punch him in the stomach.

Filix let out a dramatic 'oof' before he broke out into a small fit of giggles.

"Ugh, right. Because marrying me isn't the best part of an eternal bargain," Filix rolled his eyes dramatically.

"I'm only marrying you for your money."

His mouth dropped open in shock, which had me doubling over from how hard I was laughing. I loved to tease him; it was far too easy to rile him up.

"At least tell me the sex is good!" He pleaded, his eyes nearly completely closed as he laughed.

I squinted at him and made a dramatic show of thinking hard as I tapped my lip with the tip of my finger.

"Mmm could be better," I teased him.

Filix narrowed his eyes at me as he pouted grumpily.

"If I weren't so terrified of your Mum finding out, I'd ruin you for any other man as soon as we got inside your house."

I ran my eyes up and down his body, letting my gaze linger on the growing tent in his jeans. I licked my lips as I slowly met his gaze again.

"I'll let you do whatever you want... if you can catch me," I challenged him.

I waited a singular second before I broke off into a run, being mindful of the wet pavement.

I bolted away, blindly dashing through small bushes and abandoned streets, uncaring about the noise and trail I left behind as I desperately tried to create some distance between Filix and I. Fear, excitement, and arousal made a mess of me as my thighs clenched in anticipation of what was to come while my body instinctively quivered in nervous energy at being hunted down like prey.

The thunderous sound of Filix's sneakers smacking against the pavement directly behind me had me running harder, a newfound surge of adrenaline induced giddiness washed over me. Behind me, I could hear Filix curse slightly, before he too picked up his pace, running harder.

The usual 15-minute walk from town to my street was cut in half as I ran from Filix. Rounding the slight bend in the road, I turned onto Lonely Street and zeroed my sights on the only house around for miles, my house. With a cautious but quick glance over my shoulder I searched for Filix's pursuing form. He was several paces away, with absolutely no way for him to get to me before I made it to safety. With a smirk I pushed myself harder, knowing with full confidence that I was going to win.

Arms snaked around my middle, hauling me off my feet, dragging me backwards. I let out a scream before it descended into hysterical laughter. Filix spun us around carefully on the wet pavement in front of my house.

"I win," he growled in my ear, his hot breath fanning across my cheek and down my neck. I shivered at the contrast between his heated breath and the near freezing rainy air around us.

"How did yo-"

Filix cut off my question, possessively nipping his teeth against my jaw as he growled, "Mine."

"How - how do you want me?" I panted, trying to catch my own breath.

I tilted my head slightly, trying to get a better look at Filix in the dark. He said nothing as he breathed heavily through his nose, trying to calm down after running so hard. The hands around my waist squeezed at my flesh before he released me and took a small step back.

"Let's go inside. It's cold," he said instead of answering my question.

I looped my arm around his and pulled him through the front gate and up to the front door. It took a second for Filix to find the key inside his pocket, but when he found it, he ushered me inside out of the cold.

My back collided with the closed door, the echoing sound of the lock sliding into place filled the silence that engulfed my house. I barely managed to suck in a startled breath before Filix's lips crashed against my own. He kissed me roughly, tongue plunging deeply into my unresisting mouth.

His heated kisses trailed down my jawline, ghosting over my neck before they trailed down, inching closer and closer to the sensitive spot beneath my ear that had me squirming in his arms every time.

Out of the corner of my vision, I saw something glinting in the light before the sound of tearing fabric reached my ears. Looking down, I saw that Filix had completely shredded my shirt and my bra with a knife in his hand, exposing me to his lustful stare as he licked his lips.

I couldn't even be mad about the ruined bra, I had been meaning to replace the damn thing anyway.

Carefully, he cupped my face, actions juxtaposing the dark look in his eyes.

"These tender lips are mine," he placed his own on mine in a searing kiss, as if to prove his point.

Parting from my lips, he was quick to drag his tongue down the column of my neck, nipping at the skin yet again as he murmured, "this beautiful neck is mine."

His hands slid up my sides, moving to cup my breasts. I could feel the cool press of the metal from the blade against my heated skin, causing me to shiver.

"These," he gave them an appreciative squeeze, humming in approval as a soft gasp escaped me in response, "are mine."

"Please Filix, fuck me," I begged him, pushing my chest farther into his grasp.

His hand slid up the expanse of my now naked flesh, brushing my shirt away and off my shoulders, before his large palm settled against my throat. He gently rubbed his thumb back and forth across my skin in a soft, comforting manner.

"You are mine. You're never going to leave me," he said in a low yet soft voice. "I love you too much to let you go."

"I love you Filix," I whispered back.

The sweet time lasted no more than a second before he started to softly choke me, making me crazy again.

"What did my baby say she wanted from me?" he asked teasingly as he looked deep into my eyes, enjoying every time he made me vulnerable to his touch.

"I want your cock inside me so bad, Filix."

The cold blunt end of the knife ran across my chest, stopping just above my heart. Blood pounded in my ears as I struggled to control my frightened, excited breathing. I loved when Filix brought out a knife to play with in bed.

The tip of the knife hovered over me as I looked up at Filix. His gaze was fixated on my naked chest, on the point between my breasts where the knife hovered. His eyes slowly rose to meet mine, the muddy brown orbs blown out in lust.

"Is this okay, baby?" he asked, swallowing down his own desire for a moment.

"I said you could do whatever you wanted to if you caught me. You caught me."

"Yes, but you can always change your mind or use the safe word if you need to."

I shook my head quickly, "I don't need to use them. I haven't changed my mind. Please, Filix. I want this. I want you."

Filix fixed me with an apprehensive look, trying to truly see if I meant what I said or not. After a second of contemplation, he stepped back. Disappointment and rejection bloomed in my chest. Had he changed his mind?

Using the knife he pointed behind him.

"Upstairs. Naked. On the bed. Now."

I darted past him, running through the living room before taking the stairs two at a time.

I barged into my room and quickly began to pull off my pants. My socks were harder to take off, the damn things refused to leave my feet as I yanked at them. Chucking my clothes into a pile near my bathroom, I moved in front of my bed and quickly tore off the blankets.

I would need to change the sheets once we were done.

The sound of Filix walking toward my bedroom had me jumping onto the bed, scrambling to get in the position he asked me to be in.

I looked up to see Filix leant against the doorframe, a dark, hungry smirk spread across his features. He slowly stepped inside my room, taking all the time in the world to get to me.

"I specifically remember stating 'naked' when I let you go."

I looked at him for a second, confused, before I looked down. Navy blue panties were still on my being, making me only ninety-nine percent naked in front of Filix.

"Do I have to punish you for not listening?"

I shook my head, my eyes wide in an innocent stare.

"Lay back," he said. "Eyes closed."

I laid back, settling in the middle of the bed, with my head resting against one of my pillows. I heard the rustling of clothes hitting the floor as I waited, and with a quick peek, I saw the hard planes of Filix's abs illuminated by the dim light. The bed dipped beneath us as he straddled me, being mindful not to put too much of his weight on top of me.

"Do you trust me?" he asked.

Cold metal grazed against my collarbone. My heartbeat spiked, the feeling of the blade flat against my skin sending jolts of fear and pleasure through me. We have played like this a few times before, but it had never felt like this – it had never turned me on so quickly.

As Filix dipped the knife's point into my skin, all of my focus honed in on one area, the rest of my body fading away as I waited to see what Filix would do next.

"Yes Filix," I breathed out, sounding needy to my own ears.

He applied enough pressure to prick my skin, my lips parting with a gasp before he pulled away entirely. I couldn't see the blood trickling down from the small cut, but knowing that it was there did something primal for my desire towards him. Filix grunted quietly, trying to hold back the noises he wanted to make.

His thumb and forefinger lightly pinched one of my nipples, and twisted. I gasped and arched my back at the sensation, wanting him to touch more of me. He shifted his entire body to hover over mine, letting his naked skin touch mine. His lips met the junction of my neck and shoulder, his teeth scraped over the sensitive skin there, earning him a shudder. His hot, wet tongue lapped at the small incision he'd made. There was only a tiny sting of pain as his saliva met the fresh wound before the pain faded into pleasure.

His mouth left my neck as he began to move down on the bed. He laid between my legs, kissing my inner thighs. I took a deep breath, feeling that my panties were already soaked.

Filix licked my folds through my panties, making me whine. He pulled the panties to the side, exposing my core to him. He licked me again, up and down. Then he focused on my clit, licking and sucking on it.

"Lixie," I moaned, grabbing his hair. After all the teasing Filix had put me through, it didn't take long for me to get to the edge, I desperately moved my hips against his face, watching as he ate me out.

"Filix, I'm g-gonna cu-" I tried to warn him before my orgasm hit me hard, making my whole body tremble. "Fuck, fuck," I whined, feeling my clit getting sensitive as Filix kept licking it.

Bringing his hand up, he spread my folds, giving him unrestricted access to my weeping cunt. He redoubled his efforts, eating me out like I was the best thing he had ever tasted. With my essence seeping into every fiber of his being, making him drunk on me, I did not doubt that fact for one second.

He suddenly nipped at my clit and my reaction was a gasp, hands flying to his hair to either stop him or pull him closer. I felt the vibrations of his chuckle against my pussy before slurping noises filled the room. My clit throbbed, and the pressure in my stomach returned.

"Fuck. I fucking love eating you out, baby. You taste so good," Filix hummed against me, making me squirm against him. "So creamy against my tongue. Fuck, you're my favorite meal."

The sting of being cut had me hissing through my teeth, yet the pain was gone the moment Filix's hot tongue lapped across the top of my thigh.

"And your blood tastes so delicious," He groaned as his eyes rolled to the back of his head.

"Come here," I whispered.

Filix crawled up my body, pressing kisses into my skin as he went. His lips met mine, and I could taste the sharp tang of my own blood on his tongue. Filix licked into my mouth, the hunger of the kiss growing in intensity.

In his momentary distraction, I wrapped my legs around his hips and used all of my strength to flip him beneath me. The surprised squeak that left his lips had a smile spreading across mine, a hunger ready to devour him whole.

"Fuck you're hot when you're on top."

"And you're hot when you're beneath me," I teased him. My grin spread wider as I saw his chest flushing pink, spreading up his neck.

Using gentle, slow motions I took the knife from Filix's grasp, and slowly drug the blunt end of the blade down his chest. Filix's abdomen muscles flexed as the cold metal ran over his skin, making him shudder beneath me.

Picking the knife up again, I slowly ran the cold metal over his collarbones before I lightly scratched a line against his skin, tiny rivulets of blood poking up through his skin where it was thinnest. I surged forward, hunching over Filix as I let my tongue dart out and swipe against the teeny tiny drops of blood.

Spit slick and no longer bleeding, I leant back against his thighs, grinning when Filix uncontrollably bucked up into me, so close to where he wanted to be.

"Fuck, baby," Filix hissed, squeezing his eyes closed, "Fuck. Please."

"Please what?" I questioned him, innocently.

Filix's eyes shot open, an annoyed look furrowed his brows. "Don't fucking tease me."

His sentence ended faster than he had intended, as I quickly drug the knife across the side of his abdomen, being cautious of prominent veins and veins that lurked beneath the surface of his skin that weren't clearly visible.

Blood welled quickly against the cut and began to dribble down his side, running across his skin and onto the sheets beneath his back.

I gently tossed the knife across the room, onto the pile of clothes Filix had discarded when he joined me on my bed, being mindful of where the knife landed to pick up later.

"I don't think," I began, gently pressing my fingers against his newest wound, "that you're in a position to give me demands."

I gathered his blood on my fingertips before I pressed harshly into his cut, forcing him to bleed more for me.

Grinning, I lifted a hand to my lips, leading my tongue up and down the length of my crimson fingers. Sharp copper lit up my palate, and I shivered. I wrapped my lips around one of my fingers, humming while I sucked it clean, pumping it slowly in and out before finally pulling it out with a wet pop.

"Mmm... you taste so good," I met his gaze between the long licks of my digits, coating my mouth with his blood. "Wanna try?"

Filix murmured something under his breath, eagerly nodding his head.

I placed two of my fingers above his lips, letting the pads of my digits rest against his mouth. Filix pursed his lips, gently kissing my fingers before his tongue swiped at them, drawing them inside his warm, wet mouth.

When he had licked most of his blood off my fingers, I pulled them from his mouth and gently pressed them back into the cut I had made on his abdomen. The wound bled a bit more, the warm, wet liquid coating my hand instantly.

With my free hand I leant over and grabbed a few tissues I had off my nightstand and placed them over the cut, stopping the bleeding all together. When I was satisfied that Filix wasn't going to bleed out, I tossed the soiled tissues onto the floor to clean up later.

Wrapping my fingers around his cock, I slicked the shaft with his blood, glaring at him while he jerked and shook from my touch. It was incredible, watching him trying to thrust into my fist, whimpering, head lolling while I sped up my pace. His dick was bright red, wet with the combination of pre-cum and his blood.

"So eager to please me," I cooed.

As I moved up to straddle his head, I trapped a breath in my lungs, steadying my own quaking body. My heart hammered in my chest, my cheeks flushed with heat. Filix Hallowes was under my thumb, and it was exhilarating. Staring down at him, blood drying on his face and chin, eyes bleary with bliss and pain, I grinned and my cunt pulsed in anticipation.

"If you're good, I might even let you cum inside of me."

I rocked over his cock, teasing him before I released a deep, lengthy moan; I sank onto him, stretching wide to sheathe his hard, aching cock in my wet cunt. The sound that escaped Filix's chest was somewhere between a sob and a scream, body lifting from the bed as I enveloped him to the hilt. I leaned forward, putting my palms on his stomach, shifting my weight to the heels of my hands while I began to slide up and down on his cock.

A sharp, pained hiss from Filix had me freezing completely as I bottomed out on him, his thighs pressed firmly against my ass cheeks. I looked down at him with wide, worried eyes.

One of his hands gripped my wrist and roughly pulled it away from his side, the side I had cut up. He placed it on his shoulder before giving me a small smile.

"Little too much pain?" I asked, feeling sorry for unintentionally hurting him.

"Just a bit," Filix laughed.

He lifted me up once more, laying back and grabbing my hips. I knelt up and sunk onto his length again, both of us groaning and throwing our heads back. I panted as I started to grind on his lap, leaning forward to bury my head in the crook of his neck. I kissed along his jawline, before I nipped at his earlobe.

Filix hissed in pleasure, and I failed at suppressing a smile. Filix's ears were always so sensitive, and I loved it.

He placed both hands on my bare back, guiding me as I took him. He cried out for me softly, and started to buck his hips up into me, bouncing me up and down on his cock. I moved with him, slamming down on him with force, moving to kiss him to try and shush him, despite how much I loved his little noises.

He removed a hand from my back, and gently pushed two fingers into my mouth, before moving them down to my clit and tracing around it. I cried out for him, and he started to fuck me faster.

"Cum for me," he begged, staring darkly at me.

I felt him thrust into me once more, and instantly came undone. I writhed on top of him as I coated his cock with my cum. The pleasure was so intense that I shook violently, and I couldn't stop my hips from rocking against him.

The feeling of my throbbing pussy clenching around him was the last straw for Filix, and his eyes rolled back as he came. I felt his cock twitch as he shot his cum into me, filling me up with his seed until I was completely stuffed. I collapsed onto his chest, exhausted, and he moved his hands to my back again to steady me.

We both gasped for air, trying to catch our breath for what seemed like ages, before Filix tilted my chin up and kissed me hungrily. We both fell back into the sheets and laughed as we tried to catch our breath again. I moved my head to the side to face him.

"I love you," I whispered, my voice hoarse.

"I love you too."

We stayed in that position, tangled together with no true idea where one of us ended and the other began, until I began to shiver from the cool air that circulated through my room. Filix's hand trailed up and down my spine, his fingertips dancing over the goose-bumps that erupted across my flesh.

"Do you want to shower?" Filix asked, his voice hoarse.

"No," I hummed, despite knowing that we had to get up and tend to our wounds.

"We need to clean up."

"I don't want to move," I protested with a little pout.

"We can be quick, baby."

I sat up and got off of Filix, scurrying to the bathroom as fast as I could without making a complete mess. Filix's deep laughter followed me into the confirmed room, which had me laughing as I sat on the toilet. I made quick work of wiping away excess fluids that had begun to drip down my thighs.

He joined me a moment later, dressed in a pair of boxer briefs, with his shirt and a new pair of panties for me to get dressed in. Setting the clean clothes on the bathroom counter, Filix turned and grabbed the mini first aid kit from beneath the bathroom sink. Popping open the box, he placed it on the countertop and began to pull out what he needed to clean up the wounds we had given each other.

Filix dropped to one knee on the bathroom floor and tenderly began to disinfect the cut he had made across the top of my thigh, being extra gentle when I hissed in pain as the rubbing alcohol hit such a fresh wound. When Filix finished putting a bandaid on me, I did the same to him making sure to be extra gentle with him.

I placed a quick kiss on his lips and promptly pulled him back into my room, where my pillows called our names.

GOING CRAZY

Someone had been watching me since I stepped foot outside to water the garden.

The morning had been peaceful, almost lazy. I awoke to Filix making breakfast for the two of us, and once our plates had been cleared we lounged around the living room.

In the early afternoon Filix left, going home to check in on his aunt and uncle and cousins.

I had felt a little guilty that I was stealing all of his time, taking him away from what little family he had left – his parents died when he was young. Yet he reassured me that stealing him away from his family was okay, that he would rather spend every moment he could with me before I returned to the capital to graduate from university.

His words were kind, and helped to ease my worries, but an underlying pang of guilt still pulsed within me.

In the late afternoon, I busied myself with watering Mum's garden, as a physical distraction from my overactive thoughts, knowing she'd be upset if I had let her hard work die while she was away on vacation.

As I moved from watering the herb garden and onto the flower bed, I stopped in my tracks. Something felt wrong. Turning slowly, I made it seem like I was looking over the garden to see what else needed to be watered, but I looked past the gate and the fence, searching for anything weird. It felt like someone was watching me and my every move.

A flash of red had my heart jumping in my chest, and my head whipped around to look back at the flowers I was watering. Sweat broke out across my forehead as I tried to act normal.

If the prince really was outside the front gate near my house, then there wasn't much I could do. The center of town was a ten-minute walk, and Sheriff Radley's place was another five from the town square. Phoning for him wouldn't be any faster either.

I pivoted and looked over toward the front of the pathway again, where the front gate was still closed. The glimpse of blood red that I'd seen had disappeared. My gaze bounced up and down the fence, searching for the prince. I knew he had been there, and he couldn't have disappeared like that.

Not bothering to put away the hose, I bolted through the garden and to the side entrance of the house.

Inside, I grabbed the phone in the kitchen and dialed Sheriff Radley's number. My fingers nervously played with the coiled cord as I waited.

"Tindol," Deputy Tindol answered.

"Hey Tindol! I uh…" I nervously glanced out the window in the sunroom that looked out over the side of the house, over the garden and out into the forest beyond our fence.

Off in the distance, next to the sign post that directed you to different forest trails, stood a figure.

Bright red hair. Elegant clothes.

The prince.

"Mare?" Tindol said, drawing me back.

"He's here," I breathed out. I refused to look away from his figure in the distance.

"Who's where?"

"The prince. He's in the woods by my house," I explained in a quiet voice, afraid the prince could hear me despite being so far away.

"Do you see him right now?"

"Yes."

"Stay in your house, Mare. Radley and I are on our way. Is the front door locked?"

"Yes," I said, but I was lying. The front door and the back door were definitely not locked.

"Good. Sit tight." Then the line went dead.

I slowly set the phone back onto the receiver and after a few blind tries I managed to hang up the phone.

Off in the distance, the prince paced back and forth along the tree line. He ran a hand through his vibrant red locks, tugging at the strands in frustration. His head whipped to the side as if he could sense I was staring at him. I ducked behind the curio cabinet Dad kept in the sunroom, and silently cursed myself.

Keeping to the blind spots of the windows, I crept my way through my own house toward the back door. I quickly latched the lock to the back door, and drew the blinds on all the windows within the sunroom. I kept myself hidden, and out of view from the windows in the kitchen in case the prince could potentially see me, even if he was an incredible distance away on the opposite side of the house. I did not want to meet the prince. I did not want to even think about the prince.

I should have called Filix to see if he'd be able to come back over and hangout. The possibility of facing the prince alone was not something I had planned on doing today – or ever for that matter.

The wait for Sheriff Radley and Deputy Tindol to arrive at my house felt like it took eons. Every creak of the house settling had me jumping, afraid the prince had somehow found his way inside.

A knock on the front door had me paralyzed. My eyes darted to the glass back door, where I could barely see off into the distance where the beginning of the forest began. Bright neon red was nowhere in sight, and that realization had my heart pounding in my rib cage.

Sweat beaded at my hairline as I turned my gaze in the direction of the front door.

"Mare?" Deputy Tindol called out.

I dashed for the front door, and peeked through the peephole to confirm that Neverhelm's deputy stood on my front porch instead of an ancient and confused fey prince.

I opened the front door and shakily greeted Tindol with a smile.

"Hey, Deputy."

"Miss Mare, how are you this evening?"

"A little spooked but I guess that's to be expected," I joked, reaching a hand up to scratch at the back of my neck. "I mean, how often do ancient cursed princes walk through your backyard?"

"Not every day," Tindol chuckled. His face crinkled as he laughed, revealing laugh lines and other wrinkles which showed his age. He was one of the finest silver foxes to grace this town. If I weren't so in love with Filix, perhaps he would be an option.

"Where'd you see the prince exactly? I'm gonna radio Radley to give us a better search area."

An uneasy feeling washed over me, much like the ominous one that had struck me earlier when I had watered the garden. The thought of stepping foot outside my front door had me rooted in place, afraid to move.

"Just by the signpost. He was pacing back and forth, like he was lost."

"Has he come any closer? Tried to talk to you?"

I shook my head no, despite the fact that I was certain I saw him near my gate earlier.

"Okay," Tindol hummed, "did he look hurt or in pain or anything?"

I again shook my head no. Even from far away he looked elegant and regal. How someone who had been asleep for four centuries looked so good was a mystery to me. I looked like a mess in the mornings.

"Okay honey, you sit tight while Radley and I go searching for him."

"Okay," I agreed. "Be careful."

Tindol gave me a nod before I carefully closed the door and moved into the living room to wait. My knee bounced as I tried to distract myself to keep my mind off of any horrible outcomes that could come to pass.

I threw on the sweater that Filix had left here, and cracked open the copy of *the Lone King* we had been reading.

Eternities are hard to bear. They are harder to bear alone.

I shivered at the thought of being alone forever, of having never met Filix or the few friends I had made while away at college. I would have led a miserable existence had it not been for them.

A prince cursed to rot beneath the earth until the blood of his kin awoke him.

Who had cursed the prince? What did he do to deserve such a punishment?

It made me think about the fey that resided in Neverhelm. Had they known the prince before the doors between our worlds had been sealed shut for eternity? What had their world been like before they had lost access to their home? I wondered what he was like, what he liked to do for fun? What kind of fey was he? What did he truly look like in the light?

I skimmed a few more pages of *The Lone King*, but I truthfully had not absorbed a single word I read. I must have read the same sentence three times before I finally realized I had been reading the same line over and over again.

I jumped in my seat on the couch when a knock came from the front door. I slowly closed the book and set it on the coffee table, before I slid off the couch and turned to the entryway.

"Evening Mare," Sheriff Radley smiled down at me. I smiled back at him and Deputy Tindol. The two of them stood on the front porch alone, no confused blood-soaked prince in sight.

"Good evening Sheriff, I take it you didn't find him?"

"We didn't see anything out of the ordinary," Sheriff Radley explained.

Odd. I thought to myself. *He'd been there clear as day.*

"You're certain you saw the prince?" Radley questioned me.

I nodded my head.

"We'll make another sweep before we head back into town. Is Filix staying the night?" Tindol asked.

I shook my head, "No, he had some things his aunt wanted him to do."

Radley hummed, the sound was displeased.

"Make sure you keep your doors locked, just in case the prince does come around. He's scared and is probably confused about where he is."

"I will," I reassured them.

"Brikham will be at the station all night. Don't be afraid to call him if you see the prince again," Tindol advised me. He gently reached out a hand and patted my shoulder, shooting me a half smile.

I shut and locked the front door after I bid them a goodbye.

LIGHT IN THE DARK

There had been no need to call Brikham after Deputy Tindol and Sheriff Radley left. I had moved cautiously through my own home, in my own room. The lights were dimmed in whatever room I entered, and I kept the music I played from my laptop at a minimum volume.

My sleep had been poor, and all I craved was Filix's warmth beside me. I'd tossed and turned, while my dreams had been plagued by the prince and the story of *the Lone King*.

Eternities are hard to bear. They are harder to bear alone. Their weight can break you down, strip you of yourself until there is nothing left.

How could you even begin to face an eternity alone? Certainly you would go mad; I know I would. Filix had only been gone for a day and I was beginning to go a little stir crazy.

While I was away at college, Filix and I would message everyday, so it wasn't like I missed him. He was always with me. And I had friends in most of my classes, so it wasn't like I was truly alone without anyone to talk to.

But still... Facing an eternity alone sounded cruel. Just like how the prince's curse was cruel. I could not face an eternity alone.

The majority of my day had been slow, and I craved distraction. I cleaned my room, sorting through and tossing out clothes that no longer fit me, or I no longer wanted. I reorganized my desk and bookshelves, being mindful to keep my favorite novels on full display.

I did a load of laundry that I had been neglecting to do for quite some time. I had been running low on underwear. My body was on high alert whenever the house creaked or groaned as it settled. Each noise had me jumping in fright, afraid that the prince had somehow gotten inside.

The sun had long since set when I took a break, finally allowing myself a moment to breathe, to relax and not worry about an ancient prince who may or may not have been lurking outside my house.

The kitchen was quiet as I chopped veggies and threw them in a pan. I had made sure the back door was still locked, and I had drawn the blinds inside the sunroom to avoid peeping eyes.

Music gently floated in the air as I cooked, the beat of the music keeping me company when Filix couldn't.

I ate dinner slowly, trying to distract myself from him with *the Lone King*. How a man was supposed to face eternity alone baffled me, the thought of being alone forever sounded terrible.

But the thought of *him* kept creeping into recesses of my mind, pulling me back into reality, stealing me away from the distractions I had wanted. I wasn't going to be able to sleep tonight knowing he was out there, just lurking in the darkness, possibly waiting for an opportunity to harm me. Calling Sheriff Radley felt like a waste of time, especially when they hadn't found him the last time they'd come all the way out here.

Shoving myself off the barstool at the island, I pulled Filix's sweater tightly around my shoulders before marching towards my front door.

Yanking it open, I hesitated at the threshold. Something deep within my mind was telling me to stay within the safety of my walls, but my fear and frustration with him won. Cowering inside my own home was ridiculous.

In the darkness, I could barely make out his silhouette.

"There's dangerous things that lurk in the dark," he calmly said, shrouded in shadow.

My feet remained planted in place, afraid to move. After seeing glimpses of him, the sensation of actually hearing his voice aloud made my heart flutter, my skin heat and my breath vanish. His voice was hypnotic and enigmatic.

"There are plenty of dangerous things in the light," I replied.

A laugh – his laugh – surrounded us, making a smile of my own ghost across my lips. His laugh was light and warm and safe, and I wanted to hear it again.

"Can I help you?" I asked.

He stepped closer, and his face caught the light of the lamp outside my door, setting my heart aflame. He was gorgeous, not in the way other girls in Neverhelm would have classified him as, – but that made him all the more beautiful.

Fluffy, bright blood red hair was brushed backwards, making his illuminated eyes seem brighter than I ever thought they'd be. A faint beauty mark sat beneath his left eye; his face was flawless but before I could truly commit his features to memory, he stepped backwards, back into the shadows.

I went to step forwards, not ready to lose the opportunity to look at his features.

"Don't step outside," he warned, the coldness in his tone stilling my movements.

What was with this guy?

"The only thing I want right now is your blood," he said. "And if you leave the safety of your home, I will kill you."

I glared at him. *How was a girl supposed to reply to that?* My frustration flared inside me.

"Then leave me alone. If you don't want me talking to you, then stop following me around like a lovesick puppy lurking in the shadows."

A 'tch' of air left his lungs, which I guess resembled a laugh or a scoff, or something in between.

"That's hard to do. You made things… difficult."

"Difficult? You haven't seen anything *difficult* yet."

Another 'tch' of a laugh left his plush lips. My fingers dug into the wood frame of the entryway. My breathing felt heavier as I contemplated stepping outside.

His eyes flashed in the darkness, a warning.

"Don't you have bleeding hearts to eat?" I asked.

"You weren't supposed to see that. I should have been more careful," he said.

His posture straightened, his head turning toward the direction of town and the main road. His attention was momentarily distracted by something in the distance, something I couldn't hear.

My bare foot pressed onto the stone outside my door, and immediately his eyes were back on me, a predatory look flashing in his luminescent eyes. I hastily jumped backward, into what little safety my house could provide me.

"I wish you hadn't broken my curse," he sighed.

I stared at him, annoyed and interested all at once.

"You need to leave, before I call the police."

"Stay inside, princess," He warned me, his eyes flashing again.

"Stay away, *princeling*," I sneered back, in a child-like manner.

The prince said nothing as he turned to leave. I listened to the gate squeak open, moving just far enough to allow him to leave my property.

Anxiety tightened in my chest as I watched him go; a sudden terror filling me. I could possibly never see him again despite all his stalkerish activities, and blood crazed tendencies.

I could not let him go.

I would not let him go.

"What's your name?" I called out to him.

He had a name, a reason for being trapped inside that glass coffin until the end of eternity. Something deep within me wanted – needed – to know who he was.

He stood just outside the gate, his back still to me. It was hard to distinguish where his shadow ended and the world behind him began; I could barely make out the way his shoulders rose as he inhaled.

"You can call me Hyunjin."

And then he walked off into the darkness, leaving me in the dim glow of the porch light.

HAD IT BEEN YOU

When I saw him again at the edge of the garden wall, two days later, I nearly lost my shit. I glared at him through the kitchen window over the sink, pouring all my hatred into my gaze. I hoped he could feel it.

I threw the dishrag against the countertop, and stormed out of the house. Why the hell couldn't he leave me alone? The front door banged against the wall as I yanked it open, and stepped outside into the middle of the garden.

"What the hell do you want?" I snapped.

"Get back inside," he rasped, his voice sounding rough enough to be sandpaper.

He was closer now, standing next to the mailbox just past the front gate. It'd take eight maybe five steps for him to make it to me. It'd take me twelve to get back inside the house.

"Get the hell away from my house, from me."

"You don't understand," He physically shook, his hands were clenched in tight fists, turning his knuckles bone white. His jaw clenched, strengthening his already killer jawline.

"I understand that you and your weird obsession with me need to get the hell away from here," I waved a finger in his direction.

"*Please*," he hissed, doubling over in pain.

He sank to his knees, dirt covering his pants as he screwed his eyes shut. Agony was written all over his features. With his head hung low, Hyunjin clutched at the dirt below his open palms. His breathing came in soft pants, making his chest barely move.

"Are you okay?" I asked hesitantly. He could have been faking an asthma attack to gain my sympathy before he struck.

"Your blood. Please. Go back inside where I can't get to you," he rasped.

The slow step backwards did not satisfy Hyunjin. He slammed a fist against the ground, against a large stone in the stone pathway, cracking it in two. I jumped and nearly lost my footing as I rushed back inside.

He was still crouched on the ground when I spun around in the doorframe. His chest still heaved, and his head was pressed against the ground. I gripped the edges of the door frame, holding myself back whilst also giving myself something to propel off if Hyunjin needed help.

"Hyunjin," I said, hoping it sounded more like a question.

We were quiet for some time, as Hyunjin collected himself, before sitting upright. He sat back on his heels and brushed the dirt and hair away from his forehead. His gaze was fixed against the broken stone before him, his eyes sharp and steady before he slowly looked to me.

"Don't step outside again. My self-control is hanging on by a spider's web of silk."

My temper sparked at his cryptic words, my fingers dug into the doorframe. If the blatant stalking hadn't already been a red flag as bright as his fucking hair, this was the last straw. I raised my foot and refused to look away from Hyunjin's kneeling form as I stepped hesitantly back outside. My hands shook as my feet hit stone.

"You won't do anything," I stated, leaving no room for him to argue. "If I'm safe inside my house then I'm safe out here."

Hyunjin's jaw clenched so hard I was afraid he'd shatter some teeth. His red eyes dropped to the healing cut along my collarbone that Filix had made a few days ago.

I lingered just outside the door, watching as Hyunjin's eyes burned brightly. He held my eye contact, refusing to look away for even a second. His gaze was intense.

I cocked an eyebrow at him, angrily challenging him.

A singular blink changed everything.

Hyunjin shot forward, launching his body at mine, moving faster than I could fully comprehend.

His fingers threaded through my hair, yanking my head backward to allow him more access to the column of my throat. A soft, almost surprised gasp left me as I was pulled flush against his toned body, my hands curled around the fabric of his white disheveled jacket.

His plush lips ghosted across the skin of my throat, his warm breath fanned over my pulse point which sent a shiver down my spine.

My body froze, unsure how to process just how fast he had moved, how quickly he had manhandled me into a position more to his liking, with easier access to drink from.

Hyunjin's tongue swept across my skin, warm and wet; he lowered his head more as heat, terror and lust pulsed down my spine. The briefest graze of sharp fangs scratched over my skin.

My hair rushed around my face as I was pushed backwards, toward the house. The vinyl flooring of the entryway was cool beneath my bare feet. My ribs ached just slightly as my body finally registered that I had been pushed away from Hyunjin. His hand slowly lowered to his side where it curled into a fist, his knuckles bone white again.

I felt the ghost of his lips pressed against my neck as I stared out the front of my door, my heart hammering in my chest. My hand shot up to my throat, my fingers delicate as they explored my skin, searching for any injuries. There was no pinch of pain, nor was there the sting of touching a fresh wound.

Hyunjin hadn't bit me.

"If you step outside again I won't be able to stop myself."

His words had goosebumps erupting all across my body. I had never heard a voice sound so dark, so torn before. A tightness formed in the center of my chest, each breath of air sending a flare of pain tugging at my ribs.

Despite his words and actions, Hyunjin's act of pushing me away from him stirred something deep within me. No matter how badly he wanted to sink his teeth into me, he resisted.

"I won't ask you again," I warned him. "Stay away from me."

And then I slammed the door in his face and retreated up to my bedroom for the evening.

WHEN I OPENED the door later that evening, Filix filled my vision. He looked pale, shell shocked almost. His eyes slowly rose to meet mine when he registered that I had opened the front door. The porch light illuminated his profile harshly.

"What's wrong?" I asked, cautiously.

He had been gone for three days, helping out around his aunt's house and somehow within that time, he'd changed. Something was off about him, and I couldn't pinpoint what was wrong.

Filix blinked a couple of times, trying to wrap his mind around something – perhaps how to break whatever news to me gently. He licked his lips apart before he answered me.

"Clé was murdered two nights ago," Filix said, his voice hollow.

"What? But we just sa–"

A bleeding, bloody heart dripped in his hands as he sat on the rooftop. His glowing eyes pierced through the darkness and me. Muffled screams and the wet, cracking sound of bones being ripped apart echoed in my mind.

Pieces clicked together faster than I could keep up with them. My mind was racing, yet I was as shell-shocked as Filix was.

"He was found in the alley behind his bar. The alley you were in," Filix said, his eyes flickered away from mine.

A wave of guilt washed over me. I knew exactly who had murdered Clé Jekeil, and I hadn't told anyone. The Sheriff had been at my house — I could have told him then. I should have.

Filix's arms engulfed me in a tight hug, crushing me against him. He buried his nose into my neck and nuzzled into me as I wrapped an arm around his waist and brought the other up to play with the ends of his hair.

Hot waves of breath ghosted over my skin as Filix held me. After a few seconds Filix's breathing became harder. The wet feeling of water dripping against my skin had me pulling back to glance at Filix.

"Lixie, why are you crying?" I moved my hand over the back of his head in a comforting manner.

He refused to pull away from me, mumbling into my skin as he pressed his face harder against my shoulder. The action had my heart melting. I rubbed his back, waiting for him to calm down.

"It could have been you," he muttered, sniffling hard.

"But it wasn't."

Filix pulled away from me. His eyes were bloodshot and puffy, tears still brimmed at his waterline and clung to his lashes. His face was flushed and his chest rose and fell in odd intervals.

"It could have been. Mother help me...If it had been you..." he trailed off, his eyes falling to the ground.

His words from a couple days ago echoed in my mind.

It hurts to be alone. I never want to be without you.

"I'm not going anywhere Filix. I promise I'm staying by your side."

"If I had been a second too late... or if I hadn't left you in the alley by yourself..."

More tears fell from his eyes, their color reflecting silvery-blue behind the glossiness of his tears before they returned to muddy brown.

My hands pressed against the side of his face, trying to anchor him back in reality to escape from the horrors his mind was playing out for him. I brushed my thumbs across his cheeks, wiping his tear lines away, giving me better access to admire his smattering of freckles.

I had always had this theory that Filix's eyes were meant to hold the stars, but no matter how hard they tried, there were just too many, and so they leaked onto his face in the form of freckles.

"I love you," I said. "I'm safe."

Filix's shoulders relaxed, and his watery eyes closed tightly as he focused on his breathing, on the grounding effect my touch had on him. Relief washed over him as he gathered himself and came back to me.

I let my hands fall from his face, but I slid one back to toy with his hair.

"I am sorry about Clé," I said, as Filix opened his eyes again. "He didn't deserve to go like that."

Something dark passed over Filix's flushed features, a memory or a thought had his face morphing into a frown. A smidgen of disgust had his lips curling to reveal his sharp teeth.

"No... he didn't," Filix muttered, his voice a near snarl.

It should have been much worse. Filix's voice seethed in my mind.

I tried to keep the surprise off my face but Filix saw it immediately.

"Let's go inside," he prompted, "I have been instructed to smother you with cuddles."

"Oh instructed by who?"

"Hmmm... well you wouldn't believe me if I told you."

With my free hand, I laced my fingers through his and tugged him inside my house, laughing quietly as his arms wrapped around me from behind.

"Oh yeah, try me!"

"This guy. He's really handsome. He has such pretty brown eyes, and his hair is this dazzling silver color – but his roots need to be touched up soon."

"Oh wow. He does sound pretty," I mused, holding in my laughter.

"He's tall too. Really strong and manly."

We flopped onto the couch, my head buried into his neck, breathing in his scent.

"Is he single?" I mumbled.

"Oh..." Filix groaned, "He is unfortunately almost engaged to this incredible woman."

I let out a dramatic sigh, which sent my breath across Filix's neck making him squirm beneath me.

"Almost engaged?" I questioned, teasing Filix. I wanted to see where he would take this.

"Yeah. He's waiting for the perfect moment. Plus he kinda wants to be proposed to."

I broke out into laughter hearing Filix's words. "You know maybe they should propose to each other, so they can both have it," I suggested.

"Oh good idea. I'll let him know," Filix hummed in a smile.

BREAD AND FINGER PAINTING

I had been pulled from slumber, having found it hard to breathe with Filix suffocating me in my sleep.

His muscular arms were wrapped tightly around my middle, his grip on me tight and unbreakable. The entire length of his body was pressed up against my side. I welcomed the warmth that radiated from his grasp, which made it hard for me to be too upset about Filix unconsciously suffocating me.

I twisted slightly, loosening his death grip. I shifted onto my back, and turned my head to look down at Filix's sleeping form.

I laid there for a while, soaking in the peaceful atmosphere that lingered in the air of my bedroom. I ran my fingers through his hair, as I admired the freckles that adorned his lightly tanned skin.

A small, tired smile spread across my face as I watched Filix dream, his eyebrows scrunching every few seconds. I hoped he dreamt of pleasant things. He deserved restful, rejuvenating sleep.

When it seemed like sleep was not going to come to me again, I decided to get up. An empty canvas on the easel in front of my windows called to me, begging for me to put color on it. To bring an image in my subconscious to life.

I carefully slid off the bed and waited to see if I had accidentally woken Filix. He barely stirred as I adjusted the blankets to rest over him again. I leant down and pressed a soft kiss to his forehead before I moved away and got dressed for the day.

I squeezed several dollops of varying colors of oil paint onto my palette before I set that aside to gather my brushes. Once I had my brushes, I poured a bit of paint thinner inside a coffee mug and laid out a dozen paper towels for cleaning later.

Pulling up an old bar stool, I sat down and simultaneously picked up a 2-inch flat brush. I dipped the flat brush into a separate small container of linseed oil and titanium white, and spread it across the surface of the canvas, being generous with its application.

I absentmindedly let my hands move across the canvas, letting the brush hit wherever it wanted. The white canvas soon began to morph into a darker work in progress, dark blues and muted purples blotted out most of the canvas.

"Whoa, that's creepy," Filix yawned behind me.

I turned on my stool and looked behind me. Filix sat up in bed, tiredly rubbing his eyes as he slowly began to wake. His hair stuck up in random places, and he was shirtless - which was always a welcome sight.

I turned back to the painting I had been working on. I jerked back when I looked at what I had created. My mouth ran dry as I blinked several times, trying to see if the image would change magically.

A hand holding a bleeding heart was the main focus on the canvas, the background a mixture of swirling blacks and blues, creating a dark thunderous sky. Rivulets of blood ran down the heart onto the person's hand, running over the silver rings on his forefingers and thumb.

I refused to tear my gaze away from the canvas.

I knew that hand... and I was pretty sure I knew whose heart that was. My stomach churned violently, like I was going to be sick at any moment.

Why the fuck did I paint this? Why hadn't I noticed sooner?

The rustling of sheets and the weight of Filix's hand on my shoulder had me jolting in my seat.

"Is that my hand?" Filix asked, holding out his free hand for me to look at.

My gaze fell to his hand and zeroed in on the two thin bands on his pointer finger. The lighter silver band sat above the darker ring on Filix's hand, where it was the opposite in the painting... on Hyunjin's hand.

"The rings are backwards," Filix muttered, drawing his hand away from my field of view.

I turned on my stool and watched him rake his hand through his growing locks. Even with messy bedhead, puffy eyes and an incredibly deep morning voice, he looked pretty. Perhaps even divine. It was definitely unfair to the rest of us for him to look so good.

"I'm going to shower," Filix said as he leaned closer and pressed a kiss to my temple. "You're welcome to join me."

I didn't answer him, just turned back to the painting as I heard the shower turn on.

It still needed a lot of work: more details added to define the skin texture, metallic paint to make the rings actually pop off the canvas, more fine lines to deepen the veins that ran within the heart, more highlights and shadows. More blending was needed to make transitions between colors seamless. Yet it was hard to mistake the painting for anything else than what it was.

There was no way I could keep this painting – or even finish it. How could I explain that it was Hyunjin's hand grasping a bleeding heart? I had to change it when I had more time.

I am never mindlessly painting again. I thought to myself as I stood from the stool and moved to drop my paint brush into a small container of paint thinner to clean later. I set my palette on the dresser in front of my windows and immediately froze.

In the back garden was none other than the prince, himself.

The bastard.

His nose was pressed into the tiny red rose bush. He breathed in the sweet smell of the few red roses that had bloomed recently. He looked peaceful and content in the garden.

Fear and anger waged a minor battle inside me. I feared Filix would find out that the prince was in my backyard - that he would find out that Hyunjin had been to my house for almost five days now. I was angry at Hyunjin for stepping foot in my yard - again. Disappointment, fear and anger swirled together in a dangerous concoction within me as I gazed out my window. Hyunjin had murdered someone innocent.

The anger stamped out the fear rather quickly as I darted out of my room, and flew down the stairs. As I stormed into the sunroom, I swiped a loaf of bread off the breakfast nook table and moved to the back door.

Yanking open the sliding glass door, I heaved the bread in Hyunjin's direction, wishing it were a brick rather than a loaf of gluten free white bread. Hyunjin's eyes met mine as I chucked the bread, surprise wrapped across his features as he fumbled to catch the thing I had thrown at him.

The loaf of bread smacked him directly in the face, and the wide-eyed expression he pulled would have been one I would have cried laughing at, had I not been so fucking angry and disappointed in him.

"You murdered Clé," I spat at him.

Hyunjin stared at me, a confused look spread across his face; like his brain was buffering as it tried to process what had just happened. His lips pressed into a soft pout as his eyes widened, his eyebrows rose.

"You threw a loaf of bread at me?"

"I'm gonna throw my entire pantry at you," I threatened him.

Hyunjin turned the loaf of bread over in his hands, as if he were fascinated by gluten free white bread.

"You murdered Clé the night I first saw you. You – you ate his heart."

The painting I had subconsciously painted flashed in my mind before the image morphed into the night I had witnessed a murder and said nothing.

"I did. He deserved it."

"Deserved it?" I reeled back, disturbed and cautious now. Filix had said Clé deserved a worse death... had he been a terrible person before I had met him?

I had thought Clé had been one of the nicest people to live in Neverhelm. What crime warranted his murder, his heart eaten from his chest?

Hyunjin looked up from the bread and stared intensely at me. He blinked a couple of times before he fidgeted under my disturbed gaze.

"He was one of the people who put me in that box for eternity."

"You've only been asleep for li—"

"Three hundred and twenty years. I know how long I've been cursed."

Sympathy bloomed in my chest as Hyunjin acknowledged exactly how long he had been asleep. Filix and I had woken the prince up earlier than anyone was ever supposed to... but it had been a complete accident.

"Jekeil got the death he brought upon himself. And the rest of them shall perish too," Hyunjin declared, authority ringing out from his tone.

"The rest of them?" I snapped. "You gonna murder the entire town then? There are humans here who don't believe you're real!"

In the midst of my rage and fire, I stepped out into the back garden, my arms flung wide as I yelled at Hyunjin. "*I* don't believe you're real half the time!"

The color drained from his face as he tensed and pulled his head backwards, trying to arch away from me.

"We've forgotten you Hyunjin! The door to the Feywild was closed half a millennia ago. We've adapted, we have moved on from believing in fey and fairytales. They're myths, stories you tell to children."

I stalked closer to him, further leaving the safety of my house.

"The few fey who remain are slowly dying out. There are only a handful of fey left here," My shouts had quieted down, the anger I had felt toward him beginning to dim into pity.

Hyunjin tipped his head away, turning his nose from me. His eyes glowed violently bright as they stared down at me, a frenzied panic burned in his gaze.

"There is no way to open the door to the Feywild," I said. "You're supposed to be alone for eternity."

Hyunjin physically flinched at my words, his eyes pressed tightly together as he held back tears and vicious words he wanted to spit back at me. When he reopened his eyes I shrunk away from him, purely on instinct.

Fear seeped through my chest, completely snuffing out the candle of anger that I burned for Hyunjin. I stood rooted in place, no longer within the safety of my walls.

"Be lucky it was not your heart I ate. The temptation is still very real."

I took a step backwards, but froze again when I saw Hyunjin's eyes pulse, ready for a chase. My fingers felt clammy as I stood a few feet from safety. I swallowed, the sound embarrassingly loud.

"That's not very 'princely'," I tried to jab at him again, but it fell short.

Hyunjin sneered. "You're incredibly rude for a human."

"At least I don't murder and stalk people."

"No, you just break curses before they're meant to be broken."

He spun and began to walk away from me, moving to leave through the broken section of brick wall that Dad had never bothered to fix, that led off into the forest where the prince's coffin lay.

"You should be thanking me!" I exclaimed, getting heated again.

Anger radiated off Hyunjin in thick waves, as he stopped just before the wall. His shoulders rose and fell as he tried to control his anger, which made my skin crawl and my stomach sink. He pivoted, glaring at me over his shoulder, his eyes burning at a painful luminosity. I suddenly had no desire to be the center of Hyunjin's attention.

"I should eat your heart," he spat, barely suppressing a deep snarl that had his lip curling. The barest flash of a pointed canine glinted in the light of the late morning sun that rose in the north.

"Hey," Filix's voice echoed, coming into the sunroom.

My eyes widened in surprise and fear as I whipped around to look at the house, completely putting my back to Hyunjin.

Filix's hair was damp and hung in his eyes. He looked at me with a concerned expression. His eyes raked up and down my body, searching for anything wrong. When he found nothing physically wrong with me, he stepped outside and began to scan the garden. He kept his eyes raking across the budding greenery as he stepped up to me, and invaded my personal space.

My eyes darted to the edge of the garden, searching for bright red hair but found nothing where he stood.

"What's wrong?" he questioned, his head tipped down to look at me yet his eyes were elsewhere, gazing off in the direction Hyunjin had disappeared in.

I let out an exasperated exhale, "Nothing's wrong."

Filix's eyes immediately flicked to meet mine. I held his gaze and tried to wipe the annoyance off my face. It would do me no good to snap or take my anger out on Filix. I was mad at Hyunjin, and at myself. We were both equally to blame for Clé's murder.

There was a beat of silence as Filix stared down at me as he tried to put together a reason for why I was upset. I watched him as he watched me, his eyes moving across my face for any signs, any tells to give him even the slightest of hints to what was wrong.

"Why is the bread out here?" he asked instead.

Wise move, I thought to Filix, complimenting him for not prying even when he wanted to.

"I was going to make us sandwiches but then I saw a weasel digging around my rose bush, and that was the first thing I grabbed to scare him off."

Filix threw yet another confused look in my direction. "We don't have weasels in this area. They aren't native to Neverhelm."

"Oh, well maybe it was a fox."

We stared at each other, fully aware that we both knew I was lying. I picked at the skin on my thumbs, worrying.

Hyunjin knew how to throw a girl off her game, that was for sure.

We were quiet after that, and the two of us moved inside the house again. I locked the back door and drew the blinds. I did not want to see Hyunjin again. I'd been mean - down right cruel to him.

I should apologize, I thought to myself before I remembered that the fey were offended when apologized to or thanked. But I hated being mean when it wasn't warranted. I hated how mean I could get when I didn't control myself.

Filix absentmindedly opened the fridge and began to jot down things we needed to grab from the farmers market that was going on later in the day. I moved to the sink and began to wash the dishes from last night.

"What do you want for breakfast?" Filix asked from directly behind me. He back hugged me, pressing a gentle kiss to my neck just below my ear. I turned my head to look at him over my shoulder.

"You?"

Filix rolled his eyes at my hopeful yet teasing tone. He glided right past my proposition and moved back to the topic of breakfast. "You need to eat something. I will not go to the market with you hangry."

"But if we–"

"There's only like twenty-five calories in sperm and you burn about four calories per minute during sex," Filix said, having facts

66

ready to shut me down. "If we're fucking you definitely need to eat something. And that means we have to go to the market first."

I shut off the water as I put the last dish on the rack to dry before I grabbed the dish rag and began to dry my hands. Leaning against the countertop I shamelessly looked at Filix, letting my eyes wander across his body.

"Surprise me then," I challenged him.

"Challenge accepted," Filix beamed as he whirled around and moved back to the refrigerator.

"Cute ass."

Filix shook his ass playfully as he rummaged in the fridge, pulling out several ingredients from various drawers and shelves. I laughed as Filix moved to set his ingredients on the island, kicking the fridge door with his foot.

Two eggs, finely shredded cabbage, some green onions and carrots sat on the countertop. Along with a few slices of cheddar cheese and ham.

As Filix got out a pan from above the stove, he looked over at me.

"Do you have any bread that wasn't used to scare off non-native weasels?"

"Ha, ha *so* funny!" Sarcasm laced my words as I uncrossed my arms and moved around in the kitchen.

Filix said nothing as he pulled out a bowl and began to crack open the eggs. He quickly began to whisk them with a fork as he waited for the frying pan to heat on the stove.

"Are you making gilgeori toast?" I questioned him as I moved to the pantry to remove the last loaf of gluten free white bread I had. I definitely needed to buy more at the market.

Filix gave a non-committal hum.

Sliding up next to Filix, I passed him the loaf of bread before I moved out of his way. While we were good in the kitchen together, I was no good at making gilgeori toast, no matter how easy the recipe was to follow. I picked up the discarded grocery list Filix had been jotting down, and scanned over what he'd written. I added a couple things, letting my mind wander as I tried to plan out our meals until my parents returned home.

The sizzle of butter melting had me glancing up at Filix.

"Hey, go grab a jacket. These are almost done, and we can eat on the way," he advised me as he picked up a spatula.

I gave him a nod and disappeared upstairs to grab his jacket and a hoodie for me.

Stepping inside my bedroom felt weird. The bloody heart in hand painting felt ominous and suffocating. Especially when I knew exactly who and what was depicted upon the canvas. Half of me wanted to take my palette knife and scrape off the oil paint to start again, but the other half of me was proud of the amount of detail I had been able to capture in the few short hours I had been slaving away.

With a shake of my head, and perhaps a dramatic eye roll aimed solely at my own reaction, I grabbed Filix's leather jacket off the floor and moved to my closet to grab a hoodie.

Filix's voice drifted from the kitchen as I descended the stairs and turned left to cut through the living room. I hesitated just inside the archway, listening as Filix spoke. I strained my ears to hear what Filix was talking about, but his low voice made it hard to discern what he was saying clearly.

"...I'm saying, you'll need to return with an explanation."

With a puzzled expression I stepped inside the kitchen and glanced around the room, subtly looking for someone else. When I found the room empty, I threw the puzzled look in Filix's direction.

"Were you talking to someone or just yourself?"

"Just talking to the voices in my head," he said, laughing a bit.

I watched as he wrapped two sandwiches in paper towels before he set them on a cutting board to cool for a few minutes. We met each other halfway; I extended his jacket out to him with one hand while I simultaneously worked on sliding my arms into the hoodie's sleeves. When both my hands were free, I slipped the hoodie over my head, getting stuck in the process.

Filix stood before me, a maroon beanie in his hands. He sheepishly looked up at me as he waited for me to finish fighting with my hoodie.

"Here. You don't wanna get a cold," He said as he held the hat out to me.

"It's not even that cold out," I laughed but still took the beanie and slid it onto my head, being mindful of my curtain bangs.

Filix watched me with attentive eyes. He reached out a hand to gently untucked my bangs from being caught in the beanie, obscuring my vision just slightly. His fingers ran through my hair, dragging the long locks over my shoulders to rest against my chest.

"There. Perfect," Filix smiled as he took a step backwards to give me a once over.

I playfully gave him a twirl, which earned me a chuckle.

"Ready to go?" I questioned him, my hand extended as I wiggled my fingers at him to entice him to take it. Not that he wouldn't.

He stepped away and grabbed our gilgeori toast before he handed one to me.

"Always with you," He said as he grabbed my hand.

I smiled at him over my shoulder as I tugged him outside the front door and waited for him to close it. Filix locked the door, and we began to walk the fifteen minutes it would take to get into town.

THE WEATHER WAS SLIGHTLY chilly as we wandered through Neverhelm's town square. Laughter and conversation filled the air, yet underneath it all was a sense of dread and urgency.

As people mulled about, everyone was on high alert, searching for anything out of the ordinary; all while trying to keep a semblance of normalcy alive.

My eyes raked over everyone as they moved through the farmer's market, the hairs on my neck stood on end – waiting for something to happen. A couple people lingered around Aleiah's bakery stand, nibbling on lemon squares she'd made earlier in the morning. Near Aleiah's stand was Callie's drink booth. She moved quickly and efficiently as she prepared drinks for those who lined up. Sympathy bloomed in my chest as I watched her work.

Clé's murder had been a shock to the entire town... but Callie... Callie was the one who took the news of Clé's passing the hardest. The poor pink haired half-pixie had been close to Clé, and seen him almost like a second father - especially since her entire family was on the other side of the Veil.

Despite the underlying uneasiness that put the entire town on edge, there was an odd sense of comfort that also lingered in the air, perfuming it nicely. It felt good to be home after being away for so many months.

I kept to myself as I slowly walked past Mayor Kim's flower stand, moving toward the exit with my basket of goodies. Dividing the shopping list in half with Filix made it incredibly easy to wander through the stalls and gather what we needed for the upcoming week. The faster we got what we needed, the faster we could return home.

I caught Filix's eye from where I'd left him, stood at his aunt and uncle's wood carving table, and waved. He beamed as he waved back at me, throwing a finger heart in my direction before his aunt called his attention away from me.

My gaze darted nervously as I watched my neighbors move about the square as I waited for Filix to finish talking with his aunt. Laughter caught my attention, drawing my gaze off Kyomi's wood carving and toward the other side of the center square.

His bright red hair was a dead giveaway as he walked through the market, passing Aleiah's bakery stand and heading away from the center of the market. Dressed in a cropped, white blazer that was hollowed at the sides, thin silver chains linked together to create an intricate diamond pattern where the remainder of the jacket should have been. The white jacket was a huge contrast to the black pants and vibrant red hair. He stood out, and it was painfully obvious.

He shouldn't be here. He'll be caught!

"You okay Mare?" Filix asked from beside me. His brown eyes looked silvery-blue for a second before they returned to normal. I hadn't even realized he'd walked across the square to meet me.

"Yup! Everything's great!" I said, blindly passing him my basket. "Start heading home. I forgot to tell Aleiah something!"

I took off across the market before Filix even had a solid grip on the wicker handle. I heard him curse slightly as he fumbled to keep the items I had purchased from scattering across the ground.

Cutting back through Mayor Kim's flower stand, I continued to look at the back of Hyunjin's head as he moved further away from me. I darted past a couple looking at some plums, and peaches and nearly ran into Mr. Una, pushing a wheelbarrow down the walkway.

"Woah!" he exclaimed as he came to an abrupt stop.

"Sorry!" I called out, as I glanced back over my shoulder to make sure Mr. Una wasn't hurt. I hurried my pace when I deemed Mr. Una was unharmed.

I stumbled to a complete stop when I realized I couldn't see Hyunjin anywhere. My head whipped around, searching the crowd I'd just run through in case he'd somehow slipped past me.

Not seeing him made my head throb. He had been right there - where was he? My heartbeat drowned out the noise of the market-place as I spun in a circle searching for Hyunjin, the anxiety of not knowing where he was beginning to grow.

Why do you care so much?

I wasn't going to even think about that, about why I even cared to find Hyunjin in the first place.

A flash of red caught my attention again, just a few paces away at

Poppiri's art supply stand. Relief seeped through my chest as I licked my lips and weaved my way over to Hyunjin.

"Hey!" I beamed as I slid up to his side and tried to control my heavy breathing. I had to act completely normal in case anyone was looking in or near our direction.

Hyunjin turned to me, a tube of blood red oil paint in his hand much like the beating heart he'd had in his palm three nights ago. My brain supplied the blood that dripped off the heart and ran down his chin and a flash of neon eyes before my flashback was broken by Hyunjin speaking.

"Hey princess," he said calmly, like I hadn't cursed him out a couple hours ago.

The bloody, beating heart in his hand was a paint tube again and his eyes weren't glowing as they had been a couple hours ago. He looked so incredibly normal here at the market, even if his hair stood out among the rest of the people here.

My eyes flickered over to his ears, my heart beating nervously again. Hyunjin gently put the tube of red oil paint he was inspecting back down onto the display and turned fully toward me.

"Come to yell at me more? You look delicious when you're angry," he teased.

I ignored him and instead offered him my beanie. "Hey, put this on."

Hyunjin's eyes dropped to look at the maroon beanie in my hands, outstretched for him to take. His brows pinched together, confused and offended.

"What for?" he asked, sounding aloof.

I put on a pleasant, friendly smile as I caught Mr. Park and Mrs. Kim staring at Hyunjin and I. My eyes whipped to where I had last seen Sheriff Radley. He was thankfully watching over the crowd on the northern side of the square. I gently looked back up at Hyunjin, hoping he wouldn't protest anymore.

"Your ears, Hyunjin. They're—"

Hyunjin wasn't able to keep the disapproval off his face. I felt guilty as I stared up at him. The guilt I felt from yelling at him earlier began to double in on itself, like an ouroboros.

"That hat... have you even washed your hair recently?" he asked, striking out because I'd hurt his feelings trying to help him.

"Please, I don't want you to get hurt."

Mr. Park and Mayor Kim had begun to make their way over to Hyunjin and I, and I began to panic even more. If they saw his ears – I had no idea what they would do with him. His curse was never supposed to be broken. No one was even supposed to go near his coffin. If they recognized him – if they even had an inkling of who he was – then that would mean they'd figure out that Filix and I broke the prince's curse, and had lied about it to their faces.

I pushed myself up onto my tiptoes and slung my beanie over Hyunjin's head before he could protest or process what I was doing. I pulled it down quickly, and accidentally covered his eyes for a brief second.

Hyunjin let out a yelp of surprise as he drew backwards, his hands flying to the beanie now secure on his head. He gently pushed the fabric away from his eyes before glaring down at me. The maroon beanie did an excellent job hiding Hyunjin's pointed ears, which was the goal; though I hadn't expected him to look so good in the hat.

"Happy?" Hyunjin asked, clearly displeased.

"Very," I answered him. "And for your information I washed my hair last night."

Hyunjin rolled his eyes at me, and adjusted the beanie to rest more over his forehead, leaving his thick dark eyebrows to rest against the edge of the fabric, just slightly hidden.

"So that's why you smell?" he snapped.

"If you want to get caught then give me the hat back," I bit back, sinking to his level. I shouldn't have snapped back at him.

"No," he scoffed, staring at me like I'd lost my head.

"Why are you eve–"

"Mare? Who's this?" Mayor Kim asked as she and Mr. Park stopped behind Hyunjin.

His eyes widened in fright as he pivoted on his heel to face our elders. I reached out for him, my hand landing on his bicep. As Mr. Park and Mayor Kim watched, I slid my arm through Hyunjin's arm and side hugged him.

"Oh this is..." I faltered, unsure of how to refer to Hyunjin.

"I– I'm Sam— It's a pleasure to meet you, sir," Hyunjin said, extending his hand to Mr. Park.

Mr. Park hesitated for a moment before he shook Hyunjin's hand firmly. When Mr. Park released Hyunjin's hand, Hyunjin turned his attention to Mayor Kim. When she stretched her hand out to shake his, Hyunjin brought her hand up to his lips where he pressed a gentle kiss to her knuckles. She blushed a bit and refused to look at him directly.

"Sam goes to university with me. He's visiting family nearby and wanted to come say hi," I lied with a pleasant smile.

Mr. Park hummed before Mayor Kim cut in, "That's quite the hair color, Sam."

"Yes, I—" Hyunjin's cheeks flushed as he raised his hand to scratch at his neck, playing with the ends, "I changed it for a party a long time ago."

"Well it looks good on you. How long are you staying in Neverhelm?" Mayor Kim questioned him.

"I'm not sure. I'm expected to return home soon," he answered honestly. I squeezed his arm a bit tighter, warning him to be careful. The fey couldn't lie, so he was going to have to be careful with his answers. I needed to talk more.

"I was just showing him around the marketplace."

Hyunjin nodded his head in agreement, "It's very lovely here."

"Thank you, our town doesn't get many visitors this time of year. Usually more in the late summer," Mr. Park said.

"I hope you don't mind, I promised Filix that we'd meet for brownies," I said, hoping to cut this awkward confrontation short.

"Oh, of course," Mayor Kim said with wide eyes. "We just couldn't help but meet someone so... dazzling."

Hyunjin stiffened beside me. I tightened my grip on his bicep and slid one hand down to rest in his own. The rings that adorned his fingers were cold against my skin and they clinked softly against my own rings. I gave him a reassuring squeeze, which he returned.

I laughed, "Sam's pretty captivating. I mean I was speechless when I first met him."

Hyunjin and I shared a look as we recalled a couple nights ago, with him eating a bloody heart right in front of me. Hyunjin's expression softened as he looked down at me, something in his eyes shifted.

"And you're invigorating. You make me feel alive again," Hyunjin answered, giving me a compliment in return. His eyes never left mine, their softness holding a hint of seriousness in them I hadn't seen on him before.

My eyes narrowed at his answer. Had he really just lied to my face to keep up the cover of being a friend from school? My chest felt hot as I blinked, recalling that fey could not lie. I hardly knew him, but his words made my heart feel warm and soft and fuzzy. I was momentarily stunned.

"Really?" I softly asked, not believing him.

Hyunjin's gaze flickered from my eyes to my lips for a brief second before Mayor Kim spoke up and broke whatever trance had been cast over the two of us and locked us in our own little world for a moment.

"Come Simon, let's leave these two lovebirds alone," Mayor Kim said, gripping Mr. Park's arm to drag him away.

Mr. Park grumbled under his breath as he was led away but he was polite enough to throw a "have fun you kids!" over his shoulder before getting distracted by Jae's ice cream stand.

I laughed under my breath at Mr. Park. My head tipped sideways slightly, my cheek rested against Hyunjin's shoulder as I watched everyone walk around the marketplace.

Callie was at her drink stand across the square where a small line had formed behind Emily and Violet and the dozen children they were babysitting today. Mr. Una had stopped with his cart in front of Aleiah's bakery stand, his eyes scanning every loaf of bread for the perfect gift to take home to his wife. Sheriff Radley stood off to the side of the crowd, watching over everyone, trying to keep them safe. Radley's husband Oliver stood with Lydia and a few others, huddled around a table full of books from the library that were for sale. The only person I couldn't see was Filix, but I had told him to head home.

Ignoring Mayor Kim's incorrect comment about Hyunjin and I being a couple, everything felt right. Neverhelm had never felt so much like home before, even if things were tense.

"You said I was visiting, that we go to the same university together. What do you study?" Hyunjin asked, his entire focus on me as I people-watched.

"My parents wanted me to study something important and beneficial to society," I huffed in disappointment.

"But you are not?" Hyunjin questioned.

"Nah, my mum's made up her mind that I'm a disappointment and my dad doesn't care what I like. So I'm studying what I want. Not what they want."

I glanced up at him as I realized I had unveiled a lot to Hyunjin at that moment, more than I should have revealed to a blood drinking, murdering stranger.

His gaze was still as soft as it had been when we were pretending to be close classmates from school for Mayor Kim and Mr. Park, but a dramatic eye roll and a huff of a laugh left him.

"Trying to appease people who don't value the skills you excel at are not worthy of your kindness or your heart. Besides...why study boring or complicated topics when you could finger paint?"

A small smile spread across my face at Hyunjin's attempt to comfort me. It felt weird how easy it was to joke around with him, despite knowing who he really was. What he really was.

"What are you studying?" he asked in a more serious manner.

"Finger painting."

He gave me a pointed look, one thick straight brow arched just slightly.

"Art history. I have a job lined up to be an archivist once I graduate."

"Do you have a favorite time period for art? Or a favorite artist?" Hyunjin questioned, sounding genuinely intrigued.

Something within me clicked off, and my mouth began to ramble as I was able to talk about my passions. "Oh yes! There's this fey artist from like nine hundred years ago. We only have a handful of his pieces on this side of the Veil but his work is beautiful. The way he paints such expansive worlds of darkness, stripped of color but you can feel something alive in the shadows on the canvas. You stare into the abyss of the paint strokes and you just want to know more, to fall into the piece."

A large gust of wind rushed through the marketplace, whipping my hair over my shoulder and into my face stopping me from speaking. I tried to tame it with one hand but found it to be impossible until the wind died down. Hyunjin stiffened beside me and refused to breathe. As the wind died down, he spoke up.

"Let go of me," he seethed, his voice strained.

I looked at him with a confused expression before I glanced down and realized our hands were still intertwined. When I realized I was gripping the hand that had held Clé's bleeding heart not three days ago, I shoved myself away from Hyunjin. Even with a few feet of space between us he still looked tense and uncomfortable.

"What's wrong?" I asked.

Hyunjin pressed his lips into a thin line and he clamped his eyes closed, turning his head away from me slightly like he was trying to control himself. His face scrunched up, wrinkles appeared around his nose and eyes in disgust. He looked to be in a lot of pain.

"You stink," he said, his words dripping with distaste.

Fighting with him wasn't helpful, our little conflict a couple minutes ago had proven that. I grabbed the collar of my shirt and brought it up to my nose, inhaling. I only smelt the fabric softener mum loved to use, lavender and chamomile.

"Not your clothes," Hyunjin hissed. "Your blood."

His hands were curled into tight fists, his knuckles bone white. That look of disgust hadn't vanished from his face either.

"My blood?" I asked.

"I want to throw you across that fountain over there and strip yo —" he cut himself off, pressing his lips together before he licked them apart. "I want to sink my teeth into you and drink until I'm satisfied," Hyunjin said, his eyes opening slightly. Even if he was heavy lidded I could still see the eerie glow of his red eyes blazing bright before he looked away from me.

"How much blood would satisfy you?" I whispered, curious yet scared.

"Every last drop."

"What's stopping you?"

I shouldn't have said that. What was stopping Hyunjin from sinking his incredibly sharp fangs into my tender flesh? If my blood called to him like he said it did, I don't think I could have controlled myself. I would have succumbed to desire long ago.

"It has come to my attention that I may need your blood later when I am to return to the Feywild."

I blinked. I had not expected that answer.

"Wha- how much?" I heard myself ask.

Another sideways glance answered my idiotic question.

Every last drop.

I awkwardly smiled at Hyunjin and purposefully stepped farther away from him. His head followed my movements, making my awkward smile even more forced.

"Don't follow me home," I warned him, despite smiling.

"My coffin is in the same direction your house is in."

I took another step away from him, beginning to panic a bit. I wanted to be very, very far from Hyunjin.

"Didn't you want to murder more of the people in this town?" I questioned him. As soon as the words left my mouth I regretted them. I cringed. "I mean, isn't there like... I don't know... anything else for you to do in town?"

"You are incredibly ruthless for a human filled with compassion and empathy."

I blinked again. I had not expected that answer either.

"You don't know me."

"I know you better than you think."

And then he began to walk across the marketplace, leaving me dumbfounded in front of Poppiri's art stand.

YOU CAN'T RESIST IT

I stumbled backwards as I pulled open the back door to go water the garden while I waited for Filix to get here. Hyunjin was slumped against the door frame, nearly collapsed. His body was leant against an invisible barrier at the door's threshold, his hairline slick with sweat. It didn't slip past me that Hyunjin did not have my beanie that I leant him yesterday. His usually tanned skin looked paler than normal, even in the direct sunlight. His chest moved in shallow pants as he hunched over and gripped the doorframe.

He looked sick.

He looked like he was dying.

"Hyunjin," My voice was hard, a warning that's laced with caution and curiosity.

"Don't invite me in," he warned, braced against the frame of the back door.

"You're dying, Hyunjin!"

Hyunjin grumbled under his breath, something sarcastic but I didn't catch all of it.

I moved into the kitchen, blindly searching for something to

collect my blood and a knife. I grabbed the xacto knife off my countertop and grabbed an unused coffee spoon. I moved to the back door
again. Hyunjin's fingers were bone white as he crushed the wood
siding. He looked up at me when I returned.

"What are yo—?"

"How much?" I asked.

"What?"

"To make you better, how much of my blood do you need?"

"I'm not taking your blood."

"Hyunjin!" I protested with a groan.

"No."

Inhaling deeply I pressed the xacto into the pad of my pinky
finger and quickly sliced upwards. The line cutting my fingerprint in
two took a moment to bleed. Shakily holding the spoon in my usable
fingers, I used my free hand to gently pry apart the cut skin. The
blood began to flow freely, making me shakily scramble to catch my
blood in the small coffee spoon. My blood dribbled into the metal
spoon, pooling quicker than I thought it would.

I pulled my pinky away, pressing it into my T-shirt to staunch the
bleeding. With my other hand I held the spoon out to Hyunjin.

"Mare, I can't."

"You can and you will," I argue, shoving the spoon towards Hyunjin's face.

A bit of the blood missed his mouth, the spoon bumping into his
lip, making the liquid dribble down his chin until his tongue swiped
out to lick it up. His thumb brushed against the edge of his chin and
caught the rest of the droplet that he had missed. Two silver rings
adorned his pointer finger - the darker band sat atop the lighter
silver one. The rings looked nearly identical to the ones Filix had.

His crimson neon eyes bore into my own as he placed his thumb
against his tongue and savored the little bit of blood I'd given him.
His eyes rolled to the back of his head as he sucked on his thumb
and moaned quietly.

I watched as he sank down onto his knees and slumped backwards, resting his hands on either of his thighs. The veins in his hands flexed as he tried to regain his composure. His head was tipped forward as he breathed deeply.

"I wish you hadn't done that," Hyunjin sighed, sounding upset.

"You wanted to die on my back porch?"

A 'tch' of a laugh escaped his lips, before he looked up at me, some of his hair falling into his eyes. He looked good down on his knees for me.

"I wouldn't have died," he sighed, like he wasn't dying just moments ago. "And now you're bound to me."

"Bound to you? You're the one on your knees, handsome."

Awkward silence hung in the air before I laughed, surprised at my own words.

Those haunting red orbs stared up at me, his monolid eyes displeased.

"I'm bound to you?" I asked, hoping to move on from the weird flirty comment I had made.

"It's complicated," he settled on.

"You better make it uncomplicated really fast."

Hyunjin remained on his knees, with his mouth shut as he stared up at me.

I returned the stare, crossing my arms across my chest, waiting. The longer the silence stretched between us, the clearer it became that Hyunjin was not in the mood for sharing perhaps vital information with me. I let out a displeased huff of air as I rolled my eyes and grabbed the edge of the door.

"Right, okay. Next time I offer you a favor, remind me not to," I said, and then I slammed the door in his face for a second time.

WANNA COME IN?

our knocks resonated from the front door seconds before I
opened it.

"Hey, you wanna come in?" Filix asked, despite him
being outside.

"Step out," I joked with him, continuing an odd tradition we had
started when we first met. By asking whoever was inside the house
to 'come in' to the outside, while asking whoever was outside the
house to 'step out'; it made no sense, but it made us laugh at
ourselves. Opposites had become sort of our thing.

A smile tugged at his lips as he waited for me to step back and
allow him inside. I opened the door wider, and let him slip past me.
As Filix kicked off his shoes in the entryway, I cautiously looked out
into the garden searching for Hyunjin.

"Waiting for anyone else?" Filix asked, his voice directly
behind me.

I jumped a little, surprised that he was so close when I had heard
him walk off into the living room. Closing the door, I turned to
face him.

"No, I was making sure the lights came on outside in the garden. Dad said they've been acting up recently," I lied.

Filix's eyebrows dipped together as a shiver wracked his body, despite the clear effort in which he tried to suppress it. In fact whatever happened to Filix didn't look like a shiver, it looked like he flinched, as if I had hit him or something.

"You okay?"

Filix put on a fake smile for me, trying to get me to ignore whatever had upset him. He held up a paper bag, one I hadn't seen him walk in the door with.

"I bought gluten free brownie mix," he said, with a real smile.

"And to think I couldn't love you any more," I teased him, willing to let his strange reaction go for the time being.

Holding out his other hand, he wiggled his fingers trying to entice me to join him on his baking adventures. I hesitated, staring down at his hands, flicking between his offer and the bag he'd suddenly manifested. I was certain Filix walked inside my house empty handed.

Where had he gotten the brownie mix?

"You know you want to," Filix tempted me, "I'll even let you lick the spatula afterwards."

"Ohh tempting, do you think I could lick your abs too?"

"Only if I get to eat you out while we wait for the brownies to bake," Filix countered my offer.

I stared down at his waiting hand, my eyes lingering on the double stacked silver rings on his pointer finger. My mind flickered back to yesterday when Hyunjin was dying on my back porch. When he had swiped up the blood droplet that had run down his chin when I had missed his mouth with the coffee spoon full of my blood.

Filix began to lower his hand when mine slipped into his own, silently accepting his counteroffer. And then he tugged me across the living room and into the kitchen.

We fell into a rhythm in the kitchen. I began to gather the bowl, the pan and all measuring cups and utensils we would need while Filix rummaged inside the fridge for the eggs, before he slid over to the pantry. He pulled out espresso, castor sugar, brown sugar, and cocoa powder before he moved back to the island to begin measuring and mixing.

As I set up our workstation, I playfully twirled away from the island and moved toward the oven. With quick fingers I had the oven preheating as Filix began to crack an egg.

Together we made quick work of creating the brownie batter, and soon we were just waiting for the oven to finish preheating.

Licking the spatula, I glanced over at Filix. He stood at the sink, washing out the bowl so we wouldn't have to do it later.

"Wanna watch a movie?" I questioned, my mouth full of leftover batter.

Filix shifted to glance over his shoulder as he continued to scrub the bowl clean. He nodded his head as he straightened and turned off the water. Setting the bowl on the drying rack, he picked up a dishrag and began to dry off his wet hands.

"You pick while I go grab blankets?" he suggested.

"But I chose last time," I reminded him.

"I never choose something that keeps you awake, so you pick something."

"I fell asleep like one time!" I protested, laughing as I moved toward the sink to wash the spatula.

Filix laughed as he walked away, heading toward the living room.

"Yeah sure. Once when I put on that documentary. Once *again* when I chose that cheesy romance flick. Once *more* when I said I wanted to watch a horror movie." His voice echoed through the living room as he moved to the hallway to get to the stairs.

"Yeah, yeah, yeah! I get it!" I shouted back at him.

I turned back to the sink and began to scrub the spatula clean. Placing the utensil onto the drying rack, I grabbed the dishrag and dried my hands. With my hands no longer dripping wet, I began to clean up the few things we had yet to put away, like the chocolate chips, the vanilla extract, the espresso.

"H-h-hey yo-ou wa–" came the rasp of a man's voice.

I froze in the kitchen, listening intensely to every sound within the house.

The refrigerator and coffee maker sounded the loudest as they were right beside me, but despite that, underneath the hum of electricity and the gentle rumble of the air conditioning the distinct sound of heavy breathing – heavy yet shallow panting – could be heard.

I slowly set the bag of chocolate chips back down on the countertop, and pivoted on my heel, straining to listen harder, to hear more over the natural sounds that resonated throughout the house. Upstairs I could hear Filix moving around in my room as he gathered blankets and a couple extra pillows.

I strained my ears, listening for whoever's voice I knew I had heard coming from just beyond the archway in the sunroom, near the back door.

Filix's footsteps thumped down the stairs and darted off into the living room before the house grew silent again.

"Lix?" I called out quietly, afraid to make too much noise.

"Yeah?" he called back, his words loud and unaware.

I moved to the archway that connected the living room and the kitchen, and kept an eye on the archway that led back into the hallway. Filix's head popped up from the couch where he was arranging pillows and blankets for a mini sleepover.

He stopped fluffing the pillows when he saw how worried I looked.

"What's wrong?" he asked, his voice quieter now, more concerned than it had been.

"N-nothing," I lied. "Did you want me to add extra chocolate chips to the brownies or do you think they'll be good enough?"

Another minor flinch wracked through Filix's body, but I chose to ignore it. Hyunjin's presence over the past couple of days has put me on edge. I needed to relax and stop worrying about every tiny thing that seemed abnormal or out of place.

"They'll be fine without any," Filix said as the oven beeped, signaling it was done preheating.

I threw a distrustful look in the direction of the kitchen, but continued to walk inside the room while Filix began to assemble our makeshift cuddle pile.

My head immediately turned to the dark sunroom, searching for anything lingering in the shadows as I moved toward the oven. When I was certain nothing was inside my house without my knowledge, I turned my attention to the brownies.

Placing the square pan inside the oven, I set a timer and walked back into the living room where Filix had finished setting up an obnoxious amount of blankets. He looked back at me with his head hanging off the back of the loveseat. He smiled brightly as he watched me walk around the couch, and made grabby hands at me when I neared the couch.

It was a struggle to get over the copious amount of blankets, but once I managed to climb over them, I fell into Filix's side, his arms immediately wrapping around me, dragging me against his chest.

With nimble fingers, Filix passed me the remote to choose which movie we would try. It took me a few minutes to pick what we wanted to watch, I had wanted to watch something Filix would want — yet every time I asked his opinion he deflected and said he was good with whatever. Each time I thought I had chosen a good movie to watch Filix would answer the same way, putting us back at square one. Fed up and hungry for our baking brownies, I randomly settled on a movie, not caring what it was anymore.

Filix shifted on the couch, pulling yet another blanket on top of us as he pressed more of his body against mine.

"If you snuggle me any harder I'm going to melt."

"Ew. That would be so gross to clean up," Filix chuckled.

"I thought you liked it when I was 'messy'," I teased him, sticking my tongue out at him.

"Don't say things that will get you fucked. I don't care if your mum finds out I took you here on the—"

Frantic knocking on the front door pulled Filix and I from our conversation. Were we expecting someone? I shot a confused glance in Filix's direction as I rose from the couch, letting the blankets pool on the floor. I cautiously moved toward the entry to answer the door.

Filix shot off the couch and dashed to get in front of me, blocking my path. With his arms pressed against the archway frame, he made it impossible for me to pass into the entryway and greet whoever was banging incessantly on the door.

"Dude, move your incredibly delicious ass."

Filix shook his head at my request.

I stared at his face, even more confused. He threw a nervous glance over his shoulder as the knocking grew louder. He gulped and blinked hard before he looked back at me.

"FILIX!" Hyunjin's voice came from the other side of the door, his voice desperate.

Distrust and uncertainty rippled through me as I watched Filix fidget. His eyes darted around the living room, avoiding my eyes at any cost. His knuckles were bone white as he flexed and strained his fingers against the archway, either holding himself back or grounding himself.

"FILIX!" Hyunjin shouted. "Open the door! Something got through the Veil!"

Filix licked his lips and breathed heavily through his nose, a war of conflicting choices and emotions written across his face. Worry filled his eyes as he looked down at the ground, his head turned slightly back toward the front door.

In his momentary distraction, I ducked beneath one of his arms and moved to open the door.

"No!" Filix shouted.

I managed to flip open the lock and was beginning to yank open the door when Filix's arms wrapped around my waist and yanked me backward, trying to stop me.

"Relax! It's not like I'm gonna tell him to come in."

The door swung open, revealing a disheveled Hyunjin, arms braced on the doorframe as he panted heavily. His blazing red eyes slowly rose from the ground, drinking in the close, nearly intimate position Filix and I were in.

Hyunjin looked at Filix before he dropped his gaze to meet mine. The sound of his ragged breath filled the silence that lingered around us for several seconds.

He lowered one hand to his side but let the other hover in the air at chest height, his palm reaching toward the threshold that kept him out.

Hyunjin's hand met no boundary, allowing him inside.

His eyes snapped up to meet mine in shock, our faces a reflection of the other.

Filix's arms tightened around my waist, as he pivoted, putting himself in between Hyunjin and I.

"Hyunjin don't," Filix warned in a deep growl.

I struggled against Filix's grip, peeking over his shoulder to watch Hyunjin.

Hyunjin's eyes never left my half hidden figure, the intensity of the glow was hard to look at as they bit into my very soul. A hungry bloodlust craze clouded Hyunjin's eyes.

He stepped inside the foyer, his polished boots thumped heavily against the hardwood as he stepped further inside. His chest rose and fell, making his shoulders move in great heaving motions.

"Hyunjin," Filix growled again, another warning.

Hyunjin's eyebrows twitched, which was the only evidence I had that let me know he was fighting against what his entire body was screaming for.

"Go to your room," Filix whispered.

His hands around me pressed hard into my shoulders, shoving

me violently into the living room. I barely braced myself before I collided with the couch, my upper half toppling over the back of it.

A hand brushed against my ankle before it was yanked away, the heavy sounds of grunts and snarls filling the air inside the living room.

I scrambled to my feet and dashed for the hallway, my leg giving out as I hit the edge of the coffee table.

I tripped headfirst toward the hallway, but was saved when a strong hand came down on my shoulder. That saving hand was ripped away not seconds later as Filix pulled Hyunjin back, away from me.

The sounds of wrestling filled the room, rivaled only by Filix and Hyunjin's growls. The pair of them sounded more animalistic than I'd known a human could sound. I recovered onto wobbly feet, my back pressed up against the wall nearest the archway into the hallway. With fearful cautious eyes I watched as Filix fought against Hyunjin, his size and strength nearly identical despite being human.

"I told you to stay away from her," Filix snarled, shoving his hands against Hyunjin's chest.

Hyunjin stumbled backwards, slamming into the bookcase beside the fireplace. I flinched as I watched Nana's urn teeter back and forth, threatening to fall.

"You know I can't stay away," Hyunjin snapped back. "All I want is her."

"If any of them find her I—" Filix threatened, cutting his own sentence off.

A deep, wet rumbling growl breathed around them, the sound shuffling inside the kitchen opposite all of us off to my right.

Our heads whipped around to look at the archway that led into the dark kitchen.

Filix opened his mouth, his eyes trained solely on me, but Hyunjin surged forward using the distraction in the kitchen to his advantage. He gripped Filix by the collar and using his own body weight against him, slammed him up against the bookshelves.

Hyunjin hovered over Filix, using the couple extra inches he had on him to invade Filix's personal space; his hand pressed firmly over Filix's mouth. The two of them were nearly inseparable. I could hardly see where one ended and the other began. Hyunjin's lips hovered over the back of his hand, directly over Filix's lips on the other side of his palm.

Filix's eyes filled with tears, muddying his brown irises as he looked from Hyunjin to me. A tear trickled down his cheek as Hyunjin kept him pressed against the wall, trying to keep him quiet. Hyunjin tilted his head slightly, drawing Filix's attention back to him.

A silent conversation passed between the two of them, one I wasn't able to decipher fully. Filix's eyebrows furrowed as he watched Hyunjin before his eyes flickered to me and then back again. And when I had expected Filix to look in my direction again, his focus remained on Hyunjin.

Hot air blew down my neck, sending my hair into my face as I hastily shot forward a step. The lights within my house flickered before they shut off completely. Tensing, I held my breath hoping it would keep me from shaking. A deep growl rumbled behind me, making me curl in on myself, my hand over my mouth doing little to muffle the whimper I let out.

Hyunjin and Filix immediately stiffened when they realized something was directly behind me, as close as they were.

My heartbeat drowned out a lot of the white noise around us, but failed to erase the heavy panting of the creature. It huffed behind me, sending more of my hair over my shoulders and into my face as it scented the air.

I pivoted slightly, glancing up behind me.

A vast monster hovered in a mass of thick inky smoke inside the center of the wall in the living room.

It was mostly shadow as it undulated inside the wall except for brief seconds when the smoke thinned. When the smoke thinned, different animal skulls with varying layers of jagged teeth filled my vision before shadows descended and distorted everything.

Black spit oozed from the monster's ever shifting mouth, dripping onto the ground in the minimal space between us. The saliva pooled on the floor, sizzling and bubbling as it began to erode away the fibers of the carpet.

I took a step backwards, drawing the beast's attention to me. My muscles locked up as fear burst inside my chest, cold spreading through my veins.

The creature's head slowly swung back and forth, obscured by smoke, as it scented the air. A continuous growl rumbled within the monster's chest, the sound grating.

What the fuck is that?

The shadow monster stuck inside my walls roared loudly, the force of it shaking the walls, rattling the paintings and picture frames. Black viscous spit and thick mucus flung from the creature's mouth, flying toward my person as several clawed hands reached outwards from within the darkness.

A body collided with mine, knocking me out of the way, but simultaneously crushed me beneath their weight. They grunted above me as they struggled to stay upright. My hands and elbows scraped roughly over the carpet, giving me a nasty case of rug burn. Yet a hand on the back of my head kept me from getting a concussion, cradling me gently.

A pained cry from Filix sounded through the living room, making my heart squeeze tight in my chest. If Hyunjin had hurt him I was going to lose it... but Hyunjin's blazing eyes bore into my own. The body that had knocked me from the monster's path had been his.

My heart stuttered in my chest when I realized just how close Hyunjin and I were. How the natural scent of him, sandalwood and fresh roses, filled the space between us. His cool breath fanned across my cheeks.

A panicked, pained expression knit its way onto Hyunjin's features, furrowing his straight brows.

The beast roared again, stepping out of the wall into the living room. As it emerged from the wall, it solidified, its body doubling in size.

My focus zeroed in on Filix, who clutched his forearm in pain. Black saliva seeped between his fingers, staining his skin an inky black mess.

I inhaled loudly, shocked to see Filix had gotten hurt. Hyunjin's palm pressed over my mouth, his body hunched over mine as he looked over his shoulder.

The monster lunged toward Filix, its ever shifting jaws snapped in the air, smoke curled around it. The sound of bone hitting bone clacked together.

I screamed.

Hyunjin's arms wrapped around my waist and hauled me upwards off the floor, robbing me of the opportunity to see if Filix had gotten out of the way fast enough or not.

My heart wrenched as Filix let out another pained cry. I shoved my entire body weight back against Hyunjin to stop him. His grip managed to loosen greatly, giving me the chance to slip free of his arms. Using my hands I braced myself against the back of the couch, and looked across the room. My heart sank deep into my stomach as I took in the sight before me.

No, my heart whispered.

Filix hung limply from the monster's mouth, its sharp teeth had sunk into Filix's flesh, its viscous black saliva infecting the puncture wounds. Filix's blood dripped steadily onto the carpet, mixing with the erosive spit the monster had already drooled. His face was scrunched in a permanent grimace as he tried to keep from screaming out. The pain he was in must have been unbearable.

The monster loosened its jaws just slightly before it bit down again, sinking its fangs deeper into Filix's torso. A series of cracks popped off as the monster broke Filix's ribcage. The beast shook its massive head, throwing Filix about like a dog's chew toy. He cried out, jerking within the monster's maw.

"Hey!" I screamed at the monster, trying to distract it.

My body moved before my mind could second guess myself; I grabbed the closest object near me, which happened to be the TV remote on the arm of the couch. The remote sailed across the air and smacked the beast between its eyes.

The monster snarled in my direction despite its mouth being full.

Hyunjin's arms wrapped around my waist again, and hauled me backwards out the front door, as the beast reared its ugly head and began to charge after us.

"No!" I cried out. "Get off me! Filix!"

My hair whipped around my face as Hyunjin hauled me across the threshold of the front door – only we weren't in my front yard. The cold night air nipped at my fingertips as the scent of pine trees assaulted my senses. The trees in Neverhelm had no scent, wherever we were was not home.

"Filix!"

I thrashed in Hyunjin's arms, trying to break free to get back to Filix. My desperate movement only made Hyunjin tighten his grip on me, his arms crushing down on my ribs, leaving possible bruises.

My limbs shook as my chest felt tight, the ability to breathe vanished as my mouth became dry. The pain in my chest hurt, and every labored breath I took stoked a fire beneath my veins, and allowed it to spread further within me.

Hyunjin refused to let me go as he hauled me through the mysterious forest, trying to put distance between us and the monster that had taken Filix.

I cried, struggling against Hyunjin's grip. "Hyunjin, please!"

Hyunjin dropped me when we reached a relatively small clearing in the thick of the trees, causing me to stumble forward. I barely caught my footing as I spun around. Hyunjin's gaze was focused on the treeline behind me, searching for something. Tears clouded my vision as I glared back at him.

"We have to go back," I pleaded with him.

"We can't," Hyunjin said, somberly.

Filix's body in the jaws of the monster flashed in my mind, his blood drooling from the creatures' smoky mouth. I smashed my hand over my mouth as my mind continued to relive the last half hour. Filix's cries echoed inside my skull the longer we stood inside the empty clearing. I whimpered and felt tears dribble down my cheeks before it dripped off my chin and onto the ground.

"Wha– What if he's dead?" I mumbled behind my hand.

My mind was whirling but my body refused to move, completely shell shocked. Hyunjin's hand settled against my shoulder, the action making me flinch as I dropped my hand.

"I need you to take a deep breath," Hyunjin said, refusing to let me look away from him.

"There was so much blood. There's no way he..." I trailed off, my voice cracking at the end.

Hyunjin's hand slid beneath my chin and tipped my head to look up at him. His gaze was surprisingly soft as he studied my features. His hand drifted across my skin, his thumb brushing across a tear that had trailed down my cheek.

"He's probably fine. Smogbodies are collectors. They don't kill their prey, they take them back to their masters," Hyunjin pulled his hand away from my face and studied the wetness on the pad of his thumb. He rubbed my tears between his fingers, feeling the texture against his skin.

"So what they're like bounty hunters?" I asked, disgusted and frightened.

Hyunjin hesitated but nodded his head as he returned his attention to me.

"In a sense," he confirmed.

I took a small step away from him and ran a hand over my face, trying to wipe away my tears. Closing my eyes, I focused on taking deep breaths to calm myself down.

The smell of pine trees filled my nose, the scent was sharp yet sweet and refreshing, reminding me we were not in Neverhelm.

"Who took him?" I asked, needing a distraction.

"I don't know who the Smogbody is bound to, Mare. Smogbodies serve one master until their debts are paid. It's impossible to know who their masters are unless you speak to a mage."

I glared at him, pressing my lips into a thin line to keep from yelling at him. Yelling and crying wasn't going to save Filix, and being at odds with Hyunjin wasn't what I wanted.

"There has to be a way, Hyunjin."

He said nothing as he looked at me.

I swallowed the lump in my throat and tried again. "Where are we?"

"We're in the Feywild, home of the fey. I opened a portal to get us away from the Smogbody."

I chose to ignore exactly how Hyunjin opened a portal, and promised to revisit it later when I wasn't about to completely break. "Can Smogbodies open portals too?"

Hyunjin shook his head. "They can only use an established, solidified portal. There's only one that connects our worlds together permanently, but that door has been closed since I was cursed."

A beat of silence passed before I spoke again. "You said something slipped through the Veil. Obviously that was the Smogbody... can't it come back the way it came?"

"We don't know if the Smogbody brought Filix back this way. They could still be on the other side of the Veil," Hyunjin pointed out.

The lump resurfaced along with the urge to scream.

If Filix was on the other side of the Veil with the Smogbody, then maybe that was a good thing. With him safe in Neverhelm, whoever had sent the Smogbody wouldn't be able to get their hands on Filix.

That is, if he was still alive.

Another problem presented itself as I stared at Hyunjin, a heavy sense of dread sunk in my stomach. If Hyunjin opened a temporary portal to get here, and the official 'door' between our worlds was sealed, then how was I supposed to get home?

"Am I trapped here?"

Hyunjin's gaze slipped away from me as he stayed silent.

"I'm stuck here?!" I screeched, panicking. "Filix is–"

I cut myself off as a new wave of hysterical, panicked tears blurred my vision. I squeezed my eyes shut for several long seconds, willing them away. I inhaled slowly, holding my breath until I released it slowly. I looked back at Hyunjin.

"There has to be someone nearby who knows someone that can help us."

"You don't even know where we are," Hyunjin pointed out.

I opened my mouth to protest but Hyunjin cut me off.

"I think we're close to Kiruna. We can see if anyone there can help us."

Hyunjin gestured in front of us, urging me to begin down the pathway that led toward the mountains in the distance.

I gazed down the overgrown road taking in the dazzling columbines and the vibrant lilacs of every color. The path before me was enchanting and enticing, just like the prince beside me.

Turning back to Hyunjin stole my thoughts. He was beautiful. I wanted to run my fingers through his hair and commit every detail of his face to memory. It had been obvious that he knew Filix – somehow – so how was he so calm about witnessing such a traumatic event? I was barely keeping it together.

"We go to Kiruna and see if anyone can help us," I said, restating what our loose plan was, shaking myself from the spell the prince's beauty had cast over me.

"Yes."

"And if no one can help us there?"

Hyunjin blinked a couple times before he spoke again. "If there's no one to help us in Kiruna, I will be surprised."

And then he stepped around me and began down the pathway.

THE PATHWAY toward Kiruna was beautiful. Even in the glow of the two moons' light, the forest was bursting with colorful flowers. Every flower we passed called to me, begged me to stop and smell its sweet scent. It enticed me, promising to fulfill hidden desires the longer we walked. I had half a mind to try and recreate their beauty when I returned to Neverhelm.

While the call of the wildflowers was tempting, the desire to find a way to save Filix and send me home was more pressing.

When we reached the two-hour mark I had grown bored of the silence that had settled between Hyunjin and I. Not knowing about Filix's fate was slowly driving me insane. I needed a distraction, something to keep me from breaking down and crying.

"Can I ask you a couple questions?" I asked.

"If you must."

"What? You have somewhere better to be?"

Hyunjin glared at me, his eyes flashing in warning. I pressed my lips together to stop myself from apologizing.

"Smogbodies. Their spit is corrosive?"

"A Smogbody's bite is poisonous to fey, and I suspect to humans as well."

So Filix was in an incredible amount of pain then. Fuck. I watched the ground in front of my feet, demanding the tears away.

"So... Smogbodies are beasts then? They aren't sentient like you and I?"

A judgemental look passed over Hyunjin's features as his eyes darted up and down my body.

"I guess... It is the equivalent of having a pet, like a dog or a dragon. They are loyal to one master until whatever bargain between beast and man has been fulfilled."

I ignored the idea of pet dragons, though was determined to

revisit it later and decided to switch gears. Something had been bugging me for a while.

"You called yourself 'Sam' when we first met in the marketplace back in Neverhelm," I said, walking beside him down the pathway.

"I did," Hyunjin agreed, but offered no explanation.

"But... is Hyunjin not your name?" I asked, feeling a bit stupid. I knew fey could not lie. They could manipulate their words and speak half-truths... There was something I was missing.

"Sam is my..." he trailed off, his face in deep concentration as he tried to find the words to explain this to me. "Sam's the name our Mother gave to me."

"*Our* mother?"

Hyunjin looked at me, his red neon eyes burning a hole into the side of my head as we continued to walk in the direction of Kiruna. I glanced over at him, concerned.

"What?" I asked.

Hyunjin said nothing, which confused me further.

"Did - did I do something wrong?"

If I had asked him a question that was supposed to be a secret then I would feel incredibly bad. I had been trying to ask polite questions, trying to alter my words so Hyunjin wouldn't be obligated to be polite back to me.

I opened my mouth to apologize, but quickly pressed my lips together before a single sound could come out. Apologizing was considered rude to the fey... but I felt rude not apologizing.

I let out a soft groan, frustrated with myself. Fey rules were confusing and were beginning to give me a headache.

"Something wrong, princess?"

"Nothing's wrong, princeling!" I sassed him, the two of us fully aware I was lying.

Hyunjin's eyes flickered up and down my body, trying to get a read on what was wrong. When he found nothing physically wrong with me, he rolled his eyes and began walking faster down the pathway.

I needed to swallow my pride and get along with Hyunjin.

I let him walk ahead of me, the two of us could use a few minutes away from each other to cool off. The past twelve hours had been intense for the both of us. Things were likely only going to get crazier when we reached Kiruna.

I jogged to meet with Hyunjin, who was several paces ahead of me, when my mind began to slip back to my house. Images of Filix limp in the Smogbody's mouth threatened to undo me where I stood.

When I reached his side again, I decided that in order to get by in this unfamiliar world, I needed more information about the Feywild and its people. What I had learned as a child wasn't going to help me get back to Neverhelm – and who better to ask than the Feywild's prince himself?

"I have another question. One that might be offensive, but I don't know any other way to ask," I said.

Hyunjin raised a brow, urging me to speak. I had the slightest inkling not to ask, but I pushed aside my awkwardness in favor of trying to learn something vital.

"Why do you need my blood? Are you a vampire?"

"I'm not a vampire," he said seriously before he sighed, "But if it helps you wrap your mortal brain around what I am... then you may call me a vampire."

"Then what are you?"

Hyunjin came to a full stop, turned and stared at me, his gaze fully judgmental.

"Did Filix teach you nothing?" he hissed.

"What does Filix have to do with this?" I fired back.

Hyunjin inhaled, the action sounding more like a pained hiss. He held his breath for several seconds before he released it slowly.

"I have not the patience, nor the energy to explain every rule you should follow here in the Feywild. But since you're a fragile human I will tell you the few that might save your incredibly short, obnoxious life."

I took a slight step backward, the hurt visible on my face.

Hyunjin's eyes flashed as he registered he'd offended me, but he continued as if nothing had happened.

"Don't apologize. Don't offer anyone your name. Don't eat or drink anything offered to you," Hyunjin listed off, counting on his fingers. "Don't accept any gifts, and never thank someone, but don't forget your manners. Don't dance with one of us. Most importantly, try not to kill anyone or anything. A life for a life, and all that."

I blinked. There were a lot of rules to remember. The rules I had learned as a kid felt useless now.

"And don't ask what species of fey someone is," he added.

It's rude. Hyunjin did not have to say that for me to get the jist of things.

I nodded my head, silently repeating the rules he'd laid out for me. I wasn't certain I could remember all - or any - of them, but I would certainly try.

"Just a few more questions and then I'll shut up, I promise."

Hyunjin's face grew serious as he shook his head, his red hair flopping about. "Don't make promises either."

I nodded, "Okay. Do you still want to rip my throat out?"

Hyunjin's eyes settled on my neck, his gaze focusing on my jugular vein. I swallowed nervously, unsure if I wanted an actual answer to my question or not.

"The hunger has died down since we've returned to the Feywild. I suspect it has to do with the magic in the air, it helps curb the cravings. But I will need to feed in a few days."

"Why my blood specifically?"

Hyunjin drew his gaze away from my neck and met my eyes. "You were the one who woke me when your blood touched my coffin."

A prince cursed to rot beneath the earth until the blood of his kin awoke him.

I subconsciously rubbed my thumb over the nearly healed cut on my finger as Hyunjin spoke. Filix's cut had healed in a matter of days – three tops, while mine was slowly healing.

"The only way for you to be woken up was by the blood of your kin," I said, repeating back the age old myth that had surrounded the prince and his mysterious glass coffin.

It dawned on me then that the myth surrounding the prince's coffin hadn't been entirely true. Hyunjin had not been buried beneath the earth and he hadn't been woken up by the 'blood of his kin'.

What I knew of the fey and the Feywild has turned out to be wrong.

"Who do we need to talk to in Kiruna?" I asked, shaking myself from my thoughts.

"A mage. They should be able to tell us who sent the Smogbody through the Veil. And once we figure that out, we can then go to the Kingdom."

I had never heard of the Kingdom, but my tired, stressed-out mind stored that question away for later. My legs were killing me, and I was beginning to slow down as I walked beside Hyunjin.

"How much farther do you want to travel tonight? I don't think I can go much further. I'm exhausted," I admitted, feeling my eyes growing heavy.

"I forgot how fragile humans are. You need to sleep so often."

"Says the vampire who's been asleep for nearly half a millennia," I muttered under my breath.

"What did you say?" Hyunjin questioned.

"Nothing!" I sing-songed in reply.

Hyunjin fixed me with a puzzling glare, trying to get a read on what I had said moments ago. "Whatever it was… it is beneath me."

I pursed my lips, unsure if I should reply or not. I kept my mouth shut, which gave Hyunjin the opportunity to fill the silence.

"Not much farther. We can rest for the night soon."

We continued down the pathway as a steady stream of worried thoughts plagued my mind. I was satisfied with the answers Hyunjin had answered, but the questions I still had about Filix's fate couldn't be answered by the prince at my side. And that bothered me.

"Oh fuck!" I gasped.

"What?" Hyunjin asked, whipping his head to look at me, worry and apprehension in his burning eyes.

"I left the oven on!"

Hyunjin cocked his head to one side.

"We were baking brownies," I panicked. "If I burn down the house my mum is going to kill me."

She was gonna kill me if the Smogbody fucked up her wall too.

Hyunjin stared at me for several long seconds, his glowing eyes dimmed drastically until only embers burned behind his gaze.

"The oven is off," he said, cryptically.

"And how do you know?" I asked.

"Fil- I was taught how to look into your world," Hyunjin said, but I could tell he had wanted to say something else when he had started his sentence. "A picture had been painted in my mind about what your world was like."

Hyunjin's word choice left me swimming in my own thoughts as we continued to walk through the forest; the distraction my brain had been in need of since we stepped foot in the Feywild.

Pictures were not necessarily painted in one's mind unless another person was telling a story, explaining how things worked. Words had a power of their own, being able to take the simplest of ideas and fleshing them into emotions and worlds beyond our imaginations. They were powerful, and I guess that was why the fey valued them.

With the prince trapped inside the glass coffin for half a millennium, I wondered how a picture was painted for him. Had someone been visiting him besides when Filix and I visited to clean up the clearing? Who told him stories while he slept?

"Okay, weird. How do you know my oven is off?"

"Smogbodies consume a number of things in order to make themselves corporeal. Rubber ducks, honeycombs, dragon scales, hag eyes, electricity."

"That does not answer my question... also how do you know what electricity is?"

"The Smogbody was the reason your power went out seconds before it appeared. The oven turned off." Hyunjin explained before he scoffed, walking ahead of me. "The Feywild might be behind in terms of technological advancements but we have electricity in most cities."

WHEN WE STOPPED for the night, I had not expected Hyunjin to suggest we sleep together. In fact, his suggestion had me blue screening for a few moments as I tried to process what he had said.

"You will freeze in your sleep. I can keep you warm," Hyunjin explained when I took too long to reply.

"Promise you won't bite me? No midnight snacks?"

Hyunjin dramatically rolled his eyes as he heaved out a heavy sigh. Hadn't we just gone over the rules — no making promises and all that?

"I won't bite you in your sleep," Hyunjin said.

"Well, okay," I agreed hesitantly.

Hyunjin brought his hand to his mouth and bit down, blood rapidly dribbling from his mouth, splattering onto the blades of grass beneath his feet.

"What the fuck?" I asked, my filter no longer working. I pulled back, putting a bit of space between us.

Hyunjin pulled his hand away from his mouth and squeezed, forcing more blood from his self-inflicted wound. When a small puddle had formed near his feet, he brought his hand to his mouth again and licked the wound.

Hyunjin looked at me and paused mid-lick. I guess it had not dawned on him that purposefully licking your own blood was not a common thing humans did.

"The magic in my blood will conceal us from predators during the night, and my saliva heals wounds."

I blinked at him. "I guess, of all the things I have seen today, this has to be one of the more 'weirder' things I've witnessed."

"We have very different definitions of 'weird', princess," Hyunjin laughed under his breath.

We moved several feet away from the blood puddle, sinking beneath a large pine tree.

I curled near the base of the tree, laying on my side with my back facing Hyunjin. Hyunjin laid down beside me, keeping a few inches of space between us, while allowing me to steal his warmth from him. Tucking my arms beneath my armpits to keep them warm, I closed my eyes and focused on breathing.

In and out.

In and out.

Focusing on breathing would keep me from thinking about what happened during the day, about what had happened to Filix.

Guilt settled in my stomach, making my chest feel tight.

The Smogbody's fangs pierced into Filix's limb body. The viscous black venom that oozed and dripped from its maw. The pain etched on his face as Hyunjin pulled me away from him.

Stop, I hissed at myself. *Go the fuck to sleep. You— you can't change anything now.*

I forced my brain to focus on the world around us, listening to what the Feywild sounded like.

In and out.

Hyunjin shifted behind me, rolling from one side to another as he let out a soft huff.

In and out.

Crickets chirped off in the distance, and every so often the jingling of bells could be heard just beneath the gentle rustle of the leaves shifting in the wind. The rustling of fabric and grass behind me caught my attention as Hyunjin moved around again.

In and out.

The gurgling of a nearby creek had my brain quieting down, lulling me toward sleep after an incredibly stressful day.

Hyunjin shifted behind me again, and another huff left him.

"What is wrong?" I snapped. I was exhausted and wanted to fall asleep but Hyunjin's fidgeting wasn't helping.

"I need to feed," he sighed, annoyed.

"I assume you can't just go find a squirrel to eat?" I sighed as I rolled over to face him.

"I honestly wish it were that easy."

I swallowed, nervously. I doubted that this was going to be an easy thing for either of us.

"I know I said I wouldn't bite you in your sleep, but..." he trailed off, letting silence fill the small space between us.

"But I smell," I finished for him.

He had said that my blood smells delectable in the marketplace back in Neverhelm. And while the magic in the air here in the Feywild was helping to curve his cravings, desire was winning out for him. I could see it in the way his eyes pulsed more frequently, burning brighter and brighter at increasing intervals.

"This is going to put a strain on our already rough relationship," Hyunjin said, tipping his head back to glance up at the canopy of trees above us.

"How so?" I asked.

"My bite– when I feed it's–" Hyunjin trailed off, and I knew he was holding something back.

"Hyunjin, just tell me. I'm too tired to play riddles with you."

"It's erotic. You'll – you'll have an orgasm."

His blunt words had my throat going dry. How - what was I supposed to say to that?

Hyunjin let out a noise, something between a groan and a whine, as he shifted beside me. He ran a hand over his face before he peeked at me from behind his fingers. He let out another embarrassed noise as our eyes locked.

"Will it hurt?" I asked.

Hyunjin dropped his hands away from his face and looked at me. "Well, no I don't think an orgasm has ever hurt somebody."

I reached over and smacked the back of my hand across his chest, laughing in embarrassment. "No! I meant the bite."

Hyunjin threw his head back and laughed, almost as embarrassed as I was.

"Oh! That– that might hurt. A pinch if nothing else," Hyunjin said between laughs.

I was quiet for a moment, contemplating whether I wanted to give Hyunjin my blood or not. I wasn't worried that he would try and eat me in my sleep. Despite saying that promises shouldn't be made in the Feywild, I believed his words. I was more worried about what he could do when we arrived in Kiruna. Would he be as blood crazed as he seemed back when he murdered Clé?

"Can we go to sleep after this?" I asked.

"Of course."

"Okay, come here," I relented, shifting closer to him.

He moved, molding his body against mine. I shuddered at the warmth that radiated steadily off his body and let my eyes fall closed. Despite Hyunjin being a monster of sorts, I felt safe in his arms.

"Princess," Hyunjin coaxed me from my tired thoughts. "I want you to know I didn't– I hadn't meant to– earlier, when I had said that I wou–"

"Hyunjin," I sighed, barely opening one eye to look at him. "It's okay. I freely give you my blood or whatever it is you need to hear. I give you permission and I don't think you were lying to me earlier."

I licked my lips as I opened both my eyes to fully look at him. "I'm guessing you used whatever magic is in your blood to keep us safe for the night."

Hyunjin hummed in agreement. "I thought the taste I had gotten of you back in Neverhelm would give me enough strength to last until we arrived at the Kingdom."

He hesitated, glancing away from me, staring off into the dark.

"I doubt a teaspoon of blood is enough to satiate your appetite. If I remember correctly I believe you said 'every last drop.'"

Hyunjin's breath fanned across my cheeks, his body covering mine as he tipped his head down. One of his hands came to cradle the back of my head, while the other rested against my waist.

"I did say that, didn't I?"

I felt him breathe above me, as he let the seconds tick by.

His fangs pushed into my neck, pushing through the skin to get to what he craved most, giving way to fresh blood.

I gasped as my eyes rolled to the back of my head, my hand shot out and my fingers dug into Hyunjin's bicep, trying to keep myself grounded as my orgasm over took my senses. My pussy clenched around nothing as pleasure washed over my body.

Hyunjin's tongue was hot against my skin as he lapped up my blood, gulping down mouthful after mouthful. The sting of his bite ebbed away into heated pleasure, the feeling coursed down my spine. He groaned above me as his cravings were finally satisfied. The hand he had on my waist gripped me firmly, keeping me from bucking my hips against him as I rode out my orgasm.

My grip on Hyunjin's arm loosened the longer Hyunjin drank from me, and as my hand fell from him, he pulled away. His tongue sweeping across my skin, his saliva healing the puncture marks from his bite in a matter of seconds. He hovered above me, his breath ghosting across my wet skin, sending a cool shiver over my body.

My panties were damp, and sticking to me uncomfortably. Hyunjin's fingers flexed against me, his grip still strong and grounding. A wave of lust-addled confusion washed over me as I tried to come to my senses. A pang of guilt let a bitter aftertaste in my mouth.

How could I have an orgasm when Filix was in excruciating pain or possibly dead?

Hyunjin pressed a couple soft kisses against my skin as my senses slowly came back to me. He whispered things in my ears that I couldn't fully understand.

"Hyunjin?" I whimpered as I blinked up at him, still dazed from the orgasm he pulled from me with a simple bite.

"Sleep princess," Hyunjin urged me. "You're okay. I'll keep you safe."

I nodded my head, agreeing with his words. I curled against his side, fisting my hand around the fabric of his jacket to keep him close.

My eyes slipped shut before I could stop myself.

THE GOBLIN MARKET

Morning came faster than I thought it would.

Hyunjin was already awake when I managed to crack open my eyes. His body was still close to mine, but continued to leave a couple of respectful inches between the two of us. When we had parted, I was unsure. He studied me with a soft expression as I sat up and rubbed the sleep from my eyes.

"Good morning," he said, his voice deeper from hours of disuse.

"Morning," I whispered back. I had a feeling Hyunjin had not slept at all last night.

Stretching my arms above my head, I let out a large yawn that I barely managed to cover with a hand over my mouth. My back hurt and my legs felt like they were moments away from an unbearable muscle spasm. My neck hurt, the bite from last night throbbed. A twinge of hunger gnawed at the back of my mind, but I chose to ignore it – there was nothing I could do about food here in the Feywild.

Hyunjin's body heat left my side, leaving me to shiver slightly as the cool morning air settled in his place. My eyes drifted down his back as he stretched away his own sore muscles. The white strappy jacket he wore shifted, revealing tiny gaps of his flawless, tanned skin. I licked my lips, as I caught more glimpses of skin that had been hidden away.

A knowing smirk spread across his face as he turned and caught me openly staring at him.

"Shut up," I grumbled, embarrassed.

Hyunjin let out a small laugh and turned to completely face me. He bent forward and extended a hand down to me, offering to help me off the ground. I eyed his hand for a second, curious if he was testing me or truly being nice, before I grasped his open palm and hauled myself off the ground.

"We aren't far from Kiruna," he said. " I suspect we can get there just after dusk."

"And you're sure that there is someone in Kiruna that can tell us what happened to Filix? How a smoke body was on my side of the Veil?"

"*Smog*body," Hyunjin corrected me. "And yes."

I took a deep breath, grounding myself before we took off for the day. With a nod of my head, I began to head in the direction the pathway had been before we had veered off it to find a safe place to sleep.

No footsteps followed behind me, which had me glancing back over my shoulder at Hyunjin.

He stood several paces away. I cocked an eyebrow in his direction. "You coming?"

Hyunjin snapped out of his trance, blinking several times as he focused on what was before him and not whatever had been conjured in his mind. He shook his head and trotted to my side again.

He said nothing as we continued our way to Kiruna.

I FELT eyes following us through the forest. Chills ran down my spine, urging me to glance behind us, to search for what was moving with us. I had stopped a handful of times to see if I could hear what was behind us, but my ears couldn't pick up anything other than the faint bells that jingled off in the far distance.

Curiosity nipped at my heels. I wanted to know what was following us in the woods. Yet something unpleasant gnawed at the back of my mind, telling me it was a bad idea to look.

With my curiosity unable to be satiated, my thoughts began to wander leading me down a dark path to what happened yesterday and last night.

What if that was the last time I saw Filix? With venom spreading through his veins, pain etched onto his gorgeous freckled face. Was my last memory of him going to be something terrible?

And then the orgasm I had from Hyunjin feasting on my blood had me wanting to curl up and die. The initial guilt I had felt immediately afterwards had continued to fester within me. My best friend was probably dead and here I was experiencing an incredible, mind blowing orgasm when I should have been fighting harder to save him.

I didn't deserve Filix in the slightest.

"Fuck," Hyunjin hissed.

My eyes snapped up to look at the back of his head, pulled from the thoughts that swirled in my mind. I had never heard him curse before.

"What?"

A growl rumbled in his chest. He stopped walking and ran a hand through his hair. He quickly spun on his heel to look back at me.

Behind him was a large tent, reminding me of a big top tent at a circus. Only the grand tent had a million holes in the grime stained white fabric. Creatures and fey alike wandered through the open panels of the big top, mulling about in stalls and crude little shops. At the center of the big top raged a massive pyre, one that had thick plumes of smoke rolling from the center of the tent's peak.

"What's wrong? I need you to talk with me."

"It's the Goblin Market."

"You cannot be serious," I said, glaring at Hyunjin's back. His shoulder blades flexed underneath his jacket, giving away his discomfort.

"I am," Hyunjin snarled.

"The Goblin Market? What is that?"

"It's a marketplace run by the goblins."

"You can't be serious," I repeated.

The Goblin Market was only ever mentioned in *The Lone King*. It was never described, but it was dark and dangerous. And nothing good ever happened there. I had no idea it was a real place.

Hyunjin glared down the path we'd just come down, his eyes bright and murderous.

"This is bad, isn't it?" I questioned as I looked past him toward the open air market.

"For you."

I hurt my neck with how fast I snapped my head up to look at Hyunjin. "Excuse me?"

Hyunjin growled again, running his hand through his red locks. "We need to make you look fey."

"Absolutely not," I started, crossing my arms over my chest. Hyunjin's eyes flickered downwards for a fraction of a second before meeting and holding my eyes. His cheeks held a faint pink tint, but it could have been the lighting.

"Why not?" Hyunjin asked, swallowing, trying to keep himself composed.

"I'm human, and I'm not going to change how I look to appease some fucking goblins or fairies." I snapped before adding, "No offense."

"If you don't change your appearance then the trolls will kill you," Hyunjin stated.

"I'd like to see them try."

"You are going to get us both killed. The Goblin Market plays by a different set of rules. Ones, even I can't get out of." he said, his eyes looking wet, like a burning ruby in the dusky lighting. I'd never seen his eyes so bright, so decorative. I suddenly had a new favorite color.

"We just have to be careful. How bad could it be?" I asked, reaching out towards his hand, wanting to hold it. I dropped my hand at the last possible second, afraid to act on my feelings.

Hyunjin stared at me as I stared back at him. I wasn't going to change how I looked.

"Mare, I don't want you to get hurt," he stepped closer to me.

"I have you to protect me."

"And what if we get separated? What if something happens to you? I can't go home without you."

"You can't get home without my blood," I corrected him, "and if something does happen, I'm sure you'll just take my blood and leave. All you need is an explanation about what happened back at the coffin."

A deeper frown passed across Hyunjin's face, making me regret my choice of words. Maybe Hyunjin wouldn't abandon me if things went south. But then again, I didn't know him well enough to possibly predict what he'd do.

"At least put your hair down. Cover your ears," he pleaded, his hand reaching out towards my face. He dropped his outstretched hand before it could touch me, much to my disappointment. "Your round ears will draw more attention to us."

I yanked the hair tie from my hair, placing it on my wrist. My eyes darted over to his pointed ears, my gaze lingering on the silver jewelry that he had artfully stacked there. It was a little eerie how we had piercings in a similar pattern.

"Actually, here," Hyunjin pulled something from behind his back and extended it to me.

The maroon beanie I had leant him at the farmers market rested in the palm of his hand, waiting for me to take it back. My eyes lifted from the beanie to Hyunjin's face as I reached out and took the hat back.

"You kept it?" I was absolutely certain Hyunjin had thrown it away the second he left the marketplace.

"I had to return it," he said in a soft voice.

I slipped the beanie over my head, being mindful to keep my ears covered while keeping my hair out of my face.

Hyunjin reached out and adjusted my hair over my chest, being careful not to touch me. His brows furrowed as he pursed his lips, studying me carefully.

Hyunjin placed his hands on either side of the top of my head and brought the beanie down farther down my forehead, blinding me in the process.

"There," he said, satisfied.

"Hyunjin!" I laughed, using my own hand to raise the beanie off my eyes. "I can't see."

A smile graced Hyunjin's flawless features, making the fey prince before me more beautiful than I had ever seen him. Dimples appeared on his cheeks as his smile widened, revealing sharp canines.

"Think you can stay out of trouble for me?" Hyunjin questioned.

"No promises," I teased him, the smile still on my face.

Hyunjin rolled his eyes like he was annoyed, but chuckled under his breath.

THE GOBLIN MARKET was exactly as I imagined it.

Fey of all kinds walked through the straw covered ground. The smell of roasting meat wafted in places around the market, while other areas stunk of rot and decay. An underlying danger lingered in the air around us, something sinister lurked in every shadow, around every corner. Conversations in languages I couldn't even begin to fathom floated in the air as fey bartered and bargained amongst themselves.

Signs hung from market stalls and crudely made shops alike, the more notable ones were written in English – which had me doing a double take. A sign that read: 'Goblin's Teeth' hung above a stall directly next to another stall that advertised 'Lost Potential' and 'Mustaches.'

While my curiosity was piqued, I had no desire to leave Hyunjin's side. We walked through the marketplace, acting like the fey around us. A wide variety of goods were laid out on tables and set up in displays that had seen better days; although I figured the Goblin Market had never seen 'better days' before.

Fat bat-like hobgoblins fluttered about in the air, their clawed hands a mess of juice as they noisily munched on fruits and varying meats. Giant creatures with deer-wolf hybrid skulls lumbered past me, a wave of rot had me gagging in their wake. Armed ogres marched through the stalls, knocking over those who were unfortunate enough to be in their way. Ghastly banshees and women dressed in bloodied gowns floated about aimlessly, wailing and shrieking every so often; although no one seemed to react to the outbursts.

My eyes were naturally drawn across the crowd to a small stall filled with art supplies down the way, tucked away between larger booths. I initially wanted to venture over and see what the Feywild had to offer in the way of art supplies, but the ominous sign that read 'Ageless Children' nearby had me second guessing my interest.

I turned to ask Hyunjin where we were going, but found he was not next to me like I had thought. My head whipped around, searching rapidly for his vibrant red hair. Relief flooded my chest when I spotted him a few feet from me. I had to keep a better eye on him.

I watched as Hyunjin drifted down the way, also automatically drawn to the little art stall. Gliding behind him, I watched as he reached for a tube of red oil paint. A smile spread across my face as it dawned on me that he liked to paint. He liked art, oil painting to be specific.

He turned the tube over in his palm, bringing it up into the pyre light to get a better sense of what the color looked like in different lighting. His head cocked to the side as he shifted the tube, watching all the ways the red color shifted and changed within the light.

Hyunjin returned the oil paint tube to the little art stand, before running his fingers across a fluffy blending brush. A small laugh escaped me, which had his head popping up to look at me. He quickly withdrew his hand from the brush, opting to shove it into his pants pocket instead.

"Something funny?" he asked.

The smile remained on my face as I drank in the knowledge that we shared a passion for the arts, shared a hobby. He had also picked up a paint tube back in Neverhelm when we met at the farmer's market. I was not sure who else knew Hyunjin liked to paint, but I liked knowing. I liked that through even the smallest, simplest acts I knew more about Hyunjin than I had before.

"Why are you looking at me like that?" Hyunjin asked, growing more concerned.

"I just... know nothing about you. I had no idea you liked to paint."

"I love to paint," Hyunjin answered me honestly.

"I wish I had known sooner. I bet you're an amazing artist. I would love to see you work someday."

Hyunjin raised a hand to his face, using his forefinger and thumb to press against the tips of his nostrils. His pointed ears began to turn pink and he refused to meet my eyes.

"Maybe you shall one day."

Hyunjin and I looked at each other for a moment, our differences cast aside over a few tubes of pigmented oil as we stood in front of a tiny art supply stand in the midst of the Goblin Market.

The soft moment between us was shattered when a burst of

commotion sounded across the center of the Goblin Market, a scuffle breaking out.

Hyunjin stepped into me, into my personal space; his arm wrapped around my side, drawing me close to him in a protective manner as he scanned those around us for any sign of potential threat. My hands rested against his chest, one curled around the fabric of his strappy jacket, while the other hovered over his abdomen, ghosting over his skin.

The scent of him filled my nose, deep sandalwood and fresh roses and something distinctly Hyunjin that I couldn't put a name to.

Hyunjin looked down at me, his pillow-soft lips parted as he breathed out. His breath fanned across my face gently, and I realized just how close we were to one another. My eyes flickered from the tips of his fangs to his glowing red eyes, although neither sight frightened me, even though they very much should have.

"We need to go meet with someone," Hyunjin said, his arm still tight around my side. "Someone who can point us in the right direction of Kiruna. There should still be a shop labeled 'Side Effects' around here."

Hyunjin scanned the crowd again, searching for the shop he was looking for.

"Do you know the owner or something?" I questioned, enjoying how close he was still.

"Yeah," Hyunjin said, avoiding my gaze. "Something like that."

"Lead the way, princeling."

Hyunjin's arm fell from my side, leaving me cold; just like it had this morning. He stepped away from the art stall and began to weave through the fey in the market. I moved after him, making sure to keep my head low as I followed in his shadow. I had no desire to draw any sort of attention to myself while we were in the Goblin Market. Hyunjin moved down the street, walking like he was supposed to be there. I lingered just behind him, subtly trying to take everything in at once.

Through the sea of goblins, trolls, pixies and other creatures straight out of a fairytale, I looked across the big top to a figure amidst several captive fey, all chained up and bound. My stomach churned violently as I watched a goblin spit on a poor pixie's face, before he threw coins at a minotaur and yanked her away into the crowd.

As I glanced over the other fey for sale, I caught glimpses of a man's arms; they were battered and bloody, strung up and bound with painful looking irons. His head of dark hair hung low, not bothering to interact with the fey that mulled about and mocked the other captured people around him. He looked most human among the other fey that were on display.

A shoulder knocked into my own, causing me to stumble forward into several other creatures that were wandering the Goblin Market. They grumbled and cursed and hissed in my direction, and I had to physically bite my lips to keep from apologizing. I threw a glare over my shoulder at the large creature that had bumped into me. Straightening my beanie, double checking my ears haven't been uncovered, I surveyed the Goblin Market again.

My heart sank when I did not spot Hyunjin's vibrant red hair amongst the sea of fey that mulled about. I spun from left to right, jumping onto my tiptoes to see over the crowd. Despair rapidly settled between my bones as I began to panic.

Hyunjin was nowhere to be found.

Taking a couple deep breaths, I forced myself to remain calm. Having a panic attack in the middle of the Goblin Market was not an option at the moment. If I had been brave and not broken down when I saw Filix attacked, I could find that courage again and find the prince.

I began to scan the crowds again, taking extra time to search for Hyunjin's face amongst the unfamiliar fey that moved around me, going about their lives. The fat bat-like hobgoblins fluttered above my head, which I shooed away with a careless wave of my hand. Those pesky fat little blobs were bothersome and distracting.

I was all alone.

Beneath my steadily rising panic was a strange pull that tugged against my chest. Our eyes met across the square, and I found myself frozen in place, staring at the human-esque man for sale. His eyes blazed molten silver despite the haunted faraway look that glazed over them, like he was physically present yet a million miles away in his mind.

Nothing about his appearance gave away what type of fey he was, but my mind immediately supplied 'wolf shifter' – as if I knew that was an actual species of fey to exist or not.

Warmth bloomed in my chest, yet it was faint – like it was locked behind a million glass doors and I had no keys. The warmth was grounding, giving me a moment to breathe, to realize that everything would be okay.

The feeling tugged at my heart, pulling me deeper and deeper in a sense of comfort. It settled between my bones, like crawling into a warm bed after being out in the cold all day.

"Mmm, something smells human," growled a large ogre a few feet behind me at a meat stall.

My eyes darted sideways, taking in the array of food that lined the walkway. My stomach tightened when I saw a mountain of brownies, which reminded me of Filix.

A smaller fey beside him yipped and howled in maniacal laughter as it plucked a chunk of meat off of a skewer. He popped it in his maw and messily began eating, his tongue darting out every now and again to lick his chops.

A second ogre piped up as he slurped down a string of sausages like noodles. "Don't be foolish. Human meat is unavailable."

"I'm tellings ye. Human is in the air," the first ogre grumbled, sniffling the air again. The smaller fey and the second ogre paused in their feast to scent the air as well. "Don't ye smell it?"

My heart leapt into my throat as the smaller fey's head turned in my direction. The probability of finding me amongst the dozens of fey that moved around me was slim, but if three dark fey a few feet from me could smell my human scent in the air, then others could too. I had promised Hyunjin to stay out of trouble.

The warm, cozy sensation tugged at something in my chest, urging me to turn around and hurry down the narrow, crowded streets. To hide until I could find Hyunjin again.

"Mmm, human meat." The smaller fey began to head toward me, getting closer than I was comfortable with.

The warm feeling urged me to go, which spurred me into action. Twisting on the balls of my feet, I took off in the opposite direction Hyunjin and I had originally been going. I darted up the makeshift street, ducking between fey and stall alike, hoping to throw anyone who could smell my scent off the trail.

Cutting left, I tripped, my foot having caught on a jagged piece of rotten, splintered wood that had been carelessly tossed on the ground. I caught myself, and awkwardly tried to play it off as I came to stand before an alcove that was tucked between two unoccupied booths.

A woman turned to look at me, her hands shuffling a deck of cards over a low table covered in various crystals and herbs. A large crystal ball sat on the center of the table, cluing me into the fact that I had just unintentionally stumbled into a fortune teller's booth.

I smiled nervously at her as I glanced around the hidden alcove I'd ended up in, searching for an easy way to get out.

The Fortune Teller gazed up at me, her eyes changing from green to blazing purple. A tiny shiver of apprehension ran down my spine as I watched her eyes pulse, burning brighter and brighter. I had only ever seen Hyunjin and the wolf shifter's eyes burn like that.

Who was she?

Glitter was smattered in her long black hair, the tiny particles reflecting the light wherever she moved, giving her an ethereal cosmic vibe.

Tilting my head, I looked closer at her, watching as the glitter in her hair pulsed randomly.

They're stars! I realized, my face morphing into one of surprise.

Tiny, luminescent stars burned in her hair, the sparkling dots mesmerizing me. The Fortune Teller was gorgeous, with strong brows and full pillow-soft lips that oddly reminded me of Hyunjin.

She stood from her seat, abandoning the tarot deck she had in her hands on the table. The dress she wore was made of shifting, shimmering tulle; the semi-gray tint to the see through fabric left nothing to the imagination. Instead of being distracting, or embarrassing, the dress did nothing but compliment the Fortune Teller's natural beauty, making her more delicate.

Her purple eyes appraised me, looking at the tiny details I tried to hide from people, and tried to ignore myself. She stepped around the small table, invading the limited personal space I had inside her tiny section of the Goblin Market.

"Oh you've been with the Prophet for a long time now..." she mused as she reached out and gripped my wrist, bringing my palm up to her face to see clearly.

I watched her with wide, nervous eyes as I chewed on my lip to keep me from saying something I shouldn't. The Fortune Teller's long nail trailed gently over the lines on my palm, before she ghosted the pad of her fingers against the cut I had sustained from the prince's coffin a few days prior.

Her eyes slowly rose to meet mine as she gently put my hand down. She shifted closer to me, nearly engulfing me in an embrace, almost like a hug. Her hands ran through my hair, playing with the ends in a tender manner. I couldn't tear my eyes off of her as she stared at me with a loving gaze that left me feeling oddly warm and fuzzy inside my chest. She just looked so soft and ethereal.

"You are perfect. I knew I was right," she said in a sweet voice, talking to herself.

"I'm sorry?" I asked.

Her glowing purple eyes met mine again, yet there was nothing malicious in her gaze. The hand she had playing with strands of my hair came to cup the side of my face. The skin of her palm was soft and smooth, her actions were demure and feather light. She ran her thumb over my cheekbone, gently stroking the skin.

"You are their compass. Remind them of that," she whispered to me.

She then spun around and disappeared into the crowd. I tried to follow her, searching for the mysterious woman with glowing eyes.

"Wait! Come back!" I pleaded with her retreating form.

My body was thrashed about as I shouldered into people. I stepped on someone's hooves, before my body was shoved into a gargoyle's sharp wings. I tripped over my own two feet more times than I could count as I tried to find a safe path out of the chaos I had been pushed into. A hand cupped my elbow, which had me whirling around to snap at whoever had the audacity to touch me without my permission.

Familiar ruby eyes met mine, which had me heaving a sigh of relief. I had never been happier, more relieved to see someone before.

"Where did you go? I thought I lost you," I questioned him.

Hyunjin's eyes tracked along the curves of my face before they fell to the ends of my hair. His free hand came up and gently touched the ends, his fingers brushing against the soft strands. His eyes dimmed for a moment as he studied something I couldn't see.

"You have stars in yo–"

Hyunjin's head snapped up as he cut his own sentence off, his blazing eyes scanning the crowds around us. His grip on my elbow tightened. I watched him as his eyes tracked someone weaving through the stalls.

"We need to go," he said in a quiet voice, looking down at me for a fraction of a second. His hand slid from my elbow to grip my hand in his. "Now."

Hyunjin tugged me behind him as we weaved through the throngs of fey, trying to put distance between us and whoever Hyunjin was trying to avoid. I glanced behind me, over my shoulder trying to see who we were running from. My efforts were in vain, I wasn't able to spot whoever was hot on our heels.

"Did you get what you needed?" I asked as I nearly tripped over a hobgoblin pushing a cart of rotting fruit through a busy intersection.

"Yes, we need to visit the Den."

"The Den?" I asked.

Hyunjin tugged me sideways, cutting back across the Goblin Market, using a surge of people to hide us away. My legs protested, my strides could barely keep up with Hyunjin's long legs.

"Hyunjin, slow down. I can't –"

"There!" shouted someone behind us.

I gripped Hyunjin's hand tightly as he took off, pulling me behind him at a rapid rate.

I struggled as we ran through the center of the market, running through stalls and throngs of people. Chaos swarmed in the air, as the shouts of our pursuers echoed behind us.

People tried to move out of our way, but some fey were unfortunate enough to run into us. My sweat-slick palm slipped from Hyunjin's grip, which sent him careening across the street. I stumbled over my own feet, trying to reach for his hand again, but he slipped from within my reach. He tried to turn and correct the mistake we had made, but he wasn't looking where he was going as he turned back to help me.

Hyunjin crashed, full force, into a nymph carrying a bucket of live fish, sending the contents splattering across the dirty, hay strewn ground. The poor nymph girl collided with a stall behind her, making her cry out.

Hyunjin easily caught his footing, and reached for my hand again.

But before I could take it, an arrow sunk into the stall next to my head, missing me by an inch. Hyunjin and I stared at the embedded arrow for a moment before we locked eyes. I had almost died. He surged forwards again, gripping my hand tighter as he took off again.

We weaved through the streets, running hard as the shouts of whoever Hyunjin pissed off grew closer.

With a jerk, my body was yanked backwards. We stood in a vacant makeshift alleyway, not far from the main center of the Goblin Market. Enough people buzzed past the entrance to conceal us away from prying eyes, and thankfully no one looked too closely at us.

"Something isn't right," Hyunjin panted, bending to rest his hands against his knees as he tried to gain control of his breathing again.

"What? Besides the fact that someone is actively trying to kill us?"

His eyes narrowed and lips thinned as he threw a distasteful glare in my direction.

"I was expecting someone to recognize me. Someone to greet us since you broke the curse too soon."

"Oh, I'm sorry I bled all over your glass coffin, princeling. I'll be sure to leave your coffin covered in vines to be forgotten about next time."

Hyunjin ran a hand through his hair, as he drew in steadying breaths to calm himself down. I watched in awe as he ran his hand through his hair again, the red began to fade into a perfectly bleached blonde color. The color magically disappearing in a matter of seconds as Hyunjin cast a glamor over himself. He looked like an entirely different person without his vibrant red hair.

"You're not listening," he snapped, his eyes glowing brightly. "They wouldn't leave me behind like this. Something is wrong."

"It's been half a millennia, Hyunjin!"

The glare intensified and I shut my mouth immediately.

"Even if you had not broken my curse before the initial time frame was up, I still should be getting escorted to the Kingdom right now, not hunted down like an animal. Something's —"

Hyunjin was cut off by shouting.

"Down here," I suggested, dragging Hyunjin down an adjacent makeshift alley.

We ducked into the shadows, hiding behind several haphazardly stacked crates that had definitely seen better days.

Hyunjin pressed me up against a wall of an abandoned market stall as we tried to catch our breath. Our pursuers were shouting a street away, searching frantically for the two of us. My heart hammered in my chest as I tried to think of a way to get us out of this situation.

We had run into a dead end, the only way out was back in the direction of where our pursuers were. Their commotion got louder, the sound of their feet against the ground growing heavier with each passing second.

We just had to stay hidden long enough for them to pass us so we could slip away undetected.

"Kiss me," I said.

"How will that help?" he snarled down at me.

He looked ravenous and terrifying, and I wasn't sure which one I was more afraid of at that moment.

"People tend to look away from physical displays of affection. We'll be fine unless they're into voyeurism, which is a whole different problem, and then —"

His hands caged either side of my face, and tipped it upward to meet his. His lips pressed harshly against mine as he swept down to save me from having to strain to reach his face due to his height. I melted into him, and refused to let him go. The rough fabric of his jacket felt soft beneath my fingers as I curled them into a fist to keep him from moving away from me. His hands tugged my head towards his, as if he couldn't get enough of me.

The sound of pattering feet ran past us, not bothering to double check down the dead-end alleyway.

"What's voyeurism?" he asked, pulling away as if he was completely unaffected by the kiss we'd just shared.

"It's the– the– you get sexual pleasure from watching others when they are naked or engaged in sexual activities," I explained.

A smirk tugged at his lips as he looked down at me, his eyes full of amusement and mischief. As soon as I saw Hyunjin's expression, I regretted it. Of course he knew what voyeurism was - he was four hundred some odd years old and not uneducated.

"And are you into that kind of thing?" He asked quietly as he tipped his head downward, and invaded my personal space. My breathing became heavier as my eyes dropped to his lips. Was he gonna kiss me again? I decided that since he wanted to play with me like that, then I'd play with him right back.

"Watching others isn't really my thing."

"And what is?"

"Biting, for one," I said bluntly.

His jaw clenched as his eyes fell lower, and watched as I deeply inhaled, which pushed my breasts together.

"You want to know what my bite feels like?"

"I want you to know what mine feels like princeling," I purred. "I wanna know what you taste like."

Hyunjin stepped away, bringing a hand up to his nose. He pressed his forefinger and thumb against the tips of his nostrils as he avoided my gaze. I watched in fascination as his hair slowly began to bleed, changing back to the vibrant red it had been.

My chest felt tight as guilt stirred in my stomach. How could I do that to Filix? My best friend whom I loved with everything I had.

If Filix was in my shoes he wouldn't be flirting with the Prince. He would be exhausting every resource he could to ensure I was alive and could be rescued. And yet here I was flirting with the Feywild's prince, kissing him and freely offering him my blood in exchange for orgasms.

How could I keep betraying Filix like this? It wasn't fair to anyone.

I cleared my throat, ready to move on from the weird tension that hung in the air between us.

"We should go before they come back."

Hyunjin nodded, agreeing with my decision to leave the Goblin Market as fast as possible.

TO BE HIS FATE

N ight fell quickly across the sky, the warmth from the
earlier sun's rays had already begun to slip from the
earth, leaving everything chilly and crisp in the spring-
time air.

Hyunjin had indirectly apologized when the sun had dipped
below the horizon line. Our little detour through the Goblin Market
had eaten up hours of our time, putting us behind our self-inflicted
schedule. There was a split second where I was angry, but the
circumstances were out of my control and losing myself to my anger
would put us back even farther.

My anxiety was harder to quell. A dozen 'what if' thoughts had
managed to creep past my defenses, and had me nervously sweating.
What if Filix was on this side of the Veil? What if the Smogbody had
turned him over to its master already? What if Filix was dead and we
had been chasing after a ghost?

When the cold had begun to seep into my bones, settling beneath
my skin, when Hyunjin turned to me.

"We need to stop for the night."

I nodded in agreement. We'd yet another exciting day in the

Feywild. I could only imagine what the next day held for us. Definitely more surprises for sure.

Walking off the road, we began to search for a place to spend the night.

"How about over there?" I asked, my stomach growling loudly.

I pressed a hand against my abdomen, startled by the ravenous sound my body had made. I hadn't felt hungry since this morning, and even then I had pushed aside the thought of eating anything. Fey food was off limits.

Hyunjin stared at me, his eyes trained on my stomach.

I shifted, uncomfortable in his line of sight.

"You need food."

"I'm not hungry," I lied. Hyunjin flinched as if burned, and I felt guilty. I had momentarily forgotten that lying to the fey was one of the rules he had warned me about.

"You need to eat something, Mare."

"The first rule in the Feywild is not to eat anything here," I stressed.

Hyunjin stared at me, annoyance and anger clear on his gorgeous features.

"How long do you think you'll last without food or water? I can guarantee it won't be much longer before you pass out from dehydration. You're no good to me unconscious, or dead."

My own annoyance settled on my face, I could feel it in the way my teeth ground together and my nose flared out as I huffed. I hated that Hyunjin was right, but I couldn't consume anything here.

"If you're not going to eat, you're going to drink," Hyunjin stated, leaving no room for me to argue with him.

I stared at him, confused.

He walked toward me and raised his wrist toward his mouth, where he bit down violently. Blood smeared across his pillow-soft lips as he dragged his wrist from his mouth and shoved it toward my face. His other hand gripped the back of my head, keeping me from jerking away from him in a panic.

His blood was rich against my tongue. The tang of iron filled my mouth as it slid down my throat. Hyunjin held me tightly, his grip strong and unwavering as I reached up to hold his wrist. My chest felt hot, the more blood I consumed.

I dug my fingers into his forearm, trying to escape his hold. A dark wave of lust ran down my spine, my clit pulsed in desperate need of friction. A whine was tugged from within me; I was scared at how my body was reacting to his blood. He gently shushed me as he pulled me closer to his chest to steady me.

"That's it, princess. Take what you need from me," Hyunjin hummed into my hair.

Giving in to his hold, my lips pressed against his skin as I lapped up more of his blood. The biting tang of iron tasted rich against my tongue, subtle hints of earthy tones lingered at the back of my throat. His blood was intoxicating; it made me wonder if my blood was as addictive as his was.

I squirmed in his grasp, sucking harder against his wrist, drinking down his free-flowing blood.

Hyunjin's hand at the back of my skull disappeared for a second before I felt its weight settle against my hip, his fingers digging into the soft flesh beneath my clothes. Goosebumps erupted across my skin despite how hot I felt in my own skin.

I pressed my thighs together, trying to appease the ache that had manifested out of nowhere. My panties were damp, and sticking to me uncomfortably. Hyunjin's fingers flexed against me, his grip still strong and grounding. A wave of embarrassment washed over me without warning and I snapped to my senses.

Shoving my hands into his chest, I pushed Hyunjin away from me with more force than I had meant to. He stumbled backward, nearly tripping over his own two feet.

I was seething in my own embarrassment. And I was certain he could hear how loud my heart was beating.

"How was drinking your blood supposed to help?!" I yelled at him. I pulled my sleeve down over my hand and dragged it across my lips, trying to wipe away the taste of Hyunjin in my mouth.

Hyunjin stared at me for a moment, his pupils blown wide revealing a sliver of a glowing ring around his iris.

"Fey blood has magical properties to it, it will curb your hunger. And it was the last thing I ate was your blood. You should be okay."

My mind went completely blank in rage as I tried to process his words and the implications they had. I was dumbfounded and wanted to drive my fist into his pretty features or have him fuck me senseless.

"'Should be' is not reassuring enough. Filix and I have a life back in Neverhelm. One I would really like to get back to."

Hyunjin fixed me with a stare, his lips parted just slightly.

"Have I ever lied to you?"

"Fey can't lie," I deadpanned.

"Exactly. If I didn't think you would still be able to return home I wouldn't have fed you my blood. No fey food is in your system. I'll get you home."

I narrowed my eyes at him, though the urge to punch him had lessened slightly.

"You look good covered in my blood," he said.

The urge to punch him returned with a fervor.

"I'm going to rip your heart out and eat it."

A teasing, flirty smile spread across Hyunjin's face as his eyes lit up. "I would love nothing more."

I turned from him, surveying the forest around us.

We were going to have to find a safe place to sleep for the night. Going back into the Goblin Market sounded like our worst option, and the very thought of having to step foot inside that horrid place had me shivering. I would much rather sleep outside than beneath the gigantic tent.

I turned back to Hyunjin, mouth open to ask him where he wanted to sleep for the night but I no longer stood within the forest.

A massive crowd of fey swarmed around me, dancing and mingling inside a massive ballroom.

Sweet, soft music filled the Grand Hall as people from all over the Feywild danced, drank and talked amongst themselves. Dozens of species of fey I'd never even heard of danced around me. Everyone was dressed to the nines, vibrant colors were everywhere you looked.

At the head of the room was a large pool of milky white water, the miniature lake surrounded by a dozen small rocks and mushrooms, creating a massive fairy ring. Yet despite the size of the pool, only a gentle gurgle of water flowing could be heard throughout the entire hall. Off to the side of the head of the room sat an empty throne, the King supposedly off mingling with his kin.

This place was magnificent. Laughter and peace filled the air as everyone continued to enjoy their night. Drinks flowed freely as feet glided across the dance floor in effortless patterns to the music that floated in the air.

Turning my head, my eyes immediately found Hyunjin amongst the sea of fey that surrounded us. My heart flipped in my chest as I drank in his appearance.

He was beautiful.

Long vibrant red hair was brushed back, with pieces at his temples pulled down to frame his face. An earring hung from Hyunjin's left ear, the diamonds glinting brightly whenever he moved and caught the light.

My eyes drifted down, eyeing the thick silver chain around his neck before I moved to the white blazer he wore. The blazer was cropped and hollowed at the sides, where thin silver chains linked together to create an intricate diamond pattern where the remainder of the jacket should have been.

As he moved, the jacket rode up, revealing tiny slivers of his stomach, making me eager to watch him more; hoping for another glimpse of his toned body. I forced my eyes away for a moment when I caught my gaze drifting down to his ass, taking in the black leather pants he wore.

He waltzed across the ballroom floor, his arms around a beautiful woman draped in a soft flowing red gown. Her fox-like ears twitched as they danced, moving across the room as they weaved through the other couples.

Together they looked ethereal. I was mesmerized as I followed them. Their movements were graceful and well controlled, showing exactly how much power they commanded. And based on how many people I could see that were also mesmerized by their dancing, they held a significant amount of it.

A hot spike of jealousy ran through me as I forced myself to ignore the pretty fox in Hyunjin's arms. I hoped she wasn't important to him.

I gazed out into the crowd around us, fighting the urge to glance back at the prince and his princess. A cluster of sea nymphs giggled nearby, their beady black eyes trained on the prince beside me, not that I blamed them.

He's in his funeral clothes, I realized as I whipped my head back to look at him. A haunted feeling crept over my shoulders and wound its way around my neck, nearly suffocating me.

The story of the Lone King had briefly mentioned the night that they were all cursed, dressed all in white in celebration before it turned into a nightmare – but I had never bothered to think much more about it other than a tragic night. I didn't want to watch this.

The song the prince and his companion were dancing to came to an end. Hyunjin bowed slightly to the kitsune he danced with, and she gave him a polite, almost needy smile in return. When they straightened, the kitsune girl went to speak but a satyr swept up beside her, stealing her attention. That momentary distraction gave Hyunjin the perfect opportunity to escape.

He slipped from the dance floor and moved through the crowd. His hand darted out and swept a flute of honey-wine off a tray held by one of the servants before he continued walking. He came to a gradual stop beside me on the aisle way.

"Tonight's the night you're cursed," I stated, looking at him for confirmation.

Hyunjin said nothing as he brought a flute of honey-wine to his lips, taking a small sip. His lips glistened as he pulled the glass away from his face.

"Hyunjin," I stressed, "This is the nig-"

He can't hear me. I realized as I watched him. I'm in one of his memories.

"Hyunjin, I don't want to see this, please," I pleaded with him. I was met with no reaction once again.

A man dressed in similar clothes to Hyunjin - only the shoulders of his white suit jacket were hollowed out, the same silver chains were draped across the empty space giving just a glimpse of the lightly tanned skin he had - weaved his way toward us. His puppy-dog features were relaxed and at ease.

"Seiji," Hyunjin greeted the man with a gentle raise of his drink.

"That's a bold color, even for you," Seiji said, sliding up beside Hyunjin and myself.

Hyunjin brought his flute of honey-wine to his lips and took a gentle sip before he spoke to the healer. His hand rose to brush the strands of bright red hair that had fallen into his eyes away, being mindful of how roughly he straightened his locks.

"If people are going to talk about me, why not give them something to actually talk about?" Hyunjin asked.

Seiji chuckled.

"You could have gone blonde again. Why red?" Seiji asked.

Hyunjin stared out across the sea of people inside the Grand Hall, his heart thumping slowly in his chest, a heavy weight had settled itself within Hyunjin some time ago.

A distinct lack of something weighed on his shoulders, and pressed at the back of his mind at all times. Hours spent in his chambers with his brushes and canvas hadn't been able to relieve Hyunjin of such a hefty, depressing feeling.

"Something had to change, Seiji. My hair color is one of the few things I have control over right now."

The man beside us stared up at Hyunjin, his features still and neutral. Yet behind Seiji's eyes was a look of deep concern.

Are you still concerned with what Iyena said? About the message Mother sent to our Prophet? Seiji questioned.

That obvious? Hyunjin raised an eyebrow in Seiji's direction. I'm worried for all of us. For Wolf mostly. He's still missi–

From the throne, a bloodcurdling scream cut through the room, rising above the chatter and the orchestra, cutting Hyunjin off. Every voice inside the Grand Hall quieted down, leaving the room completely silent.

Hyunjin and Seiji darted through the crowd, weaving their way toward where the scream had originated.

The King stood at the bottom of the dias with two others at his side, each of them dressed in a similar fashion to Hyunjin and Seiji. The King, himself, was *dressed in a rather revealing cropped suit jacket - the sleeves cut off as well. It was such an odd style to see amongst the elegant gowns and sharply pressed suits; it looked more like an outfit from my side of the Veil than this one.*

The two other men beside the King were dressed similarly in a monochromatic style – white blazers decked with silver accents and black leather pants – making them stand out in the crowd. I realized that those in a variation of white were of some royal status, while the rest of the room was bursting with vibrant colors and hues.

They stood out, and for good reason too. They were all beautiful.

The taller of the two immediately shifted closer to the King - to Wolf. The shorter man was surveying the entire room, watching as ogres, and hobgoblins had filed into the room, lining the walls and blocking the entrance, awaiting orders.

The second man's round features zeroed in on us – on Hyunjin and Seiji – a single, subtle jerk of his head had the two of them moving through the crowd again. Seiji broke off to the right, disappearing behind the cluster of nymphs who had huddled together, afraid of what was happening around them.

Atop the dias, slumped on the throne was a body – and a woman stood proudly next to it. Several Smogbodies lurked in the shadows outside the Grand Hall, peering in through the large windows behind the gigantic pool of water.

The body slumped on the throne was headless, completely covered in blood. Black veins spread beneath the poor fey's corpse. The poor thing had suffered greatly before its death.

I gasped and slapped a hand over my mouth to stop myself from vomiting. The corpse's body was disgusting – and I couldn't help but think of Filix, and how he had looked similar after the Smogbody had bit him.

Was that to be his fate?

A hand rested against the corpse's shoulder, extremely long, spindly fingers spanned downwards. The hand's owner laughed loudly as every eye settled on her and the body. A dark ominous wave radiated from her as she gazed down at everyone.

She was eerily beautiful. Her purple-black hair was luscious and shiny, the wispy bangs she had gave her a gentle, friendly appearance, yet the spindly horns that curled around the back of her head in a crown-like spiral spoke to her authority. Her skin was smooth and looked like glass. The gown she wore was breathtaking, made of pure white silk and sparkling lace details.

Two extra pairs of eyes on her face resembling an arachnid, had my stomach churning. I felt like crawling out of my skin the longer I stared at her extra beady eyes and ungodly long fingers. It made me self-conscious despite this being a memory - one that wasn't even my own.

"My dearest King," hissed the woman in a deep sultry rasp.

My stomach twisted in knots as I listened to her, addressing the King.

A lingering wave of uneasy anticipation washed over Hyunjin as everyone began to rush towards the blocked doors.

"Lady Iseul," Wolf said, looking up at her from the bottom of the dias. "To what do I owe the pleasure of hosting the Jotkai's Queen?"

He casually held his flute of honey-wine in his hand, the other shoved into his dress pants pocket. He looked calm but he was anything but.

A sense of urgency pulsed within Hyunjin's chest as he tracked and counted the guards that had filed into the Grand Hall. There were dozens of dark fey awaiting orders from the arachnid queen.

Seiji, Iyena, get everyone out. Now. Wolf's voice rang out in Hyunjin's head and subsequently mine. Hyunjin, listen closely. Be ready to negotiate.

"It's not what I want, Your Majesty," Lady Iseul said, "But what our people need."

Her spindly hand slipped from the corpse, letting it fall forward. It thunked onto the ground letting blood and black venom seep onto the ground, pooling beneath the body.

I took an involuntary step backwards, disgusted and frightened. More and more fey began to retreat, frightened just like I was. Their bodies piled up against the blocked entrance. Terrified screams and pained cries echoed around the room as the dark fey guards began attacking those who got too close to fleeing.

"Your ambassador for the humans has failed to protect us. Hundreds of fey have lost their homes, their crops, their livestock... their lives," Iseul said, her *voice ringing throughout the room, rising above the screams and cries of the fey.*

Don't listen to her words. You haven't failed us, *Wolf's voice rang out, speaking to the Human Ambassador.* This is the first I am hearing about this.

She's not wrong. The humans haven't been kind to us, to you, *replied a deep voice inside Hyunjin's head, one that belonged to the Human Ambassador. The voice sounded sad, defeated. I craned my neck, searching for the owner of the voice that sounded incredibly familiar.*

Hyunjin stiffened beside me. His head subtly swiveled back and forth, searching the crowd for someone just like I was. A burning desire to protect washed over him as he surveyed the frantic crowd.

Where are you? *Hyunjin questioned.*

Just inside the Maze, *replied that oddly familiar voice.* I'm coming.

Stay there, *Wolf commanded him.* Hyunjin, go. Keep him safe.

Hyunjin melted into the crowd, weaving his way through his frightened kin as he made to move toward an exit, one that other fey hadn't known was there. He slipped toward the edge of the room, glancing over his shoulder only once.

I hurried after him, curious as to where he was going.

"What is it that you want, Iseul? They have yet to break our treaty. You know my hands are tied. I won't risk war with them," Wolf reminded her.

Iseul's eyes narrowed in Wolf's direction.

"They must be made to pay," she hissed. "I want our people to prosper. Humans stifle that progress."

"What do you plan to do, Lady Iseul? Start a war that will kill thousands?" Wolf asked, his tone sounded cocky but I could sense he was trying to reach Iseul, trying to get her to see reason. "What good could that accomplish? We are no better than humans sometimes. They have yet to break my trust."

All six of Iseul's eyes glared at Wolf. The weight of her gaze was bone chilling.

Haunting howls broke free of the Smogbodies, the piercing sound splintered the grand windows that led out into the hedge maze. The glass shattered, flying everywhere as the Smogbodies burst into the Grand Hall. People continued screaming as the Smogbodies began to chase them across the Grand Hall.

Wolf and the two other royal fey at his side jumped into action, rushing to cut the Smogbodies off before anyone got hurt. Seiji and Iyena managed to take down the guards that had blocked the entrance, and were quickly ushering people out of the Grand Hall.

I lost sight of Hyunjin, too many bodies blocked my vision. I darted for the front of the room, stopping at the base of the dias. I rose onto my tiptoes and tried to scan the crowd. Through the frightened fey I could see the two other fey fighting against a Smogbody, their swords sailing through air and shadows, trying to drive the monsters back so their people could escape safely.

On the opposite side of the Grand Hall, Wolf was fairing only slightly better than the rest of his kin. The Smogbody Wolf faced was the largest of them all; its body undulated in smoke and mist, transforming into different monsters with every passing second. Wolf's own sword sank into the Smogbody's side, viscous black blood oozing from the wound and splattered against the ground.

In rage and agony, the beast knocked Wolf off his feet, sending the King flying across the room. His body landed atop the dias, where Iseul stood proudly.

Amidst the fighting and fleeing, another wave of goblins and ogres and other hideous looking fey flooded through shattered windows. Some of the dark fey rushed toward Seiji and Iyena, while more broke off and ran at the other royal fey, while others ran through the Grand Hall, heading straight toward Wolf.

My vision swam as chaos erupted around me.

And then as soon as it had started, the chaos stopped.

Another swarm of dark fey fell into a line, awaiting new orders. The Smog-bodies stopped their pursuit of the guests and slowly lumbered back toward the head of the room to stand by Iseul's side.

I dared not even breathe as they walked past me, my eyes never leaving their massive smoke riddled bodies.

Seiji and three others I had never seen before were at the top of the dias, forced onto their knees and shackled- yet the taller fey I had first seen at Wolf's side was nowhere in sight. Dark veins spread across the skin of their necks and ran up their jawlines, a clear sign of a rapidly spreading infection from a Smog-

body bite. The four of them had different expressions of pain written across their features, each one at a different severity and tolerance.

Grunts and thrashing limbs thumped up the grand strip of red red carpet that divided the room in half. I pivoted at the waist and watched as Hyunjin was wrestled toward the front of the room by two dark fey. His vibrant hair was wild, and his chest rose and fell in heavy drags as he struggled to catch his breath. The guards stopped directly beside me, leaving Hyunjin and I at the bottom of the stairs.

"You haven't listened to your people, Your Majesty. So we will make you listen, starting with the Captain of your guard, your healer, your Ward and your right hand."

Don't fight her. Let me handle this, *Wolf's voice rang out in everyone's head.*

I felt my stomach churn as a wave of nausea crawled up my throat. I pressed my lips together to resist the urge to give in and vomit as my eyes trailed over them all, finally moving up to Wolf.

He was on his knees, struggling against several fey that held him down while others worked quickly, stringing up massive chains that mounted to the walls. Seiji and the others yanked viciously at their bonds, desperate to get to Wolf to aid him. But it was no use. The chains they were trapped in refused to budge.

In a matter of moments, Wolf's own hands were bound in iron bonds. His arms were spread wide with no give at all. He was at Iseul's mercy.

Her eyes burned brightly in wicked glee.

Her heels clicked against the flooring as she walked toward Wolf. She stopped before him, looking down at the King of the Feywild on his knees before her. Raising a spindly hand, she roughly cupped his jawline and forced his head back to gaze up at her. Wolf clenched his teeth as he glared at her, a hatred I'd never seen before raged in his eyes.

"After tonight the door between our worlds will be sealed until the humans can learn to be respectful."

"The humans haven't —"

"The humans are foul, loathsome creatures that don't deserve our help or

kindness. You should be able to see that, Wolf. They have no respect for our customs, our culture..."

"They're learning, adapting to be more mindful of the fey."

"Not fast enough."

My heart began to beat faster as my anxiety grew. I felt like I was trapped inside a nightmare, one I wasn't able to wake from. I didn't want to be here anymore.

Wolf, let us fight, *A voice spoke clearly in Hyunjin's - and my - mind.*

We can take her out, *Spoke another's voice.*

You'll do as I say, *Wolf snapped at them, but there was no venom in his words. He was enduring this punishment to give them all a lesser sentence. The dead body at the base of his throne sent a clear and concise message. Wolf was playing into Iseul's plan to protect those he loved.*

Iseul pushed Wolf away from her, and turned her focus to the four others chained on the dias. She turned to look at Wolf after she stopped counting how many she had wrangled up.

"I might not have your historian and I may not have your Human Ambassador in my grasp, but I'll have him soon. I have a special plan for him."

The entryway doors groaned open, the sudden noise making everyone flich. Several goblins and ragged ogres pushed a glass box through the entryway; my heart sank as goosebumps erupted across my skin.

It's his coffin.

Iseul's laughter echoed through the Grand Hall.

My mind went numb as tears welled in my eyes. My hand shot out, reaching for Hyunjin's but this was a memory and I wasn't really here. I was unable to save him. My anxiety still shot through the roof, my blood running cold.

"And you princeling," purred Iseul. Her eyes were fathomless pits as her gaze landed on Hyunjin.

"A thousand years spent sleeping shall be punishment enough. Don't you think, Wolf?" Iseul asked, her white teeth flashing a wicked smile in Wolf's direction.

Wolf tossed his head back, a wild look blazed in his dark eyes. He pulled hard against the chains he was in, trying desperately to get to his mates.

"Don't worry, Your Majesty. All this is meant to teach them a lesson. When

their time is up, Hyunjin may be awoken and will be allowed to return home. But not a moment before."

"Punish me. Not them. They've done nothing wrong."

Iseul stared down at Wolf, her chin pushed upwards proudly. Her lip curled into a disgusted sneer as something shifted in her.

Claws wrapped around Hyunjin's arms, ripping him from my side as they forced him backwards, away from his mates and any possible aid they could provide. He thrashed and struggled, his movements were violent as he began to panic.

"I am. By punishing them, I punish you. Perhaps you will learn to care for your people more than you care for humans when this is all over." She turned her gaze back to Hyunjin and I.

I stood frozen in place, watching helplessly as Hyunjin fought against his assailants, trying desperately to break free. Tears tracked down my face as he was pulled down the aisle, toward the glass coffin he'd be trapped inside of for the next three hundred and twenty years.

Hyunjin was no better than I was. Panic filled tears streamed down his cheeks and ran down his neck the harder he struggled. His chest felt tight, like the hands wrapped around his arms pulling him to his doom; each breath he took felt like he was fighting two battles at once: one physically here as he was forced toward the glass coffin and the other a silent cry no one else but he could hear.

I felt useless as I stood there, watching as the past began to unfold; writing what I once thought to be a myth into fact. A happy ending hadn't been written for them and I wasn't sure one ever would be.

Look at me, *Wolf's voice echoed in my mind.*

Hyunjin and I looked at Wolf, the sight of him on his knees making my heart sink more. Hyunjin stopped struggling, and willed himself to stop crying. To be strong for however long Wolf needed him to be, despite Hyunjin being woefully unprepared and terrified.

Wolf's wet eyes met mine for a moment, and despite this being a memory that belonged to Hyunjin, I couldn't shake the strange feeling that Wolf actually saw me, actually had his focus trained on me.

"Always find me, yeah?" Wolf's voice rang out, a promise made. "I

won't leave you behind."

Something I'd never felt before rushed down the bond that Hyunjin and Wolf shared. Something I wasn't able to describe.

Hyunjin's heart felt heavy in his chest, that missing piece that had been weighing him down suddenly felt soul crushing. In the span of a couple minutes, his entire world had changed and wouldn't return to normal for centuries.

They were losing everything.

I blinked several times, trying to clear my vision that had been skewed by my endless tears. My heart physically ached inside my chest for Hyunjin's future. He didn't deserve such a punishment. None of them did.

"Farewell dear prince. May the Feywild be a better place when you wake," Iseul called out, with a graceful, mocking wave of her hand. A proud, triumphant smile spread across her face again as Hyunjin was pulled away again.

The clang of snapping bonds broke the resounding silence in the throne room. In a flurry of motion, one of them rushed at Iseul. She wasn't able to react fast enough to block the assault.

The shortest fey's teeth sank into Iseul's neck, ripping into her carotid artery. Blood poured from her neck and ran down her chest, staining her white dress.

Her loyal followers surrounded the fey and pried him away from Iseul's body. They wrestled him back into his bonds, where he was vulnerable and unable to defend himself. One of their fists met his nose, which had the fey doubling over in pain as blood poured down his face.

I turned from the front of the room to look at Hyunjin.

He had stopped struggling as he was brought over to the glass coffin. Silent tears streamed down his cheeks, yet held his head high. He kept his eyes trained on Wolf at the opposite side of the room, and refused to look anywhere else.

He stepped inside the coffin and slowly lowered himself down until he was laying down. I watched as the lid of the coffin slowly slid into place. Hyunjin was trapped.

I quickly spun around, turning from the image that would surely haunt my memories for years to come... perhaps for the rest of my life. I wrapped my *arms around myself and pressed a hand over my mouth to muffle my sobs and huddled into a ball as I cried.*

My chest felt tight, and I found it hard to breathe properly.

Arms wrapped around me from behind, a wave of heat radiated at my back warming me. I pressed back, seeking more contact with them. Lips pressed against the top of my head, trying to offer whatever means of comfort they could provide to me.

He didn't deserve that. I repeated to myself, over and over and over again. *They didn't deserve that.*

"Shhh, it's okay, princess," Hyunjin whispered, his grip around me tightening.

I shifted in his grasp, spinning so I was able to wrap my arms around him. My hands fisted the material of his jacket and refused to let go of him.

"You–" I cried, cutting myself off.

I knew it was pathetic to cry like this, but I couldn't help it. An onslaught of raw emotions crippled me.

My tears fell freely as I tried to forget the terrified look on Hyunjin's face as he was forced to accept a wrongful punishment; I tried to forget the pain etched across his mate's features, and Wolf's heartbroken expression as he was betrayed. Sobs racked my body as I clung to Hyunjin, his shirt clutched tightly in my fingers.

He didn't deserve that. None of them did.

"I'm sorry. I should have warned you," Hyunjin apologized.

He kept me close, his arms wrapped tightly around my body while one of his hands gently stroked my hair, petting me in a calming, comforting manner.

Why the hell are you apologizing? I thought, fisting more of his jacket in my grasp.

I should have warned you about blood bonds. When created, they can establish strong connections; sometimes memories can be shared. Hyunjin whispered, his voice rang out in my mind.

"A warning would have been nice," I muttered, sniffling.

Hyunjin chuckled and I felt it in his chest, which in turn made me laugh a little.

"I will warn you next time," he promised me with a kiss on my forehead.

I kept my arms around Hyunjin, afraid he'd disappear if I let go of him even for a second.

"How many memories will I see now? How do blood bonds work?" I questioned him.

Hyunjin opened his mouth to answer me but I cut him off, pushing back to look up at his pretty face. "Is this what you meant by being bound to you?"

"Yes, this is a blood bond. It's– close your eyes for me," Hyunjin instructed me, choosing to do something other than explain.

"Hyunjin."

"Please, close your eyes."

I stared at his glowing orbs for several seconds, admiring the bright ruby color before I slowly let my eyes close.

"Good girl," he praised quietly.

A frown appeared on my face which had the prince chuckling slightly. His laugh echoed inside my mind.

I want you to focus on the feelings between us, on how it feels to hear my voice in your mind, feel my emotions as if they were yours.

Foreign was the word I wanted to initially describe it as; feeling the calmness that radiated from within Hyunjin so I wouldn't freak out. I felt the underlying excitement he felt at having a blood bond with someone again.

Deep within the bond, nestled beneath everything I was feeling, was something else. Something familiar and grounding, but I couldn't reach it, couldn't figure out what was so familiar yet foreign to me. And a lingering ache of sadness thrummed beneath his skin, the dull ache never truly disappearing but no longer crippling him.

What is that? I questioned, reaching to find the source of his sadness.

I miss my family.

Empathy filled my chest as I thought of the circumstances that had brought us to this very moment.

Iseul cursed Hyunjin. Her manipulation and betrayal of Wolf. Bleeding on top of the prince's coffin. The Smogbody biting Filix. Almost getting caught in the Goblin Market.

Filix! Fuck. I hissed.

Shhhh... focus on us, Hyunjin redirected my wandering thoughts.

I swallowed and took a steadying breath before focusing back on us, on the bond we shared.

A singular string tugged at my heart, the rhythm matching with Hyunjin's heartbeat beneath my hand. And the familiar feeling lingered just out of reach, leaving me puzzled.

Warmth and heat radiated down the bond, much like the hug Hyunjin and I were wrapped in. There was nowhere else I would have rather been at that moment.

Warmth. Home. Those are what I feel when I'm with you. You make me feel less alone, Hyunjin said.

A pant of guilt hit me hard when I realized I felt the same way when I was with Filix. Everything with him had been easy, I could be *me* around him. The guilt intensified when I realized I felt the same way with Hyunjin.

Blood bonds are complex, Hyunjin said. *You don't need to feel guilty.*

"That's easier said than done, princeling." I whispered, trying to push away the guilt until I could process my emotions properly.

A soft, infatuated look had spread across Hyunjin's face as he looked at me. His eyes glowed, the ruby color sparkling bright.

An image of a thin red string appeared in my mind, and with nimble fingers I reached for it, allowing my fingers to twist and tangle around the singular strand. I gave it a gentle pull, half afraid it would lose its tension.

A purposeful tug at the opposite end of the string had my heart swelling in my chest, a smile spreading wider across my face.

"We can hear each other's thoughts. Feel what the other feels. This is the same type of bond you share with Filix. The same one I share with my family."

"Is there any way to turn it off? What if I don't want you to see the dark stuff? The things that I want to never think about again?"

Hyunjin reached up and brushed my hair away from my chest, sending the locks over my shoulder to expose my throat.

"It takes an incredible amount of magic to sever a bond like this. But boundaries exist and are followed by any means. Tell me if I wander too far inside your mind, inside your heart and I will stop."

His head came closer to my own, his nose nudged at the junction of my jaw and neck just below my ear. His pillow-soft lips barely ghosted across my skin, leaving me wanting.

"I'm sorry," He muttered against my skin.

"I've never heard a fey apologize so much in one day."

A 'tch' of a laugh left him as he snuggled closer.

I know I forced this blood bond on you. It was never my intention to do so. I– I had no idea you were my blood marked.

Blood marked? That was a term I'd never heard before.

It was explained to me a very long time ago by our healer, Seiji. Our heart-strings are made of the same thing in order to find one another. It's not just a connection between two people, although that is most common among those who share blood bonds. There can be people with multiple heartstrings, like us. I believe your world calls them 'soulmates'.

A fleeting thought from earlier flickered across my mind, before it vanished completely.

Hyunjin was happy to have a blood bond *again*.

"Why couldn't I hear you before? When I fed you my blood back in Neverhelm?" I needed to distract myself from that thought.

Again... who had been Hyunjin's first?

"Blood marked bonds are only solidified when both parties consume each other's blood. I've heard that due to the magic that lingers in the air here in the Feywild, it's easier to feel the bond – easier to hear little snippets of your other half inside your mind, or feel their emotions as your own – even if the bond hasn't been completely completed."

"We should find somewhere to sleep for the night. I'm tired," I said, distracting myself. I had so much to process.

Hyunjin pulled away, but kept his arms around my waist as he looked at me. His eyes glowed a little brighter than they had before, but my own eyes could have been playing tricks on me.

How are you so calm about this? I thought, the question more posed as rhetorical but Hyunjin answered anyway.

"I'm not. I never was. I was a nervous wreck when I first bonded. You're taking this surprisingly well. Way better than Miro had when he first bonded to Taesung," Hyunjin chuckled.

"Did Miro not want to be with Taesung?"

"No, he was ecstatic. It's just..." Hyunjin trailed off before he sighed. "Blood bonds are rare... for me... I felt like I didn't deserve this. Sometimes I still feel unworthy."

We were quiet after that. So much had changed, it was overwhelming to think about any of it. We had such a long road ahead of us to get to Kiruna and find out about the Smogbodies, about Filix's fate.

The guilt I had felt minutes ago pulsed within me.

My best friend was most likely dead. I had seen the way the Smogbody had sunk its teeth into Filix's flesh. I had seen the agony written across his freckled features. He had been tortured when Hyunjin had pulled me away from him, separating us.

And the prince. He was something else entirely. He wasn't like the murderous vampire I had first met back in Neverhelm. He had me feeling certain ways, ways only Filix had ever made me feel. And I wasn't sure what to do with that information. I did, however, feel guilty. I was betraying Filix by flirting, kissing and offering Hyunjin my blood.

I laid down, ready to fall asleep. Thinking anymore about this was going to drive me crazy. Hyunjin remained standing as he walked a few feet away from the spot we had claimed.

I watched as Hyunjin brought his hand to his mouth and bit down, blood rapidly dribbled from his mouth, splattering onto the blades of grass beneath his feet.

Hyunjin pulled his hand away from his mouth and squeezed, forcing more blood from his self-inflicted wound. When a small puddle had formed near his feet, he brought his hand to his mouth again and licked the wound.

"I don't know if I will ever get used to that," I commented.

Hyunjin's head popped up and tipped to the side in confusion.

"Blood magic. Magic is hard to find in my world." I explained.

Hyunjin hummed as he came closer, settling down beside me. He kept a couple inches of respectable distance between us, for my sake mostly. He leaned most of his weight on one elbow as he looked down at me. His eyes dimmed drastically, the flaming ruby color almost completely extinguished.

"Magic is everywhere. You just need to know how to look at it to see it," he said. "I hope you learn someday."

He rolled over onto his back and closed his eyes, leaving me to my racing thoughts.

WOLF'S WORDS continued to run through my mind, the promise he made echoing across my thoughts, keeping me awake despite how tired my body was. My mind was running in circles as I tried to process everything that had happened during the day.

When my thoughts wandered away from the vow Wolf had made, it looped back around to blood bonds. I wasn't even sure where to begin comprehending those.

"Can you explain something to me?" I asked, rolling over.

Hyunjin's eyes stayed closed but he shifted beside me and hummed. For a moment I thought he had fallen asleep on me.

"Wolf," I started, a bit unsure how to ask my question.

"What about him?" Hyunjin asked as he cracked open one eye to glare at me.

"He's the King of the Feywild?"

"Leader," he corrected me, closing his eyes again, "Technically, yes he is. It's just we don't call him a 'king'. It's not derogatory, but Wolf just prefers 'leader' over 'king'."

I stayed silent, waiting for more of an explanation to the questions I hadn't given to him.

"So as the legend says, long ago, Our Mother, the mother of all fey, realized her children were suffering without a real leader, someone to protect them from the cruelties that humanity faced us with," Hyunjin began to explain.

He was right, humans had not been kind to the fey when our worlds were connected and intertwined tightly. In every history lesson and made up myth, it had been clear we weren't good for each other.

Humanity had moved on quickly once the door between our worlds was sealed shut, the few fey that had been caught on the human side had suffered or were forced to adapt to our ways. After we'd severed ties, I wondered how the fey on their side fared. I hoped they had thrived like we had.

"She gifted Wolf to the fey to be that protector. And he was– is a great leader," Hyunjin's voice got quieter, seeming to get lost in his memories, replaying what had happened the night he got cursed.

"Wolf's ruled over the fey for nearly two thousand years. At first he was a magnificent leader... but three hundred years into his reign, things changed, he lost a bit of himself as more and more years passed. Until we came along."

"I thought you've all ruled since the beginning."

"No," he denied.

I stayed quiet, as Hyunjin had not actually answered my question.

"Wolf took the throne when he was really young. I believe he had just turned fifty. Fey at that time had been skeptical at Our Mother's decision... but despite what Wolf lost, he never failed our people. Not once."

I knew the fey lived longer than humans, but I had no idea that

Wolf had taken over at such a young age. Fifty years was nothing to the fey. "Did– did you help him get back to himself after he had been lost?"

"He did. He lost himself, lost little pieces of the puzzle that made him him. He was in such a dark place when we each came into his life."

"Who came first?"

"Seok came first, seven hundred years into Wolf's reign," Hyunjin said with a small smile on his tired features.

"And what did Wolf find again in Seok?"

Hyunjin cracked open his eyes, and let them burn brightly in the vast darkness around us.

"What do you want most when you've lost yourself?"

I stayed quiet, thinking about what I would want most, had I lost myself. Loneliness was the emotion that resonated with me most. I wouldn't want to be alone as I tried to figure out who or what I was again.

"If I've lost everything, including myself, then I would want a friend to help me get back to who I was."

A huff of a laugh left Hyunjin, and for a second I thought I had answered him wrong. But a proud smirk spread across his features, and I felt butterflies in my stomach.

"Exactly. Wolf found a friend in Seok first."

"What did Wolf find next?"

"These are long stories, princess. We don't have all night," Hyunjin reminded me.

I yawned as he said, which further emphasized his point. We needed rest.

"Just one more. I like listening to your voice," I said, admitting a small truth. It felt a little like betrayal though. I liked hearing Filix read me to sleep, and having Hyunjin take his place felt odd.

I hoped I could get to hear Filix read me to sleep again.

"Who did Wolf find next?" Hyunjin mused, thinking. "Wolf found Taesung, our loud mouthed historian next."

"And what did Taesung give Wolf?"

"Taesung gave Wolf hope," Hyunjin said quietly. He curled closer to me, his fingers playing with the ends of my hair.

"Despite Seok being there for him, Wolf was still in a dark place. He was consumed with dark thoughts," Hyunjin let out a deep sigh. "Taesung gave him hope for a brighter future for all of us."

"It must have been hard for him, all that pressure to take care of your people by himself." My hand rested against his chest, pressing against the very edge of his jacket. His chest was warm and firm, and beneath my fingertips I could feel his heart beating hard.

I felt Hyunjin swallow and take a labored breath. Soft sniffles were loud in my ears as I looked up at him. He was crying.

"I wish I had been there for him sooner. He didn't deserve to take on all that without us."

I shifted closer to Hyunjin, using my elbows to rise up to look down at him, my hand on his chest slid up to cradle the side of his face. Using my thumb, I brushed away hot tears that tracked down his cheeks.

Hyunjin's arms wrapped around my middle and he pulled me against his chest, his head burying in my neck as he cried. I rubbed his back in a comforting manner as I let my other hand run through his hair, my nails trailing against his skull in an attempt to calm him.

"What did Wolf find in you?" I asked quietly.

Hyunjin inhaled, ready to tell me, but I shushed him.

"Don't tell me, but think about it. What did he find in you? What did you get in return? Because I think your Mother sent you to Wolf at the exact time the two of you needed each other. That goes for all of you."

Hyunjin said nothing, but his arms tightened around me and held me close. We were quiet for a long while, so long I was certain Hyunjin had fallen asleep in my arms.

"I promise I'll get home Hyunjin. I'll bring you back to them," I vowed.

THE PRICE OF PLEASURE

Unlike the Goblin Market, Kiruna was not what I expected. I had expected a clean, sprawling city with a calming atmosphere. Butterflies and bubbles floating in the perfumed air.

What I got instead was a Goblin Market 2.0, only this time it was inside a sprawling, shit filled city.

In the shadows, terrified screams bounced off the walls of the city's buildings, only to be followed by the haunting crunch of bones breaking. Each cry had me flinching, afraid of whatever was causing said harm. My hands felt cold as I huddled closer to Hyunjin for protection and security.

The smell of roasting meat wafted in places around the market, while other areas stunk of shit, rot and decay. An underlying vibe lingered in the air around us, something felt off, like we were always two steps away from chaos being unleashed.

Music danced in the air, giving tiny pixies and itty-bitty horseflies – that were actually horses – the opportunity to dance and flutter about. I was dazzled, in an oddly frightening way.

We walked down the main street of the market in Kiruna,

weaving our way through the endless roads farther into the heart of the city.

Hyunjin had disappeared from my side, leaving me alone in the middle of the streets. It had made my heart stutter in my chest for a moment, until I felt a purposeful, almost teasing tug, urging me through a small cluster of fey that had gathered around a section of market stalls. Keeping my head down, I walked through the people, squeezing past several moss-covered dryads.

I spotted Hyunjin's frame in front of a flower stand. He had his nose buried in a blue rose, inhaling its sweet scent. He breathed deeply, letting his eyes fall closed for several seconds. He twirled the stem between his fingers as his eyes slowly opened. A small, content smile quirked at the corners of his full lips.

A similar smile spread across my face as I came to the realization he liked flowers and the beauty they held. This was the second time I had seen him smelling roses.

Excitement washed over me. I loved learning about Hyunjin. I hoped to learn more.

He turned his head, looking over at me with an unexplainable expression – a mixture of happiness and adoration and wistfulness. He tipped the blue rose in my direction, offering me a chance to smell it as well.

I quickly stepped up to his side, gently raising on my tiptoes as I gently held onto the rose's stem to bring the budding petals underneath my nose. A sweet, delicate scent of honey mixed with fruit notes hit my nose first, a soft dewy meadow whispered amongst the delicate scents. Beneath the honey and meadow, was a muskier, spicier smell I had not expected from an ordinary rose.

Darker notes of clove and musk filled my nostrils, mixing beautifully with the softer, more feminine notes I had first identified.

I pulled my nose away from the rose, my eyes wide in astonishment as I looked up at Hyunjin. I had never smelt a rose with so many different scents before.

Hyunjin chuckled at my reaction, which had my cheeks growing hot. I dropped my gaze, taking the flower from Hyunjin's fingers. I twisted the flower in my grasp, just as Hyunjin had done, admiring the deep navy petal tips before it faded down to a crisp white color at the base. Deep veins of purple ran through the petals, giving an incredible amount of depth and detail to such a small ordinary object.

The urge to try and recreate this on a canvas back in Neverhelm itched at the tips of my fingers. A good feeling washed over me as I committed its details to my memory, knowing I could paint it if I returned home.

"It's called a Terephine rose. They're only native to Everacre."

"Everacre?" I questioned.

"It's where I was born."

I looked back up at him, warmed that he would share something so personal with me.

"I've never seen naturally blue roses before," I said.

Hyunjin took the Terephine rose back, gently rubbing his fingers against the petals, feeling the softness beneath his skin. A far away look stole him away, traveling somewhere deep within his memories. I tensed, waiting to be sucked away into a vision of something that happened eons ago.

"It's blue because of Terephine. She was heartbroken that she left her mate alone, to face this world by himself. Terephine loved roses, and these roses reminded her family that she was never too faraway from them."

"That's so sad," I whispered, blinking back the tears that sprung in my eyes. A wave of immense heartbreak had me choking on my words.

"It was. I miss her," he said sadly.

"Was Terephine your mate?"

The tears I had tried to hold back came rushing into my eyes again. My entire chest ached as empathy ate away at me, and while a tiny flame of jealousy sparked within my chest, I pushed it away.

First, having to feel the immense, life shattering hurt that Hyunjin had experienced when he had to leave Wolf when he had been cursed to sleep for eternity had nearly destroyed me. To learn that Hyunjin had experienced more hardships, more pain in his life hurt worse. It was nearly unbearable.

"No, no... she was my..." Hyunjin pressed his lips together as tears sprung in his eyes. "She was my birth mother. She died when I was very young."

I wondered how many times my heart could break before I dropped dead in the streets. I blinked hard, forcefully willing the tears away as I placed a hand on his shoulder before it slid upward to cup his cheek.

He silently protested, trying to turn away from me to stop me from seeing him cry. But I stepped into him, the hand on his cheek grounding yet gentle.

He didn't have to hide from me.

My thumb once more brushed away a couple tears that tracked down his face.

I hated seeing him cry. I never wanted to see him cry again.

Hyunjin tipped his head to look down at me. That faraway look lingered in his eyes, like it was hard for him to return to the present.

"I'm so sorry, Hyunjin," I whispered, forgetting about the fey that moved freely around us. My throat felt tight as I suppressed more tears.

Hyunjin closed his eyes, squeezing them tight, releasing more tears. I rose onto my tiptoes and cupped his face in both of my hands, brushing away his tears quietly.

We stood there for a moment, in our own little space without a care.

"Your mom would be proud of who you've become," I gently released his face and took a step away from him as he opened his eyes.

"She is," he said quietly.

He put the rose back in the bucket of water it had originally been put in. Hyunjin turned to me, blinking several times. I waited, watching him gently as he gathered himself again.

I had very little knowledge on how our blood bond worked, on how our heartstrings were connected, but I sent warm, fuzzy, comforting feelings in his direction – hoping he'd be able to feel them.

He sent me a soft half smile, where his eyes turned to crescent moons for a moment. Gratefulness pulsed down the bond between us, which had me smiling softly at him in return.

With a jerk of his head, Hyunjin urged me onwards, away from the flower stand. I made sure to keep my head down, avoiding eye contact with anyone as I followed closely behind Hyunjin's frame as he suddenly moved out of the flow of traffic and over toward several open air tables piled high with fabrics. I stepped around him, standing on his opposite side, looking at the various fabrics that were laid out.

Hyunjin's hand darted out, swiping something from the table as he urged me forwards with a nudge to my lower back. I stepped forward, moving in front of him as I smiled kindly at the shop vendors we passed.

We walked several paces, moving with the thick crowd, before Hyunjin's hand at my back snaked around my waist and settled against my lower stomach, dragging me backwards. I let out a small, startled yelp as I was pulled into an alleyway.

"Change into this," Hyunjin whispered to me, pressing a long piece of fabric into my hands.

My back hit the wall as Hyunjin crowded against me, blocking anyone from seeing me if they dared to look into the shadows in the alley. My eyes dropped to the fabric in his hands, confused. "What? Why?"

"You look a little too human for my liking."

"Did you forget the entire conversation we had yesterday about how I wasn't going to change my appearance to appease some fucking fairies? You're included in that."

Hyunjin sighed as a tiny twinge of annoyance flared down the bond. I clearly had not gotten something.

"Where we need to go has certain expectations. What you're wearing won't be permitted inside."

I took the fabric from his hands and held it up. The bundle of fabric was actually a long, off the shoulder gown in a deep navy blue. The color of the dress actually complimented my skin tone quite nicely, much to my surprise. It had two high slits along the skirt, leaving every opportunity to accidentally flash someone if we had to flee again.

"Is what you're wearing appropriate?" I questioned as I inspected the dress more. Hyunjin hadn't chosen something terrible for me to change into. It could have been a lot worse.

My eyes settled on Hyunjin's form, taking in the outfit he'd been in for the past three hundred and twenty years. A cropped, white blazer was hollowed at the sides, where thin silver chains linked together to create an intricate diamond pattern where the remainder of the jacket should have been. Black dress pants made the silver chains at his neck stand out more, just like the jewelry that dangled from his left ear.

"I'll be using glamor," Hyunjin said. He gripped the lapels of his jacket and roughly adjusted them, the white jacket shifting styles before my eyes.

The silver chains in an intricate diamond pattern disappeared. Instead, long white straps appeared at the base of the cropped jacket. Hyunjin gripped them and began to lace them around his abdomen, criss crossing them over one another. I could see tiny slivers of his toned stomach, which I appreciated silently.

Hyunjin's black dress pants faded to a pure white color, and rectangular cut outs along his left thigh appeared. Thick muscles strained against how tight the pants were; and I snapped my gaze back to the dress in my hands when I noticed my gaze drifting.

"Fine. Turn around," I said, yanking off the beanie and shoving it into his hand.

Hyunjin turned and I hurried to undress.

"I'm never gonna see these clothes again, am I?" I questioned, not expecting a real answer. I kicked off my shoes and quickly stripped out of my pants, leaving them in a pile against the wall.

"No. I can replace them once we figure this mess out," Hyunjin offered.

"That's sweet of you," I said quietly.

I slipped the dress over my head, taking a moment to figure out the sleeves. Hyunjin spun around the moment I finished adjusting the dress across my chest.

"No," he said immediately.

I looked up at him, annoyed and slightly embarrassed.

"Take off the bra. That looks ridiculous."

I glanced down at myself, taking note of the bra straps that were obviously sticking out of the dress. The dark straps could easily be seen against my skin, even with my hair trying to cover them.

"Ugh. Fine. You are so replacing this though. It was like fifty dollars," I complained.

Dropping the bra onto the pile of clothes I had made, I stared at Hyunjin, irritation still burned inside of me.

"Happy?"

"Very."

A silly wave of déjà vu washed over me. Hyunjin and I had had the same conversation back in Neverhelm when I had forced my beanie onto his head.

Reaching forward, I held out my hand for the beanie again.

Hyunjin held onto the fabric, not moving to give it back to me. I eyed him, confused and guarded.

"Give me the hat."

"It's too human," Hyunjin denied me.

"Filix gave it to me. Give it back," I repeated, sterner.

Hyunjin looked down at the maroon beanie before he looked up at me, our eyes locking. "It will be safe with me. I promise."

Something shifted in the air between us, as a vow had been pledged and awaited acceptance.

My eyes wander over Hyunjin's body, shocked he would make a promise so freely. He had warned me not to make bargains in the Feywild, but he hadn't said why… and now I wondered exactly what was going to happen between us if I did accept it.

"I'll get it back? Undamaged and exactly as I left it?"

"Yes."

"No tricks? What happened to not making promises?" I asked, letting my eyes rake over his body again, silently judging his motives.

"No tricks," he started, "but you will owe me something in return in the future."

"Owe you something, like what? My first born child?"

I had heard creepy tales from babysitters back in Neverhelm when I was younger. Fey would creep into our world and snatch newborn human babies, only to replace them with their own fey children. Those that were kidnapped and, left behind were known as changelings.

Other stories spoke of how sometimes fey would take a human child out of pure curiosity. To play with it like a toy, or show it off like a shiny new trophy. My babysitters never had to explain what happened to those kids afterwards, deep down I knew they didn't last long in the Feywild.

Hyunjin barked out a soft laugh. "No, no first born children."

My eyes narrowed suspiciously at him. "I can't give you my virginity, I gave that away a long time ago."

Hyunjin cringed as he laughed. "Fey don't covet virgins like the giants do."

I couldn't help but awkwardly laugh with him, making a mental note to steer clear of any and all giants I happened to come across.

"Okay, fine. What do you want?" I relented. Hyunjin had given it back before, he would give it back again.

Hyunjin tipped his head sideways, thinking as his eyes traveled across my face. He hummed softly as he tucked the beanie into the front pocket of his pants, the hat disappearing. My eyebrows rose, shocked yet again to see Hyunjin openly using magic.

It was rather impressive.

"I'm not sure what I want," Hyunjin admitted as he stepped forwards. "But I'll tell you when I figure it out."

Hyunjin bent over and hooked a finger through one strap of my bra. He held it up at eye level and smiled, like he'd been given all the answers he needed.

"Where are we going that you need my bra?" I questioned.

The smile on Hyunjin's face vanished for a moment. "Somewhere dark."

"And you need my bra because?"

"I'm not known as Wolf's negotiator for fun. I am useful, besides my looks."

"Negotiator? This is the first I'm hearing of this."

Hyunjin's eyes burned brightly as a large, nearly energetic smile spread across his face. He extended a hand out to me, waiting for me to take it. "Trust me."

I TRUSTED HYUNJIN. I really did, but the grimy brick building before us had me pulling my hand from his as I came to a complete stop.

Hyunjin stopped when my hand slipped from his, turning back to see what was wrong.

I stared wide eyed at the bright red door at the bottom of the small staircase, leading down into what reminded me of a speakeasy. Every hair on the back of my neck and arms stood on end.

Something dark and enticing lingered just behind that door.

Hidden promises and illicit desires were just within reach. One turn of that black door knob, and every worry that weighed down my shoulders would disappear. Every fantasy I could imagine could be brought to life, even the hidden desires I kept locked away deep inside my heart.

Hyunjin stepped into my line of sight, cutting off my spiraling thoughts. I blinked owlishly at him, surprised I had disappeared within my mind for a few moments.

His eyes lingering on my neck for several long seconds. He gently bit his plush bottom lip, as a hungry look settled in his monolid eyes. I stared at the little mole beneath his left eye, finding it cute despite the salacious look on his face.

Suppressing a shiver, I said, "Stop looking at me like that."

"Like what?" he questioned, his voice low and teasing.

"Like I'm dinner."

"Maybe you are," Hyunjin's eyes flashed brightly, the action further teasing me. "I'm starving."

I felt my face heating up, and I turned my head away to stop Hyunjin from seeing me blush. A lighthearted, teasing caress brushed against my cheek down the blood bond, Hyunjin's ghost of a touch was gentle.

"I don't need to feed right now," he reassured me. "Now, why are you nervous?"

"I feel like I'm missing something. Who are we here to see? You haven't explained a single thing."

Hyunjin fiddled with one of the straps of my bra, looking down at it instead of looking at me. "We're going to visit Madam Mezarae."

The atmosphere in front of the Den became heavy as I watched Hyunjin's long fingers rub against the fabric of the strap. The silver rings he wore caught my attention, reminding me of the rings Filix wore. I wondered how the Feywild's prince and a human from Neverhelm could have an identical set of jewelry.

It seemed nearly impossible, and way too weird to be a coincidence.

"Madam?" I asked, hoping for more of an answer.

Hyunjin's eyes rose to meet mine, his eyebrows pinched in worry.

"The Den is a pleasure house. Madam Mezarae uses it as a front for many things, but what she covets most is information," Hyunjin explained.

I waited, even as anxiety began to eat away at me. Pleasure house? The only person I had ever been with was Filix; and even having an orgasm because of Hyunjin's bite had me feeling guilty and abashed. How was I going to survive in a pleasure house?

Hyunjin lifted the bra with two fingers, bringing it into my line of sight. "This is our entry ticket."

"And how are we going to get the information we need?" I asked, my eyebrows cocked in question.

Hyunjin lowered the bra and lifted his opposite hand to his face, his fingers touching the tip of his nostrils. His eyes cut away from me for a moment, before he sheepishly looked in my direction but not at me.

"You are not going to enjoy it," he started. "I– I mean you'll *enjoy it* but you won't enjoy it."

I felt my brain bluescreening as Hyunjin's words clicked in my mind. I stepped backwards, as my skin bristled.

"No way. We are not fucking," I denied him.

Hyunjin blushed, his face nearly matching the intensity of his vibrant hair. Hyunjin burst out in nervous laughter, throwing his head back.

"We don't have to," Hyunjin said as he collected himself. He fixed me with a determined look, one that had my nerves calming slightly. "But I do need you to act like a paramour."

"A whore?" I hissed, disgusted. How could he ask that of me?

Hyunjin stepped forward, panic written across his beautiful features. His free hand was raised, reaching toward me to comfort me and fix the damage he had caused.

"No, no, no. It's– that's not what I meant–" he rambled. "No one outside my blood bonds knows me."

I arched an eyebrow. He still hadn't explained a single thing, which was beginning to get on my nerves.

"The 'prince' that the Feywild knows is a mask, one I use to keep my mates safe. A reputation that has been assumed for me, about what I'm like, about who I am."

If I wasn't lost before when Hyunjin hadn't explained what we were doing, I certainly was lost now.

Hyunjin continued when he saw the skeptical look on my face. "The Feywild assumes I'm a womanizer based on my looks alone. Someone who has a new pet on his arm whenever I grow bored of the last one."

"Why haven't you corrected them? Isn't that a lie?"

"Fey cannot *tell* lies," he stated, "And I'm more than just my looks."

A darker look passed across his features, annoyance simmered at the back of our blood bond. I wondered how many people had dismissed him and his actions, and only focused on his looks to judge him by.

"Their assumptions about my reputation behind closed doors has only ever been that, a speculation. Keeping people at arms length gives me the privacy I deserve," he stated.

"What does that have to do with me? Am I supposed to walk through that door and be your newest bitch?"

Hyunjin's face hardened at my harsh words, "Don't talk about yourself like that. It's not true in the slightest."

"But that's what you're implying," I said quietly, hugging myself tighter.

"Madam Mezarae seeks information. She craves it. If she knew you were human she'd never let you leave. You would be trapped beneath her claws until your body perished."

"I don't see how Madam could possibly know what happened to Filix."

"She will know if any Smogbodies have been across the Veil. And that information will tell us about Filix's whereabouts, and more importantly: who was hunting us."

I shifted my weight around, my eyes slipped back down to look at the red door at the bottom of the stairs. Nerves from earlier doubled down within my chest. My palms were clammy as I let my arms fall to my sides. Any number of things could happen behind that red door.

I looked back to Hyunjin, needing reassurance. "We don't have to fuck?"

"No, but pleasure is the only price Madam accepts," Hyunjin said, making it clear that I would have to give him yet another orgasm.

I apprehensively looked back at the Den's entrance.

Facing Smogbodies and running for our lives through a Goblin Market had been one thing, and I had a feeling whatever we were about to do was going to be much harder to face. But having watched my best friend, the love of my life, possibly die before my eyes was perhaps the hardest thing I had ever faced.

I nodded at Hyunjin, giving him permission to do whatever he needed in order to get what we needed for Filix's sake.

Hyunjin stepped close to me, his crimson eyes burning softly as his gaze glided across my features before he settled on my ears. Raising a free hand, his fingers tucked some of my hair behind my round ears.

With my hair out of the way, his fingers were free to ghost across my skin. It felt different than the phantom touch he had pushed down the bond when he had touched my cheeks a few moments ago. His fingers against the curve of my ear had tingles rushing down my spine, causing goosebumps to erupt across my skin.

I shivered underneath his ministrations, my neck ducking into my shoulders like a turtle to escape his fingers.

Hyunjin chuckled and gently gripped my chin, turning my head in order to gain access to my opposite ear. The same tingles danced across the surface of my skin as his fingers trailed over the shell of my ear.

A larger smile spread across Hyunjin's features as he took a small step backwards, admiring his work.

Touching my ears, I was surprised to find they were pointed like his were.

"A glamor. It will only last an hour or two," he explained.

"How do they look?" I asked, feeling them again.

Hyunjin's face softened as he looked at me, an warm, enamored feeling pulsed within our blood bond.

"You look like you belong to the Feywild."

And for a couple fleeting moments, I felt like I belonged here.

I WAS NOT sure where to look when we stepped inside the Den. The air was infused with vanilla and musk, but it did very little to mask the scent of sex that lingered just below the surface.

My attention narrowed on a pair of nymphs on a bench across the room. A large, curvy water nymph was bent over it, her forearms braced on the shorter blocks. The smaller woman behind them wielded a paddle with surprising ease, each smack of contact slightly overlapping the one before it, leaving her ass and upper thighs a deep shade of blue.

"This is a lot to take in," I breathed out over the thump of music.

"I'm here," Hyunjin reassured me.

Hyunjin's hand rested against the small of my back, guiding me forward through the throng of people that loitered in various places. He steered us toward a corner of the large playroom. There were a couple deep chairs and a long couch nestled against the wall, and I could only imagine what kinds of different sinful acts had been played out here.

Hyunjin immediately dropped onto one of the chairs, settling me on his lap. I squirmed and tried to rise but Hyunjin's arm around my waist stopped me.

"Mare, this will be easier if you relax. Breathe."

"It's a little overwhelming," I admitted.

"There's nothing happening within these walls that isn't completely consensual," Hyunjin said, as he held me tight.

"Okay," I responded, but I didn't truly listen to what Hyunjin had said. My posture was stiff and uncomfortable as my eyes darted around the dimly lit sex den.

"Mare," Hyunjin called, pulling me back to the present with him.

I twisted in his lap in order to look at him. A darkness had settled in his glowing red eyes, a heavy mixture of lust and something else had made a home in his gaze as he looked up at me.

"Is this okay?"

My silence was not the answer he was searching for.

"Princess, I won't do this if you're not comfortable. But I don't know another way to get the information we need."

"No, no it's fine. I trust you," I ducked my head down slightly, a bit embarrassed to admit such a thing aloud. "I'm just nervous. I've only ever been with Filix."

Hyunjin was silent for several moments before he hummed thoughtfully.

"Tell me what he does that you like."

I felt my ears getting hot at the mere thought of exposing even a tiny fantasy I liked or had done with Filix in the past. I could feel my heartbeat underneath my skin as the seconds ticked by.

Where had the flirty, teasing girl I had been back in the Goblin Market gone? I could have used her confidence.

Hyunjin's hands wandered, one slid against the skin on the inside of my thigh, dipping beneath the high slit in my skirt. His other hand stayed splayed against my ribs, keeping me close against his chest and gently caged in his arms.

"I like when..." I trailed off, my attention stolen away by the Domme nymph across the room.

She gently caressed her submissive's ass, her touch gentle as her fingers glided across the other nymph's skin before the Domme plunged two fingers inside the sub's glistening pussy. The submissive mewled loudly at the action, clearly enjoying the pleasure she had earned.

I shifted in Hyunjin's lap, pushing my thighs together to try and relieve some pressure. His cock was hard against my ass but he simply kept me firmly grounded on his thighs. The hand on my ribs shifted just slightly to where his thumb could ghost over my hardened nipple. His other hand stroked the soft skin of my inner thigh, dangerously close to where I ached.

I wondered if he'd touch me. Wondered if he could hear how hard my heart was beating. How fast my blood was pumping. I wondered if he could smell my arousal or feel the heat radiating from between my legs.

I hadn't been prepared for this. Hyunjin had warned me we were going somewhere dark, but I hadn't imagined this. There were a dozen things to look at and simultaneously shy away from at the same time.

Besides the spanking scene across the room from us, a pair of couples were tangled together making out. And beside them, tucked around the bar farthest from my sight was a satyr receiving a blow job from a harpy.

I inhaled deeply and closed my eyes as I tried to calm my nerves. I needed to focus and play my part when Hyunjin's contact arrived. One wrong move would ruin us.

"I like it when Filix…" I trailed off again, unsure if I wanted to reveal what Filix was also into. It felt too weird, too invasive to reveal what we had done together to Hyunjin.

"I like a little bit of pain. I like being hurt, and drawing blood from shallow wounds."

The hand on my thigh stopped moving as my words sunk in. The seconds of silence had my stomach dropping, afraid I had said something wrong. The moment I had decided to get up and scurry from the Den, two of Hyunjin's fingers pressed against my panties.

A deep hum rumbled in his chest, the pleased sound had my clit pulsing in need.

"You're wet. Did you see something you liked?" Hyunjin asked, his lips grazing against my ear.

His fingers continued to rub against my clit over my panties, the action was simultaneously overwhelming and not enough.

"Tell me, princess."

I ground back against his hard cock, letting myself sink into his chest a bit. I hummed in delight, a soft moan escaping with it.

"Was it the satyr getting his cock sucked? Or was it the pretty little water nymph getting finger fucked by her Domme? Or maybe the pixies doing body shots on the bar?"

His fingers continued to circle around my clit, his pace steady as my arousal continued to soak my panties. A knot had formed in my stomach and was beginning to build.

"No one here," I mewled.

"No one in here has you hot and bothered? Hmm, then what has made you such a mess on just my fingers?"

The knot in my stomach grew tighter and it became harder to hold back my moans and little whimpers. Hyunjin's voice in my ear wasn't helping either.

"You– just you Hyune–" I gasped out.

"Never thought I'd see you back little one," purred a soft feline voice.

I tensed and moved to slide off of Hyunjin. Yet his arms trapped me against him and kept me close.

Hyunjin's fingers slowed in their ministrations, but never completely stopped. My hand shot down to grip his wrist to try and stop him from fingering me in front of a complete stranger while I shot a glare in his direction over my shoulder.

"Madam Mezarae," Hyunjin acknowledged the Den's owner.

A tall woman with all the grace of a feline sat down on the long couch across from us. Her long, bony tail curled over her lap where she gently stroked the prehensile body part as she gazed at the two of us. Her hollowed out eyes somehow held the gaze of a predator zeroed in on its prey, ready to strike, to kill.

"Please, don't stop," Madam Mezarae encouraged us, a hungry look on her cat-like features.

She was off putting. A walking cat corpse come to life. Her body was entirely humanesque, an exposed black ribcage connected to emaciated arms that morphed into dangerous clawed hands. Her head was that of a sphynx cat, wrinkles and all.

My skin was crawling. There was nothing inside of her. No lungs, no heart, no eyes, nothing. How she was alive was beyond me.

"I'm afraid my angel here is shy around others," Hyunjin apologized, trying to save me from any embarrassment.

Not into voyeurism… got it, Hyunjin muttered down the blood bond, more to himself than to me.

I jolted in his lap, surprised he was speaking to me. We hadn't really needed to use the blood bond; it was going to be difficult to get used to hearing him inside my head, along with my own thoughts.

Only with the right people watching, I whispered, enjoying the way Hyunjin's thighs flexed beneath my ass.

"Mmm, give her to me for the night and she'll never be shy again," Madam Mezarae proposed.

"We don't have all night. I've come for some information that only you know."

"Only I know, hmm? Must be juicy gossip to know."

I couldn't decipher whether I was panting due to Hyunjin's fingers as they dipped below my panties and actually touched my clit, or because of the dangerous and sultry gaze Madam had glued to us – even with no eyes.

A surprised and ravenous feeling pulsed down the blood bond as Hyunjin touched me.

Soft, he growled. *Soft and bare. Fuck.*

Fuck indeed. My eyes wanted to roll to the back of my head as Hyunjin's fingers teased my clit. His pleased words had me clenching around nothing.

Hyunjin's arm flexed beneath my hand, which made me realize just how tight my grip was, how hard I had been digging my nails into the meat of his forearm. I released his arm but kept my hand at his wrist, silently begging him not to continue, even if it felt incredible.

A woman floated towards us, her entire aura radiating that of mist and fog, like the silver hair that cascaded down her shoulder in an intricate braid. Her skin was the color of dusky purple-gray and it was barely hidden beneath a flowy gossamer dress; the see-through fabric left nothing to the imagination and accentuated the woman's unnatural beauty.

Pale, milky white eyes slid from Madam Mezarae to me then settled on Hyunjin. A seductive, dark smile spread across her darkly painted lips, revealing blinding white teeth.

If Madam Mezarae had me feeling slightly insecure, this mysterious woman certainly amplified that feeling tenfold. It was hard to look away from her, like my eyes were naturally drawn in her direction.

She's a Night Mate, Hyunjin whispered in my mind through the blood bond.

She's terrifying, that's for sure, I whispered back, tracking her as she approached.

"Xana," Madam Mezarae purred happily. "Where is your brother?"

"Dal is coming," The Night Mate spoke, her words echoing around us despite her mouth not moving, and the implications of her words were not lost to me.

Night Mate's are dark fey. They play with fantasies and dreams and manipulate them into night terrors, Hyunjin explained to me. *But here in the Den they're mainly focused on pleasuring the clientele. Bringing fantasies to life.*

Come here often? I snarked. Guilt immediately ate at me. I was stressed and worried about being in such a vulnerable position in an unfamiliar place, and I was taking that out on Hyunjin when he didn't deserve that.

The hand against my ribcage slid slowly upward until his entire palm was cupping one breast, his thumb circling my nipple over the soft fabric of my dress. My nipple pebbled instantly under his gentle ministrations.

Once. Never wanted to come back, Hyunjin admitted.

"My information *comes* at a price," Madam stated as she stared us down, her hollowed out eye sockets focused solely on us.

"You always want the same thing," Hyunjin grumbled, his thumb and forefinger gently pinching my nipple as he slid his other hand down my slit, gathering my wetness on the pads of his fingers.

Madam Mezarae laughed, the sound was unpleasant and itchy.

The Night Mate glided past us, the scent of petrichor following in her wake, before she settled on the other side of Hyunjin. Her body hovered beside his, getting close but never truly touching him. With graceful, haunting moves, she raised a purple-gray hand and let her fingers glide down his arm, never truly making contact.

"Please, you know my prices are always fair," Madam said.

A dulled wave of displeasure ebbed through the blood bond; Hyunjin hated this as much as I did.

Hyunjin huffed through his nose and shifted slightly beneath me, giving the Night Mate at his side no mind. He refocused, his thumb and forefinger pinched my nipple hard above the fabric of my dress, causing me to let out an embarrassing squeak.

Arousal pooled between my legs, making my folds drip as Hyunjin barely teased two fingers inside my entrance.

I just need you to cum, Hyunjin informed me, his words strained even in my mind. *Cum for me and we can leave.*

I want to, I breathed out through the bond, letting my eyes fall closed for a second, trying to block out the world around us as I leaned back into him. To focus solely on Hyunjin and his long fingers. His cock was hard beneath me, and it took most of my self-control not to rut back against him, to roll my hips into him to gain more friction.

I dropped my head back and nuzzled my nose into his jawline, playing up my neediness for Madam Mezarae; afterall she wanted a show, didn't she?

"It's not her pleasure I want," Madam spoke up. Her words had us both freezing. My eyes shot open and Hyunjin slid two fingers farther inside me before he stilled.

"What use do my fantasies offer you?" Hyunjin growled.

"They're not for Madam," the Night Mate spoke up, the words echoed beside us.

Despite how hot I felt within my own skin, goosebumps erupted across my body for the thousandth time. I felt a little scatter brained as I tried to figure out Madam Mezarae's game.

Orgasms hold a lot of power. If used correctly they can influence and benefit magical needs or desires, Hyunjin whispered to me. He leaned forward and rested his head on my shoulder, his lips nibbling at the skin beneath my ear.

Why does the walking ghost want your pleasure? This doesn't sound very consensual, I snapped.

Another wave of displeasure pulsed down the blood bond, this one much stronger than the last. I felt my stomach tighten into knots, the urge to vomit stirred within me. Doubt settled in my mind, had I asked something I shouldn't have?

"Let me make you feel good, my prince," hummed the Night Mate. She raised a hand again, her manicured fingers reaching toward his face.

I felt the disgust that Hyunjin felt as he anticipated the Night Mate's cold, haunting touch.

My fingers curled around her wrist before she could touch him. A cold burning stung my skin the longer I held onto the Night Mare's arm, but I ignored my body's protest to let go of the thing hurting me.

The Night Mate's pupil-less white eyes focused on me with a tiny tilt of her head, the atmosphere around us growing thick with unwanted tension. Her expressionless face stared at me, as if she were surprised anyone dared stop her from doing something. I met her gaze head on, a stern look set across my features.

"Hands to yourself."

Mare, Hyunjin warned me through the bond.

The word *'mine'* pushed and echoed through the blood bond, the masculine voice neither mine nor Hyunjin's. A nearly crippling jolt of possessiveness flared white hot in my chest.

The unfamiliar voice had me glancing away from the Night Mate, giving her a false victory in our fight over Hyunjin.

Hyunjin's hands slid to my waist, giving me a gentle, reassuring squeeze. He didn't seem afraid or affected by the strange voice or wave of possessiveness that had come through *our* blood bond.

"There's nothing else I can offer you?" Hyunjin asked. For a moment I felt him considering, weighing the options of revealing I was a human to Madam Mezarae – magic produced from a human had been inaccessible for over five hundred years. Surely that magic – that information was useful to Madam Mezarae. But Hyunjin dismissed the idea entirely just as Madam shook her head, waiting impatiently.

"Go sit with Madam Mezarae," he encouraged gently. I slid off his lap and stood, turning to glance back when his hand caught my wrist.

Hyunjin stared up at me, his eyes full of worry and wonder; and for a moment I wondered what else I could give Madam Mezarae so Hyunjin wouldn't have to be left alone with the Night Mate. Whatever that ghastly bitch was going to show him made my skin crawl.

Hyunjin was always allowed to have his fantasies that he wanted to indulge in, but he should be free to explore them on his own, on his own terms. Not because someone else wanted to exploit them later on. This felt dirty, cheap even.

Is this okay? I asked, using his words from earlier.

Hyunjin hesitated for a second as uncertainty came through the bond. *Don't - don't look at what she creates. Stay out of my mind... please.*

I gave him a soft smile, one that I forced to reach my eyes as I sent calm vibes through the blood bond. It hurt, to say the least, to be rejected by Hyunjin like that... but I understood his reasoning and I wasn't going to violate his private thoughts like this, even if we were bound together. I bent at the waist, pressed my free hand to his cheek and kissed him.

"Cute," the Night Mate spat out as I pulled away from Hyunjin, a bit kiss-drunk.

I had used all the confidence I had to kiss Hyunjin, because when I turned to face Madam I felt nervous and weak. Like I was prey. I was a fragile human in the Feywild, and I suddenly felt that danger thrum in my veins.

A pointy wicked smile spread across Madam's face as I approached her, the tips of her sharp canines poked through her lips. Her clawed hands shot out and gripped my waist when I was within reach.

I yelped as she spun me around and positioned me on her lap, exactly like I had been on Hyunjin's. Madam's body was bony beneath my ass, and for a moment I worried my weight would become too much. All thoughts and concerns about my weight vanished when I felt her lithe skin covered tail tickling at my neckline, teasingly stroking the skin across my collarbones and atop my cleavage.

"Relax, my prince," Madam said. "I won't hurt your little pet."

My eyes refocused on Hyunjin, who was at the edge of his seat. His eyes pulsed as the intensity of their glow undulated. His posture was rigid as he glared at Madam Mezarae behind me.

I'm okay. Let's get this over with, I whispered down the bond, keeping my voice calm and soft.

Hyunjin's glowing eyes softened as he flicked his gaze over to mine.

I watched as he forced his shoulders to droop, to relax. He

shifted, pulling his jacket off to expose his toned stomach, before slinking back against the chair's backrest. The Night Mate surged forward, invading his personal space, but never touching him.

A shudder wracked through Hyunjin, but he was good at hiding his disgust at the dark fey next to him. He took one last look at me before turning his head to meet the Night Mate's fathomless gaze.

"Watch," Madam purred in my ear.

And I did.

Hyunjin's eyes dimmed drastically as he fell under the Night Mate's spell. A look of peace and pleasure spread across his pretty features.

"You'll experience the same thing when Dal joins us," Madam said to me.

Silence fell around us, the distant sounds of pleasure in the other room barely reaching my ears. Blood rushed in my ears as I watched Hyunjin under the Night Mate's spell.

The Night Mate hovered over him, her gaze focused on Hyunjin's features as she created the perfect fantasy for him. My curiosity was piqued; how was she able to peer into someone and draw out the perfect fantasy for them? And what had she conjured up for Hyunjin?

I was certain I would never fit into any of his desires or dreams.

Sharp pin pricks sinking into my thighs had my body tensing, nearly leaping off of Madam's lap at the sudden pain. Her claws dug into my flesh, tiny beads of blood pooling at her fingertips.

A throaty moan left Hyunjin when he smelt my blood in the air; his hands quickly worked at his pants, tugging them down to expose himself.

I swallowed thickly, keeping my eyes transfixed on Hyunjin's chest. On the small mole beneath his left pec, nearly identical to the one I had on my own body... and surprisingly also on Filix's chest as well. It felt wrong to look at him like this, but my blood pulsed with desire for him and my cunt was wet, desperate for him to fuck me.

I wanted him, needed him, but not like this. Not when I knew I

175

couldn't compete with whatever fantasies the Night Mate had conjured up for him.

Not when I had a lover – one who might be dead.

Guilt at my lust for Hyunjin had me tearing my eyes off Hyunjin's beautiful body. I settled my gaze on the Night Mate, watching, enraptured as she manipulated Hyunjin into seeing his deepest, dirtiest desires.

"Doesn't he look good like this?" Madam purred behind me.

My skin felt as if it were on fire, the constant sting of Madam Mezarae's claws dug into the meat of my thighs, keeping me trapped against her lithe body. I kept my eyes on the Night Mate, her eyes glazed over as she refused to look away from Hyunjin. Her head tipped to one side, which had Hyunjin gasping out.

My eyes met his, half-lidded and brimming with tears as he fisted his cock. Hyunjin's hands were glorious. My eyes followed their every movement, eyeing up the veins that scattered across his forearms. His knuckles were scraped slightly - most likely from our grand detour through the Goblin Market to get to Kiruna. His fingers were the perfect length, and I *knew* what they were capable of. The memory of his fingers toying with my clit just a few moments ago before we were interrupted surfaced in my mind. I wasn't even upset over being robbed of an orgasm.

I wanted him. I needed him.

His thumb circled the head of his cock, smearing precum across the sensitive skin. His cock was pretty, just like him - long and thick with a few prominent veins running along the underside. He was completely clean shaven - which threw me off guard. *How could he have manscaped when he'd been asleep for three hundred and twenty years? Where had he found the time?*

The head of his cock was a bright red, another bead of precum had already collected along the slit and it made my mouth water. I wanted to taste him.

He removed his hand from his cock and, using the tip of his pointer finger, he smeared around his precum, then pulled off slightly, watching how a string of the milky substance still connected his digit and his dick.

Hyunjin's hand wrapped around his cock again, his fingers enveloping it completely. He began slowly dragging his fist up and down the length of his cock, spending a couple of extra seconds near his sensitive head, using his pointer finger to tease his slit whenever he neared it.

His hips bucked up into his hand every couple of strokes, chasing the pleasure and whatever fantasy had been conjured up specifically for him.

"You see how worked up he is? Don't you wonder what fantasies Xana is playing out for him?" Madam hissed in my ear. She tried to make her words so sweet and enticing, but all I felt was jealousy. White hot jealousy and a strong sense of possessiveness.

Hyunjin's chest rose and fell in heavy drafts, the occasional grunt or muffled moan leaving his pillow-soft lips. Sweat beaded at his hairline and ran down the side of his face, and I wanted nothing more than to lick it off him.

Swallowing thickly, I squirmed against her hold.

"You haven't– haven't held up your end of the deal," My voice came out breathier than I had intended, but the sight of Hyunjin masturbating in front of me had me in a tailspin.

"He hasn't cum for me yet," the Night Mate jabbed at me.

If Madam Mezarae hadn't been holding me, I would have punched the Night Mate in her hauntingly beautiful face.

Madam's claws fingers left one of my thighs, finding their way up to my face. With a rough grip, she jerked my chin back to Hyunjin, to focus solely on him.

Watching him get himself off made me shiver with want and intensity. A desperate, whiny moan of Hyunjin's name left my mouth as Madam Mezarae dug her claws deeper into my thighs. The sting of pain barely distracted me from the erotic sight before me.

Look at me, I urged him through the bond.

My whole body tensed as his orgasm approached, toes curling as shockwaves of pleasure coursed through Hyunjin - and me simultaneously. It was as if a coil was tightening more and more, threatening to snap.

Hyunjin licked his lips apart as he struggled to fight against the fantasy the Night Mate was showing him, and my plea for him to look at me. His eyes rolled to the back of his head as he stroked himself faster. His body shook as pleasure coursed through him.

Look at me, I pleaded again. *Please.*

A brief image flashed through my mind as Hyunjin's eyes connected with mine: his body pressed against mine laid upon silken sheets, with another man beneath me as the two of them had their way with me. And an additional figure lingered at the head of the bed, watching with rapt attention, brown eyes never leaving my face for a second.

The image was gone before I could fully appreciate it.

His hand jerked violently as his orgasm hit him, cum spilling out from his tip, spurting onto his toned stomach, and he fell back into the chair, his hand still clutching his cock as he came down from his high.

The Night Mate waved a purple-gray hand across Hyunjin's torso, evaporating his cum into a wisp of smoke, cleaning the mess in a matter of seconds as his body stopped shaking.

A snarl threatened to rip from Hyunjin's throat as he panted, trying to control his breathing. His eyes glowed, narrowing in on Madam Mezarae behind me.

"You know what I've come for," he growled. I felt a wave of disgust roll across his body as he hiked up his pants and buttoned them, re-buckling his belt quickly.

"And what might that be?" Madam Mezarae questioned, a mischievous smile spreading across her feline features.

Hyunjin yanked his jacket off the back of the couch, roughly shoving his arms through the sleeves before he took the straps at the waist and began to wind them around his body again.

"Has a Smogbody been through the Veil recently? Has anyone sent them out to collect anyone?" Hyunjin asked.

"No Smogbodies have traveled through the Veil. If one has, it must have slipped through a crack," Madam said, her bone tail twitching. "The only ones in contract are summoned to the Kingdom."

"It does not seem like the thing you seek is here," The Night Mate's voice echoed around us, her lips never moving.

My heart dropped as I realized we had nothing on Filix and what could have possibly happened to him.

Hyunjin stood up, his eyes bright.

Madam Mezarae's claws retracted from my thighs, allowing me off her bony lap. I leapt up and wrapped my arms around Hyunjin's bicep, giving him a half hug of sorts.

I knew exactly why Hyunjin had only ever stepped foot in here once and never wanted to return.

"It's a shame you don't want to stay longer," Madam pouted, "I would love to play with your little pet."

Hyunjin's arm snaked around my waist, keeping me tucked against his side and away from the dark fey around us.

"I never should have come back. You never have what I desire," Hyunjin said, barely holding back a snarl.

Hyunjin pulled me behind him as he weaved through the other scenes that were being played out in the Den, moving toward the exit as fast as he could.

I purposefully ignored the pleasured cries that came from the submissive nymph I watched earlier, keeping my eyes on Hyunjin's back as we moved through the dimly lit area. I was worried about our next step, about what we could do now to figure out what happened to Filix... but that could wait, what was one more moment when Hyunjin was hurting?

"Hyunjin stop," I tugged at his arm, pulling against him roughly.

Hyunjin stopped, looking down at me. Disgust plagued our blood bond, suffocating any other emotion I wanted to send to him.

I can't apologize - but if I overstepped... if I made you uncomfortable when I begged you to look at me....

You did nothing wrong, Hyunjin reassured me.

His words did nothing to ease the guilt that had my stomach twisting in knots. I couldn't shake the feeling that I had overstepped. That I had asked too much of him.

I don't believe you.

I can't lie, princess. You did nothing wrong, Hyunjin repeated. *In fact you made my orgasm so much more intense.*

I dropped my eyes to the floor beneath our feet, embarrassed and slightly aroused.

I've never cum so hard. I hope you can help me again someday.

My cheeks grew hotter and I playfully hit his chest. His arms snaked around my sides, one hand coming to rest against my hip.

I'm serious, princess.

You can't just say things like that! I squirmed in his arms.

A small laugh escaped him, clearly enjoying the reaction he was getting out of me.

"I wish I could take you in the art room," he whispered, his hand squeezing my hip. Arousal pulsed down the bond, replacing the disgust that tainted it moments ago.

"Why don't you?" I question him.

He stared down at me, his eyes burned bright, full of desire.

"The first time I fuck you covered in paint will be in *my* studio in the Kingdom. Not here... not where I cannot take my sweet time with you."

I imagined him covered in paint: a line of lilac across his toned stomach, a smear of blue across his collarbone. A tiny smudge of yellow on his cheek. A swipe of red along his thigh in the shape of my handprint.

He'd look adorable covered in paint.

Don't do that! Hyunjin whined in my mind.

I met his eyes again, he was blushing. He brought a hand to his nose, gently touching it with his pointer and thumb. I had come to recognize it as a response to his embarrassment. It was cute.

Stop! he whined again.

It was fascinating how fast he could go from being shameless to being embarrassed.

I shook my head as I held back a laugh. I laced my fingers through his and nodded toward the door.

Come on princeling. We have to get you home.

Lead the way princess.

ONE OF YOUR KIND

<p style="text-indent: 0;">

eat licked against my skin, burning the hairs off my arms. Smoke curled through the lobby of the inn, wafting up toward the rafters as fire ate away at the walls.

I sputtered and coughed as I breathed in toxic air, searching blindly for anyone who had not escaped from the inn as it burned. The furniture in the lobby had quickly taken flame, the fabric curtains and plush carpeting in front of the fireplace was completely ash.

Picking my way over to the stairs, I doubled over, coughing violently. I had to get out of here soon.

Smoke had risen through the trees not too far off in the distance when Hyunjin and I crested over a hill, winding through the forest. The thick, dark smoke rose into the air, swirling up and up and up.

"Hyunjin, look," I had blindly reached for his hand, refusing to look away from the smoke.

Hyunjin had glanced down at our entwined hands before he followed my gaze.

"Oh shit," he breathed out.

The rising smoke plume had begun to grow in size the longer we stared at it. My heart sank at the thought of a forest fire eating away at the Feywild's beauty.

But then a rush of blind panic hit me in the back, like being hit with a snowball. I tore my eyes off of the smoke to look at Hyunjin.

What's wrong? I had questioned him.

Yellow Wood is that way, Hyunjin looked worried. Conflicted feelings burst inside his chest, and despite how he tried to hide them from me I felt them.

Is Yellow Wood a town? I guessed.

Hyunjin wanted to go and help, but he had a duty to return to the Kingdom as soon as he could. He had a responsibility to send me back to Neverhelm.

It's Miro's hometown. His family still lives there, Hyunjin replied.

Let's go, I said.

Hyunjin's eyes had met mine, blazing brightly. He still seemed so puzzled, so conflicted about getting home or going to help. He wanted to go– needed to get to Yellow Wood and help those who had helped Miro... but he was worried about me and my safety.

"Hyunjin, we have to help. If there are people over there..." I glanced back at the dark angry cloud of smoke.

The giant plume had begun to tint the sky a dirty, ugly brown color, casting a grimy filter over the land. Soon the ash in the sky would tint the world an ominous red.

"We have to go help," I pleaded.

Hyunjin's eyes darted back and forth, between me and Yellow Wood, contemplating on whether or not we should go help.

Hyunjin! I stressed, urging him to go and help through the bond.

A disgruntled huff left his pillow-soft lips, his resolve finally crumbling. He tore his eyes off of Yellow Wood to glare at me, a serious expression on his pretty prince-like features.

"You will stay out of trouble. You won't put yourself in danger. You won't leave my sight," Hyunjin demanded me.

"Yeah, okay. Sure. Let's go!" I agreed, knowing it had been an empty promise.

And then we took off, running down the winding pathway that led to Yellow Wood.

The streets were chaotic when we arrived.

Dozens of people were running about, some taking preventative measures to contain a blazing fire that had accidentally begun in the bakery and had spread to the only inn in town. They tossed bucket after bucket of water onto the surrounding buildings and onto the fire itself in an attempt to put it out. Others were tending to those who had managed to escape the blaze, treating them for mild burns and smoke inhalation.

Hyunjin and I ran toward the blaze, stopping to speak to several dwarves that continuously lugged water toward the burning buildings.

"Is anyone else inside?" Hyunjin demanded, the prince in him coming out.

"There are several unaccounted for in the bakery and from the inn," grunted a dwarf as he hauled away a heavy bucket of water.

Hyunjin and I shared a look – silently questioning whether we were actually going to help or not. I gave Hyunjin a nod, sending reassurance down the blood bond to ease his overactive nerves. Hyunjin craned his neck, scanning our surroundings for an easy way to get inside either of the buildings. I watched as his eyes widened when he found what he was looking for.

He darted off, surging forward through the bustling crowd running toward the bakery. I ran after him before I darted left, running toward the inn. The fire had not spread as far as it had in the bakery, giving me more time to search for the other missing fey that hadn't been accounted for.

I burst through the door of the inn, instantly raising an arm to shield myself from the flames that roared as more oxygen was introduced to the environment. Smoke filled my lungs as I hurried through the burning lobby, carefully picking my way through the debris.

The furniture had quickly taken flame, the fabric curtains and plush carpeting in front of the fireplace was completely ash. Books on the built-in shelves had been reduced to nothing, and the wood was quickly adding more fuel to the ever burning fire.

Bracing myself on my knees I doubled over, coughing violently before the front desk.

"Help!" called a voice from across the room, "Is someone there?"

My head popped up, scanning the room for the owner of the voice. Crushed beneath a beam that had fallen from the archway overhead lay a man, his legs trapped beneath the burning wood.

Our eyes met through flames, an urgent pull tugged at my chest.

"I'm trapped, my legs a–" the fey cried, his voice nearly buried beneath the crackle and roar of the fires around us.

"I'm coming, hang on."

My watery eyes darted up to the rafters, worried more beams could fall at any moment. Fire ate away at the support beams that arched over the ceiling, giving me only minutes to get to the trapped fey and get him out of here.

Debris blocked each path that I had wanted to take to get to him. Couches burned in one direction, and toppled chairs were crushed beneath a collapsed wagon wheel chandelier in another.

"Please!" the fey begged.

It hurt to breathe as I moved through the room, being careful not to catch myself on fire. I coughed hard, an ache in my lungs making my body shake as I inhaled more smoke.

Hurrying to his side, I crouched beside him and tried to see if his legs were broken from being crushed. No bones jutted out from his skin, and it didn't look like he was bleeding at all. He was just trapped, unable to escape on his own.

"Are you hurt?" I asked over the roar of the fire.

"No," coughed the fey.

Bracing myself, I pushed against the beam, hissing in pain as heat licked at my back. The fire mere inches from my body. The fey slid free of the fallen beam and rolled out of the way as beams overhead came crashing down.

I flew forward, toward the fallen chandelier, my arms flailed in front of me in an effort to steady myself. Arms wrapped around my midsection, yanking me backwards to keep me from crashing head-first into the burning chandelier. Twisting in his arms, I stared up at the fey, surprised he had helped me.

"We need to go," he coughed, searching for a safe way out of the burning inn.

"Was– was there anyone else in here?" I coughed, gagging on the thick smoke in the air.

"No. I got them out," the fey coughed. His arms loosened around me, letting me stand on my own. I slid one arm around his back, keeping him close.

Cracking noises crunched above us, the roof moments away from collapse. The fey and I shared a look, knowing we had to get out of this death trap right now. We took off, running through the flames, squeezing past the burning couches that had first blocked my pathway. The ceiling came crashing down behind us as we burst through the front entrance, stumbling far away from the fire and onto desolated streets.

I crouched on the ground, collapsing next to the fey, the two of us struggling to breathe as we gulped down fresh air.

With a free hand, I pushed my hair behind my ears, away from my face in an effort to cool down. I tried to focus on breathing, focus on pulling in clean lungfuls of air. Closing my eyes, I focused on the pounding of my heartbeat against my chest, and let it console me.

"You're human," coughed out the fey.

My eyes cut to his, the irises glowing a vibrant, warm yellow back at me. I jerked away from him, frightened at what he would do.

My hair had been pushed behind my ears - my very round, very human ears. The glamor Hyunjin had cast on them had fizzled out hours ago. My heart hammered in my chest as fear slowly spread through my veins.

"Wolf's been betrayed before, by someone that had been really close to him before. One– one of your kind," he whispered in fear.

I refused to blink as I stared at the fey, a sick feeling sinking in my stomach like a large stone. The flickering fire light illuminated his dark blue hair, making it glow almost. Soot and ash stuck to his sweat slick skin, smudged across his round cheeks and over his nose.

"Mare?!" Hyunjin shouted, his voice echoing from down the street.

"Hyunjin!" I called out.

My voice was scratchy, my throat was tight and burned from the smoke I had inhaled. Relief washed over me, my shoulders dropped as Hyunjin rounded the corner and came into my sight.

His footsteps pounded against the ground as he ran toward us, his white suit smudged with black soot and singed in certain places. His vibrant red hair was pushed back from his forehead, sweat dripping off his chin. Hyunjin didn't seem to be hurt, only mild bumps and scratches were visible.

His burning red eyes cut to the fey beside me when he got within a couple of feet of us. Hyunjin jerked to a stop, his feet planted on the ground firmly. A scared look ruptured on his face: his eyes widened, his eyebrows furrowed as his nostrils flared and he tugged his full lips down into a frown.

"Taesung?" Hyunjin whispered, scared like he had seen a ghost.

The fey I had rescued stared up at Hyunjin, his face full of awe and wonder. Tears filled his warm yellow glowing eyes as he shakily got to his feet.

"You're... you're here. You're home," Taesung said, his sentence ending in a giddy, disbelieving laugh.

I watched as Hyunjin launched himself at Taesung, his arms wrapping tightly around the other fey. Taesung wrapped his arms protectively around Hyunjin, despite being shorter than the prince. Hyunjin buried his face against Taesung's shoulder, shrinking down to melt into the short fey's embrace.

A myriad of emotions rushed down the blood bond: elation, relief, nostalgia, disbelief, confusion. Each battered against my heart, barely giving me a moment to process them before a new one was overwhelming the blood bond.

Hyunjin slammed a door closed, effectively cutting me off from feeling what he was feeling before it began to become too much for me to process. A tiny flicker of sadness bloomed in my chest, but I stamped it out before it could burn any brighter.

Taesung pulled away from Hyunjin, his hands on either side of the prince's face. Tears streamed down Hyunjin's face as he refused to leave Taesung's embrace. Taesung looked no better, happy tears falling from his yellow eyes. A wet, watery smile spread across Taesung's round features as he looked at Hyunjin.

"You're home, Jinnie," Taesung laughed.

A new rush of tears poured down Hyunjin's cheeks as he pulled Taesung back into a tight hug. Taesung began to laugh, but wrapped his arms tighter around Hyunjin. Over Hyunjin's shoulder, Taesung smiled at me.

I smiled back, happy to see Hyunjin so elated being reunited with someone he knew.

Hyunjin yanked himself out of Taesung's grasp and whirled around to face me. His ruby eyes scanned over my tired body, searching for any injuries. His rapid, near crazed gaze landed on my face.

We stared at each other for a moment, basking in the fact that neither of us had been hurt in our efforts to help.

Hyunjin stepped away from Taesung and pulled me into his body by the wrist. I hadn't expected his strength and ended up face-planting into his chest. My arms awkwardly wrapped around his torso and Hyunjin pressed his face against my hair.

"I smell like fire," I complained into his chest.

Hyunjin groaned, completely ignoring my words. He adjusted his arms, wrapping them over my shoulders, trying to pull me closer to him.

I'm not going anywhere, I laughed. *And we can't get any closer.*

We can try, Hyunjin sighed down the blood bond.

He pulled back just slightly and looked down at me, his fingers brushing soot from my cheek.

You're dirty, He teased me.

I gently punched him in the arm as I whispered, "Don't leave me again."

"Never," Hyunjin whispered back, his eyes dropped to my lips before he met my eyes again.

How did you find me?

You called.

I called?

Not consciously, but your heartstrings called out when you were having a panic attack.

That wasn't a panic attack. A panic attack would have been much worse, that was nothing.

Hyunjin said nothing as he studied my face for a moment.

"If I had known you were bringing home a pretty girl, I would have burnt the inn down myself," Taesung laughed, cutting our private conversation short.

Hyunjin rolled his eyes as Taesung continued to laugh.

Using his free hand, Hyunjin gently ran his fingers through my hair, pulling the strands from behind my ears to cover them again. He gently adjusted my curtain bangs to delicately frame my face, taking his time to get them in their proper place.

He's already seen, I whispered through the bond. The fear I had felt moments ago had lessened into nervousness.

Taesung's laughter died down as he stared at the two of us. His eyes pulsed as he looked us up and down, growing serious. "If you're awake... where's our Prophet?"

Hyunjin snapped his head toward Taesung, his own eyes burning bright. The two of them stared at each other. A silent conversation passed between the two of them, one I wasn't able to decipher fully. Taesung's eyebrows furrowed as he watched Hyunjin before his eyes flickered to me and then back again.

"I was headed back to the Kingdom, the– my– my campsite isn't too far away," Taesung offered, seeing as the inn had burnt to the ground.

He shifted on his feet, raising a hand to scratch at the back of his neck. He nervously smiled at us, his eyes lingering on Hyunjin – like he still couldn't believe the prince had returned to the Feywild.

An apprehensive, questioning feeling nudged at my side through the blood bond. The feeling Hyunjin sent my way had me keeping my guard up, despite how deeply Hyunjin trusted Taesung – something was up.

"Lead the way, Taesung," Hyunjin smiled, waiting to see exactly what Taesung was hiding.

I STARED at Hyunjin across the fire, whilst the wood nymphs and dryads and brownies around me giggled, and drank merrily.

For a moment, my breath caught in my throat as my eyes connected with a person that sat next to Hyunjin, who had not been there seconds ago.

The wolf shifter from the Goblin Market.

He stared at me, his face half hidden by the shadows from the blazing fire. His eyes flashed a molten silver, a tired look on his otherwise beautiful face. His features, the ones I could see, were familiar – like I had seen them in a dream before.

The warm, fuzzy feeling I had felt in the Goblin Market that had guided me toward the Fortune Teller tugged at my chest. It was pulling against a string that was nestled deep inside my heart, intertwined and tangled with others around it.

I had the urge to get off my stump and walk around the firepit to go and sit next to him, but I forced myself to remain in my seat. It felt strange to feel such a sudden, unprompted urge. A desire I had no idea I had wanted until it had been offered to me.

The purposeful tugging against a certain heartstring became more insistent, guiding me toward something I had been missing, something I had been searching for.

I pulled back against the desire that tempted me to get up and move, hoping to put a little distance between myself and it. I wanted a second to breathe, to get an outside view of the sudden shift in my emotions.

A calmer, gentler sense of warmth ebbed over my skin, giving me the space I wanted. I felt comforted and cared for, which brought a soft smile to my lips as I kept my gaze locked on the wolf shifter's.

I blinked, and he was gone.

I looked away from the fire, away from Hyunjin and where the wolf shifter had been as a mixture of unsure rejection and disappointment twisted inside my chest. Where had the wolf shifter gone? Why had he left so suddenly?

I purposefully put up a wall, being subtle about it. I didn't want Hyunjin to notice that anything was off.

I eyed him, watching as he laughed with Taesung. He threw his head back, his higher pitched laugh filled the air. It warmed my heart to know he had reunited with someone from his past. He truly looked happier.

He belonged here, amongst his people where he was free to be himself. He belonged to the Feywild.

I slipped away, walking from the bonfire and ducking into the tree line.

I moved through the trees, being mindful to keep an ear out for monsters that lurked where I wandered. I was also mindful to not stray too far from the noise of the bonfire.

Soon I came upon a small clearing in the trees, giving me the perfect opportunity to stare up at the stars.

Settling down in the center of the clearing, I brought my knees up to my chest and hugged myself as I tipped my head back to look up.

Two moons, one white and the other red, hung low in the sky, their luminescence not as bright as they could have been if both moons were complete.

The stars were beautiful here. I'd never seen these constellations before.

Deep blues were painted across the sky, with little pockets of oranges and yellows that hinted at stars burning brighter than others. Purples of varying warm toned hues blended between the midnight blues and the vibrant oranges, creating a gorgeous night sky.

The sky was riddle with blazing white dots, as if the sky had been scattered with diamonds when everything had been created.

A cool breeze rushed through the trees, the scent of pine caressed over my skin. I closed my eyes as the wind blew through my hair, letting myself feel the ground beneath me.

A sense of melancholy ebbed in my chest, growing larger with each beat of my heart. My time in the Feywild was coming to an end.

Soon we would know what happened to Filix. An answer to whether Hyunjin and I were in trouble for breaking his curse too soon. An answer on how to get me home, because I clearly did not belong here.

The stars above me twinkled softly, reminding me of the Fortune Teller's hair from the Goblin Market.

I wanted to stay.

I wanted to stay despite everything that had gone wrong since this adventure had begun. A huff escaped me. I could not even begin to describe why I felt so at home in the Feywild. Why a sense of warmth and comfort and pure happiness had spread through me the longer I spent here, connected to Hyunjin.

I wanted to stay with him.

Guilt was quick to flare in my chest, mixing negatively with the melancholy. I had a life back in Neverhelm with Filix – a man who loved me. A man I could not live without. Wanting – desiring –

another person when I had everything my soul could ask for was selfish. I couldn't keep Hyunjin like that.

He deserved better.

Was it wrong to want Hyunjin like I wanted Filix? It couldn't be... not when I felt like this, free to be myself.

You better be nearby and not have gotten yourself kidnapped or killed, Hyunjin spoke down our bond, his voice slipping through the cracks in the wall I had tried to put up.

Not dead. Not kidnapped either I'm afraid. Just needed some air.

Hyunjin hummed, *Come back to me.*

I hesitated to answer him. I wanted a few more minutes to myself.

Five minutes and then I come looking for you, Hyunjin bargained. *I don't care how long or how far I have to search to find you again.*

I send a wave of gratitude down the bond, being mindful not to outright thank him as I minded my manners. A soft feeling buzzed against my forehead, reminding me of receiving a kiss on the forehead.

I smiled softly at Hyunjin's sweet gestures as I tipped my head back to look up at the sky.

"YOU LOOK A LITTLE STAR LOST," Hyunjin said, coming up behind me.

I turned my head to glance back at him over my shoulder. "Star lost?"

He laughed softly, the bright sound filling the air around us as he moved to my side and sat beside me. The warmth of the campfire from earlier still warmed my skin despite the chill that had settled across the land the higher the crescent moons rose in the sky.

"It's a saying we have..." Hyunjin began as he crossed his long legs and tipped his head back to look up at the stars with me.

Hyunjin grew quiet as his eyes slowly scanned across the sky, lazily drinking in the sight of a sky he had not seen in many, many years. I knew I could never get tired of seeing this sky above me.

I waited patiently for Hyunjin to explain as my eyes tracked over different stars, connecting them to others to create constellations.

A quiet, easy silence filled the air between us as we gazed up at the stars.

I had nearly given up hope of getting an explanation when he broke the silence.

"Being star lost... It's like– like I'm lost, stuck in the dark almost. Wandering in a deep fog, searching for something."

Hyunjin tipped his head to the side, letting it rest on his shoulder as he looked at me. I rested my cheek against my knees, hugging them close to my body.

What are you searching for? I asked as I looked over at him.

It's different for everyone, Hyunjin smiled softly. *For me, personally...*

His eyes dropped to the grass beneath us as a warm, giddy feeling of love burst down the blood bond. Hyunjin chuckled under his breath and brought a hand up to his face, his fingers touching his nose.

"Before the coffin... before Wolf found me, I was wandering down a road and ended up going back to the same place, over and over again. Searching for a purpose. Searching for where I belonged."

Hyunjin's eyes began to glow, barely simmering as he spoke.

"I found where I belonged with Wolf – with everyone," he said, looking up from the ground. Our eyes met, and an overwhelming, near suffocating wave of love and adoration flowed back and forth through the blood bond.

"I found something else entirely with you."

My eyes filled with tears as my chest grew tight with an onslaught of emotions.

That's the sweetest thing someone's ever said to me, I whimpered as emotional, happy tears slipped down my cheeks. I straightened my posture, and turned from Hyunjin, embarrassed that he had to see me like that.

Hyunjin shifted closer to me as my fingers swiped against my cheeks, trying to stop the tears that flowed freely. He chuckled under his breath as he wrapped his long, muscular arms around me, pulling me back against his chest. His pillow-soft lips pressed into my hair, comforting me.

I no longer feel empty without you. Everything makes sense again, Hyunjin hummed into my hair.

His sweet words made me cry more. I shifted in his arms, pivoting to wrap my arms around his torso so I could bury my face against his chest. Hyunjin's arms wound their way around my back, and held me close as I cried.

Hyunjin gently stroked my back in a comforting manner, pressing kisses into my hair every now and again as he held me close.

"Taesung said we're only a day or two from the Kingdom. We should be able to get you home soon. I don't think too much time has passed on your side of the Veil. Maybe a week or two?"

Oh shit, I had not thought about the different time passages in our worlds. *My mum is going to be so mad at me. She better not have eaten my brownies.*

Hyunjin threw his head back as he laughed, the sound filling the space around us. My mouth dropped open in mock shock as I tried to hold back my own laughter – how dare he laugh at me.

"I'm serious," I pouted as I shoved him over. His laughter continued.

I rolled my eyes at him, but could not keep the smile off my face. He had such a wonderful laugh.

"I know you are," Hyunjin said, sobering up for a second. I stared at him and waited for him to crack. He burst out into laughter not a moment later, throwing his head back again.

I tackled him to the ground, laughing with him despite the lingering worry that nagged at the back of my mind. My thighs settled on either side of his hips, my hair fell over my shoulder and pooled to one side as I gazed down at him. Hyunjin's hands gripped my waist, his grip tight and grounding.

My gaze fell from his glowing eyes to his pillow-soft lips. I wanted to know what they felt like again. Kissing him once in the Goblin Market hadn't been enough for me. I wanted more of him.

He kissed me, hard, his brows furrowing passionately and his jaw clenching at the intensity.

When his tongue slipped into my mouth, I couldn't help but thread my fingers through his hair. I yanked at the tendrils, trying to suppress whatever sounds that wanted to spill from my lips.

Desire burned through our blood bond. I wasn't sure where my need for him ended and his craving for me began. Or even if the two were exclusive to one another. My fingers eagerly pulled at the material of Hyunjin's coat, pushing and tugging at the fabric until I shoved it off his shoulders, letting it pool on the ground behind him.

I felt hot in my own skin, the desire to feel more of Hyunjin against me consumed nearly all of my thoughts as I briefly pulled away from him, from his searing kisses to discard my dress.

Hyunjin shamelessly followed after me, stealing a quick peck from my lips as his fingers gently helped bunch the fabric of my dress in his hands as he pulled it off my body. As soon as the dress was gone, his hands were wandering; groping and gripping whatever expanse of skin his fingers could find.

I surged forward, pulling him back into a heated kiss.

I could feel his erection, straining painfully against the thin material of his pants, twitching against my leg as the distance between our laps closed. I sank down and rubbed my clothed heat over his bulge, desperate for some friction. His hands flew to my waist, gripping painfully onto me as I ground against him. As I moved backwards and forwards, I kissed and sucked against his collarbone, encouraged by Hyunjin nibbling at the side of my neck.

His hand roamed against my skin, fingers ghosting hotly against the surface before he gave my waist a brief squeeze. And while one hand remained around my waist to keep me close on his lap, his other hand flew up to cup my breast in his hand. I moaned into his mouth at the pressure, pleasantly surprised and thoroughly enjoying the way his tender palm kneaded my flesh.

His hand left my breast and slid up to my neck before he cupped the back of my head, his fingers threaded through my dark strands. He tugged just hard enough to earn a moan from me, my hips grinding down against his. Hyunjin's grip against me grew harder, and then my naked back met the soft material of his jacket that I had pushed off his shoulders moments ago.

I heard him sigh softly, happily as he stared down at my naked form. From where he crouched in between my legs, he could see my arousal coating my folds, nearly coating the insides of my thighs. Hyunjin growled quietly in pure approval, his grip on my thighs tightening as he took in the sight of my dripping pussy.

"You look... fucking good like this... all wet for me and my cock."

I squirmed slightly, hyper aware of the fact that Hyunjin could now see all of me. I tried to close my legs, but between his broad shoulders and his strong hands on my thighs, it was impossible.

"None of that now, princess. I'm going to make you feel good," he promised as he shifted lower.

Hyunjin mouthed at my inner thigh, leaving a few more little bites and hickeys. Then he was using his thumbs to spread open the lips of my cunt. I could feel my arousal dripping out of me already and he'd barely done anything.

Hyunjin dragged his tongue against my folds, nibbling at the skin softly. Whimpering, I grabbed him by his hair, tugging it lightly and making him groan against my throbbing pussy.

Hyunjin traced his large hands across my thighs, massaged the skin, while his tongue worked against me. He sucked on my clit, making me gasp out in pleasure. He had a cocky smile on his face.

"You're so wet for me princess..." he teased me.

Shut up, I whined. Hyunjin pushed his tongue inside my cunt, stuffing me for a moment.

I groaned, pushing his head back against me, cheeks heating up from embarrassment. He started teasing my pussy with his finger, dipping just inside my aching walls before he'd pull out again and barely ghost the pad of his fingers over my clit when his tongue left.

I pulled at his hair harder but he didn't seem to mind as I struggled to keep still. He finally put his finger inside me, his tongue never leaving my clit. I threw my head back and squeezed my eyes shut, breathing heavily.

You taste so good. I love this pussy, Hyunjin growled in my mind, a hungry fervor rushed down the blood bond.

My pussy clamped down on his fingers at his possessive tone, the growl making me melt beneath his fingertips.

"Princess, you're such a good girl," he panted, wet fingers lingering down to my exposed core, rubbing circles against my clit.

I couldn't help but buck my hips against him, whining at the contact I had been needing. He broke our stare to place sloppy kisses along my neck and jaw, sucking lightly against my skin, claiming what he knew was his. His mouth traveled lower to my breasts, taking a sensitive peak in his mouth, swirling his tongue around it, biting softly. He kept a torturous pace against my clit, my moans echoing across the clearing we were in.

"Gonna make you feel so good, princess. Do you want that? Does my little human want to feel good?" he questioned, moving his fingers from my clit directly into me, causing me to cry out in pleasure.

I could only whine in response, hips moving in an attempt to feel more, needing Hyunjin more than ever. I nodded my head, eyes shutting tightly as he quickened his pace in and out of me.

"Tell me what you want, Mare. Use your words," Hyunjin said sternly, his free hand moving up to my jaw, holding in place to keep me from looking away from his intense gaze.

I moaned deeply in response, tightening slightly around his

fingers. The action had Hyunjin groaning – my eyes fell down the expanse of his half naked body, staring at his hidden erection. He was so hard that he strained visibly against the fabric of his pants, and I whimpered at the sight of it.

"I need you, please," I begged, crying out as he removed his fingers from inside my pussy, going back to rubbing my clit once more. "Please fuck me, I need you."

Hyunjin pulled back, discarding his pants as quickly as he could before he invaded my personal space again. He kissed me, his sharp teeth biting down on my lower lip, drawing out a small gasp when I tasted the tang of copper against my tongue. Hyunjin licked into my mouth, savoring the way my blood mixed with his saliva.

Hyunjin, I whined, which sounded far needier than I had intended it to sound.

Hyunjin smirked against my lips, kissing me harder, hungrier before he pulled back. He hovered above me, his eyes burning bright.

The head of his cock was a deep shade of red, precum covering it lightly. I licked my lips as I stared at his toned body. Muscular arms reached down to pump himself as he stared down at me, his eyes glowing brightly, burning intensely with lust and passion. Hyunjin leant down to give me a quick kiss before lining himself at my entrance, groaning loudly as he began to push inside.

He peppered my neck and chest with kisses, reaching down to lift my legs up when he felt me relax around him. I wrapped my legs around his waist as he began to pull out slowly. A broken whine escaped me as Hyunjin slammed back inside me, filling me completely.

"Hyun- Hyu- Jinnie!" I gasped out, my fingers curling into the grass.

"Fuck," Hyunjin shuddered above me. *Call me that again.*

"Jinnie?" I whimpered.

Fuck, Hyunjin shuddered again, biting down on his lips as he lost the rhythm he had started to pound into me.

I tried to lift my hips to meet his thrusts but his movements only forced them back down. Every time he thrust into me, it drew out more sounds, more heavy breaths. The sound of his hips slapping against mine had me shuddering, clenching around him. He kissed once more at my neck, sucking and biting a dark mark into it, one I knew would be there for a few days at least.

When he started to lose his rhythm, he pushed his entire length into me, pressing his body as close as he possibly could, grinding himself into me. The new position pushed his pelvis against my clit, and I squirmed beneath him at the nearly overwhelming stimulation.

My hands slid up the muscles on his back, up his neck, and my fingers tangled in his hair, tugging harshly. He moaned, his eyes fluttering slightly as they rolled to the back of his head. His fingers squeezed harder against my thighs and I knew there were going to be bruises there in the morning. I whined at the pain, the mix of sensations sent waves of heat through my veins.

Hyunjin's cock twitched inside me when I clenched around him again. The pleasured look on his face, combined with the overwhelming waves of pleasure that he kept sending me, had my moans getting louder and louder, echoing off into the distance in the trees.

"Bite me," I breathed out.

Hyunjin hovered above me, his hair damp from sweat as he panted, breathing through his swollen lips.

"Ask nicely."

"Please, Hyunjin. Bite me," I begged, blinking up at him with big doe eyes.

My fingernails raked down his spine leaving small trails of blood in their wake, my back arched off the ground as my pussy constricted his thick cock until I felt like I was hurting the both of us. Hyunjin's breath caught in my ear as he rasped out, "good girl" before he sank his teeth into the crook of my neck, and bit down hard.

Fangs pushed into my neck. Ripping skin and the savage push of them dug deep. Diving into hot, giving flesh. He wrapped his arms around my back, and drew me flush against his chest.

I came hard for him, on him, around him. I downright drowned his cock, suffocated him and worked out the aching tightness in my cunt all over him until I felt like I couldn't breathe anymore. I came around him with a drawn out whine, tightening around him repeatedly as I ground against him to chase my high.

We were panting, tears lightly lined the sides of my cheeks, lips swollen and plump as I came down. Through the blood bond, I caught the briefest glimpse of myself through his eyes as he hovered above me.

To Hyunjin, I look beautiful that way; so blissfully fucked out that just the sight of me was enough to make him moan out, thrusting sloppily into my shaking core as he spilled into me. His warm cum made me cry out in delicious overstimulation.

He stilled his movements, allowing himself to catch his breath as his cock twitched softly inside me. After a moment of silence, he slipped out of me with a hiss. He groaned as his cum leaked out slightly, barely visible in the dark.

I looked up at him with sleepy eyes, giving him a small smile. With a gentle wave of his hand, Hyunjin used a tiny dose of blood magic to clean us both up, like the Night Mate had done back in the Den.

We shuffled around in the dark searching for our clothes, getting dressed before we laid down beside each other. Hyunjin draped his arms around me, pulling me against his chest. I curled into his warm embrace and let my eyes fall closed.

MY GAZE WAS DRAWN to a tiny blinking yellow light that hovered in the air, much closer than any star could get as I tried to fall asleep.

I shifted in Hyunjin's grasp, propping myself up on my elbows slightly to get a better look at what I was seeing.

The light danced slowly through the air, blinking every so often.

"Jinnie..." I reached with a hand to shake him slightly awake.

He hummed, having barely dozed off. He cracked open an eye, his face scrunching up as he came back to reality.

"What is that?" I questioned him, pointing off in the direction of the blinking light.

Hyunjin grumbled as he sat up and blinked the sleep from his eyes as he followed my finger. His eyes grew wide when he saw the tiny dot blink, his mouth dropping open in awe.

"It's an emberbug," he whispered, scrambling to get up.

"An emberbug?" I questioned, a bit unimpressed. We had fireflies back home - not native in Neverhelm but I had seen photos of them before.

Hyunjin jogged over to the emberbug and cupped it in his palms, being incredibly gentle with it. His eyes lit up, burning brightly as he stared at the flashing bug in his hands.

"Emberbugs are rare. It's an honor to see one," Hyunjin said, still looking at the bug in his hands.

I got up off the ground and made my way over to him, curious to see the tiny insect myself. As I got closer I could see the emberbugs light blinking in Hyunjin's pupils, watching in rapt fascination as Hyunjin's eyes began to pulse in the same intervals that the emberbug did.

"Your eyes are blinking like the firef– emberbug."

Hyunjin looked at me, an elated yet soft smile on his face. My eyes dropped to the beauty mark beneath his left eyes before I stole a glance at his semi-swollen lips - lips I had kissed senseless only hours ago.

I'm happy. For the first time in a very long time, Hyunjin said.

"Why is it an honor to see an emberbug?" I questioned, hoping I hadn't asked another stupid question.

None of the questions you've asked have been stupid, Hyunjin scolded me, before he began to speak aloud.

He looked back down at the emberbug in his hand, shifting his palms as the bug crawled over him. "Emberbugs have been in the Feywild since the beginning. There are a finite number of them, as they cannot reproduce. I am surprised to see one. It was rumored they had all died out."

My gaze was pulled away from watching Hyunjin take in every detail he could about the small emberbug in his hand, committing this once in a long lifetime moment to his memory forever. A dozen tiny flickers of light had begun to bloom across the empty field, filling the air with specks of light. My eyes darted back and forth, shocked at how many emberbugs there were. They were beautiful.

"Hyunjin," I whispered, afraid to speak too louder and break the peace that had settled across the clearing.

Hyunjin continued to look at his hands, enraptured with the one emberbug he could see.

"Hyunjin," I tried again.

He hummed but refused to look up.

I stepped closer to him and tipped his chin up with my fingers. He was confused for half a second before his eyes widened again, taking in the hundreds of emberbugs that danced around us, lighting up the area.

The elation Hyunjin had shown when he reunited with Taesung was nothing compared to how he looked as a few emberbugs floated around his head, dancing closer to us.

A small laugh escaped me when I noticed one of the emberbugs had landed in his hair.

Hyunjin looked back at me, his own smile still on his face. I gently reached up and removed the emberbug from his hair; being mindful to be delicate with the tiny bug. I cupped the insect for a moment before I opened my palms and let it go. The itty bitty emberbug buzzed off into the air in a dizzying pattern, bumping into another emberbug as it took off.

Our laughter filled the air, which attracted more emberbugs towards us.

Why can't they reproduce? I asked Hyunjin as I looked over at him.

I was a little startled that he was already looking at me, but I let it slide as I had emberbugs hovering all around me.

Our Mother. They're meant to remind us to be humble and kind during our long lives. When they are all gone, they can never come back.

The emberbugs danced around us, spinning slowly in a lazy circle. Hyunjin gently released the one emberbug he held delicately in his palm, watching in rapt fascination as it joined the others.

Hyunjins' burning eyes met mine, and I couldn't help but smile at him. He stepped closer to me, looking down at his feet as his hands reached for my own.

"I'm honored to share this moment with you."

I wasn't sure what to say in response to such a confession, but I felt how humbled and blessed Hyunjin was. Instead of using words, I poured what I wanted to convey to him into actions.

I surged onto my tiptoes and pressed my lips against his, letting my heart whisper to him.

I love you.

YOU ARE DANGEROUS

When Hyunjin and I returned to Taesung's camp just after sunrise, I was surprised to see many of the night's party goers were up and mulling about. Several of the dryads and nymphs I had danced with bounced around their makeshift kitchen, pouring chopped vegetables and chunks of cooked meat into a hearty stew that boiled over a hearty fire. Hyunjin and I waited patiently in line, moving closer and closer to the front as food was served.

My stomach growled softly, which had Hyunjin glancing worriedly at me, his eyes dropped to my stomach before he cast a sorrowful glance at the food being cooked. I gave his hand a reassuring squeeze.

I know. I wasn't going to eat any of it.

Surviving off my blood isn't healthy. You need to eat real food, Hyunjin argued with me.

I can live off of your blood for as long as I need to, I reasoned, despite knowing I needed real food, and soon.

It's not healthy, Hyunjin repeated.

That's all I can have here.

Hyunjin gracefully accepted two bowls of stew from the brownie that was serving everyone, and began to lead me across the campsite to a less crowded area to eat in peace. Hyunjin let me take the free stump, while he sat down on the ground, pressing his side into my legs.

"Jinnie!!" Taesung beamed as he spotted us seated hand in hand before a smaller fire that had yet to die out in the night. "And our princess! You are looking lovely on this fine day!"

Taesung's smile widened when he stopped before us, his round eyes staring at our entwined hands.

"Aren't the two of you adorable," he teased us.

I felt my face grow hot, and from the corner of my vision I could see Hyunjin pressing his finger against the edge of his nose. I let go of Hyunjin's hand, smoothing out my hair, making sure my ears were covered and hidden away.

"Yeah, yeah," Hyunjin dismissed Taesung's comment as he scooped a mouthful of potatoes into his mouth with a free hand.

Taesung casually scanned the surrounding area, watching as everyone slowly began to wake for the day. Hyunjin reached down and grabbed his tankard of water, and slowly brought it to his plush lips.

"I'm afraid none of this will suit you, little human," Taesung said quietly, dropping his voice so as to not be overheard.

"It's quite alright Taesung. I prefer to be hand fed anyway."

Hyunjin choked on his water, spilling the cold liquid across his jacket.

Taesung burst out laughing as Hyunjin coughed and sputtered. I pat his back, trying to get him to expel the water he had unintentionally inhaled.

You devilish little minx, Hyunjin said, glaring up at me.

I gave him a big, cute innocent smile, hoping it would distract him. Or at least lessen whatever he planned to get back at me with.

Taesung's laughter echoed around camp, much like it had done the night before.

"My," he chuckled, his laughter dying down a bit, "You two are quite a pair."

When Hyunjin had stopped coughing, and his breathing had returned to normal, he glanced up at perhaps his oldest friend. A soft look settled over Hyunjin's pretty features, a smile broke out across his face.

"We certainly are," Hyunjin confirmed.

Taesung looked between the two of us, a proud smile made his face squish cutely.

"Don't let me interrupt your breakfast you two. Remember you've got to rest up before we head off!" Taesung called out, moving away from us to check on others in his camp.

When Taesung was out of earshot, I leant down and whispered in Hyunjin's ear. "I want to taste you."

Hyunjin stiffened, his mug of water hovered just before his mouth.

And not just your blood.

"Mother," he hissed, dragging the mug of water from his face. He twisted to look at me over his shoulder. "You are dangerous."

A wicked, hungry smirk spread across my lips as I looked down at him.

Can you blame me? You're tasty.

Hyunjin rolled his eyes at me, and turned back to the second bowl of stew that he had yet to consume.

Behave yourself, He grumbled, forcing himself not to react to my teasing.

My laughter bubbled out and across the little clearing we were in, earning a few glances in our direction.

We fell into a comfortable silence, listening as the camp began to wake up. Conversations began to flow freely as more and more fey began to go about their chores for the day.

A couple of ogre children played tag with a satyr kid and a sphinx kid. Their shrieks of laughter filled the peaceful morning air, bringing a smile to my face. A mini pack of dwarfs slung axes over their shoulders and headed off into the forest with several tall, ghastly looking elves with bows and arrows strung across their backs. Dryads basked in the early morning sun, soaking up as much sun as they could before Taesung could yell at them to get to work helping around camp.

As Hyunjin finished the last of his meal, I reached out and took the bowls from him, ready to take them to be washed out to be used again later, when a pair of hands pressed hard against my shoulders, keeping me pinned to my chair.

I let out a yelp of surprise as a hood was hastily thrown over my head, blocking my vision completely. Hyunjin struggled and cursed beside me for a moment until everything fell silent.

Silent and dark.

THE HOODS WERE YANKED off of our heads, bright lights blinding us. I squinted and blinked several times, trying to get my eyes to adjust to the harsh change in lighting.

A weird sense of *déjà vu* washed over me as I recognized the room we were in – the Grand Hall in the Kingdom. At the head of the room was a large pool of nearly milky water, the miniature lake surrounded by a dozen small rocks and mushrooms, creating a massive fairy ring. Yet despite the size of the pool, only a gentle gurgle of water flowing could be heard throughout the entire hall. Our eyes were drawn to the first person we saw, sitting just before the pool.

Wolf's arms were spread wide and shackled tightly, his head hung low as he knelt on his knees in a defeated pose.

Their best leader had been brought to his knees.

Hyunjin stood beside me, our eyes never leaving Wolf's bound form. My hand shot out and slid into Hyunjin's, our fingers interlocking.

My tear-filled eyes glanced to the right, to the row of four men bound and chained like animals.

The very fey who helped Wolf find himself again.

Each one looked to be in pain, collars of iron were wound around their necks and wrist, rivulets of fresh and dried blood trickled down their necks and stained their clothes. They were painfully chained to the wall behind them. I had no way of knowing all of them, but I recognized Seiji from the memories Hyunjin had shared with me.

I looked back at Wolf.

His arms and shoulders shook slightly, the strain of being chained up for so long had finally taken its toll on his body. A single tear slipped from my eye and trickled down my cheek as I stood there, practically helpless.

"Don't cry beautiful," mocked a voice, his words echoing loudly through the hall. "Tears don't suit you."

A figure emerged from the shadows behind Wolf and stepped into the light, coming to stand beside the grand throne off to the left.

Hyunjin's hand tightened around mine as he stared at the man who had revealed himself. Disbelief ran down our bond. The prince's entire posture went rigid, ready to fight if need be as he stepped in front of me, protecting me.

The man who stood beside the throne had an air of aloofness to him. He looked calm and unbothered by our arrival but I sensed something different. It was all an act; he was frightened and angry.

Light orange-brown hair hung over his forehead and hung in his eyes, which made him look younger than I had expected. He looked no older than Hyunjin or I, but then again there was almost a five hundred year age difference between us. And there was nearly a thousand year difference between Wolf and I. I had no true way of knowing who he was or how old he could truly be.

His face reminded me of a sun bear; his features were short and stunted. This man looked nearly ridiculous: with undefined, thin lips, wide set monolid eyes and a slightly snubbed nose. And his ears were large, and very very round – not pointy like the fey at all.

My eyes darted back to Wolf as something Taesung had said a few days prior rang in my mind.

"Wolf's been betrayed before, by someone that had been really close to him before. One– one of your kind."

I glared back at this new face as pieces clicked together.

"Hyunjin," he said with a fake, beaming smile. He threw his arms wide, "Welcome home, brother."

The echoing crack of snapping fingers filled the hall. The sound made me flinch as I clung to Hyunjin tighter. Then hands grabbed me and yanked me away from Hyunjin, my grip on his hand ripped away in the blink of an eye. My knees hit the hard flooring as hands shoved at my shoulders, pushing me down.

"I see you brought home a little pet too," mused the man.

"Leave her out of this Jakob," Hyunjin snarled as he thrashed against the hands that held him down and away from me.

The guards behind me yanked at my arms and brought them behind my back, quickly locking them in handcuffs to hinder any of my movements. The clicking sound of more shackles had me glancing at my side. Hyunjin hissed as the iron in his own bonds met his skin, burning him.

"Tell me Hyunjin," Jakob said, in a taunting voice, "how did you get out of the coffin? Was it her?"

Hyunjin said nothing, but continued to struggle against the guard's grip on his shoulders. A grimace was nearly permanent on his face from the iron cuffs that rested against his skin.

The chains Wolf was bound in looked similar to the ones Hyunjin wore, which had me quickly looking at the guys by the wall. The collars that wrapped around their necks and arms looked to be coated, or even made out of the same iron that burned Wolf and Hyunjin. The same iron that was used by humans against the fey under the guise of protection from their trickery and charms.

"Because the way I heard it, Mare Cozen wasn't the only one to release you from your prison."

My eyes met Jakob's at the mention of my full name, my heart hammered loudly in my chest. How did he know my name?

"Let me explain!" Hyunjin pleaded.

Another falsely pleasant smile spread across Jakob's flat features, a wicked gleam burned in his dark eyes. Jakob leant his weight against the arm of the throne, crossing a leg lazily over the other like he had all the time in the world.

Jakob snapped his fingers again. The entrance doors swung open with a deep groan only to be replaced by the heavy, haunting wet growl of a Smogbody.

Its body thumped ominously up the aisle before it came to a stop directly behind me. A heavy thump of something hitting the ground had me flinching again. A soft groan of pain barely reached my ears over the roar of my own blood.

Movement behind Wolf's tired, strung up body caught my attention; and I watched as a second Smogbody emerged from the same doorway Jakob had entered from. A figure hung limply from the second Smogbody's mouth, before the Smogbody dropped it unceremoniously to the ground, exactly like the first Smogbody behind us had done.

The second figure groaned as well, but struggled to sit up more than the person behind me. Silver hair caught my eye.

"Filix!" I called out, tugging hard at my bonds.

The men bound to the wall shifted at my outburst, each one seeming to slowly register what was going on around them.

Jakob laughed wholeheartedly as he stood from the throne and walked a few feet toward Filix. He turned to face me fully as he squatted down beside Filix's exhausted form. With one hand, Jakob violently gripped Filix's hair and yanked his head up to force him to look at us.

Jakob turned his attention to Hyunjin, his eyes burning with a cold gaze.

"Filix, here, told me what happened. How he and Mare were cleaning up your coffin and then things got a little heated, and one thing led to another...then bam! You're free!"

"That's not what happened!" I lashed out, struggling harder.

Filix's gaze met mine. Yet his eyes weren't his usual brown, but instead were a wet silver-blue. Dark circles were heavy beneath his eyes, and dark spindly black veins crept up his neck and ran down his chest.

The Smogbody had bit him when we were first separated, and the venom from the bite had been spreading through his body killing him slowly.

My eyes bounced around his entire being, trying to see what else he'd been put through, what torture he'd endured because of me. I did a double take when I saw his ears. They were pointed. They'd never been pointed before... just like his eyes they were different.

He was fey.

His eyes filled with new tears as he watched my expression fall and morph into one of frightened confusion. He tried to push himself upright but Jakob's grasp on his hair held him back.

"Mare, let me explain. Please!" Filix begged in a broken tone.

"No, you've done enough explaining," Jakob shoved Filix's head down in a violent push.

Disbelief had my mind going numb as I helplessly watched Filix get pushed around. My heart sank in my chest as everything I had known and shared with Filix had been a lie. Were there clues I hadn't seen? How had I missed this?

He was fey.

Jakob rose to his full height again, his flat features pulled into a fake smile as he gazed back at Hyunjin.

"I'm disappointed, Hyunjin. You only had six hundred and eighty years left. You were so close. Our Mother would be disappointed in you."

"Don't speak about her. You have no right to talk about her like that. You're not one of us!" Hyunjin fired back. A dark, murderous look blazed behind his eyes, one that resembled his blood lust gaze.

A displeased smile was thrown in Hyunjin's direction. With a wave of Jakob's hand, the guards holding us back began hauling him forward.

"String them all up next to *our Leader*. I want them all to watch what I have planned for our little *human*," Jakob sneered.

Hyunjin and Filix struggled harder, the two of them fighting with whatever strength they had left to fight to get to me, to keep me from Jakob's wrath.

The man groaned behind me, struggling to move to help protect me. The guard that had dragged him in here simply stepped forward and yanked him back by the nap of his neck.

Don't! I pleaded with Hyunjin. *Please!*

I refused to meet his eyes as he looked at me, confused as to why I would ask him not to protect me. I couldn't watch him get hurt because of me.

"I know we've only just met, but I want to play a game with you," Jakob declared, a new spark of fire had ignited behind his eyes.

Don't play Mare, Hyunjin's voice broke through my scrambled thoughts.

"What kind of game?" I questioned.

"I want to know what makes you so worthy of what's rightfully mine."

I had no idea what he was talking about. What was rightfully his? I didn't get an opportunity to voice my questions.

"Jakob don't! You're angry with us, not her!" The man behind me protested as he was forced to his knees.

Jakob huffed, sounding truly puzzled like he was considering the man's words.

"Truest words you've ever spoken, Taesung. Doesn't stop me from wanting to see what's so special about *this* human."

He cut his eyes to me before he sent a pointed look to Hyunjin, an eyebrow arched in challenge.

"Shall we play?"

"You haven't explained the rules, or what we're playing," I piped up.

"Oh, you'll catch on quickly," Jakob said, as he jerked his head.

A jackal stepped down from the dias and settled in front of me, the emaciated dog hybrid stared down his snout at me. He bared his rotting yellow teeth in a snarl as he reached down and hauled me to my feet.

Hyunjin, Taesung and Filix began shouting at Jakob, begging him to release me. The three of them struggled against their bonds, the metal creaking against the strain. I tried to see how the others were fairing, but my focus was pulled as pain flared in my arm as the jackal's claws pierced my skin.

The jackal pulled me up the dias steps, and I barely managed to make it to my feet as we neared the giant pool of water surrounded by mushrooms. Heavy drafts of magic pulsed from within the depths of the pool but were kept at bay by the ring of mushrooms.

The call of the magic was intoxicating, like a song made specifically for my ears alone. It tugged gently at my heart strings, teasing me, tempting me to step foot inside the chilled waters. Stepping inside the fairy ring, sinking into the waters would ease all the worries I had. It would soothe my aching muscles and calm my messy feelings. It would send me home, back to the comfort and safety of my own world.

Stay with me, Hyunjin pleaded.

Panic screeched inside me, every warning bell that Hyunjin had warned me about when we first arrived in the Feywild began to blare.

Digging my heels into the polished ground beneath my feet did nothing to slow the jackal's quick pace or strong grip. I jerked and tried to pry the jackals' paw off my arm. I was not going in the water.

"Relax, I'm not sending you home just yet," Jakob scoffed. "Where's the fun in that?"

I was pulled past the pool of water and to the large windows behind it. Through the glass panes I could see a hedge maze just beyond the courtyard, illuminated by the fading light of the setting sun. I struggled against the jackal's grip as Jakob walked up behind us, his shoes softly thudding against the wooden flooring.

He passed by me, walking straight to the windows. His hands pressed against trim and pushed, the windows opening in a large sweeping arc. Cool air rushed inside, rustling the dress I wore, pushing my hair over my shoulders.

The jackal released me, but his clawed hand pressed roughly behind my back, sending me stumbling forward out the open windows. My arms flailed as I tripped over the dress and fell harshly onto my knees on damp grass. I was thankful the drop hadn't been more than a couple steps high.

I threw a glare over my shoulder at Jakob, who stood at the threshold, his arms behind his back looking proud and regal. The jackal that had manhandled me stood directly beside him, watching me intensely.

"I hope you're able to escape the maze. Dangerous things lurk inside."

With a snap of his fingers, magic rippled upwards in front of him. An ugly shimmer of yellow crackled in a spindly pattern, arching like lightning as it traveled to the ceiling – a barrier had been made to keep me out and the others in, unable to help me.

And then a rush of that same magic shot through the windows, the spindly pattern tangled against my limbs, roughly hauling my body across the ground. I tumbled, unable to keep myself upright against an intense onslaught of magic. I rolled to a stop, the ground beneath me no longer stone but soft moss.

I shot to my feet despite the protests my body shouted at me, and looked around. Shrubbery ran for a few feet in either direction, before sharp turns cut the sprawling, overgrown walls off. I was in the middle of a pathway inside the hedge maze, with no true way of knowing where I was or where I could go.

Leaving me entirely on my own.

THE SEA OF OLD MEMORIES

"What the fuck?" I hissed under my breath as I walked a few paces in one direction before stopping, only to walk back to where I had started.

Who the hell was Jakob? And what the fuck was his problem?

I had never felt such hatred toward someone before. I could barely kill the spiders that I'd occasionally find inside my home, let alone actually murder a fellow human being. But the way my blood boiled within my veins, the way I was fueled by heat and rage, with it aimed at a single person had me terrified of what I could truly be capable of.

"Hurry Mare! You have to get through the maze to earn your freedom!" Jakob called out, echoing over the hedges.

I glanced around, back towards where I had just left. A heaviness radiated from within the hedge walls, the uneasy feeling ebbed around me, warning me to stay away from the direction Jakob's voice had come from.

Hyunjin? I whispered, a primal fear seeping into my bones.

Don't follow the voice. Go forwards, and keep your hands on the wall, Hyunjin encouraged me.

I had no way of knowing how he knew where to go, but I trusted him. And that was all I had at the moment, so I would take it.

With an exhale of breath, I took a step forwards, deeper down the pathway.

Go left, Hyunjin advised me.

I took two steps further down the pathway I was already following, before Hyunjin shouted in my mind.

Wait!

What? I exclaimed, startled by how loud he had been.

T–take a right, Hyunjin corrected himself.

My hand grazed against the boxwood shrubs, letting my fingers ghost and glide over the soft greenery as I pivoted to follow Hyunjin's corrected directions. A singular lantern burned several feet from me, illuminating a tiny corner of this endless maze.

No, wait, Hyunjin said, sounding as confused as I felt. *Take a left.*

Is it a left or a right? I snapped. Silence lingered in the chilled air of the hedge maze as I waited for Hyunjin's help.

Behind me, the muted, rhythmic thump of something stalking through the halls caught my attention. Fear spread slowly through my chest as I whipped around and peered down the darkened corridor, silently begging for nothing to be lurking in the shadows.

Mare, Hyunjin warned, his voice strained and near panicked. *You need to go. Now.*

Why? What is it? I questioned.

You don't want to know. Please, go!

The nearest lantern behind me flickered violently, as if a giant gust of wind had whipped through the air – yet everything was still and quiet, except for the thumping sounds of something walking, getting closer.

Something large shifted in the shadows in front of me, from where I had just come from. Not wanting to get a closer look, I spun around and quickly darted left, running as fast as I could across the moss covered ground, searching for a safer path – one that wasn't near whatever stalked behind me.

A wail of a cry pierced through the air, before the creature behind me gave chase.

I bolted, taking twist and twist, turn after turn, blindly running through the shrubs, searching for somewhere safe to hide.

The moss beneath my feet began to disappear slowly, morphing into a cobblestone path the further I ran. I kept my hand hovering over the foliage of the wall, keeping contact at all times to stop the walls from moving, from changing and throwing my sense of direction off.

A distant, muted roar of crackling flames came from somewhere farther in the maze, the sound only a few rows away from where I was.

What is that sound? I questioned Hyunjin.

I don't hear anything. What do you hear? Hyunjin questioned.

A flare of pain rippled down the blood bond, and a phantom throbbing radiated across my cheek. My eyes watered violently. My free hand shot up to cradle my face as I flinched at the residual pain, stopping in my tracks as I kept my other hand on the wall.

Had Hyunjin been punched? Were any of the men hurt?

I gently rubbed my skin, sending soothing, comforting tingles back down the blood bond to help ease the hurt Hyunjin felt and ignored the pang of betrayal that ebbed in my chest when I thought about Filix, about his pointed fey ears, about the lies he had told me.

Keep going, princess. Don't worry about us, Hyunjin whispered, gently nudging my back with a ghosting touch to urge me forward.

That's easier said than done, I said as I hurried down the moss covered stone, intrigued by the sounds only I could hear.

I had taken two rights before I had to lift my hand off the walls, in order to make a left like I wanted. But as I lifted my hand from the boxwood shrubs, the entire maze began to shift, again.

The pathway before me was no longer a left turn, but an unending corridor. It seemed to span for miles in one direction, and as I glanced over my shoulder saw that it spanned on for miles in the opposite direction too.

Annoyance and confusion spread throughout my body, leaving me as lost as I had been when I started.

"Fuck!" I shouted, raking my hands through my hair, no longer caring if the walls around me changed when I wasn't touching the shrubbery; or if monsters lurked nearby. At this point I was never going to escape.

Keep going, Hyunjin encouraged me, but his attempt to calm and refocus me only angered me further.

Everything looked the same: the same long endless roads, with no place to go. Even if the pathways were ever changing, I was still trapped deep within the labyrinth, no closer to finding a way out than when I started.

I'm fucking lost Hyunjin. I don't know where to fucking go! I snapped at him.

Hyunjin was quiet, which wasn't comforting in the slightest.

I clamped my eyes closed and inhaled through my nose, trying to calm myself down. Snapping at Hyunjin wasn't helping, and letting my anger control me wasn't going to get me out of the labyrinth. The pang of Filix's betrayal ate away at my heart, consuming me as my emotions ran high, leaving me aching and hollow.

How could Filix do that to me?

The rustling of the hedge maze changing shape again had my eyes popping open, and I watched with rapt fascination as the shrubs rippled into place before they solidified. I gently touched the tiny leaves of the boxwood, and waited for the end of the hallway to come into sight.

A long corridor spanned out in front of me, and a shorter one led off to my right, before it cut off into another direction, the corners sharp and limiting my sight.

Warmth settled at my back, the same warmth that I had felt back in the Goblin Market when I had first seen Wolf. The warmth shifted against my skin, traveling across my back, moving to rest against my right shoulder. My eyes fell to the shorter, sharp cut pathway to my right.

That way? I asked, the words flowing toward a string nestled deep within me. Toward a bond that had yet to be completed.

Wolf's warmth slid down my arm, ghosting across my skin like slow, teasing fingers before it pooled in my palm. Reminding me of holding hands, which answered my question.

I took the shorter pathway, peeking around the corners when I arrived at them, searching for creatures that lurked in the dark that may have been alerted to my presence when I screamed out in frustration. With nothing lurking in the bushes, I continued on, and the warmth of Wolf's hand in mine slowly left me.

A singular streetlight poked above the hedges, just around the corner, the bulb burning a soft amber-yellow. I came to a stop as my eyes scanned the streetlight. I could hear the hum of electricity coming from the lamp, which shocked me.

Most of our cities have electricity, including the Kingdom, Hyunjin reminded me. *Remember?*

I could recall our last and only conversation about electricity, but the electricity wasn't what shocked me. The singular streetlight in the middle of a dark hedge maze was what had my skin crawling, my senses on high alert.

Why is a streetlight in the middle of a hedge maze? I questioned, taking a singular step towards it, rounding the corner.

A full length, standing mirror stood at the end of the corridor, just below the lamppost. I froze at the corner, suddenly afraid to move any closer to the illuminated mirror.

The muted roar of flames I had heard earlier hit my ears, the sound coming from the direction of the mirror. Yet no actual fire burned near or around it.

Mare? What is it? Hyunjin questioned.

Smoke swirled around the frame of the golden mirror, the fog hypnotizing. I took several steps forward, enchanted by the twisting smoke surrounding the mirror.

As I stopped before it, I was confused when I couldn't see my reflection looking back at me. Instead the mirror was completely blank, reflecting only the hedge maze behind me – as if I didn't exist.

Cocking my head to the side, I shifted to glance behind the mirror, trying to see if this was a trick of some kind. Yet the mirror looked like any other ordinary mirror back in Neverhelm. It wasn't broken or in need of any repairs. It was in excellent condition despite it being outside in the elements.

Standing before the mirror's reflective surface again, I stared into the glass. Vague, half-blurred images rippled across the surface of the mirror before they stilled and came into focus – the scenery around me changing completely.

Warmth washed over my skin as I spun in a rapid circle, taking in the new surroundings. A large window to my left sat on the adjacent wall to the door, where bookshelves lined the walls. Any blank space was filled with paintings that looked oddly similar to the ones created by my favorite fey artist. Behind me sat a large fireplace, with the same eerie mirror standing next to it.

A reflection within the mirror caught my focus, and I turned to look at it fully.

Wolf cradled Filix's body against his own inside a large bed. Hyunjin and Seiji sat on Wolf's other side, the latter gently pressing a cloth against Filix's forehead.

Hyunjin – with light brown hair – refused to leave Filix's side for even a second, afraid he would miss even the smallest of moments. He gently stroked the back of Filix's head, trying to comfort him. Tears burned in his red eyes, the ruby color wet and vibrant.

Filix looked sick; his lips blue and skin deathly pale, his freckles faded away into near nothingness. His – then – dark hair was plastered to his sweaty forehead as his body shook, fighting off a vicious infection.

And his ears... they were round.

He was human.

Seiji shared a dire look with Wolf, one that didn't show any sign of hope for Filix's recovery. Whatever killing him was winning.

Wolf squeezed his eyes shut as he tried to keep himself from crying. He shifted on the plush bedding, cradling Filix tighter, as if he were afraid to lose him.

I blindly reached out toward Wolf, wanting to comfort him. The moment my fingers reached for him, the world around me rippled and the image changed.

Yanking my hand back, I watched as the world tried to come into focus again.

And when the image sharpened, I only saw Wolf.

He sat beneath the stars, tears burning in his eyes. His mouth moved, but I wasn't able to hear anything. A bone chilling gust of wind rushed through the air, blowing my hair away from my face. Wolf's shoulders shook the longer he spoke and the tears he had been trying to hold back finally fell down his cheeks.

He looked broken, and lost. My heart ached for him.

The image rippled once more, the world shifting to reveal Filix.

He laid in a milky pool of water, the color not completely white nor completely blue either, somewhere in between, shifting with a hint of a metallic hue oil slicked over the surface. Terephine roses floated around his body, the occasional rose bud or petal would bump against him.

The water soaked into the bottom of my dress, and I shivered at how cold it was against my skin. I tore my eyes off of Filix for a moment, unable to look at him without my heart aching, and forced my eyes on the lake we sat in.

In the distance, behind layers of fog and mist I could make out the shore line, and above that I could barely see the outline of mountains. The milky lake we were in was silent, no birds chirped off in the distance, no lapping waves brushed against the shore. Everything was quiet here.

Pivoting, I froze as I stared at another body in the water – only this time it was me.

My second self's eyes were closed, her lips and skin a pale color, nearly blending into the water that surrounded us.

With a quick glance over my shoulder, I checked if Filix still floated behind me. His body was exactly where I had last seen it, but as I turned back around my second self had disappeared. No water ripples or bubbles indicated that my second self's body had submerged beneath the water, leaving me to wonder where she had gone.

I jerked back around to look for Filix, afraid he had somehow disappeared too, but found him still in the water with me.

He had lied to me.

He had lied to me about everything.

His eyes were closed, his skin looked brighter. His freckles had returned and his lips no longer blue like the water around him.

He looked peaceful.

Filix shot up, his eyes burning bright silver-blue, his entire body dripping wet. He ran a hand through his dark hair that was plastered against his forehead and neck. And his ears – they were pointed.

His gaze met mine.

My heart constricted, as I flinched backwards.

He was fey.

Mare? Hyunjin called.

Hearing his voice pulled me out of the spell I had been cast under when I looked into the mirror. I spun around, the bottom of my dress soaking wet, suddenly afraid to look at the standing mirror. Betrayal and disappointment burned within me.

Mare? He screamed. *Princess?!*

I'm here, I tried to reassure him. Although I didn't sound convincing even to myself.

Mother, thank you, Hyunjin breathed out a heavy sigh of relief. *Where did you go? I couldn't hear your thoughts, but I could feel you.*

The urge to glance behind me at the golden mirror was tempting, but I kept my back turned. What that mirror had shown me wasn't something I wanted to experience again.

There's this mirror, I trailed off, unsure if I should even bring it up. *Filix wa–*

Beside me, a creature growled, its voice clicking almost like a bat. I couldn't see it, but I could hear it as it brushed against the shrubs, moving down an adjacent pathway.

Oh fuck, I whispered, panicking. Whatever lay on the opposite side of the shrub wall was too close for my liking.

Let's keep going, Hyunjin suggested. *Go left.*

IT FELT impossible to find my way out of this fucking maze, and Hyunjin's words were not helping me. His voice filled my head with varying opinions and ideas, trying to help me escape the maze in his own way.

Keep going straight. No, wait. Turn around.

His voice filled the silence that I needed in order to hear the monsters that stalked through the same halls I was lost in.

Shut up! I screamed. I felt my panic, and anxiety race down the bond before I couldn't hear at all – a wall had been put up, silencing him completely.

A different kind of fear shot through me.

I had done that.

I had blocked him out without meaning to. That certainly hadn't been my intention, I just needed him to be quiet. So I could hear, and could pinpoint where the monsters were that were loose inside the hedge maze.

I had to beat Jakob at his own game. He didn't expect much from me, if anything at all.

A flash of light against metal, sharp fangs and vicious claws blurred before my eyes. I flinched, and tripped backward into the open space of a clearing.

A woman, stark naked except for the metal bat shaped mask that covered her eyes and nose pinned me to the dew-covered ground, her claws raking down my forearms. I cried out, in pain and panic. I bucked and thrashed, but her weight kept me pinned beneath her.

The sight of her thin razor sharp teeth behind perfectly painted red lips had me frozen, completely stunned for several seconds. A beautiful, swirling filigree pattern had been intricately blended into the metal of the eyeless mask she wore.

Surging forward, the monstrous bat-masked woman sank her teeth into my shoulder, using my momentary pause to attack.

I screamed, and the sound cut across the maze.

Twisting, I tried to break the woman's hold, which only ended in more agony. Her teeth stayed in my skin, the needle-sharp points ripped through me, leaving gashes in a gruesome trail that led to my back.

The creature scrambled to keep her hold on me, her hands met my shoulders, using her strength to pin me face down. Her claws sank into my skin, ripping into the meat of my back.

I screamed again, and I felt hysteria shoot through the bond from Hyunjin.

Bucking against the creature on top of me, I slipped against the ground, losing my shoes in the process. Wolf's warmth settled in my palm again, only this time it felt more tangible, like his hand was actually in mine, guiding me through the maze. I ran, taking twist after twist, turn after turn, running through the shrubs, searching for the exit.

A clawed hand wrapped around my ankle, and yanked me off my feet. I fell onto my knees, skidding across the hard cobblestone, chest heaving as I shakily raised a hand to my neck and touched the blood that slipped from the gash. I flinched, the pain flaring at the barest touch.

Slow clapping had me flinching again. I looked up at the windows Jakob had sealed with his magic. He stood there smugly clapping as I sat dying.

"Good job! You made it!" he beamed.

I had gotten out of the maze, but at what cost?

"Let them go!" I forced out. I shivered as more of my blood began to slide across my skin as I bled out.

"Let them– oh," Jakob laughed and waved a hand over the windows, breaking the seal he had made.

"You misunderstood me. I said if you made it through the maze you could *earn* your freedom. You haven't earned it yet."

A pained glare spread across my features as I tried to keep myself from crying out at how agonizing the wound at my neck and back felt. It pulsed, an infection waited to settle beneath my skin.

"You bastard," I hissed.

"Biroo!" Jakob called out. The jackal behind him popped his head up, straightening his hunched over posture.

"Take her to the dungeon," Jakob's voice called out as he waltzed from the windows in Grand Hall.

I was yanked forward by Jakob's magic and into Biroo's waiting claws, before he was dragging me across the ground, down to the dungeons.

I GRIT my teeth and pressed my lips together to keep myself from letting any noise out, from giving Jakob any kind of satisfaction knowing he'd hurt me. But my efforts were wasted as tears tracked down my skin and slid into my hair as a fire in my veins burned hotter.

"Ow. Ow. Ow," I repeated to myself, while actively trying not to think about the pain that made the muscles in my back twitch and ache or how I felt like clawing my own skin off.

I smacked my fist against the ground repeatedly, trying to work through the pain, to give myself anything else to think about.

Breathe princess, Hyunjin's voice coaxed me out of my own mind. He sounded faint and far away.

"Hyunjin?" I asked aloud, confused in the darkness.

I'm here, he reassured me.

I tried to do as Hyunjin had asked. I focused on controlling my breathing, in through my nose and out through my mouth. In and out, in and out. Yet every time my chest rose it felt like I was breathing in broken glass.

The fire beneath my skin was growing hotter. Sweat broke out across my brow, running down the side of my face. Tears continued to streak back into my hairline as I shifted my posture, trying to muster up the strength to get off the ground. My limbs shook and quivered as venom from whatever monstrosity had bitten me had begun to take full effect, coursing through my body.

Get up, pup, Wolf's voice whispered, his voice the faintest.

The effort alone of thinking to sit up off the ground nearly wiped out the last remaining dregs of energy I had left. It hurt to breathe. It hurt to blink. It hurt to even think. Everything was too much.

I can't.

Despite protesting, I tried to sit up like Wolf asked of me. Using my elbows to push my upper half into a hunched over position, I moved to sit upright.

A scream tore through me as a new wave of unbearable heat spread across my body, each wave lapping hotter and hotter beneath my skin, within my blood. Agony blanketed my senses as I collapsed back against the cold stone ground.

I couldn't focus on anything around me. Hyunjin whispered only faintly in the back of my mind, trying to comfort me but his words were lost the longer I screamed. The pain I felt was excruciating; growing hotter and hotter and hotter.

Wolf! Hyunjin's voice rang out in my head, his tone broken and distressed. *What can I do to help her? Please!*

It's fine. Doesn't hurt! I pushed the thought out, trying to ease the worry Hyunjin was riddled with. It was an obvious lie based on the way I was screaming. My throat was raw and I could taste blood at the back of my throat.

Focus on me princess, Hyunjin's voice was barely a whisper, the bond between us growing weaker. *Focus on my voice. I'll get you out of there.*

I could barely hear him. Could barely feel him at the other end of our blood bond. The blood bond was fraying, unraveling faster and faster the longer the seconds ticked by.

Hyunjin? I called out.

I was scared and worried about what the guys were enduring because of Jakob. And I was terrified about losing what Hyunjin and I had together.

I'm here, came his faint reply. *Always.*

And then the bond was gone, as if it had never existed in the first place.

GONE AWAY

At some point the world went dark. When I could open my eyes again, when tears no longer blurred my vision completely I could barely tell the difference between them being closed and open. If it weren't for the sconces outside in the hallway, I would not have been able to tell the difference.

The cell had become eerily quiet as I searched for the bond. I desperately reached for it, yet my fingers met air, slipping through nothing, only a faint lingering essence remained like the wisps of smoke once a candle had been blown out.

Staring at the cell door, I blinked several times. I felt hot and clammy and the world looked fuzzy. It seemed to sway, its lines rippling. My head felt heavy and my eyes stung as tears welled in my ducts. Exhaustion settled in my bones, lulling me to curl up and rest.

I couldn't go to sleep. I needed someone's help cleaning my wounds before I bled out.

I couldn't go to sleep...

I couldn't...

I awoke some time later to a warm, wet cloth being dabbed across my forehead. My eyelids were heavy and crusty from my tears, and took several attempts to open fully.

Pain no longer burned through my body, but the dull throbbing ache a deep wound leaves behind ebbed through my upper back.

Cold air helped to lessen the pain I was in, but being trapped did not. Nothing could erase the fact that I had lost my blood bond with Hyunjin. It didn't answer my unspoken question about what kind of bond Wolf and I shared.

And Filix…

"You're awake," spoke a soft voice.

I flinched, startled by how close the voice was. However, I was thankful for the distraction. Thinking about Filix hurt too much.

"How do you feel?" the man in the dark questioned gently.

"Terrible doesn't even begin to cover how I feel," I told him honestly.

"I can imagine. Hyunjin seemed no better when I left him."

A deep hollow ache gaped in my chest at the mention of Hyunjin's name. A massive hole had been carved into my very soul, the endless well descending into nothingness.

"Is he okay? Are all of you?"

The man chuckled in the darkness, "They asked if you were okay too."

I heard the man's clothes shuffling as he dipped a cloth into a small bowl of water and rang it out again. The warmth of the rag was dabbed against my cheeks and moved down the expanse of my neck, wiping away the sweat and blood that had dried against my skin.

"You're Seiji… the healer, yes?"

"I am," Seiji replied gently.

"I've seen you before, in a memory of Hyunjin's."

"I've been Wolf's healer for several centuries now."

I appreciated the calm aura Seiji radiated. It kept the anxiety I felt creeping in my chest at bay as he tended to me.

"Have you come to ensure that I've been properly poisoned by whatever attacked me in the maze?"

"No, I've been sent to cure you, actually. Jakob is eager to play with another human after being surrounded by fey for so long."

"Are they okay?" I repeated, needing to know and simultaneously distract myself. The throbbing at my back was gradually becoming more noticeable, more persistent in its annoyance.

"The venom from the Smogbody resulted in some nerve damage to Filix, but that's nothing I can't fix when Jakob allows it. Wolf is strong, he's exhausted but he can handle anything."

"He's a good leader."

Seiji was quiet and I could feel the judgmental look he threw my way as he dropped the rag into the bowl again. I shifted in the dark, a hiss escaping me when the jagged skin at my back tugged open again.

"What?" I questioned.

"You called Wolf our leader. Not King or Ruler... leader."

"You say that like I've said something wrong. Hyunjin said Wolf preferred it."

"I'm impressed actually," Seiji scoffed.

He shifted, his clothes rustling as he turned and began rummaging in his medicine bag. I was puzzled about why Seiji was impressed, especially over something as simple as a title. It took zero effort for me to correctly address Wolf.

"You're impressed by the bare minimum?" I asked, huffing out a laugh, a bit delirious.

"I am impressed you even bothered," Seiji corrected.

A pang of guilt flared inside me as I realized that Seiji did not like humans. I had no way of knowing what cruelties humanity had forced the fey into in the past... but based upon the contained, controlled hostility in Seiji's words I could only guess how horrible we had been.

I kept quiet, unsure how to respond to him, but I understood why he said what he had.

When the doors between our worlds had been sealed shut, we both moved on without the other. And the fey who had been trapped on the human side of the Veil had been forced to adapt to our ways in order to survive.

Any future interactions between fey and humans was going to be rough.

"Is Hyunjin okay?" I asked, keeping my voice small and quiet.

I felt so alone despite Seiji being in the cell with me. The empty hole inside me yawned wide, and I felt the absence of Hyunjin's presence. I tugged at the end of our bond, the silky red string dangled limply, the end was frayed and unraveled.

"No better than you," he said, his voice sounded thicker, like he was holding back tears.

The emptiness yawned wider hearing those words. Tears flooded my eyes, and for once I was thankful for the darkness.

"Breaking a blood bond takes an incredible amount of power. I'm surprised Jakob has succeeded in breaking yours when he's only been able to suppress ours."

"You have a blood bond?" My curiosity was reignited, especially after the strange interaction I'd had in the Goblin Market before I'd seen an apparition of Wolf chained up.

"You'll find blood bonds are quite rare despite all eight of us sharing one."

My brain ran with that information, trying to grasp the fact that eight of them shared a bond together like Hyunjin and I had shared. All eight of them shared their feelings with one another. Shared their thoughts and memories.

A nitpicky feeling jabbed at the back of my mind, something didn't sit right with me, with the information I'd just learned.

Eight of them shared a bond... but I'd met nine of them.

"Jakob... he doesn't share the bond with you at all, does he?" I questioned. "Is it because he's human?"

"Humans are not built for our world," Seiji began. "They simply don't belong."

He crouched beside me and continued to rifle through the medicine bag he'd brought with him.

"They either get trapped by consuming fey food, or tricked by a bargain or a promise, or they get sick and die. Jakob and Filix were brought to our world in exchange for changelings that were left behind in yours."

The tales my babysitters used to tell me before bed flared in my mind; how the fey left their children behind while they stole human babies in their place.

"Neither one was supposed to live past infancy, and yet they did. And then Wolf found them. He knew that one of them held a string in his bond, the only question was who," he pulled out a rag and a murky bottle of a strange looking liquid. "Wolf had asked Our Mother for guidance, and for a long time nothing happened."

Seiji gently dabbed the rag over the exposed bit of my shoulder that had gotten ripped open while fighting to escape. I flinched and let out a hiss as I tried to work through the pain.

"My intentions are never to hurt you," Seiji explained, in a way of an apology. "The last thing I wish to do is hurt my patients. To hurt those my mates care about."

"I know," I reassured him. I tugged my hair over one shoulder, exposing the other to Seiji so he could tend to more of the wound Jakob's monster inflicted on me.

"Why would– is Fel-" I cut myself off, a sob choking me off. I couldn't bring myself to ask about Filix. That wound was too raw to touch right now. "Why isn't Jakob fey then? What happened?"

"Our Mother had them participate in the Rite and the outcome enraged Jakob. He swore Our Mother made a mistake."

"The Rite?" I questioned, "What is that?"

"I cannot answer your questions about the Rite. It has been forbidden by Our Mother. But what I can tell you is that Filix succeeded where Jakob failed."

I jerked away from Seiji when he gently cleaned up a particularly sensitive spot on my back. One of his hands came to my opposite shoulder to steady me as he continued to wipe away blood, dirt and grime so I wouldn't get an infection.

That information made my head hurt as a dozen new questions bloomed in my mind. It also answered a few of the unspoken questions I had lingering in the back of my mind: like why Filix had pointed fey ears instead of the rounded human ears I had grown so used to seeing on his person. It also answered why Filix's eyes would flash to silver-blue every once and a while. Why he would flinch when I lied to him or made him a promise, or thanked him.

It reconfirmed what I already knew.

Filix was fey.

"I don't understand," I admitted, blinded by the pain that ebbed at my back.

Water dripped and echoed in a nearby section of the dungeon, the stone walls made the tiny droplet of water sound so much louder than it really was. In the distance a rat squeaked as it ran along the endless stone corridors that plagued the Kingdom.

I couldn't believe what I was hearing. My best friend had *lied* to me from the very beginning. He had spent years lying to me, and I had spent those years unintentionally hurting him. Every white lie, every promise made, every heartfelt thank you.

Everything we had together had been built on lies.

Did I know Filix at all?

"I can't tell you much more about Filix. It is his story to tell... but he was incredibly sick when he was your age. He was dying, and Wolf was hopeless when he learned there was no cure for a human in our realm."

Fingers gently pressed into the scrapes and cuts along my back and shoulders, as Seiji applied a thick layer of cream.

"Is that what I saw in the mirror? Filix dying in a lake of Terephine roses?" I pushed, hoping I could get more of an explanation.

Seiji's fingers stopped moving, and his silence had me shifting to look at him over my shoulder in worry. In the dim lighting, his puppy-dog features were lined with shock, and apprehension.

"You saw Yenta Ga?"

"Yenta Ga?" I repeated, feeling stupid every time I had to ask for something to be clarified.

"The Sou– the lake. The lake of Terephine roses and white water? You saw it?" Seiji questioned, nearly frantic.

"Saw it? Seiji I was there. The mirror showed me a couple memories of– of when he was sick."

Seiji leaned away from me quickly, a look of concern passed over his features. He quickly dove for his medicine bag, and began searching for something hidden at the bottom of the bag. He quickly pulled out a teeny tiny tube of oil, flicking off the cap and spread it across his fingers.

I barely had time to flinch away before Seiji was smearing his fingers over my eyes. The oil stung as it seeped into my eyes. I yelped at the sudden assault, trying to scoot away from Seiji's reach.

"What the fuck, Seiji?" I hissed, reaching up to swipe at my eyes.

"It goes away in a few minutes," Seiji said. "Yenta Ga isn't somewhere fey come back from. I'm surprised Our Mother allowed a human to see such a place."

"What was that for Seiji?!" I spat out, annoyed and in pain.

"It's a blessing oil. I can't have you getting sick like Filix did."

Seiji offered no other explanation, which infuriated me further. But my body was exhausted and my mind was running in circles as I tried to piece everything I had recently learnt together. And I supposed I was grateful for Seiji taking care of me. I was drained and couldn't do it myself.

I stared at the wall, flinching every now and again as the cream Seiji spread across my back began to take effect, numbing the pain away into nothingness.

"Why was Jakob mad at your Mother?" I asked in a near whisper.

"It was obvious that either he or Filix was another missing piece that Wolf had lost. And Jakob knew he wasn't the one, despite how desperately he tried to change Wolf's mind, all our minds. He is not one of us."

I was silent for the rest of the time Seiji applied gauze to my back. I had no more energy left to ask him the burning questions that repeated over and over again in my mind. And the guilt from earlier still lingered within me, leaving a bitter taste in my mouth.

Seiji was quiet as he cleaned up his medical supplies. He moved slowly, trying to delay leaving for as long as he possibly could. Biroo or another hideous monstrosity would eventually return to the dungeons to retrieve him, to bring him back to wherever Jakob had them locked away.

"I've never repaired a blood bond before. I've never known a fated pair that's had their bond broken and lived," Seiji said somberly.

An unexpected rush of tears had my throat closing as I tried to keep the whimper that threatened to escape me from leaving. That intense lonely feeling yawned wider, reminding me that Hyunjin wasn't with me anymore.

"I never expected..." I choked on my own words, "It just slipped away. I had expected it to hurt more."

A disbelieving laugh burst out of Seiji. "You had expected it to hurt *more?*"

I stayed quiet, unsure how to answer Seiji's question, but the answer was yes. I had expected it to hurt more, even if what I'd just gone through was hell. I had expected losing something life changing to have a greater exit... considering what it meant to me, but it just fizzled out like it was nothing.

"I envy you, Seiji. This is something I hope you never experience."

Seiji said nothing as he finished packing up his supplies. The heavy, rough drag of Biroo's paws could be heard, descending the stairs coming toward us.

"I will try to find a cure. You and Hyunjin deserve that much... if not more," he said before he closed my cell door and left.

WHOLE HEARTED

A pungent odor wafted from the entrance of the dungeons as Biroo stepped into the darkness. The jackal sniffled the air, his body hunched over. He growled beneath his breath as he fiddled with several keys on a keyring, searching for the one that belonged to my cell.

"Come on. Bath time," he muttered unhappily, letting the cell door swing open.

"Bath time?" I questioned the jackal.

Biroo gave me a deadpan expression, not bothering to explain. I refused to move from the spot I stood in.

Biroo was having none of it. He reached out with one long arm and yanked me out of the cell. He hauled me behind him as we ascended the stairs. We twisted through the halls, ascending and descending a dozen staircases until we came to a grand bathroom on the third level of the castle.

Throwing open the bathroom door, Biroo shoved me inside and promptly shut the door, a haunting click locking me inside.

Taking in the bathroom, my eyes were drawn to the massive chandelier that hung above a grand pool of water and a massive waterfall that spewed from the wall, acting like a shower, yet the water never overflowed and spilled out onto the floor. The air was warm and inviting, the lighting was dim and cozy.

A massive, sunken glass object sat on the bathroom floor at the back of the room, every bit of attention being drawn to it. For a second my heart dropped into my stomach, mistaking the glass tub for a glass coffin. But water gently lapped at the edges of the tub, reminding me the coffin Hyunjin had been buried in was in a completely different world.

I stepped forward, letting the warm tile beneath my feet seep into my cold toes. Despite the tub being nearly translucent, I still cautiously leaned over it in case something lurked just beneath the surface of the water.

Terephine roses and lavender floated on top of the steaming water, but I still had a clear view to the bottom of the tub in the ground. The water was tinted a soft periwinkle color, probably from the flowers that had been added to it.

A cautious scan of the water put my nerves at ease as I shifted to undress myself. The end of my dress had been ruined while running through the hedge maze, the fabric had been ripped and torn to shreds. I slipped my arms out of the sleeves and yanked the damn thing over my head, getting rid of it. I let it pool on the ground as I striped off my underwear, quickly stepping into the warm water.

Shifting within the bathtub, I submerged myself up to the base of my neck, relishing within the intensity of the water's warmth. I sat on one of the small stairs, keeping most of my torso submerged beneath the surface.

A soft gurgling from the waterfall into the bath was relaxing. It gave me a few moments of peace and quiet, true tranquility in the madness I had been through recently.

And yet the silence was deafening, and I hated it.

I pulled my knees up to my chest and hugged myself. I focused inwards, and searched for the strings Hyunjin and I shared. I gingerly tugged at the thread, hoping something else would happen. Instead sadness bloomed in my chest, as I stared at the frayed, limp string in my mind. Tears blurred my vision, running down my cheeks as I stared across the bathroom, looking at nothing, letting my mind spiral.

Filix had lied to me since the very beginning.

My heart felt heavy in my chest as more tears fell and dripped off my chin into the water.

Filix's pointed fey ears flashed in my mind as I squeezed my eyes closed, trying to keep from crying. I hated crying, or feeling weak.

Another image of Filix resurfaced in my mind, of his eyes flashing from muddy brown to silver-blue. I had always associated the weird eye color change to be a trick of the light.

But this whole time...

Did I know him at all?

How could I have missed every sign, every clue that pointed to him being fey. I slapped a hand over my mouth to keep quiet.

He had been lying to me from the moment we met.

He would flinch whenever I made him a promise, or thanked him, or inadvertently lied to him. He had needed explicit permission to enter my house the first time ever he came over.

And the last time he entered my house I had been suspicious of him. He'd entered empty handed, and then the next moment he had gluten free brownie mix in his hands, when they had been so clearly empty before.

Had I truly been that stupid? How could I have been so blind?

Why would he do that to me? Did he not trust me enough to tell me? Did he think I would think differently of him if he had?

An image of Hyunjin's glass coffin flashed before my mind, throwing me back to the last time Filix and I had been there together. Filix had stared at the coffin, and talked about what the prince was dreaming about.

A soft sob escaped me as I realized that Hyunjin and Filix shared a bond together. That was how they spoke over the centuries

Hyunjin was trapped. It explained the silent conversation they had in my living room before the Smogbody attacked us.

My heart felt messy inside my chest, far messier than I had ever felt before. My feelings for Hyunjin were clear. My feelings for Filix had been clear.

But now... everything ached and all I wanted to do was forget.

Forget Filix. Forget how he betrayed me. Forget how I loved him.

I stayed there for a few minutes, giving myself a few moments to collect myself, and then I focused on cleaning myself up.

When I stepped out of the bath, the dress I had stepped out of was no longer on the floor and a different dress hung on the back of the locked door. I cautiously approached, not having seen or heard anyone enter while I bathed.

The dress that hung up was similar to the one that Hyunjin had stolen for me back in Kiruna - only this one was a soft beige color with softer look tulle draped across the bust and arms. It was incredibly beautiful, and it fit perfectly.

As soon as I had finished, Biroo burst through the door and escorted me back to the dungeons.

I FROZE inside my cell as I met Taesung's gaze through the bars. Biroo's clawed hand scraped across his back, and the force of his hand at Taesung's back had him stumbling forward, tripping over the jagged uneven stones on the floor.

"Hey man!" Taesung called out, his hands shooting out to try to save his fall.

Biroo cackled as he lunged forward and snapped cuffs around his ankles, not bothering to be gentle or kind in the slightest. And then he was slinking through the shadows, slamming the cell door closed and walking out of the dungeon, leaving Taesung and I alone.

"Are you okay?" I asked as I sat back on my heels, and brought my hands up to the bars that separated our respective cells.

"I've been better," he said, sniffling. I heard him shuffling around, the tiny clink and jingle of the chains cuffed to his ankles the only other sound that broke up the silence of the dungeons.

"What are you doing down here?"

Taesung lowered himself to the ground, picking up his hands to inspect the damage. He let out a sigh and let his head thunk against the stone wall behind him.

"I told Jakob the same thing you'll tell him."

"How do you know what we will discuss?"

Taesung huffed out an unamused laugh. "Because we have the same conversation almost every month. He wants a blood bond, and he's unfit for one."

"And why would he ask me about blood bonds? I don't know anything about them."

"You have what he wants. He won't listen to me anymore. He won't listen to any of us anymore."

"I never asked to be bonded to Hyunjin."

"Or any of us," Taesung muttered quietly, a bitter tone beneath his words.

How did he know Wolf and I had some kind of connection? Did he know what kind of blood bond we had? Was that what he and that fortune teller had meant when they said I had a messy heart?

Silence stretched between us – I was too nervous to ask about Wolf, about messy hearts, and Taesung made no effort to fill the silence like he had done when we first met near Kiruna. But I had other questions, questions I hadn't been able to ask Seiji when he had come to tend to my wounds a few days ago.

I couldn't let an opportunity to get answers go to waste. Taesung might not be stuck in a cell with me for very long.

"Seiji mentioned it was nearly impossible to break a blood bond. That Jakob is only able to suppress the bond you share with the rest of the guys..." I trailed off, unsure how to phrase the question I wanted to ask. Thankfully Taesung knew what I was getting at, knew what I wanted to ask without actually having to speak aloud.

"Our bonds are cracked, but not broken like yours is with Hyun-jin. It lingers... just beneath the skin. Like I can..." Taesung sighed. "I can feel them at the opposite end of the bond if I reach far enough... but there's this barrier that's blocking me from fully feeling them, from being able to speak or hear them. It's like there's a massive glass wall separating us."

Trapping them like the glass coffin trapped Hyunjin.

"Is it one blood bond between all of you or..." I cut myself off, still a bit too confused and embarrassed about having more than one heart string.

"We're just like you," Taesung said in a comforting manner. "We all have messy hearts."

I had expected hearing an answer to my unspoken questions to give me some kind of relief, some kind of pressure would be taken off my shoulders. But all I felt was more confusion, more uncertainty about what it entailed for the future.

If I had a future with Hyunjin. A future with all of them.

"Do you... can you feel Hyunjin?"

Silence hung heavy in the damp air around us. I figured he was reaching out, trying to feel Hyunjin through the glass barrier that kept them all apart. I wanted nothing more than to shatter the barrier with my bare hands. I wanted nothing more than to make Jakob pay for what he had done to Wolf and his mates.

"I can," Taesung said. "It's harder to feel him since he's been on the opposite side of the Veil for so long. I kinda forgot what he feels like."

"What does he feel like?" I asked, intrigued. Did blood bonds feel different to each person?

"He's a muse, like the safest space to be yourself is to be in his arms."

It warmed my heart to know that I wasn't the only one who thought of Hyunjin like that. Like being by his side was the one and only spot made for me to be in the universe. It made heart ache to know I didn't have that connection with him any longer.

"And Jakob's keeping you from them? He's blocking your blood bonds?"

"He's manipulative, even for a human," Taesung spat out bitterly, "No offense."

"None taken," I reassured him.

"We need a plan. You have two trials left... and Jakob is malicious in his punishments," Taesung hummed, "I wish Seok or Iyena were here. They're so much better at planning than I am."

"Wolf's ward is good at planning things?" I questioned. I had seen a lot of people in the Grand Hall when we first arrived in the Kingdom. I had no way of knowing who was who, or what they did or who they were to Wolf. That left me puzzled.

Taesung barked out a short, quick laugh. "Iyena isn't Wolf's ward. He's our Royal Advisor. He's the one Wolf runs all our plans through."

"But..." I trailed off, more confused that I had no face to put to name.

Taesung barked out another laugh, this one much softer and more amused – if that were even possible. "Don't feel bad. It's a secret. Everyone assumes that Seok or Miro are Wolf's advisors. No one expects our youngest mate to be the one that calls most of the shots."

It's intentional. I realized as Taesung finished speaking.

"That's... wow," An impressed smile spread across my face. That was inventive, so creative and unexpected. I had assumed – like everyone else – that Iyena wasn't as involved as Wolf's other mates.

The sound of the door leading down to the dungeon boomed above us. A set of footsteps could be heard as they thunked against the stone stairs, marching closer to us.

My heart leapt into my throat, and I couldn't stop my hands from shaking as I grew nervous. Whatever trial Jakob had prepared for me was going to be difficult, and the last trial had already been the toughest thing I'd ever faced before.

And I had lost so much during the first trial. I did not have much left to lose.

"I'll think of something," Taesung said in a hurried, hushed tone. "I'll try to have a plan when you come back."

The thunk of footsteps got closer, and the unease I felt grew tenfold.

"Don't accept anything that's offered to you," Taesung added.

The footsteps were louder, and I could hear Biroo's heavy huffing as he descended the last section of stairs. I nervously glanced from the cell door to Taesung, my palms growing sweaty.

"I'm scared," I whispered.

"Jakob just wants to play," Taesung reassured me, but his words fell on deaf ears. My heartbeat pounded in my chest as Biroo's shadow loomed outside the doorway he drew closer to.

"Mare, look at me," Taesung urged me.

I tore my eyes off of the door and looked at him. Half of his face was hidden in the shadows, but I could see the urgency in his gaze. I could see how much passion and truth burned in his eyes.

"Jakob won't hurt you," Taesung repeated. "He's just excited to play with another human."

The heavy footsteps that belonged to Biroo stopped at the threshold, his beady chartreuse yellow eyes narrowed in my direction, sparing Taesung no mind. The jackal's hunched form stumbled forward and shoved a key inside my cell door, unlocking it. My mind went completely blank as the door squeaked open.

"Let's go," Biroo snarled, his words slurred together.

I made no move to step forward and follow the jackal out of the dungeons. Biroo had absolutely no patience for my hesitancy. He surged forward, his clawed hands wrapped around my wrist and pulled me forward.

I stumbled and tripped every step of the way as we left the dungeons, ascending hundreds of steps. As we reached the main level of the Kingdom, I was out of breath and slightly sweaty, but my nerves already had me sweating before I had been dragged away.

The same clawed hand that pulled me along collided with the center of my back. My foot caught on the hem of my dress, and I barely caught myself before I ate the lush red carpet that ran through the corridors.

"Move," Another shove had me stumbling yet again.

"Take your hands off of me," I snapped, rounding to face him.

Biroo stared down at me, a resting bitch face etched on his canine-like features. I gave him a similar look as my anger began to outweigh my anxiety. I was not going to be pushed around. I was perfectly capable of walking to whatever destination we were journeying to.

"Touch me again," I dared him.

"And what will you do, pest?"

I smiled at him, "Do you want to find out?"

The big bad jackal before me swallowed, and his eyes dropped to the ground in submission. He made no move to reach out and shove me forward again, but he did huff in annoyance.

"Jus' move."

It didn't take long to get to where Jakob wanted to meet. We entered a decently sized dining hall, one I suspected was used more often by Wolf and the guys rather than the grand dining hall. Fifty to a hundred people could have easily fit in here, unlike in the grand dining hall where I estimated a thousand or more could fit.

Thick dark velvet curtains were drawn back on certain windows, allowing the barest amount of light inside the dining room, creating an intimate, near claustrophobic atmosphere. Sconces burned along the walls, making the room feel hotter than it should have been. Freshly polished wooden floors had my bare footsteps sounding near silent as I walked farther inside the room.

"Welcome back!" Jakob beamed.

He sat alone at the end of the long dining table with enough food to feed nearly half of Neverhelm. As I neared him, my eyes scanned over the food, my stomach tightening in hunger. Each dish looked delicious. It had my mouth watering.

Crackers, various breads and cheeses were piled high, with fruits stacked in varying quantities in between. Bottles of honey-wine and what I hoped to be red wine were strewn across the grand table, with candles burning in candelabras across the table's surface. A platter of what looked like chicken wings sat at one end of the table, while an entire roasted fat bat-like hobgoblin was posed in the center of the table, stuffed with various herbs and spices.

A raw bloody heart on Jakob's plate had my appetite dying.

"Where are my manners? Wolf taught me better than this, please have a seat," Jakob gestured to the empty seat at the opposite end of the table with his fork.

I remained standing, my gaze fixated on the bloody human heart on Jakob's plate. Jakob pressed a piece of heart against his tongue and slowly chewed it, evidently savoring the flavors that danced across his tongue. His head cocked to the side when he realized I had yet to take my seat across from him. His beady dark eyes followed my line of sight, confused.

"Ah! Yes," he scoffed to himself as he set his cutlery down and dabbed a cloth napkin against his thin lips. He looked up at me with a false smile.

"Ask away," he taunted me.

I felt my throat go dry as I opened my lips to speak. I hesitated, afraid what would happen if I asked the question that was prevalent in my mind. An itchy warning crawled down my spine. Panic began to squirm within me, urging me to leave as fast as I could. I had absolutely no desire to ask such a gruesome question that had an absolutely horrifying answer.

"Is that a human heart?" I questioned, my throat tightening as bile threatened to rise.

Jakob tipped his head to the side and frowned down at his plate.

"He was a warlock to be precise," Jakob shrugged as he picked up his cutlery again. He waved the knife in the air, directing me to sit down silently as he went back to eating.

I swallowed thickly as I shifted toward the open seat at the opposite end of the table. The plate in front of my seat was thankfully empty of hearts, but that didn't help ease the nausea that tightened in my stomach as I sank down onto the seat.

"Why are you eating a warlock's heart?"

Jakob popped another juicy chunk of meat inside his mouth and chewed thoughtfully as he looked down the table at me.

"Besides the taste?" Jakob asked, "Breaking your blood bond with Hyunjin was rather difficult. It depleted my magic greatly. This is the only way to replenish what I've lost,"

A disgusted look curled on my face, and I was certain I was going to vomit. I pressed a hand to my mouth as I stared down at my empty plate, forcing myself to focus on breathing in through my nose and out through my mouth.

"That's disgusting," I breathed out.

Jakob ignored my comment. "How's your back? I know the Mournhead is not a pleasant creature to meet."

The eyeless metal bat-masked woman I had encountered inside the maze flashed before my eyes. Her razor-sharp fangs and deadly claws had my back aching as phantom pains burned alive in my nerves.

"That's what the bitch is called?" I snapped.

Jakob laughed at my outburst. He slowly cut another chunk of heart off from his plate. He stabbed it with his fork but didn't raise it toward his lips.

"You're lucky you only encountered one. Mournheads hunt in packs, never straying too far from their packmates. Color me impressed, Mare."

A disgusted shiver ran down my spine as Jakob spoke my name.

"How did you do it?" Jakob mused. The air between us shifted, as if a window had been opened in the middle of winter. The air felt cold and heavy as he stared me down.

Pure silence was all I could give him in return.

"How did you do it?" he repeated, desperation breaking through this time. "Blood bonds take years to develop and even then... they're incredibly rare."

"I don't–"

His fist slammed against the table, making the silverware and glasses rattle. His lips were pinched as his nostrils flared.

"I want–" Jakob cut himself off taking several deep breaths, as he settled back in his chair. "Seiji said they were rare. So how did you form a bond with Hyunjin?"

"We... Every year Filix and I would clean up the clearing that Hyunjin's coffin was in."

"I suppose that you connected with Hyunjin and Filix because they share a bond together... but... no..."

Jakob ran a hand over his face, clearly dissatisfied with my answer. He grumbled to himself as he pinched the bridge of his flat nose. His jaw flexed as he grit his teeth together.

"No, no, no, no, that can't be right," he muttered quietly before he looked up at me again. "What else?"

I gawked at him, unsure what else I could tell him.

"What else? Why do you have a bond with them?" Jakob shouted.

"I don't know! What do you want from me?" I shouted back at him.

Jakob's eyes were dark and glassy, his gaze filled with unshed tears. His chest rose and fell in deep, heavy pants. I could see the wheels turning in his mind, I could see he was urgently seeking an answer.

"I need to know what you've done. I need to figure out what went wrong, where did I fail?"

I watched as Jakob dropped his head, letting it hang over his lap in defeat. A thick, heavy weight settled over the dining table, leaving the air tense and charged with raw energy.

Seiji's words from the previous night echoed in my mind: *Jakob knew he wasn't the one, despite how desperately he tried to change Wolf's mind, all our minds.*

Empathy burst in my chest, making my heart flutter as realization hit me.

"You wanted to be another piece to Wolf's puzzle, didn't you?"

Jakob's wet eyes met mine again, a hatred burning in them like I'd never seen before.

"You'd feel the same way if something you'd been promised your whole life was ripped from you before you have had the chance to prove you belong."

"But," I began cautiously. "What you want…it's hurting them."

"Are you going to tell me that I'm wrong? That what I desire isn't worth the pursuit?" Jakob asked.

The empathy that bloomed in my chest churned violently inside me, changing into guilt before it morphed back into empathy. I hated how I could understand such a cruel human. How I could relate because I was perhaps the only other person who knew exactly how he felt in this situation.

"No. You're not the only human who's afraid of being alone. Who's afraid of feeling unworthy of love, despite how desperately you crave it."

The tears in Jakob's eyes finally broke through the dam and silently trekked down his round cheeks.

"I was promised a family. People who would love me despite being different from them."

The hatred in his gaze vanished for a moment. But then I blinked and it was back, burning hotter than before. His fist slammed into the table again, several apples rolled off the table and onto the floor. Glasses clinked as they fell over on the table.

"I won't be left behind again. I won't! Our Mother doesn't get to meddle in my life anymore. Her decision at the Rite was wrong."

What had happened at the Rite? What decision had seemingly ruined so many lives?

"Punishing the people you want to accept you as family isn't the way to get what you want," I said quietly.

The fire that burned in Jakob's eyes flared brightly as he stared me down. My palms started to sweat, worried about the magic he had just consumed. Was there a digestion period where he had to absorb the magic, or did he immediately replenish it?

"I'm not punishing them... I could never hurt them. I'm keeping them safe."

The disgusted nausea I felt when I saw Jakob eating a fey heart crawled back up my throat. Jakob was delusional. He couldn't see how much damage he was doing to those he claimed to love.

"You are hurting them Jakob. They're all suffering... let them go."

A scoff left Jakob as he straightened his posture in his seat. He swiped angrily at the tears that had slipped down his face, getting rid of any evidence that he indeed had a heart.

"Why did you betray them?" I asked. "Why side with Iseul? Her goals never alined with your own. She's pointless in this."

A nagging feeling had lingered at the back of my mind since I had seen the memory of that night, when Hyunjin had shared it with me. Iseul had wanted to punish humanity for being ignorant and cruel toward the fey. Jakob on the other hand... It made no sense as to why he would side with the dark fey when all he wanted was a family, a place to call home, a place that accepted him wholly.

Jakob snorted out a laugh. Uneasiness spread through my chest. I wasn't sure what was weirder: seeing Jakob consume a warlock's raw heart or him laughing at my question.

"Iseul's death was... unexpected. It was a shame Seok murdered her, but nothing I couldn't work around. The Jotkai were not happy when the news reached them," Jakob gave me a half shrug.

I shot Jakob a deadpan expression, unamused and annoyed with his answers - or lack thereof.

"I saw an opportunity to get what I deserved," Jakob huffed.

I just stared at him.

"That dress looks lovely on you by the way," Jakob said, returning to eating the warlock's heart.

I ignored this. "What am I doing here?"

"Ah! Yes!" He exclaimed, his mouth full of warlock heart. "As I said before your unfortunate run in with the Mournhead, I want to play with you."

"I'm not stupid. I'm not making a deal with you."

"No, no, no. That's not what I want."

He stared at me as he chewed, his eyes burning my skin.

I swallowed hard. I wanted to look away but couldn't.

"What," I said again, a little hoarsely now, "do you want from me? To kill me?"

The heavy sigh escaped Jakob's lips. "I wanted to see you for myself, Mare Cozen," Jakob replied. "That is all."

"Why?"

"Why not?" Jakob asked, dodging my question yet again.

I glared down the table at him, the nausea in my stomach tightening.

"How are you alive? How are you…" I trailed off, the image of Filix's pointed fey sears flashing across my mind. How could he have lied to me all those years?

"Human?" Jakob supplied.

My silence spurred him to continue speaking.

"Human adjacent would be the technical term here, I guess," Jakob posed more to himself. "I consume magic, like this warlock's heart, and I live longer while absorbing the poor fey's powers. It's really a win-win situation for me if you think about it."

I did not, in fact, want to think about it. At all… if ever. I felt bile rising in my throat.

"When I lost the Rite, I had two options," Jakob explained. "Either consume magic to stay alive, or wither and die out like every other human who has ever set foot in the Feywild."

"I haven't died," I pointed out.

Jakob scoffed, "How long do you think you could survive on

Hyunjin's blood? I can hear your stomach growling from the dungeons. So please, eat up. I want you to stay for as long as you can."

I shoved my chair backwards, and stood up. I was done listening to his bullshit and half answers. He was toying with me for his own entertainment. And I was done with it.

"I know you have one more question!" Jakob called as I reached the doorway.

I stopped in my tracks, my back still turned to him.

"Ask away," he prompted.

"Why did you send a Smogbody after us?"

"Oh, that's a little personal. More of a third date kind of thing," Jakob teased me.

I turned back to glare at him. His jokes were not funny.

"A Smogbody was always going to hunt down whoever woke Hyunjin from his sleep. You just happened to bleed on the coffin which gave the Smogbody a third person to hunt down."

"What the fuck is wrong with you?" I spat, disgusted.

Jakob slammed a fist against the table top, glaring at me with a vicious hatred in his eyes. "You were in the wrong place at the wrong time. *You* bled on the coffin. *Your* blood mixed with Filix's, not mine. You got yourself tangled in this mess."

"Any of us could have died!" I yelled, the briefest image of the Smogbody's ever shifting teeth piercing into Filix's torso crossed my mind, making my heart constrict in my chest.

Jakob huffed and rolled his eyes, leaning against the back of his seat. "They're both here now, calm down."

I glared at him for a good minute, before I spun on my heel and left him alone with his heartless thoughts.

THE LAST ROOM

I was pleasantly surprised to find Taesung still in the cell next to mine when I returned. I was even more surprised to find new clothes neatly stacked in a pile for me on the floor of my cell.

A white dress made of silk was folded nicely and while they weren't exactly my size, they looked like they could fit. I cautiously picked up the dress and dropped it immediately.

"Is this Iseul's?" I whispered in horror as I stared at the dress on the ground.

The one and only time I'd ever seen the Jotkai queen, she'd been wearing such a dress, covered in her own blood as the shortest fey in Wolf's bond ripped her throat out. There was no way I was going to wear the dress Iseul was murdered in. I would rather face the Mournhead again.

"No, pesky 'uman," Biroo grumbled with an eye roll as he stepped inside the cell. "Strip."

"I can get dressed on my own," I shot back.

"Now!" Biroo snarled in my face. I refused to break eye contact with him.

The mighty jackal before me bent over and snatched up a pair of

254

black pants off the pile of clothes and carelessly tossed them at me. I clutched them as they hit my chest, offended and surprised. I hadn't seen the pants in the darkness.

Was it in fey fashionary customs to wear pants beneath gowns and dresses?

"Turn around," I told Jakob's general.

Surprisingly, the jackal turned his back to me, giving me the briefest moment of privacy. I quickly shoved one foot into a pant leg, and then the other and shimmed into the pants, not bothering to take my dress off. I would not give Biroo a show.

Biroo spun around the moment I straightened up and fixed the skirt of the dress over the pants. He bent down and shackled my legs again, not bothering to be gentle. He then stomped away, slamming my cell door closed.

I watched him leave before I looked at Taesung, completely lost and disturbed.

I pointed to the fabric, my question still hanging in the air, needing a clear answer that this wasn't what I thought it was. Taesung shook his head, easing my worry. The dress wasn't Iseul's thankfully.

I picked up the dress again, this time with more confidence. I realized it wasn't a dress at all. It was a white dress shirt with see through lace on one breast panel, whereas the other side was solid, and beneath it still on the floor was a thin black belt, adorned with silver chains and dangling diamond accents.

I waited for Taesung to speak, as he knew when the coast was clear. That no ears were listening through the walls and no eyes were spying on us in the darkness.

"I have half a plan," Taesung announced a few minutes later. "And the shirt is Hyunjin's."

"I think I have the other half of your plan," I said, as I tried to process the fact that I was to wear some of Hyunjin's clothes. I felt giddy about being in his clothes, about being close to him somehow again.

255

"You first," we said at the same time. We laughed quietly at our synchronization, and I was thankful for the laughter after the conversation I had just endured.

"Ladies first," Taesung offered me the floor.

"When Filix and I first woke Hyunjin, the connection between them must have been unblocked. I actually suspect it was open the entire time Hyunjin was asleep."

"Filix fled to the human realm at Wolf's request to watch over Hyunjin," Taesung stated, confirming my suspicions.

They had been able to hear and feel each other, even when Hyunjin was asleep. That thought warmed my heart a bit. Neither of them had truly been alone in the centuries that they were apart from everyone else. They had each other, even if they were separated by a sleeping curse and a couple inches of glass.

"It was an accident," I said quietly, looking down at my hands. I ran my thumb over the healed cut that had awoken Hyunjin. "Filix and I bled on the coffin together, but my blood hit the glass first."

"An accident we are grateful you created," Taesung butt in, cutting off any doubt or self-deprecating thoughts I had brewing within my mind.

"I'm guessing, based on every fairytale I've ever read, that only my blood can break the curse Jakob has on the rest of you?" I questioned.

"You have weird fairytales in your world," Taesung commented. "But yes. Your blood mixed with Filix's, tangling yourself into our mess."

I shifted the shirt in my hands, feeling the soft fabric beneath the pads of my fingers.

"Based on the new clothes you have, the last trial will be soon, perhaps tomorrow. At the right moment, if we get someone else your blood, we can create a distraction and you can get to Wolf," Taesung said.

"How are–"

"Wolf's weak. He needs blood, and human blood is an incredible sustenance for fey. And if he drinks enough from you he'll be able to stop Jakob."

"Do you have a plan to get someone down here to take my blood? No one comes down here to check on us," I pointed out.

Taesung went quiet. It was obvious he had not thought that far in his plan. And I wasn't going to blame him. I hadn't thought that far either. I wasn't even sure about what kind of distraction could be caused to give me enough time to get to Wolf.

"Turn around," I said. "Please."

I heard Taesung's chains shuffle a bit. I waited a couple seconds before I began to undress myself. I practically ripped the damn thing off my body, eager to be in Hyunjin's clothes.

I missed him. I missed the way I had felt him at the back of my mind, his presence had become my favorite comfort. Now, I felt lonely, and miserable.

"Think you can scream again?" Taesung piped up as I readjusted the pants.

I opened my mouth to reply, but no words came out. I could scream again, sure, but the screams I let out when Jakob's magic had erased the blood bond between Hyunjin and I had been something I'd never done before. I wasn't certain I could do that again without being in extreme pain.

"I don't know."

"Ah, you're right. Stupid plan," Taesung muttered to himself. "Come on Taesung, think."

"Think you can scream?" I asked, an idea blooming in my mind. It was incredibly foolish, and I would be amazed if it worked.

"How loud are we talking?" he questioned.

I slipped Hyunjin's shirt over my head, and fiddled with a few of the buttons. When I had the shirt tucked into the pants properly, I reached for the belt still on the ground.

"I can't scream like you did. Your voice echoed through the entire castle... It was terrible. Hyunjin couldn't stop crying... I have never seen him so broken-hearted, so ruined and beyond repair."

I kept quiet as tears filled my eyes. Hearing that Hyunjin was as broken as I was, was not comforting. It broke my already shattered heart.

"He made Miro cry... Miro hasn't cried since he bonded with me," Taesung said.

"Why did he cry when he bonded with you?"

"He felt unworthy. He already had a bond with Wolf, and then he learned he had another blood bond with me... it was a little overwhelming for him."

"Does he still feel that way?"

"Sometimes..." Taesung's words slowed down, as he pondered how to word his thoughts. "Sometimes we all feel unworthy of the connection we share between us. It seems unfair to the rest of the Feywild for each of us to have a blood bond when most of our people won't get to experience it." Taesung laughed quietly, "It's honestly a little frightening that we each share a blood bond. Seems a bit too perfect when you think about it."

I was quiet for a while, worrying over a question that had lingered in the back of my mind since I had saved him from the burning inn.

"Did you know we would be kidnapped?"

"No. I'm not sure why we were dragged back to the Kingdom. It should not have happened," Taesung replied.

I hummed, more puzzled than I had originally been.

TAESUNG WAS AN EXCELLENT SCREAMER. Biroo and several guards had stormed into the dungeons, armed to the teeth. When they saw that I was far away from Taesung, and he was writhing in pain on the ground, they called for Seiji.

The healer appeared a few minutes later, his medical bag in hand.

He cautiously eyed me the entire time he was with Taesung. And Seiji took his time examining Taesung to determine what was wrong with him.

He made a show of doting on him, being extra dramatic with his scoldings as to throw Biroo off our trail. I watched, worriedly, as Taesung slipped his hand into Seiji's medical bag, swiping the things we needed.

Seiji stayed for a while, making sure to be thorough with his false medical examination; only leaving when Biroo forced him to.

Taesung and I waited to speak again, listening to the silence that filled the dungeons.

"This plan of ours... I can't promise you it will work," I said.

"Didn't Hyunjin teach you about making promises and bargains in the Feywild?" Taesung asked with a quiet laugh, but I knew he was serious.

"Don't make them. Don't accept them. Yeah I know... but I need you to know that this might not work. I'm only human after all."

Taesung passed me a needle, tubing and a small vial no larger than my thumb. This had to work. "That is the very reason I know we will succeed."

We had half of a plan, with vague ideas on how to alter said plan when the time arrived. Any number of things could go wrong. If I fucked up a single thing, then Jakob could rule in Wolf's place forever.

I held the needle and vial in my hands, staring down at them.

"Your heart's beating faster," Taesung commented from across the room.

"I can't do this," I admitted.

"Scared of a little needle?" He teased me.

"No," I snapped quickly. A moment of silence passed between us. "Okay, yes. And I can't see in the dark."

"Come here," Taesung said. The rustling of chains made me jump slightly, but I relaxed when I realized Taesung was just shifting in his cell, getting closer to the bars to help me.

Clutching the needle and vial in one hand, I carefully crawled to the bars that separated us. The iron chains at my ankles prevented me from fully reaching them. I shifted until my back faced the bars and then pulling against the chains, I leant backwards and extended an arm toward Taesung. This position was ridiculous and completely impractical.

He took the needle and vial from my hand, his reach feeling as strained as my own.

"I need you to talk while I do this," Taesung said in a serious manner.

"Why? About what?"

"I don't know how Hyunjin resisted you for so long. Your blood smells delicious."

He needed a distraction.

My head turned to glance back at him. I could barely see his outline in the darkness, the sconces outside our respective cells did little to illuminate the place.

"Okay," I said quietly.

Taesung's hands settled against my forearm, near the ditch of my elbow. His warm fingers ran over my skin, searching carefully for a suitable vein. When Taesung removed his fingers from my elbow, I began talking.

"I don't understand how I can have a messy heart like you claim I have."

"How so?" Taesung asked.

I took a deep breath and barely felt the pinch of pain as Taesung slid the needle into my vein and began to draw my blood.

"You're not the first person to tell me that I'm a mess. When Hyunjin and I got trapped in Kiruna, in the Goblin Market, a fortune teller said my strings were jumbled together. I just figured they meant I hadn't admitted my feelings for Hyunjin, which was messing with my head, making my emotions muddled."

"That's not completely true is it?" Taesung questioned.

"My feelings for Filix weren't complicated. I loved him."

I stopped talking seconds after that. I had loved Filix, with my whole heart... but now... after learning he had lied to me... I wasn't sure how to feel.

"What's confusing you?" Taesung asked, his voice sounded strained.

I started breathing faster, hoping it would cause my heart to beat faster, to get my blood flowing faster to get this over with for the sake of Taesung's nose.

I let out a deprecating laugh. "Me. I am confusing me. It feels wrong to..."

"To love Hyunjin?" Taesung finished for me.

I clamped my mouth shut, ashamed to admit that he was right. If I truly loved Filix like I said I had... surely I wouldn't have fallen for Hyunjin or cared so deeply for Wolf.

And yet Filix had lied through all of it. Had he even loved me to begin with? Or had I been there to pass the time until Hyunjin woke? I wasn't sure about anything he did anymore.

Laughter from outside the cell had the two of us jumping slightly. I forced myself to remain completely still as Taesung fumbled with the vial, trying to keep from spilling any of my blood.

"I take it no one's explained anything to you," spoke a new voice.

"I was getting there Miro," Taesung grumbled. "You could have warned me you were coming."

"You know I couldn't. Our bond is blocked and only Mare's blood can free us," Miro replied in a threatening tone. "I'm not the King's spy for shits and giggles."

In the dim light I could see Miro had a tray of fairy food. My stomach twisted at the thought of eating something, anything. Hunger pangs were beginning to make me hangry; and the thought of taking even a nibble of fey food was tempting.

"Explain what to me?" I asked, bringing Miro's words back to the forefront of everyone's mind. I wanted a straight answer for once, and I was going to get it one way or another.

"You have multiple heart strings," Miro said simply, like I knew what that meant.

The door to Taesung's cell opened and Miro stepped inside.

Miro crossed the cell in four steps, coming to a stop near Taesung. I twisted and craned my neck as far as I could before my back muscles began to protest, or before Taesung could tell me to quit moving while he withdrew my blood.

"This is the best the two of you could come up with?" Miro asked, a condescending tone in his voice. "How do you even plan to sneak this out of here? And how do you plan to give everyone a taste?"

"We were still working on that," Taesung muttered under his breath, clearly a bit annoyed that Miro was questioning our very loose, very sketchy, very unplanned plan.

Taesung pulled the needle from my arm and pressed his thumb against my vein to staunch the bleeding. Miro grabbed the vial from Taesung's hands. He quickly capped the bottle to avoid losing any of the blood we had collected, and passed it to me. Nestled next to the vial were two cold metal objects that I had not expected to feel.

I ran my fingers across the tiny metal objects, trying to figure out what Miro had passed to me without raising it into the light. Anyone could be watching or listening. Various bumps and curves danced beneath my fingers, the first object coming to life in my mind's eye.

Miro had passed me a key.

"Stuff that in your bra," he instructed me. I slid the vial and the key between my breasts, and then fiddled with the last object. It was circular and thin, reminding me of a ring. "And I took that from Filix."

I held one of Filix's matching rings with Hyunjin in my palm for a couple of seconds, debating whether I should chuck it back in Miro's face or simply toss it behind me to get lost in the darkness of my cell. I ended up sliding the thin band onto my forefinger.

"The two of us are more likely to be searched than you are," Miro explained. "And that's useless to you unless your shitty plan actually works."

He passed the tubing used to collect my blood to Taesung, while he licked the edge of the needle that had been in my arm, in my veins.

Taesung wrapped his lips around the tubing and sucked, drawing what little blood remained into his mouth. Taesung moaned loudly as my blood spread across his taste buds. A shudder wracked his body, and I could feel the strings that were meant to bind us together stitching themselves closed, weaving an intricate pattern that belonged solely between Taesung and I; bringing to life a friendship I had never experienced before.

It felt strange to feel more for Taesung than I had previously.

Miro huffed, a bit disgusted with my cheesy thoughts.

With his opposite hand, Miro urged Taesung up off the ground. Miro tossed the needle away, letting the sharp object clatter against the stones, discarding it entirely.

I strained to look over my shoulder to see what they were doing. I watched as Miro withdrew a set of keys from his pocket and unlocked Taesung from his bonds. The historian rubbed his raw wrists and nervously glanced at Wolf's right hand man.

"I still don't understand," I said, "Heart strings? Why are they so important?"

Miro jerked his head to the side as he closed his eyes briefly, urging Taesung to go on ahead without him. Taesung looked back at me, his body radiated anxiety. Spending another night down in the dungeons wasn't ideal. I wanted to be with people again. I wanted to be with Hyunjin again.

"Go or we'll both be punished," Miro growled, which sent Taesung scurrying out of the dungeon.

I knew Miro had to leave, he'd already been here for too long. But I had one last question.

"Why me? Why would your Mother think I'm the one who can..." I couldn't bring myself to finish my sentence.

It felt absurd that I could have had such a powerful destiny bestowed upon me from a goddess no less. I was ordinary.

Miro stared at me, a serious expression on his cat-like features as he hovered in the archway, trying to delay his departure until the last possible second.

"How does it feel when you're with Filix?"

The seconds we had were ticking away, faster and faster until I'd be left alone again. I bristled slightly at Filix's name, but knew I had to answer honestly. Not for Miro's sake, but for mine. Everything we had together couldn't have been a lie. It couldn't have.

"It felt like home."

"And with Hyunjin?"

A beat of silence passed.

"I've never felt this way before," I said.

"And Wolf?"

"I hardly know him, but…"

"But he feels like home as well. Like everything is right in the world with him by your side?" Miro suggested, speaking from experience.

"That's what scares me most."

"Heart strings are never wrong. That's how it feels between us all. Each one of us makes up a room inside a house we all call home. The *why* does not matter. There is no answer as to 'why me?' They just happen."

"Shouldn't we have a bond then?" I questioned him.

"Oh we do. Just not a romantic one. It's more of a platonic bond. It could change in the future, but underneath it all, at its rawest form you and I share an unbreakable connection to one another," Miro explained, like it was the most casual thing in the entire world.

You make up the last room missing inside Wolf's home, his voice echoed down our bond.

And then I was left alone.

THIS LOVE IS FULL OF FAIRY TALES

S harp claws dug into my biceps as they hauled me up off the cold ground in the dungeons, physically pulling me out of my slumber.

I let out a groggy yelp as the claws sunk deeper into my flesh, drawing blood. A deep grumble from a jackal had me flinching as I was pulled out of the cell, and carelessly tossed toward the stairs.

Stumbling, I caught myself before I could face-plant into the first section of stairs. I threw an annoyed glare over my shoulder as I picked myself up. The tiny puncture marks on my arms stung slightly, but the blood had already ceased bleeding.

"Mov'it," Biroo growled.

"Or what?" I snapped back.

Biroo's gnarled teeth flashed in my face, the stench of rot filling my nostrils as his breath fanned across my face. I cringed away from the jackal's jaws, swallowing the bile that threatened to leave me.

Biroo laughed at my reaction, the sound echoing into the dungeon behind him. My glare deepened as I turned from the ugly mutt and ascended the staircase.

There were more people inside the Grand Hall than I had been expecting when I stepped inside. Since arriving at the Kingdom, there had only ever been a handful of dark fey guards that I had seen apart from Wolf and the guys.

A dozen fey littered themselves throughout the room, staying a respectful and safe distance away from the front of the room. A cluster of sea nymphs and selkies lingered closest to the front of the room, drawn to the massive magical pool before the gorgeous grand windows that led out into the gardens. A couple centaurs and a pair of griffins hovered at the back of the room, situated near the entrance, acting like bodyguards. The security had been doubled.

What had Jakob planned for the last trial?

Ever the center of attention, on display like an animal, Wolf was still strung up like a martyr. His head hung low, and his chest barely moved. Everything about him screamed that he was in agony. My eyes fell to the stairs as guilt ate away at me.

The other members of Wolf's home were lined up on the larger landing that separated the dias into two smaller sections of stairs, hands bound in front of them with large orcs and burly goblins guarding them at either end. They looked rough; blood ran down their necks from where the iron collars dug into their skin, staining their white outfits crimson.

Seok had blood running from his nose, and Miro sported a nasty bruise on his cheekbone that hadn't been there last night. Taesung's left eye was swollen shut, a dark nasty bruise marred his pretty tanned skin. Iyena and Seiji looked to be in better shape, only a minor cut marred Iyena's brow and Seiji seemed to have a busted lip. Despite their rugged state, they were all dressed in regal white outfits with varying silver accents, tainted only by the blood that stained the edges of the tops.

Where was Filix?

My gaze ran down the line, taking in all of their injuries, subconsciously searching for anything that seemed out of place, anything that screamed for me to pay more attention to it – like black poisoned veins from a Smogbody bite, or vicious claw marks from a

Mournhead, or whatever else lurked inside the Feywild that I had yet to meet.

I took a relieving breath of air when I found nothing to be physically wrong with Hyunjin, save for a tiny scrape across the bridge of his nose. Hyunjin's gaze was startling, however.

His eyes looked vacant as he stared at me, his eyes briefly flickered to my arms, to the bloodstains that soaked into the shirt from Biroo's claws when I'd been literally pulled from sleep. Hyunjin looked exactly like he had the night he was cursed to sleep for eternity. The weight of the world had been placed on his shoulders again as a future he wanted no part of was thrust upon him without his consent or opinion. He looked spaced out, but I knew him. He was putting on a brave front despite how terrified he was – just like I was.

"Mare! Thanks for joining me yet again," Jakob beamed.

My face scrunched in disgust as I was forced to meet Jakob's gaze. I knew with absolute certainty that Jakob was not actually happy to see me. I had become the root of many of his problems. If anything I was a thorn in his ass.

"Ah don't give me that look. You're so close to beating all of my trials. In fact," Jakob mused as he stepped up a few steps of the dias. "I'm proud of you."

"Stop talking Jakob," Taesung spat out.

The goblin guard closest to him stepped past Seiji, Iyena and Miro before he rammed his fist into the side of Taesung's head, sending the poor historian toppling over into the healer, who struggled to stay upright and not collide with the prince. Taesung groaned loudly as he righted his posture, grimacing openly as he shook his head, trying to clear the fog from his brain.

"Serves you right," Jakob muttered, a distasteful look on his flat, bear-like features. "As I was saying, I'm proud of you, Mare Cozen."

The disgust I had felt when Jakob first praised me, tripled. My skin crawled, leaving me itchy. I liked being praised – just not by Jakob.

"I sincerely hope you don't disappoint me this time," Jakob said. "I mean, how could you? You're the first one in hundreds of years to stand up and play my games. It's exciting."

"I'm sick of playing your games. They've proved nothing," I snapped at him.

An amused huff of laughter left Jakob as he began to descend the stairs again. He looked past me and waved to a couple of guards by the entrance, urging them to bring something forward.

Dread filled me as I stared wide-eyed at Jakob.

If it's another coffin I'm going to lose it, I thought.

My heartbeat picked up as I heard several pairs of feet scuffling against the plush red carpet that ran down the length of the Grand Hall. I sunk onto my knees as icy cold hands pushed down with a heavy iron grip.

Biroo manhandled a hooded fey past me, the jackal using his strength to his advantage as the fey jerked and struggled to get out of his claws. Biroo forced the fey to stand before me at the base of the dias, just steps away from the others. When the jackal was satisfied with where the fey was, he stepped back, awaiting Jakob's next orders.

I was more than confused as I looked at the hooded figure in front of me, before I looked at Jakob. What was I supposed to do?

"Beat this last trial and I'll let Wolf go. I'll let them all go," Jakob declared with a shit eating grin.

Hyunjin and Seok flinched as if burned in my peripheral vision. A flare of pain passed across Miro's features as his face scrunched up, and Taesung and Seiji looked no better as they glared at Jakob's back.

I looked back at Jakob, fully aware he would not keep his word no matter what was promised.

"What do I have to do?" I asked, hoping to find a loophole in Jakob's words.

"It's simple," Jakob beamed, a sick smile spread across his features. "I want you to kill Filix."

The hood was yanked off the fey in front of him, revealing my first love.

The blood in my veins ran cold as our eyes connected, his flashed a silver-blue before they dimmed, whereas mine instantly filled with tears. His hair was as disheveled as his clothes - ones that looked similar to the fancy ones they'd all worn on the night Jakob betrayed them. His hands were covered in blood, yet the rest of him was clean.

My throat felt tight at the realization that Jakob had forced them all back into the clothes they wore that night – the night he betrayed them all. Like he was trying to recreate what had happened nearly half a millennium ago.

"No."

Jakob's beady narrow eyes grew smaller as he glared down at me, his head held high as he arched a brow.

"Giving up already? My court and I had high hopes you would succeed at all my trials," Jakob pouted.

"It's not your court! You stole it from the people who loved you most."

Jakob's glare turned harder, if it were even possible. A tiny pang of uncertainty flared in me, the very real feeling of needing to be cautious around Jakob had been triggered.

"They don't love me. Not like they promised," Jakob said coldly, his head turning to look back at Wolf.

This was not going the way Taesung and I had planned.

I had no idea what he was truly capable of, but I was learning. If the first two trials, and now the threat to kill Filix was anything to go by, Jakob was not a man to be trusted or toyed with.

"What does killing Filix prove? You're a coward for not doing it yourself!"

Those were the wrong words! I screamed at myself. *Shut your mouth before you say something else stupid.*

"It proves that I was the better choice all along. That Our Mother made yet another mistake... And by having you kill him, well, it's just extra sweet knowing he'll die at the hands of the human he's in love with."

I shook my head, unable to speak. I couldn't do it. I *couldn't*, and Jakob likely knew that all along. He knew I wouldn't be able to kill Filix.

Despite every lie he inadvertently told me, I knew Filix... and I loved him.

"Oh well... His death will be boring now," he surmised. "He's all yours, Biroo."

Biroo puffed out his chest as he and two other guards moved to grab Filix again, eager to kill Filix at Jakob's orders.

I struggled against the hands at my shoulders, trying to keep me in submission.

"No, no, no," I panicked, frantically trying to appease Jakob. "Please, kill me!"

Jakob raised a hand, stopping the guards from reaching Filix. He cocked his head to the side, uncertain but interested.

"Kill me," I said again, steadying my voice as I licked my lips apart. "Kill me instead... take my place- take my string in their bond."

They'll all be okay. They have each other. They won't be lonely when I'm dead.

Hyunjin snarled loudly, his vacant eyes blazing brightly as he glared at me. He looked ravenous and terrifying, and I wasn't sure which one I was more afraid of.

Miro jerked at his chains, a grunt of a growl left him. Our eyes met for a fleeting second, his flashed violent purple in warning before I cast my eyes to Jakob. A heavy, daring feeling pulsed at me – a clear unmistakable warning. *I shouldn't be doing this.*

Guilt continued to eat away at me; I was faced with two impossible decisions. Let Filix die or offer Jakob the one thing he sought out most in this world, even if it cost me what I desired most.

They will be okay. There are seven other bonds that complete each other. He will be okay. I whispered to myself, to my aching heart.

A dark look cast a shadow over Jakob's eyes, everything he'd ever wanted had been laid before him. He would be a fool not to take what I was offering him. Greed and raw desire burned in Jakob's eyes, the hunger for belonging somewhere blazed brightly. The hunt, the chase for what he craved was coming to an end.

A deeper shadow darkened his eyes, the greed and power Jakob had been in control of reared its ugly head.

"What a kind offer. I accept," Jakob said with a triumphant smile.

Seok and Iyena strained against their bonds, trying to escape before I could complete such an idiotic bargain.

Don't do this. Don't do this. Repeated over and over again in my mind, as alarm bells rang, a frantic sense of urgency beat down on my back. This was a bargain I shouldn't have made… But it was too late now.

"But Filix still has to die. I won't be bound to someone who never deserved this in the first place."

I stared at Jakob, my mind buffering at the worst possible time.

"Not– not fair."

"Fair?" Jakob laughed darkly, "Fair isn't something we know, Mare. We're human, we play dirty."

My mouth had stopped working.

"There's no way for you to win here," he continued, "So make a choice. Either Filix dies for a good cause or he dies for nothing, and so do you."

Disbelief swirled inside me as I realized I had been backed into a corner without even realizing it. I had been playing by fey rules when I should have been cheating with human loopholes.

And now things were going in the wrong direction, spiraling further and further out of my control.

"Mare," Filix softly called to me.

I looked away from him as a rush of new tears pooled in my eyes.

He had lied to me from the beginning. He had betrayed me… and yet I couldn't do this. I couldn't kill him.

"Mare it's okay, kill me."

271

I violently shook my head as I pressed my lips together. There was no way I could kill him. A few tears spilled down my cheeks but I roughly wiped them away. Jakob deserved none of my tears... but Filix... Filix would deserve them all if he died.

"Baby," Filix said, his voice softening just slightly. The minute change in his voice had me refocusing my gaze, had me focused on him and him alone as I analyzed everything about him.

"It'll be okay baby," Filix reassured me.

I swallowed as I kept my face neutral, trying to figure out exactly *what* Filix wanted me to notice. He looked up at me with wide, normal brown eyes. Dark bags sat heavy beneath his eyes, his freckles had faded from being trapped inside for so long, with no chance to see or feel the sun's warmth. The venom from the Smog-body's bite had spread more, the dark veins that had been on his neck and jaw had spread, seeping farther down his chest and had begun to creep up his cheeks. The weight of looking at Filix had begun to take its toll, I had to look away or else I would begin crying more.

Biroo snarled, stepping forwards. His clawed hand held a beautiful, intricate silver knife. A gorgeous moonstone sat mounted in the center of the hilt, glinting beautifully in the light. Biroo grabbed my wrist and slapped the dagger into my open palm.

My brain protested, wanting me to drop the knife immediately as soon as the cold metal met my skin. The metal burned in my clammy hands, biting against my skin like the Night Mate's touch had done. A warm, cozy sensation had me breaking out into an uncontrollable sweat, momentarily distracting me from the knife in my grasp. A very persistent idea repeated over and over again, pushing violently against the blood bonds that were blocked by Jakob's stolen magic.

Trick. Trick. Trick.

A shaky breath left me. I had no idea if whoever banged against the bond was trying to warn me that Jakob was going to try and trick me again; or if they were telling me to trick Jakob. I had no way of knowing, no way to get a hint at which option it was.

If I was going to trick Jakob, I would need to put my all into it, and I wasn't sure I could be very convincing. My watery eyes looked up at Jakob, praying that he would play into this new plan.

I sniffled hard, tearfully looking back down at Filix. I really hoped this would work.

"I love you, baby," Filix said quietly. His honest admission had a new wave of real tears clouding my vision. I couldn't reply to him, not when I wasn't sure where we stood. I couldn't lie to him when I wasn't sure what my heart wanted and needed in return.

I sniffled again, silently steeling my nerves as I forced myself to look at Jakob. The urge to drive the dagger in my hand through his mortal heart was tempting. Incredibly tempting – yet I expected that he was waiting for that. Waiting for me to try and betray him, so he would ultimately end up killing Filix and myself.

I wanted one last chance to try and change his mind.

"Don't do this. You already have what you want."

"You're in the Feywild, Mare. You've made a bargain that you have to uphold your end on. I don't make the rules," Jakob said, his face smug and punchable.

I silently cursed him. He wasn't budging. He wanted my blood bond. I had one last idea that I wanted to try – if anything, I wanted to try and reach out to him. Human to human. Like he had been trying with each trial. Jakob missed *human* contact.

"Please," I extended a hand out to him, a pleading look on my features. "Come home with me. Come back to *our* world. Let's find your family – your real family. You don't belong here, Jakob. We don't belong here."

The smug smile that had been etched on his face dropped, a cold hatred hardened his flat features.

"Don't," he snarled, "Any family I had on that side of the Veil is dead to me. Now stop stalling. Kill him or he'll die for nothing."

My stomach sank as my efforts failed. My eyes frantically darted from each of the shackled fey men, hoping that despite not having a solidified bond to communicate with any of them, that they would get my plan. That they would back me when I put the plan Taesung and I had made into action – even if it was altered slightly now.

My hands shook as I held the knife, my vision completely useless due to my tears. The very idea of hurting Filix – killing him–

I can't do it. I panicked, freezing as I looked down at my best friend, the one person I had loved most.

Filix gave me a reassuring look, barely moving his head to keep Jakob in the dark. His eyes burned a bright silver-blue, the luminosity intense. I had never seen Filix look so determined about something. So passionate about something, something he believed wholeheartedly.

His belief in me gave me the tiniest drop of courage that I needed.

I surged forward, dragging the knife across the heel of my palm as I shoved it toward Filix's mouth. His lips and tongue swiped against my skin, against the wet trickle of blood. A single taste had Filix's strength returning to his weakened body.

He yanked at his chains, the bonds snapping easily as he jerked upright. Filix threw his elbow back, the motion too fast for Jakob or I to see, but I heard the crack of bone breaking and the anguished cry Jakob released as blood poured from his broken nose.

A clanging snap of chains breaking had the entire room bursting into chaos. I had created the momentary distraction they had all needed to summon their strength to break free. Yelling, and fighting drowned out every noise in the room, and the sudden change in volume had my head throbbing.

Seok, was the first to be free of his cuffs, the muscular shifter wasted no time in freeing his younger brothers. With Iyena and Taesung free, the three of them broke off in different directions. Taesung worked on releasing Miro from his own chains, while Seiji and Filix slid across the stairs.

Iyena dashed for Hyunjin. The two of them barely leapt out of the way of a Smogbody as its jaws snapped through the air, the massive beast lunging for them. The two of them rolled, tumbling across the floor together in a tangled heap. My line of sight was cut short when a guard tackled me to the ground.

Jakob's guards fought hard and dirty, with no real tactic or plan. Yet their lack of preparation was easily made up by their brute strength and incredible speed.

My assailant was ripped from my body before his fists could collide with my face. Seok had torn the scruffy imp from me, throwing its body into a charging row of more guards, knocking them down like dominos.

"You okay?" he questioned, his muscular chest moving hard as he panted.

Seok reached his hand out to me, and I quickly grabbed it, yanking myself off the ground.

"I am now," I replied.

Steady on my feet again, I offered Seok my bleeding wrist as I counted down the seconds. I needed to get to Wolf.

A moment's hesitation flickered behind Seok's eyes, their color pulsing from dark brown to warmed honey-amber before they dimmed, and he took a hesitant step backwards, rejecting my blood. Rejecting my offer at a bond. He turned and launched himself at a hobgoblin.

A small pang of sadness ebbed in my chest at Seok's rejection, but I couldn't hold it against him.

Miro and Taesung appeared at Seok's side, the two of them flanking Seok as they fought against armed guards that had recovered from being plowed over. They wasted no time in turning to help their bond mates fight with renewed vigor.

Grunts and snarls bounced around the room as the clang of metal swords colliding ricocheted off the walls. I spun, trying to search for Hyunjin, or Filix and Jakob but couldn't see them through the fighting. Panicked urgency shot down my spine. If I couldn't see them, then I had a shorter time frame than I had imagined. I dashed toward Wolf, taking the stairs two at a time despite my thighs protesting such an act.

Pain flared in my knees as I dropped into a slide and came to a halt before Wolf's exhausted, defeated form. I dug into my bra and produced the tiny key that Miro had snuck to me in the dungeons. My fingers were cold and clammy, trying to hold the tiny metallic object was a challenge within itself.

Wolf made no movement to acknowledge I was there in front of him. My stomach dropped out from under me as I watched him, ignoring the fighting behind us.

His chest barely moved as he breathed, but the tiny rise and fall of his lungs working had relief washing over me.

My hands slid across his cheeks and up into his hair, trying to be gentle as I aroused him from his drowsy, exhausted state.

"Wolf," I breathed out, terrified. I had one shot to get this right.

His head tipped up, and he barely opened his eyes. His entire body twitched and shook from exhaustion and hunger. He was tired and ready to give up.

Leaning as far as I could, while still centered in front of Wolf, I shakily put the key inside the cuff's lock, and uncuffed one of his hands. His arm fell against his side with a heavy smack, and his posture shifted, slumping forward more. I surged forward, trying to counteract his actions with my body weight.

"You need to drink," I whispered to him, blocking out the sounds of war behind me. If I thought about Hyunjin, or Filix or any of the things that could go wrong I'd never succeed in my part of the plan.

My hands rested against his chest, holding him upright. Wolf's breath fanned across my neck as I shifted closer to him. I craned my head to the side to give him as much room as possible. Wolf's nose nudged against my neck, scenting me.

"Can't hurt you, pup," he murmured quietly.

My stomach fell at his refusal. Our entire plan revolved around Wolf drinking my blood. If this didn't work...

"Please, you have to," I begged him.

Wolf was silent, his chest rising and falling in heavy dregs as he panted heavily. If he was going to refuse, then I was not going to play fairly.

"I brought Hyunjin back to you, now do this for me."

Wolf shifted, and a tiny grunt escaped him as he acknowledged I'd *technically* done him a favor and he owed me one in return.

Manipulating Wolf like that had my chest feeling hot, like I wanted to collapse in on myself and never return, never recover.

It felt like an impossible task to grab the small vial of blood Taesung and I had gathered last night from my pocket while Wolf gathered his fleeting strength. My fingers were cold and clammy and wouldn't stop shaking. My chest rose and fell rapidly. I needed to move faster. I fumbled with the tiny vial, nearly dropping it.

"Easy," Wolf whispered to me. His free hand rested lazily on my waist, but the strong squeeze he gave to my side was enough to calm and ground me, "I got you."

I stopped moving and held my breath, bracing for the initial pain that always accompanied being bit.

His teeth sank into my skin, the first pinch of pain made me whimper. I could feel the pressure of his bite, and the wet drag of his tongue against my skin as he lapped up my blood.

His grip was tight, yet his hunger was stronger. A dark wave of lust rushed through my body the more Wolf drank from me, which made my thoughts cloudy and slow.

With Wolf occupied and distracted, I slowly, sluggishly slid the blood vial into the inner pocket of his cropped suit jacket. My fingers still shook, but not with the severity that they had moments ago when I didn't have Wolf's comfort.

One long last pull against my vein had Wolf releasing my neck from his bite. He stayed close, his lips hovered over my neck and pressed down in gentle, thankful, reassuring kisses.

"Thank you for bringing Hyunjin home," Wolf whispered, his grip at my waist squeezed once more as if he couldn't quite believe I was real. "For bringing them both home."

"An–"

A crackle of magic wrapped around me from behind and hauled me backwards, away from Wolf. Wolf's head snapped up, in alarm.

I thrashed around, trying to use my body weight to throw the person behind me off balance. The magic dug into my sides, the grip was painful, making me release a tiny squeak of pain. The clang and jingle of the bonds Wolf was left in broke through the sounds of fighting all around us as he struggled to free himself of the iron.

My muscles protested in pain as I was manhandled, the magic hauling me away from Wolf had shoved me forward, toward the pool of water surrounded by a fairy ring.

I stumbled, my legs gave out and my knees scraped against the ground. Darkly polished shoes appeared in my field of vision, and a hand yanked at the back of my head, forcing me to look up.

A sinister bloody smile spread across Jakob's face as I realized I was separated from everyone, and at his mercy. My eyes filled with terrified tears as I knelt before such a cruel human. My stomach sank as my heart dropped, a hysterical sense of panic hit me. My eyes darted over to the deep pool of water inside the mushroom ring, something was wrong.

"I changed my mind. Tears do suit you beautifully."

A deep chuckle resonated from Jakob as he glared down at me. That cruel smile morphed into a sneer as Jakob spit blood onto the ground and shoved me away from him. Jakob's magic wound its way around me again, hauling me up off the ground.

"You think you know me so well," Jakob hissed. His eyes narrowed in hatred, a venom lingered in his gaze. He shook his head in disgust and disappointment.

Jakob pivoted, revealing Filix's figure, magically bound and restrained, behind him. The venom from the Smogbody bite had spread further throughout his body, the veins thicker and darker the longer the venom lingered in his system.

A cut marred Filix's cheek, blood trickled slowly down his cheek as he struggled against the same magic that bound me. Tears welled in Filix's waterline as his gaze rose to meet mine.

My stomach dropped as I looked back at him; a slow, heavy dread filling my chest.

"Stop this, Jakob," Filix pleaded. "We can be a family again."

"Like we would ever be brothers again."

The magic wrapped around us constricted, squeezing the air from my lungs. I let out an involuntary squeak, feeling lightheaded. Filix and I stumbled closer to each other. I blinked, sending several tears streaming down my cheeks.

With jerking motions, my arm raised on its own. I fought against myself, trying to stop my arm from moving, being controlled like a marionette via Jakob's magic. I pulled and pulled, trying to drag my arm back to my side, and yet Jakob's magic was stronger.

My hand punched through Filix's chest, the sound wet and crunching. His hot blood rushed onto my hand, dripping down my forearm, splattering everywhere.

Filix's face scrunched in pain as his hand shot out and gripped my bicep, his eyes wide, fearful and full of agony. I reached to steady him with my free hand, trying to wrestle out of Jakob's control.

My fingers curled into a fist, wrapping around his heart. And then I yanked, ripping his heart from his chest.

A silent cry left Filix as his body slumped against my own, knocking me off balance as I tried to take all of his weight. He dropped to his knees before toppling sideways. Blood pooled beneath his body quickly.

My chest felt tight as I slowly looked to the slowly thumping heart through skewed vision.

Disbelief surged through me.

What had I done?

His heart fell out of my palm and onto the ground with a wet splat.

Jakob stepped forwards, his hand clutched at my cheeks, pushing them together as my lips puckered slightly, turning my head to force me to look into his eyes. He tipped my head to the side, staring at the bloody bite mark Wolf had given me.

"You don't belong here," he spat, giving my head a shove.

I stumbled, my limbs numb. My eyes fell, staring at his corpse as I vaguely, I heard Wolf shouting, screaming Filix's name from across the Grand Hall.

My eyes found Hyunjin's through the chaos. Sweat covered his skin, plastering a few locks to his forehead. His chest heaved as he stood on the landing that separated the stairs, yanking his sword from the chest of a goblin. His vibrant red eyes widened in horror as he stared up at us.

My body jerked under the control of Jakob's magic and hauled me backwards like I was nothing. Jakob's hold was tight, and unyielding.

Hyunjin surged forward, taking the stairs two at a time to try and get to me before I was thrown into the water.

"No!" he shouted, but it was too late.

The water invaded my mouth, my nose, my throat, cutting off my airways. I tried to expel the water from my lungs. Phantom hands gripped my ankles and dragged me deeper into the water.

I flailed and thrashed, desperately trying to swim, to get out of the water, but found my efforts making me sink faster to the bottom. My vision clouded, growing darker and darker until I couldn't see anything at all.

I SLIPPED INSIDE THE GATE, not remembering when it had fallen off its hinges. An empty, hollow feeling weighed on my shoulders and kept my eyes filled with tears. I stood in my garden, dripping wet with my eyes fixated on the cracked rock in the pathway.

How had that crack gotten there? It hadn't been there before, had it?

This was entirely wrong. Hadn't I just been...

Where had I been? How did I get outside?

The front door slammed open and seconds later arms were wrapped around me, and my mum's voice filled the air.

"Mare? Where have you been, honey?" She pulled away from me. Her hands were on either side of my face, inspecting me for any injuries. "Ciarán! Call Radley!"

I slowly looked up from the ground and at her face. She looked tired, dark circles were prominent beneath her eyes and her hair was thrown in a messy bun as if she hadn't brushed it in quite some time.

Mum's eyes focused solely on my neck, her eyes widened in horror before she threw her arms around me again. I instinctively raised a hand and hissed when my fingers met a fresh open wound.

"What are you yelling for Gwynne?" My dad asked. "Mare?!"

My father's arms wrapped around my mum and I seconds later. The two of them were crying and asking me questions about where I had been, what had happened to the house. I had numbly hugged them back, finding no words I could voice.

I only pulled away from Mum when Dad ran back inside to phone for Sheriff Radley. Something *wrong* nagged at the back of my mind as I stood in the front garden.

"Mum, what's going on?" I asked, a heavy weight pressed on my chest. "Where's Filix?"

A new wave of tears filled Mum's eyes as she stared up at me.

"Oh honey," Mum cooed, a pitying tone in her words.

The tears I had been holding onto began to spill as I tried to keep it together until I got a straight answer. I tried to swallow the lump that had formed in my throat but it still felt stuck.

"Where's Filix?" I repeated, my voice hoarse.

"We don't know honey. The two of you have been missing for a month... and the house, there was so much blood," Mum said, her words turning to cries.

The crack in the gray stone looked oddly familiar. The impact of whatever had struck it caused the cracks to splinter off in odd directions, the lines formed a flowery pattern. The only thing it was missing was color.

What was going on?

Mum's arms wrapped around me again and urged me forward. My limbs felt heavy as I was guided back inside the house.

Mum settled me on the couch, having disappeared for a couple minutes, but I wasn't sure. A towel had been wrapped around me, and a blanket was draped around my shoulders, a wet rag was pressed against my neck and a mug of tea was pressed into my palms. The cup was piping hot but I barely felt the sting of heat in my hands as I held onto it.

"Where have you been Mare?" Dad questioned me. He sat on the coffee table with a concerned expression as Mum gently wiped the damp rag against the skin on my neck. I flinched.

I recognized that the coffee table was new, which had me glancing around the living room to see what else had been replaced. The Smogbody had destroyed the entire room the last time I had been in here.

The bookshelves were new, dark wood and almost completely empty. The knick knacks Mum had kept over the fireplace were gone, along with a dozen photos that had been hung on the wall.

They were gone.

A dark shadow stained the wall beside the archway that led to the stairs. The outline matched perfectly where the Smogbody had first appeared in the living room before it had chased Filix and I out of the house. The shadow was lighter in certain places, places that Mum had probably tried to scrub away.

"Mare?" Sheriff Radley's deep voice spoke from above me.

My eyes slowly rose to meet his gaze, the shadowy stain of the Smogbody on my living room wall burned onto the back of my eyelids. A sad smile spread across Radley's face as he looked down at me.

"Hey darlin'. You up for some questions?" he asked carefully.

My head was spinning in circles as I watched myself in an out of body experience, but I forced myself to shake my head. Radley looked at me for a long second, perhaps not satisfied with my weird head shake of an answer.

"Okay Mare, we'll take this slow. Afterwards Novenol is gonna check you over, okay?"

I forced myself to nod, to give Radley a clear and concise answer.

"Do you know how long you and Filix have been missing?"

"A month? That's what my mum said."

Radley nodded and scribbled something down in his notepad.

"And did the two of you just... take off?"

Swallowing, I looked down at my mug of tea. My brain felt fuzzy and the back of my skull hurt as an impending headache began to creep up on me.

"No. We were attacked."

"Attacked? After the prince's coffin was opened?"

I didn't trust my voice, so I nodded. My movements still felt numb and sluggish. Like I was weighed down underwater, like I had been left somewhere else.

"What happened that night? Do you know what attacked you?"

"Was it the prince? Was he the one who bit you?" Mum butt in, her distaste for the fey sparking to life.

My head whipped to glare at her, my face set in a deep scowl. I wanted to snap back at her, defend the prince but the words were caught in my throat, and the longer I thought about them the faster they faded from my mind, leaving me disoriented and confused.

Who was the prince? Would he hurt me? Who had bit me?

"Please, Mrs. Cozen. I need you and your husband to wait in the kitchen. I don't want to stress Mare out any more than she already is," Novenol piped up from behind me, from the opposite side of the couch.

Dad ushered Mum out of the living room after some mild protesting on her part. She relented after a moment of worried consideration. When they had disappeared, my gaze settled on the Smogbody stain with unfocused attention.

"Mare? Do you know what attacked you and Filix that night?" Radley repeated.

"Be gentle, Rads. It's clear she's in shock," Novenol said quietly.

I was quiet for a couple seconds as I struggled to look back at the Sheriff. I opened my mouth to speak and found my words vanishing as soon as I wanted to say them. Exhaling hard, I pulled in several deep breaths to keep myself focused.

"A Smogbody," I whispered.

The room was silent.

Radley's entire body stiffened before pivoting to look at the massive shadow stain behind him. He looked a bit terrified as pieces began to connect in his mind. The Sheriff turned to look back in my direction, his eyes connecting with the doctor behind me. "A Smogbody?"

"Yes," I answered, but my voice sounded small and weak.

"Did it bite you? Did any of its saliva get on your skin?" Novenol asked quickly rounding the couch to come sit near me. He ripped open his medicine bag and began to rifle through it.

"No," I breathed out, "but it–"

It bit Filix.

The Smogbody had bit Filix, his blood had been smeared all over the living room and all over my hands.

His blood had been all over my hands?

Tears welled up in my eyes as my memory failed me. I felt like I was missing something obvious. Something I'd seen and was now drawing a blank on.

"Shh, it's alright Mare. It didn't bite you?" Novenol repeated.

Side eyeing him, I saw the glint of a vial and the bright orange cap of a syringe in his hands. I jerked away from him, sloshing tea all over myself and the blanket that had been wrapped around me.

"It didn't bite me," I snapped. "None of them hurt me. Wolf needed my blood so I gave it to him! He would never hurt me."

"Wolf? " Novenol asked, a bright spark burning behind his eyes.

Radley shifted in front us. I glanced between the two of them,

284

caught off guard at my outburst. Novenol quickly stamped down on his own excitement and put on a professional front when he realized how upset I was.

"It's okay Mare. I'm just going to give you a little dose of Duprilic. It'll help to curb your diet until you can consume mortal food again."

"I never ate fey food," I said, my train of thought trailing off at the end. I hadn't eaten any fey food, had I?

Novenol waited a couple of seconds before he moved forward at a slow pace and administered the shot. The briefest, haziest image of a man drawing my blood flashed before my mind, but before I could properly think about it the thought disappeared from my mind. I barely felt the tiny sting before Novenol was pulling away, tossing the needle into a container.

My foggy thoughts grew more distorted; the effort to keep my eyes open seemed like an impossible task. The weight of my head became too much for me as it tipped sideways, my body tiredly following the motion. I heard the thunk of the mug Mum had brought me hit the floor as my head hit the couch cushions.

My eyes slipped closed, and I was met with more darkness.

QUESTIONS

When my mum had come into my room and awoken me, telling me to get ready to meet with the Mayor and Sheriff Radley to discuss my disappearance and 'adventure' into the Feywild, all I had done was sit on the end of my bed, staring at it.

A large, half-finished painting sat on my easel, the oil paint nearly dry.

A hand holding a bleeding heart was the main focus on the canvas, the background a mixture of swirling blacks, purples and blues, creating a dark thunderous sky. Rivulets of blood dripped down the heart onto the person's hand, running over the silver rings on his forefingers and thumb.

While my mind had no recollection of creating the painting, my heart certainly did. It beat faster, and had my feelings jumbled inside my chest. A dark feeling nagged at the back of my mind, making it obvious I was missing something.

I could feel the warmth of the blood against the skin of my palm as I walked into town. I had felt the weight of the heart, heavy in my hand as I entered the town hall.

As soon as I sat down in the Mayor's office, in her meeting room, I wanted to go home. I had only been awake for an hour and I wished I had been able to grab a cup of coffee before I'd left the house. I had a feeling I was going to need the caffeine to survive this meeting.

Most of the town's remaining fey and a few humans were present on the opposite end of the long table. Their eyes continuously threw worried glances in my direction, as if they thought I couldn't fully see that they were looking at me. I fiddled with one of Filix's rings on my forefinger, trying to stop my brain from imagining a beating heart in my palm.

Mayor Kim stared at me, her under-defined, thin lips pursed and her beady eyes narrowed. She looked tired, her skin had dulled and her hair didn't have its usual shine to it.

"Mare Cozen and Filix Hallowes disappeared a month ago, just six days after the prince's coffin was opened. Six days after the door to the Feywild was opened again," Deputy Tindol began, recapping what we already knew.

"Six days after the door was opened, a Smogbody wandered onto our side of the Veil and attacked Mare and Filix inside the Cozen's house."

A chorus of murmurs and terrified whispers burst through the people in front of me. I numbly let my eyes fall across the people in front of me. A dozen fey I had not seen in years sat on either side of the conference table, mixed in with a few humans that looked to be as tired as I felt.

"Filix's whereabouts are still unknown, but we believe that he is still within the Feywild," Sheriff Radley explained, crossing his buff arms across his even broader chest. He stared everyone down, waiting for someone – anyone – to question him.

"How did you return to Neverhelm?" Mayor Kim asked, an unimpressed look on her face.

"Water. I was drowned in a pool," I said, recalling how painful it had been to inhale water as I sunk slowly in a bottomless pool.

Another burst of quiet murmurs shook through the room. Some

of the responses were startled and empathetic, while the other half of the responses were laced with underlying giddiness. Wherever I had drowned must have been important to them.

"Do you know why the Smogbody attacked the two of you?" Dantrag questioned.

My gaze slowly drifted to him, the fog that clouded my mind had barely dissipated since I had returned yesterday afternoon. I was surprised to see him seated on a pad of sticky notes, the brownie was too small to sit in one of the regular chairs inside the meeting room. I blinked hard, trying to focus.

"No, I don't know," I said.

"How did you get those wounds?" Haelra piped up.

I flinched the moment our eyes met. A burning sensation radiated across my palm and lingered at my fingertips, and the ice-cold sensation made everything feel hotter, more intense. Her pupil-less white eyes bore into my own, as an uneasy feeling ebbed in the air. My heartbeat picked up, thumping hard as if I'd just awoken from a nightmare. My hands were cold and clammy, and I drew my sweatshirt down over my hands, seeking warmth.

Tindol placed his hand on my shoulder, giving me minimal comfort – but I appreciated it nonetheless.

"Before I gave Mare a dose of Duprilic, she stated she met with our leader. She was unable to recall specific details, but I believe she offered him her blood – freely of course," he explained.

"That does not explain why Filix did not return with her," Kyomi, Filix's aunt spat.

I swallowed thickly, glancing down at the grain of the wood on the table. I had no answers to give any of the fey or the humans who had gathered together. Guilt settled in my stomach, making it churn slightly. My breathing became shallow as I pressed my lips together.

"I don't know," I said quietly, in a near whisper.

"Perhaps they were separated when they were near the fairy ring?" someone suggested.

"Do you know the whereabouts of the door to the Feywild?" Omelae questioned from the opposite of Kyomi.

My eyes settled on a water nymph, her wide black eyes never blinking as she looked at me. Her fin-ears twitched in anticipation of my answer.

"We are still searching for the access point to the Feywild. We believe it is near the prince's coffin, however we have yet to determine exactly where," Tindol cut in.

"And with Clé dead we will never know," Kyomi huffed, throwing daggers my way. I had not been responsible for Clé's death, but I still felt guilty.

"He was the last person through the Veil when the prince was brought here before the doors closed," Dantrag added.

"We are certain we can find it soon. As many of you have told me, you still feel the call of the magic that's coming from the cracked open door," Radley said, waiting for someone to argue with him.

"It's been rumored that Filix wasn't entirely human... Do you know anything about this?" Mayor Kim asked, she flipped through a stack of papers she had in front of her, not bothering to look at me.

Filix? Fey? Impossible.

"No, of course not." I scoffed, offended. I knew Filix.

"Was the King upset when you met with him? Did he seem hostile or uncooperative with you?" Mayor Kim asked, using the wrong title.

"It's 'Leader'."

There was a moment of silence as Mayor Kim looked up from her papers, a bewildered expression on her face.

"What?" she questioned, like I had the audacity to speak to her about anything other than to answer her question – let alone correct her on something she had said incorrectly.

"It's 'Leader' not 'King' or 'Ruler.' 'Leader'," I repeated for her.

Mayor Kim rolled her eyes and looked away from me, "Anyway, the King, did h-"

I slammed my fist against the table, cutting her off. *"Leader.* I won't repeat myself."

Mayor Kim looked back at me, a hard look plastered on her face. "Was the Feywild's *leader* upset that you were there?"

I blinked, unsure.

"I don't know," I repeated for the thousandth time.

"Is there anything you do know?" Mayor Kim snapped.

Anger flashed white hot in my chest, and I wanted to ram my fist into her face. I stayed quiet as I raised a brow in her direction.

The tension in the room was thick and hard to wade through.

I slowly rose from my seat, staring Mayor Kim down. I knew she had a million things on her plate. I knew she was stressed, her entire town had changed overnight and was continuing to change the longer the doors between our worlds were open.

But she didn't have to be such a cunt.

"The prince should have eaten your heart too."

Then I walked out of the room without a single glance back.

LOST IN THE DARK

One month later...

Things had not gotten easier since I had returned home.

Mum had put a strict lockdown in place. I was not allowed to go into town on my own, either Mum or Dad had to accompany me. Not that I had wanted to go anywhere the first few days I had returned home. Everyone stared at me, whispering amongst themselves like I was unable to hear them, like I had no idea what they were talking about. I had tried to stay home, but I could only stay in my room for so long before I began to go stir crazy.

The painting of the bloody heart in hand haunted me every time I stepped foot inside my room. The first few days I had been home, I actively ignored the massive half-finished painting. I tossed an old towel over the corner and avoided that half of my room. But I inevitably broke out my paints.

Something was wrong, and I needed time to distract my thoughts and let my brain rest.

It had taken another handful of days to actually continue the gruesome painting. Whatever had inspired such a dark piece of art was hard to dive back into, especially since I was not the same person I had been when I began the artwork.

When I finally finished adding the small details – like more texture to the hand, more highlights and shadows to the heart to make it stand out more – I'd been unsure what to do with it next. So I sat in my room and stared at the completed painting, wondering what to do next.

How had I become so lost?

I knew something had to change.

ASTRAY

Two months later...

With Mum and Dad out of the house, I knew there was never going to be another opportunity to slip out unnoticed. I only wanted to run into town and back – a little freedom on my own terms.

Slipping out the backdoor, I left it unlocked to sneak back in later - just in case Mum or Dad returned home early from work. I could lie and say I was out in the garden. I tugged my sweater sleeves over my hands and rounded the side of the house, heading off into town.

I hurried into the general store, throwing an uneasy smile at Vulparia at the cash register as I ducked down the aisles, absentmindedly searching for something. I let my feet wander down the aisles; I had grabbed a small box of chocolates from the third aisle I walked through.

Walking down the lighting aisle, trying to kill as much time as I could, I found myself before the holiday lights. My hand reached out, absentmindedly picked up a box of warm white string lights.

I tucked the box beneath my arm and made my way up to the checkout area. I was thankful Vulparia did not pry about my time across the Veil – I wouldn't have had much to tell her, everything was foggy, a massive blur in my memories. And I wasn't sure I could talk about what little I did know. I teared up whenever I thought about the Feywild.

I paid quickly and practically ran home, the desire to hang up the string lights had been the only thing that I had been passionate about after weeks of feeling numb and lost and astray.

A tiny flicker of hope burned in my heart, whispering about feelings I had been trying and failing to understand. I hoped the lights would unlock the memories I had blocked out.

The house was thankfully empty when I slipped in the backdoor. I tossed the grocery bag onto the counter, not caring as it slid across the surface and landed on the floor. My feet flew up the stairs, and I burst into my room as I tore open the box of string lights.

Stringing up the lights took no time at all, even if it was a bit tricky to reach my ceiling in certain places.

Flopping backwards on top of my blankets, I took in the warm glow the string lights gave off. They blink slowly like emberbugs, and with the fake foliage I had strung across the ceiling it felt magical. Like I had stepped through a fairy ring and into an enchanted forest.

The lights were dazzling and brought life into the room, but *something* was missing. My throat felt thick and tight, making it hard for me to get a satisfying breath of air. And my chest felt messy, like everything was jumbled together with no chance of being unwound or unraveled.

Tears welled in my eyes the longer I watched the lights blink on and off again at odd intervals. An intense wave of loneliness came over me, making me want to sink into my mattress and never get up again. Confusion accompanied the loneliness, which only made me cry harder.

Where was Filix? Why did it hurt to think about him? Why did it feel like *someone else* was missing too?

Curling into my side did nothing to comfort me. I gripped my blankets tightly, my knuckles turned bone white as I sobbed into pillows.

"Where are you?"

No one answered me, and that silence hurt, but the loneliness killed me.

SNEAK PEEK

M are's journey into the Feywild is far from over. Read on for a spicy sneak peek at what's to come. Below are the tropes/kinks for this specific scene:

Orgasmic vampire bites, blood play, blood consumption, voyeurism, exhibitionism, threesome, swordscrossing, raw sex, creampies

"I BET you look so pretty, underneath all these clothes," Hyunjin hummed as he ran a hand across my chest and let it travel down my sides, where they settled against my waist.

"Take them off me," I breathed, interrupted by a soft cry of pleasure as Hyunjin's teeth joined the mix of plush lips and hot tongue against my throat. Hyunjin groaned, hands crawling back from their place on my hips to knead at my ass, bringing me closer so that I could feel the hard line hidden in his pants.

"Don't test me," he whispered, lips moving up to press against my jawline. "Want to strip you bare and make you suck me off."

"Would you still like that?" I whispered but Wolf cut in before

Hyunjin could reply. He sat at the head of the bed, idly stroking his thick cock as he watched us - his blood marked mates - connecting on a deeper, more intimate level.

"No, this is about you, Mare. Hyunjin can get his dick sucked another time."

Another time, my brain whispered, shivering a little at Wolf's words despite the whine Hyunjin let out.

"But Wolf-"

"Jinnie, no," Wolf said, voice cold.

Hyunjin throbbed against my thigh, which had my clit pulsing with need. I turned my head around, trying to get a view of the look on Wolf face - the whimper I let out almost made me wish I hadn't.

Hot, My lust filled brain stupidly supplied at the sight of his clenched jaw and cocked brow, arms crossed across his broad chest. *He's so fucking hot.*

Wolf briefly locked eyes with me, a smirk on his wolf-like features before diverting his attention back to the prince before me, clinging to me, fingers digging into my ass as if it were a lifeline. "Get her undressed and then lay down so that she can sit on your face, yeah?"

Another set of hands found their way to my person, their nimble fingers working at the belt and buttons on my pants. They crowded behind me, yanking my pants and soaked underwear off all in one go.

"So pretty," Filix breathed out, his breath ghosting across my stomach, just above my pussy.

The longer it takes for you to lay down, Hyunjin, the longer you don't get to cum, Wolf growled through the blood bond.

Filix and I huddled together, scared and turned on by how hot Wolf was when he got angry. Hyunjin scrambled onto his back in the center of the large bed, being mindful not to jostle anyone too much. He licked his pillow-soft lips as he stared up at Wolf, waiting for his next order.

Come here, pup, Wolf instructed me as he continued to lazily jerk at his cock.

I slid away from Filix and straddled Hyunjin's face. I gave a nervous glance to Wolf, afraid that I could hurt Hyunjin if I put too much of my weight on his face. A reassuring, confident burst of energy flared beneath me from Hyunjin. Our eyes met - the sight of him below me, between my thighs, had my cunt clenching around nothing - a smirk spread across his half-hidden features.

"Come on princess, let me eat you out," Hyunjin begged.

Okay, I whispered, nervous yet excited all at once.

Hyunjin wasted no time in grabbing me by the hips, forcing me down onto his awaiting mouth. I moaned loudly, my brain went blank for a moment as the overwhelming feeling of Hyunjin's tongue took over any other sensation. Hyunjin moaned against me, the vibrations shooting straight through my body, making my eyes roll into the back of my head.

I gasped when soft lips pressed against my shoulder, my eyes snapping open as I glanced behind me. Filix hovered over Hyunjin's waist, his silver-blue eyes met mine as he leaned in closer to kiss my shoulder again.

"You look so good baby, getting your pretty pussy eaten out by our prince," Filix teased, his hands sliding across my waist, traveling higher across the side of my ribcage just shy of where I wanted his hands to be.

Wolf chuckled darkly behind us, which had me glancing back at him.

You want Lixie to touch you there? Wolf asked, with one eyebrow cocked.

Yes. Yes please, I begged, out of breath.

Filix cocked a brow, "Touch you where?"

Don't tease, Lix. She's been a good girl, Hyunjin jabbed at Filix through the bond. Hyunjin's tongue plunged inside my dripping folds, collecting as much slick as he could before he went back to sucking on my clit.

I surged backwards, letting my hands dart out and grip Filix's wrists. I brought them to my breasts, forcing Filix to grab handfuls of them. I moaned at the feeling of his skin against mine, just as Wolf chuckled darkly again.

"You sound just as pretty as you look baby," Filix groaned as he shifted closer to me. His lips traveled from my shoulder to my neck, his sharp teeth barely scraped against my skin, sending shivers down my spine.

Through heavy, lust-drunk lids I watched over my shoulder as Filix began to subconsciously grind against Hyunjin's stomach, trying to seek any friction he could. I wanted to help him, wanted to reach out and wrap my fingers around his straining, aching cock... but I wasn't sure Wolf would let me.

My legs relaxed just a bit, pushing my crotch farther into Hyunjin's face. Hyunjin's focus was zeroed into my core, head focusing on nothing but my pleasure. Hyunjin licked another stripe between my folds, over my slit before wrapping his lips around my clit and sucking on it.

A coil had begun to tighten my abdomen as my orgasm began to approach. My head glanced over at Wolf, my eyes hooded as pleasure consumed me. I wasn't sure if I was allowed to cum – I wasn't sure if I would be able to hold off with how fervent Hyunjin was eating me out. Filix's fingers fondled my breasts, his fingers gently pinched my nipples, making me gasp out.

"Cum on Hyunjin's face, pup. Make a mess of him," Wolf encouraged me, his voice giving me that final shove.

"Wolf, oh my fuck!" I whimpered over and over again. My whole body shook as my legs instinctively tried to close, though they just ended up pressing against Hyunjin's face, not that he minded it one bit. Hyunjin licked me out soft and slowly, helping me through my orgasm patiently waiting for me to come down.

The moment I felt like I caught my breath, sharp pinches of pain had another wave of euphoria crashing through me. Filix licked against the side of my neck, his tongue lapping at the blood that flowed from his bite. Below me, at the junction of my inner thigh was Hyunjin, his lips sucking hard against his own bite mark.

Fuck that's hot, Wolf muttered, his hand fisting his cock tightly. Filix and Hyunjin sucked against my skin, gently drinking my blood.

As the second, more intense orgasm began to disappear, Filix's arms wrapped around my naked body and pulled me forward, off of Hyunjin's face. The prince below me whined loudly, unhappy to lose access to me.

"Hush," Filix shushed him. "We have all the time in the world."

"You've had her for years! I'm making up for lost time," Hyunjin protested, leaning up on his elbow to look at the two of us near the end of the bed.

"If you two are done," Wolf cut in, shifting at the head of the bed.

My legs were shaky as I shifted to sit more comfortably on my heels, tucking my legs beneath my body. The bite mark Hyunjin had given me on my inner thigh throbbed more than the bite mark Filix gave me on my neck, the sting of both was intense yet pleasurable as I moved.

Wolf smirked, no doubt at the fact that all three of us were giving him intense bedroom eyes. His eyes connect with mine for a moment, something dark and mischievous brewing in his irises before his attention diverted to Filix.

"Come here, Lix," Wolf patted the spot beside him at the head of the bed with his free hand, his eyes never leaving Filix's naked form. Filix moved quickly, almost stumbling over his own limbs as he scrambled to sit beside Wolf.

"Hyunjin?" Wolf asked once Filix was settled.

Hyunjin hummed, rolling halfway over to look at his leader. A faraway look in his eyes had me snickering to myself. His tongue kept darting out, licking the cum from his lips as he tried to appear to be attentive to Wolf's orders.

"Why don't you help Lix out?" Wolf suggested, leaving no room for refusal.

We all perked up at that. My cheeks felt hot as I watched Hyunjin nod eagerly. A larger smile spread across Wolf's face at Hyunjin's acceptance. He snapped his fingers, and pointed at Filix's crotch.

"Here. Now."

Hyunjin nearly knocked me over as he jostled around on the bed, overly eager to suck Filix's aching cock.

I couldn't tear my eyes away from the three of them, my eyes enraptured by Hyunjin's large hands wrapping around Filix's thighs, gently stroking the skin. Something hot and wild burned through the blood bond, an ecstatic feeling bubbled beneath my skin.

My gaze followed Hyunjin's hands as he reached Filix's hip, until my eyes settled on Wolf's weeping cock. A soft whimper escaped my throat at the sight. His tip was red and angry, a large bead of precum slowly trailed down the shaft.

"Pup," Wolf called, my eyes snapped to his. He gently patted his thigh, "Come give them a show."

My movements were gentler than Hyunjin, but I was just as excited as I moved closer to Wolf. Filix whimpered as he watched me crawl across the bed and settle myself on Wolf's lap.

So needy. Even after Hyunjin and Lix made you cum?

I whined at the jab, ducking my face into Wolf's neck as my body flushed, growing hot and excited again. Wolf chuckled, turning his head toward mine, letting his teeth nibble against my earlobe. I tried to fight the urge to shudder as goosebumps erupted across my skin, the hot gust of Wolf's breath making the urge hard to resist.

My hand skimmed down the hard planes of his abs, his muscles tensed under my ministrations as I neared his cock. The tip was an angry red color, leaking copious amounts of precum, making the thick appendage shiny as the beads rolled down the length of him.

"Please," I pleaded quietly, body aching with the need to be filled with the cock in my hands. "Wolf please."

Wolf hissed as I wrapped my palm around him and gave him a gentle squeeze, dragging my hand up and down his length, jacking him off. Beside us, Hyunjin let out a whine as Filix tugged on his black locks, pulling the prince away from his cock.

Filix looked positively aching, his cock hung heavy and long between his spread thighs, the tip a light purple and half of his cock flushed red. His head was tilted back, sweat making his blonde hair cling to his forehead, and his hands balled into fists at his side, as if trying desperately not to touch himself.

They look pretty like that, don't they? Wolf asked, teasing me more. I couldn't think clearly as Wolf tapped his cock against my swollen clit, rubbing himself between my lips. "C'mon now, be good for me, pup."

I shivered at the words, nodding my head quickly before I grabbed Wolf's broad shoulders, allowing myself to sink down onto his cock as he lined himself up.

I didn't stop until I had fully sunk down, grinding needily as my cunt squeezed around his cock, which earned me a loud groan from Wolf, his head ducked down into the crook of my shoulder as his hands tightened at my waist.

Am I good? I whimper down our bond, forgetting the other two besides us. I almost missed the wet sound of Hyunjin sucking Filix's cock, my mind empty with my cunt stuffed full.

Wolf hummed, although his voice was tense, as if were in pain. He tilted his head slightly, pressing kisses against the column of my throat. "So good for us, pup."

I moaned at Wolf's words, my hips stuttering in their grind as my eyes fluttered shut.

"Let me take care of you, ok little one?"

I nodded, not truly hearing what Wolf said. I let out a surprised cry as Wolf raised me halfway off his cock before he met up with me again with his own hips; my fingers dug into his shoulders, sliding down and hugging Wolf tightly as he started at a brutally quick pace.

The wet sound of Wolf ramming into me filled the room, only occasionally broken up by the softer wetter sounds of Hyunjin plea-suring Filix. My hands reached out for them before my brain could fully process what I was doing. Filix's hand gripped at my wrist just as Hyunjin's fingers threaded through my own.

Fuck, baby, Filix whined as Hyunjin took Filix's cock deeper down his throat.

White dots danced through my vision as I came unexpectedly, suddenly, body convulsing intensely as my second high of the night hit me like a freight train. All feeling muted other than intense pleasure ripping through my body as a ringing echoed in my ears. The first thing I noticed when I came back to myself, when I returned to my body, was the feeling of Wolf's hand running up and down my spine in a comforting manner, his cock still buried deep inside me.

The second thing was the sound of Filix panting heavily beside me, one small hand holding Hyunjin down to the base of his cock as he came down his throat. Hyunjin's eyes were closed in bliss, tears seeping out of the corners; and I watched in muted fascination as the prince pulled away without a drop still on his tongue.

The third thing I noticed was the heavy pants and moans that came from the man still inside me. His thrusts were sloppy and ten times more brutal as he started to get close to his own high. I whimpered as the overstimulation started to set in, my walls aching as he continued to drive into me. I cried out as his thumb began to circle against my puffy clit, egging me on to cum again.

"Cum again, pup. Give me one more and I'll fill you up," Wolf panted, his voice exhausted and on edge.

I nodded, whimpering as another set of lips attached themselves to my neck. Heat engulfed my back, someone had straddled Wolf's legs and crowded in behind me. Hyunjin's lips pressed against my skin, gently, savoring the way he could touch me.

Cum for him princess. Cum all over his cock, Hyunjin encouraged me.

I felt the air leave my lungs as my cunt squeezed around Wolf, my orgasm washed over me - not as hard as the last - but still enough to leave me breathless and high. I moaned loudly as Wolf's hips stuttered before resting flush against my ass, cock pulsing inside my convulsing walls as he finally came.

I slumped backwards, into Hyunjin's strong arms. His nose

nuzzled into the side of my jaw, and I could feel his erection against the curve of my ass.

Don't pass out on us, baby. We have a long night ahead of us, Filix beamed with a large mischievous smile.

Oh boy, I laughed.

ACKNOWLEDGMENTS

I never actually written an acknowledgment page before... it seems a little surreal to be typing this out right now.

I am eternally grateful to my editor Morgana Stewart, thank you for taking this mess and helping me turn it into something I'm proud of. A huge shout out to Roxana Coumans for catching all the tiny mistakes I had made. I'm so glad the clock app's algorithm brought you onto my radar. And I can't forget my cover designer, Brooke Passmore. I literally have the cover of my dreams, so thank you, thank you, thank you!!

And Barb.arts, thank you for the commission of Mare and Filix. I've never been happier with character art before. You literally blew it out of the water.

Thank you to my family and friends, especially Hailey for keeping this a secret when I asked you too. And Mikayla, who will probably be mad at me for not telling her about this but will read this none-theless. Just know I thought of telling you every single day.

A special thanks to Steve, my cat, who interrupted me at every possible moment. This book could have been done sooner, but pets and cuddles were far more important in my opinion.

And to Stray Kids, who helped me find myself when I was lost. Thank you for making me *stay*.

About the Author

Hi! I'm Lore and I'm an indie author creating spicy stories inspired by the things I love. I dabble in a lot of different creative endeavors, so there's bound to be something to entertain you.

When not writing I can be found listening to Stray Kids.*

*but only when my cat Steve allows it.

Fairest in the Forest is my debut novel.

You can find more exclusive content at alittlestarlost.carrd.co

    instagram.com/lostinthelore
    tiktok.com/@thresholdguardian
    patreon.com/lostinthelore

Ingram Content Group UK Ltd.
Milton Keynes UK
UKHW011945090423
419863UK00001B/37